Will a father's final wish pull together a family of strangers . . . or drive them apart forever?

ADAM BRYANT—Handsome, intense, a street reporter burning with fire, his private life over the years never lived up to the high values he espoused on the pages of his newspaper.

ELIZABETH INGRAM BRYANT—Beautiful, rich, and passionate, she was the symbol of everything Adam ever hoped to have and the only true happiness he would ever know.

Please turn the page. . . .

LILITH BICKFORD BRYANT—Desperate to leap from society's middle strata, Adam's wife considered him a gift from Daddy, and her ticket into San Francisco's gilded upper circle.

IAN BRYANT—Adam's firstborn, his lavish life-style and brazen machinations sent the paper on a collision course with disaster. But Ian would go to devious and desperate lengths to retain complete control.

KELLEN BRYANT HILLMAN—Beautiful and independent, she alone had the vision and the ideals to restore the *Times* to its former glory—even as her heart was torn by two men: her husband, and the one true love of her life.

TYLER BRYANT—Adam's illegitimate son would finally find in the enclave of San Francisco's gay community love and happiness. Yet he could not escape his legacy of sin and scandal.

STEPHEN HILLMAN—Though Kellen Bryant shared his name and his bed, he knew her terrible secret—that their daughter belonged to another man.

GARRETT RICHARDSON—The British newspaper magnate became Kellen's shining passion—even as years of bitter rivalry and artful lies threatened to extinguish their love forever.

JEWELS OF OUR FATHER

Kristy Daniels

FAWCETT GOLD MEDAL • NEW YORK

Library of Congress Catalog Card Number: 90-93290

ISBN 0-449-14579-4

Manufactured in the United States of America

First Edition: January 1991

To Kelly Elizabeth

We would like to thank Ron Fimrite, Ena Macrae, Jim Myers, and Lauren Howard for sharing their city with us, and the research staff of the Broward County Library for its invaluable assistance.

"That which thy fathers have bequeathed to thee,
earn it anew if thou wouldst possess it."

—Goethe, Faust

Chapter
One

❦ A spear of lightning cut across the black sky, and the 727 began to shudder. The young woman opened her eyes in time to see her half-finished glass of wine skate across the tray. She grabbed it but a few drops splashed on the newspaper on her lap.

There was a sharp clap of thunder, and she leaned back in the seat, clutching the wineglass with one hand and the armrest with the other. A touch on her hand made her jump. She looked up into the face of a young steward.

"Are you all right?" he asked.

She nodded but said nothing.

"Well, we're almost home," the steward said, taking the glass.

She leaned back in her seat, listening to the strain of the jet's engines. Gradually, the thunder and lightning lessened, leaving just rain beating steadily against the window. She thought back several hours ago to when she had landed at Idylwild. The flight from Paris had been smooth, but the reservations clerk in New York had warned her about the bad Pacific storm and suggested she might stay in New York a night until the weather cleared. But something—some feeling or instinct—had told her she had to get on the plane to the coast. If she waited one more day, it might be too late.

A voice announced the plane was on its final descent to San Francisco, and from somewhere back in coach came the cry of a baby. Almost home . . . almost home.

She looked down at the newspaper in her lap. It was a four-year-old copy of the *International Herald-Tribune*. On the front page was a photograph of Jackie Kennedy in a ball gown descending a staircase with Charles de Gaulle, John Kennedy trailing behind, smiling. She started to put the paper away but stopped and opened it to the women's page. There it was, the interview with

1

Jackie. She stared at the column of type with the by-line Kellen Bryant on top of it. Her name. Her story.

She carefully folded the paper and put it back in her bag. At the last minute in Paris, she had decided to bring it with her to show her father. He would be impressed that she had met the Kennedys. The house in which she had grown up had once been a gathering place for the powerful and famous. He had always wanted to meet the young president. He would be impressed, too, she hoped, with the fact that she had written the story.

The plane landed hard in the driving rain. By the time she exited through the airport doors, the rain had slowed, but the late afternoon sky was dark. She saw a black limousine parked nearby, and a man in uniform came toward her.

"Miss Bryant, this way please." The driver put her bags in the trunk and held the door for her. Something caught her eye, standing out slick and bright yellow in the rain. It was a news rack, with the familiar blue letters painted on the front: THE TIMES IS ON YOUR SIDE! She put a dime into the box, pulled out a newspaper, and got into the limo.

The car snaked through the traffic and onto the freeway. She opened the newspaper, and as she slowly turned the pages, she smiled slightly, a little sadly, feeling suddenly as if she were being greeted by an old friend who had remained pleasantly untouched by the years. The *San Francisco Times* had not changed. It looked the same as it had the day she left five years ago. She opened to the editorial page. Her smile faded. No, not exactly the same.

She stared at the masthead, the box in the upper left column of the page that named the newspaper's executives. Her father's name, Adam Bryant, stared back at her, followed by the title Publisher Emeritus. And just below that the name Ian Bryant, her half brother, now with the title publisher. It looked strange to see it that way. It looked wrong. She tossed the paper aside.

She leaned back in the seat and closed her eyes. She knew she had no right to feel jealous of Ian, who now controlled the newspaper empire their father had spent his life building. She was, after all, the one who had run off to Paris five years ago. But still, the feeling persisted, even after all this time. She looked out the window. The congested streets of the Mission district were now giving way to the familiar sights of her childhood as the limo made its way north toward Pacific Heights. Ian now dominated her thoughts. He was a hurtful part of her past, a past that she had tried to leave behind but which was now coming alive with every streetlight, every hedge, every house she saw.

The limo stopped, and Kellen got out. She stood for a moment, looking up at the white mansion on Divisadero Street. She was home.

At the front door, Kellen was met by a maid she did not recognize. The woman took her coat and disappeared, leaving Kellen standing alone in the foyer. The house was quiet, so quiet that Kellen could hear the ticking of the old clock on the mantel in the study off to her left.

Kellen looked toward the living room and beyond to the dining room. She half expected to smell minted roast lamb and hear the sigh of champagne being uncorked. She half expected to hear the sounds of voices, all talking at once, or music, perhaps the Puccini her father so loved. But now there was nothing but quiet and a scent of must in the cool, still air.

She went to the staircase and looked up. She heard voices, soft and low, coming from upstairs. That was where he had to be. That was where her father was, in his bedroom, dying.

Slowly, she climbed the stairs and went down the long hallway toward her father's room. The room was dim and permeated with a sickly sweet smell that made her recoil. Flowers and disinfectant. It was a moment before she saw the figure lying in the bed far across the room. In the corner of her vision, she saw shadows of other figures. "Kellen . . ." Someone took her hand. Warm fingers.

She forced herself to turn her eyes from the bed. She looked up into a familiar face.

"Josh . . ."

He embraced her, holding her tightly for a moment. Finally, she pulled away but was unable to speak. She noticed Josh's face, heavily lined and slack with fatigue. She had known Josh Hillman all her life. He was her father's lawyer and his only trusted friend—like a member of the family. But she had never seen him as he looked now. His face was old, eroded by sadness. She slowly became aware of the other people in the room, staring at her. She looked again toward the bed. "How is he?" she asked.

"The doctor said—" Josh coughed slightly. "—That with this kind of cancer, at this stage, it's relentless. . . . He said he should have been dead by now but—" Josh saw Kellen's face and stopped. "I'm sorry, Kellen. It's just that, and now you—"

"Josh, it's all right." She moved past him, toward the bed. The other shadowy figures in the room stood motionless, and gradually their faces came into focus. Josh's son Stephen, standing near the window. Her younger brother Tyler, slumped in a chair. Her father's first wife, Lilith, sitting erect on a lounge in the corner. And standing behind her, Ian. Faces, familiar yet strange, floating in a fog.

Another figure in white hovered near the bed, a doctor, who moved aside as Kellen approached. Kellen stared down at the figure in the bed. She had expected to see tubes and machines, but there was little more than a skeleton. Skin like faded parchment stretched over the bones of the face, sunken eyes, mercifully closed, mouth open, pulling in air in short, desperate gasps. And strands of lank gray hair spread on the pillow.

Kellen picked up her father's hand. Next to her own, so pink with health, it looked pale and childish. She began to gently stroke it.

"What happened to his hair?" she whispered hoarsely. "It was full and beautiful. What happened to his hair?" Josh came over and put his arms around her shoulders.

She stared at her father, clutching his hand. Her father's fingers moved suddenly, curling themselves around hers. "Kellen . . ."

She quickly dropped to her knees beside the bed, straining to hear. "Daddy? Daddy? I'm here, Daddy."

He opened his eyes slowly. "Kellen," he whispered. "I knew you'd come home."

The fingers curled around hers suddenly became firm. He closed his eyes again, but his grip remained strong. The room was silent. Kellen felt his grip loosen. For a moment, she thought he was dead. Then she saw the hollow rise and fall of his chest beneath the white sheet. Then she felt Josh pulling gently on her shoulders.

"It's the painkillers. He drifts in and out. Come with me, Kellen. Let him sleep."

Slowly, she let go of her father's hand and laid it gently by his side. Josh led her away from the bed. She looked up to see Stephen Hillman standing nearby. Time continued to play its tricks. While Josh Hillman had aged terribly, his son still looked the same. He came forward to greet her with a soft kiss on the cheek.

"Stephen, why don't you take Kellen to her room," Josh said. When she started to protest, he added, "You look a little tired. I'll call you if there's any change."

Kellen glanced at the bed. "How long does he have, Josh?"

"Hours, a day maybe. When it started to get really bad last week, he said he wanted no artificial means. No tubes, no water, no food. Just the morphine." Josh glanced toward the bed. "I don't know what's keeping him alive."

Kellen looked back at Josh. "He's stubborn, Josh. You know that. He'll do it his way."

Josh nodded slightly and went over to talk to the doctor. Stephen led Kellen out of the bedroom and down the hall. Outside the door to her room, they paused. Kellen leaned against the open door, staring into the room. It was exactly the same as she had left it. The same antiques and chintz. The perfume bottles were as she had left them on the dressing table. Her tattered stuffed monkey sat in his position of honor against the bed pillows.

"I feel like I never left," she whispered.

"You've been gone a long time. Too long," Stephen said. "I'm glad you're home, Kellen."

She realized now that his face had changed a little, becoming leaner, more handsome than she remembered it. The unruly brown hair and serious hazel eyes, however, still belonged to the boy who had once fashioned a bowling alley for her in the hallway where they now stood. He had gathered ten silver candlesticks from all over the house and tried to teach her how to knock them down with a basketball. The memory made her smile slightly.

"I missed you, Stephen," she said. She impulsively threw her arms around his neck and buried her face in his shoulder. The gesture surprised him so much it was a moment before he returned her embrace. They pulled apart, both feeling awkward.

"I'll come and get you for dinner," Stephen said. He turned and disappeared down the hall.

She closed the door, went to the bed, and sat down wearily. She laid back, staring at the ceiling. It was blue, dotted with little painted clouds. Her father had it done for her tenth birthday. "Always blue skies for my Lil'bit," he had said. Strange that she should remember now her old nickname. She hadn't heard it since she was ten. It was a mispronunciation of her middle name, Elizabeth, which she had never been able to say when she was little. Her father had called her that for all her childhood. Lil'bit . . . Lil'bit.

She reached over and picked up the monkey, crushing it to her chest. She turned to her side, curled her legs to her chest, and cried.

The room was dark when Kellen woke up. She sat up slowly, momentarily disoriented, then switched on the bedside lamp. She glanced at her watch. It was after nine. She went into the bathroom and bent over the basin to splash cool water over her face. Standing up, she caught her reflection in the large mirror. Her makeup was gone. Her bare, and suddenly very young-looking face, stared back at her, pale with a faint spray of freckles across her small nose. Her large light green eyes were puffy from crying, and her long red hair was a tangled mane. The image of the sophisticated young woman she had so carefully put together that morning in Paris was gone. In her place was a child.

She quickly brushed her hair and changed into fresh clothes. Outside, she glanced toward her father's bedroom, then went downstairs. She heard the murmur of voices coming from behind the closed doors of the dining room and went toward them.

The door opened suddenly, and Ian stood there. He smiled slightly, shutting the door behind him. "We missed you at dinner," he said. Kellen stared at him. "It was a good dinner," he went on. "Fresh trout. I had them make it just for you."

"You didn't have to do that."

"I wanted you to feel welcome," he said. "A shame you missed it. Stephen said you were asleep. I wanted to come up and wake you, but he said you should be left alone. He's very thoughtful."

Ian came toward her and put his arms around her, and she stiffened. "My little sister," he whispered. "It's so good to have you home again. I'm sorry our reunion couldn't happen under happier circumstances."

"You should have gotten in touch with me sooner," Kellen said, pulling away. "I would have come if I had known."

Ian shrugged. "I didn't think you wanted anything to do with any of us. Besides, at first Father didn't want anyone to know he had cancer."

"You should have told me."

"I didn't want you to worry."

"Don't lie to me, Ian. If Josh hadn't finally called, I never would have known. You told him and Daddy a month ago that you were going to call me, but you never did. You lied and said I didn't return your calls. You wanted Daddy to think I didn't care."

"Well, if you did care, why'd you leave in the first place?" Ian said, his voice rising. "That really hurt him." Kellen winced, and Ian knew he had struck a nerve. "Listen to us, Kellen," he said. "He's lying up there dying, and here we are fighting again." He took her hand. "I'm sorry. You're right. I should have called you. Let's forget it now and put it behind us. Let's just put all the past behind us."

She pulled her hand away and stared at him. Like the house, he had remained eerily unchanged. At thirty-five, he still carried his tall, slender body with insolent grace. His face, handsome almost to the point of beauty, still had its aristocratic-like arrogance. And his brown eyes, so dark they seemed black, could still switch startlingly from soft to hard with each erratic swing of his mood. She wanted to get away from him.

"Ian, it's been a long time," she said. "Don't expect too much from me."

He smiled. "I understand." He kissed her cheek again. "Good night, little sister." He turned and went up the staircase.

She stood for a moment listening to the voices in the dining room but did not really want to face anyone. She glanced toward the study and went slowly to the door. The study had always been her favorite room of the house. With its comfortable furniture, bookcase-lined walls, and myriad mementos, it had a humility that the rest of the eccentrically grand rooms lacked. It was the only room in the house that Adam Bryant had decorated himself. It was his retreat.

The room was dark and stale smelling. She turned on the light. It looked the same. The overstuffed furniture in slightly mismatched shades of blue. The old oak desk, a homely monster standing amid the antiques. The photographs covering every inch of wall and tabletop. It was all there, exactly as it had stayed in her memory.

She went to the nearest shelf and slowly scanned the titles. She knew there was no logic to the shelves' eclectic contents. The collection was simply a testament to one man's voracious appetite for belated self-education. Guy de Maupassant. Thurber. Voltaire. Biographies of Lincoln and Einstein. A copy of *The San Francisco Giants* by Joe King, a local sportswriter. A scientific tome about the demise of the dinosaur. And next to a first edition of *Leaves of Grass* were several tattered paperbacks, mostly Old West novels.

She walked slowly around the room, examining the plaques and awards, given by the countless charities that had come to depend on Adam Bryant's largess. Then there were the framed photographs, all variations on the same theme: her father, smiling with some celebrity. Governor Culbert Olsen in 1939, Madame Chiang Kai-shek during her visit to Chinatown. Harry Truman. Soprano Renata Tebaldi backstage after her debut at the San Francisco Opera House. A young Joe DiMaggio, when he was with the minor-league San Francisco Seals.

The tour brought her full circle back to the desk. On it were other photographs. A formal prep school portrait of Ian. Tyler, when he was a gap-toothed seven-year-old. And Kellen at fourteen in riding clothes, caught in a pensive moment.

Kellen sat down in the leather chair behind the desk and withdrew a cigar from the humidor. H. Upmann's No. 4, always in plentiful, surreptitious supply from Havana. She brought the cigar up to her nose and inhaled, closing her eyes. The cigar, now stale, crumpled between her fingers.

"Kellen?"

She looked up quickly. Josh was standing at the door. "I saw the light on," he said. "I didn't mean to intrude."

"It's all right. Come in, Josh." She tossed the cigar in a wastebasket.

Josh took a chair across from her. He looked slowly around the room. "Funny," he said quietly. "I haven't been in this room for months. No one has, I think."

"Something's missing. Didn't you notice?"

Josh looked around again, frowning slightly.

"Newspapers," Kellen said. "Not one newspaper in this entire room. There used to be stacks and stacks of them. Papers from all over the world. And every day, every edition of the *Times*."

"The maid must have cleared them all out," Josh said.

Kellen was staring vacantly ahead. "Strange, isn't it. All this stuff in here from his life. No one touched a thing. But the most important thing is missing. The thing he poured his life into is gone."

He saw the tears brimming her eyes, but he felt helpless to comfort her. How could he when his own sense of loss was so great. He cleared his throat.

"Kellen, about the newspapers," he began. "Maybe this isn't the time to talk about it, but . . ."

She looked at him vacantly.

"Well, I think someone should know. I can't seem to get through to Ian, and Tyler's too young." Josh closed his eyes wearily.

"Josh, what is it?"

"I feel like I have no right to impose on you at a time like this. But you should know what's happening." He paused, taking a slow breath. "There are some problems with the paper, Kellen."

"I don't understand."

"Ian has made some bad moves while your father's been sick."

"What do you mean, Josh? Is it losing money?"

"Not exactly. But I'm afraid about the direction Ian is leading things. He doesn't care about it the way your father did. He hasn't the heart to run it the way Adam did.''

She stared at him. "Why are you telling me, Josh?''

"I thought someone . . .'' He sighed. "I don't know, Kellen. I just think if Adam were able, he would ask you to step in and help somehow—'' He stopped when he saw the sudden glacial expression on her face.

"What do you expect me to do?'' she asked flatly.

He stared at her, then dropped his eyes to his hands. "I'm sorry, Kellen,'' he said, rising slowly. "I shouldn't have brought it up. Good night.'' He went to the door, closing it behind him.

She sat rigid, staring at her hands now clasped tightly before her on the desk. She noticed a photograph in a silver frame sitting off to one corner on the desk and picked it up. It was a sepia-toned remnant from another era, a picture of her father and mother. A tall, handsome man with a wicked smile and a stunningly beautiful young woman in an ivory-colored dress with sparkling eyes. Adam Bryant and his bride, Elizabeth Ingram. The woman he had pursued with relentless passion, the woman he had waited for through both their first marriages, the woman he finally married against all odds. The woman who died in a drug-induced delirium when Kellen was thirteen.

Kellen stared at her mother's face, trying to connect the image to the memories in her head. Finally, she put the frame back in its place. She rose slowly, rubbing her neck, and walked to the door. Pausing, she looked around the room one more time, then left the study, locking the door behind her.

Early the next morning, Kellen was awakened by a knock at her bedroom door. She opened it, blinking in the hallway light. "Get dressed,'' Josh said. "Hurry.''

The urgency in his voice was like a splash of ice water in her face. She threw on a robe and went quickly to her father's room. Stephen and the doctor were bending over the bed. Adam's breathing was labored, his eyes screwed shut with pain. She grabbed his hand and held it tightly.

"Kellen . . .'' His eyes fluttered open but did not focus on her face.

Kellen was aware of other people now closing in around the bed, but she didn't look up.

"I'm sorry . . . so sorry . . .'' he murmured.

"So am I, Daddy . . . I didn't mean to hurt you.''

"I hurt you—''

"Daddy, don't—"

"Kellen . . . help . . . help me. . . ."

She quickly looked up at the doctor, then back at her father. He closed his eyes, his breathing coming now in short gasps. The room was quiet for a moment, except for the sound of muffled crying. She looked up. It was Tyler in his pajamas, leaning against a far wall. She saw Ian standing at the end of the bed, his face stony and pale.

"Kellen . . ." She looked back at her father. "Take care of everything for me," he whispered. "Take care of the newspapers for me." He paused. "And Tyler . . . take care of your brother. Take care of everything for me . . . Kellen? Promise me. . . ."

"I will, Daddy. I promise."

For several minutes, the room was quiet except for the sound of Adam's labored breathing. Then, suddenly, he gripped Kellen's hand, and his eyes opened wide. "My wife," he said.

Kellen felt someone press forward. "I'm here, Adam," Lilith said.

He glanced up at her, then slowly turned his head away on the pillow. "No, not you," he murmured. He closed his eyes. "Elizabeth. Where's Elizabeth?"

Kellen felt Lilith shrink back, retreating to Ian's side. When she looked back at her father, she realized he had stopped breathing. His eyes were closed, but his face was still creased with pain.

Dry-eyed, Kellen stared at her father's face, then gently released his hand. She reached up and stroked his brow.

"It's over, Daddy," she whispered. "You're all right now. It's over."

Chapter
Two

The funeral was held two days later. Grace Cathedral was filled with the rich, the powerful, and the curious. In the front pew was vice president Hubert Humphrey, and in the back was a sixteen-year-old *San Francisco Times* copyboy. Neither had known Adam Bryant well, but each had come out of a sense of allegiance. Adam Bryant had helped them both get their jobs.

The house on Divisadero Street was filled with cables, letters, flowers, and the constant ringing of the phone. In grief, everyone reverted to their usual behavior patterns. Josh, with typical calm efficiency, took up the burden of dealing with the funeral aftermath. Tyler retreated to his room. Ian, in a replay of one of his black childhood moods, disappeared after the funeral, returning two days later with no explanation. Stephen sequestered himself at the newspaper office, his job as managing editor providing his solace. Kellen retrieved her Alfa Romeo from the garage and took drives at all hours.

Josh finally called them all together for the reading of Adam's will. Ian, Tyler, and Kellen took their seats in the study silently and in wary distances from one another. Josh sat in a chair at the side of the oak desk and glanced at each of the children. Ian, now thirty-five, sitting erect in a chair, calmly smoking a cigarette. Tyler, at eleven, fair-haired and thin, his blue eyes cautious. And Kellen, now a beautiful woman of twenty-five. Her face, always a mirror of her emotions, was drawn with despondency and fatigue.

"I knew your father for more than thirty years," Josh began slowly. "There were a few times when I thought that I maybe knew him well. As well as anyone could." He paused. "He was a complex man. At times, difficult, stubborn, even hard."

Kellen looked up at Josh.

"But I have no doubt that he loved you three. And he wanted you to love each other. That's why, three weeks ago, he had me rewrite his will."

Ian stared at Josh, his cigarette poised in midair. "He didn't say anything to me about this," Ian said.

Josh looked at him. "He wanted nothing known until after his death, Ian." Ian took a drag on his cigarette. Josh put on his glasses and began to read. " 'I, Adam Bryant, domiciled in San Francisco County, California, do make, publish, and declare this to be my last will and testament. . . .' " Josh's voice droned on through all the preliminary articles of the will.

Kellen half listened to the strange legal language, her eyes roaming over the photographs on the walls. She heard the names mentioned of several of her father's favorite charities and servants. Generous bequests to Stanford University and the opera.

" 'Article seven,' " Josh said. He paused. " 'I bequeath to my three children, Ian Thomas Bryant, Kellen Elizabeth Bryant, and Tyler Landon Bryant, the remainder of my estate, including all personal holdings and properties of the Bryant Newspaper Corporation, to be divided equally among them.' "

Ian glanced quickly at Kellen. She stared at Josh.

" 'This bequest is made,' " Josh went on, " 'with the provision that Ian and Kellen participate jointly in the management of the *San Francisco Times* and the chain holdings, with each having an equal-voting half interest.' "

"What?" Ian blurted out.

Josh looked at him, then readjusted his glasses. " 'My son Tyler will obtain equal voting power at age twenty-one.' "

"I don't believe this," Ian said. "He said nothing to me—"

"Let me finish, Ian, please," Josh said calmly. "There is another provision. 'Article eight: I hereby decree that Stephen Hillman be named editor in chief of the *San Francisco Times*, and retain said position for his lifetime or until he deems otherwise.' " Josh put down the paper and took off his glasses. "That's the gist of it," he said.

"I can't believe he'd do this," Ian said quickly. "I'm the publisher. He didn't tell me any of this." He jumped up from his chair and began pacing.

"Ian—" Josh said.

"I've been working my ass off," Ian went on, "and now I'm expected to run things with these two?" He glanced at Tyler, who was staring at his hands, and at Kellen, who was watching him intently.

"Adam wanted you all to work together," Josh said quietly. "He knew the chain was in trouble, and he knew it was too late for him to do anything. This was his way of telling you three to work together to save it."

Ian began to laugh. "That's a good one! Why in the hell didn't he tell me? I'm his son, for chrissake! He wouldn't tell me this when he was alive, so he gets in the last word now." He glared at Josh. "This is crazy. He was crazy. This family's filled with crazy—"

"Shut up, Ian!"

Everyone turned toward Kellen. Her face was red with anger. "Don't say that," she said slowly, her voice low. "I told you a long time ago, don't ever say that."

"It's the truth," Ian said. "You know it is."

"That's enough," Josh said sharply.

"No, it's not," Ian said. "I'm not going to put up with this." He pointed at Tyler. "If you think I'm ever going to let this snot-nosed little shit have any say in the newspaper, then you're crazy, too, Josh." Tyler began to cry. "And as for my little sister," Ian went on, "You're all so ready to welcome her home with loving, open arms. Well, I'll be damned if I will! What does she know about newspapers? She's nothing but a spoiled brat! Where was she when Father needed her? I'll tell you! While he was lying up there wasting away, the beloved prodigal daughter here was fucking her way across France—"

"Stop!" Josh shouted. Everyone froze out of sheer shock at hearing Josh raise his voice. He rose and stared at Ian. "I won't let you make this something dirty, Ian," Josh said, straining to keep his voice even. "And I won't stand back and see you three tear one another apart and what your father worked his entire life to build."

Ian stared at him for a moment. "Forgive me, Josh," he said finally, "but you really have nothing to say about this. This is none of your damn business. You are not family."

He smiled slightly at the hurt look on Josh's face, then turned to Kellen and Tyler. The boy was whimpering. Kellen was ashen.

"I'm the only one who can run the newspaper," Ian said. "And I'm the only one who will. It's my right!" He stalked out of the room.

Josh gathered up his briefcase and a small box. He went to Tyler and bent down before him. He handed the boy his handkerchief. Tyler took it and wiped his eyes. "It will be all right, Tyler," Josh said gently.

"He hated me," Tyler said quietly.

Josh looked over at Kellen, then back at the boy. "Your father loved you, Tyler."

Tyler's pale blue eyes looked up at Josh. "He hated me because I was his bastard. A will doesn't change that." He began to cry again. "I'm alone. I'm all alone."

He got up off the sofa and ran out of the room. Kellen rose quickly as if to go after him, but then stopped. She looked back at Josh helplessly.

"Let him go for now, Kellen," Josh said. He handed Kellen the box he had been holding. "Adam wanted you to have these," he said. He looked at her for a long moment, as if he wanted to say something. "Think about what I told you," he said finally, "about the newspaper."

He left her alone in the study, holding the box. She stood there motionless until she heard the sound of his car going down the hill. It was quiet again. She looked at the box in weary curiosity. It was an old cigar box, its paper edges worn, its color faded to gray. Inside were photographs, most yellowed and tattered with age. She sifted slowly through them. They were mostly of her mother, in a variety of poses and dress. From the bottom, she pulled out a small creased photo. It was of a very young man on a dock. His expression was serious, but despite the slight shabbiness of his tweed suit, he looked dashing. She turned it over and read the feminine script: "Adam, Berkeley Pier, 1925."

She turned the photo back to the front and stared at her father's face, trying to imagine what he had been like then. The photograph had been taken the year he moved across the bay from Berkeley to San Francisco. She knew that much from the stories he used to tell her.

She slipped the photograph back in the box and noticed an envelope. Inside was a key and the number of a safe-deposit box in Adam's bank. She would worry later about what was in it. She put the box in a drawer of the desk and then paused to look around the study. The stunning contents of the will had still not completely registered. She felt a vague sadness over the fact that her dream of being involved in the family business had come only through her father's death. All those times they had fought about it . . . she had begged to be included, and he had always insisted that his daughter had no place in the newspaper. Now, through his will, he had given her what she had always wanted. But she had no idea what she was going to do with it.

Maybe Ian's right, she thought, maybe I have no claim to

anything. A couple of bylines over in Europe doesn't mean I can run a chain of newspapers.

She ran her hands over the worn leather of her father's chair, her throat constricting. Her eyes lingered over the photograph on the desk of Adam and Elizabeth, but finally, she left the study. In the foyer she paused, staring at the pattern in the marble floor. She knew she didn't want to stay in the house, but she had nowhere to go, no one to go to. She felt a sudden, pressing need to get out for a while and walked quickly out the front door, not pausing for a coat. Outside, the late afternoon air was cool and moist. She got in her car and raced out of the driveway. Driving aimlessly, she thought about many things, but she kept coming back to Tyler and how he had looked when he told Josh, I'm all alone. She had understood the terror in his eyes. It was exactly how she now felt. She had no one.

The car screeched to a stop. She turned off the motor. Without thinking, she had driven out to Fort Point, below the Golden Gate Bridge. It was a spot she had often sought out when she was younger, when she needed to get away and think. She got out of the car and walked out onto the concrete abutment along the rocks.

She stood watching the waves crash against the rocks, oblivious to the chilly wind blowing in from the west. The sun was nearly gone, its last light casting the city in an ochre glow. She watched as the fog moved in from the ocean, curling up over the orange spans of the bridge.

The fog spread slowly eastward over the bay. She glanced toward Berkeley and thought of the photograph of her father standing on the dock. She tried to imagine how he had felt that day, waiting for the ferry that would take him across. He had told her the story, of how he had always wanted to live on the west side of the bay, and how he had gotten the job on the *San Francisco Times*.

But he never had told her how he *felt* that day. Had he been afraid, she thought, like I am now? He was alone. And he had nothing. Nothing but giant, terrifying, exhilarating dreams.

The yellow lights of the East Bay glimmered through the fog. In her mind she could see her father clearly now, standing on the dock waiting for the ferry. Just dreams, that was all he had had forty years ago, dreams he had now passed on to her. Dreams that she had inherited, whether she wanted them or not. Dreams that he had asked her to protect, whether she was able to or not.

"I can't do it," she whispered. "I can't do it alone."

She stood there staring across the bay until it was dark. Then she turned and started for home.

Chapter
Three

Adam, 1925

❦ The bay waters churned, green-gray and white, and the flat, slate sky was broken only by a small flock of gulls straining against the wind. Adam Bryant pulled up his lapels to protect his neck, so nakedly exposed by the fresh haircut, and tucked his hands into his armpits. He watched the last car roll onto the ferry. The men on the pier began to cast off the lines. The ferry was, as usual, behind schedule. He glanced at his wristwatch. Still plenty of time. But he did not want to be late, not this morning.

The ferry finally sputtered away from the pier and although his teeth were chattering, Adam stayed on the stern and watched the slow retreat of the East Bay waterfront. He had lived across the bay from San Francisco nearly all his life, yet he had never really looked at his home from this vantage point. On the few times he had been on the ferry, he had always looked at the San Francisco side, where the view was so enticing.

Now he searched for landmarks, anything that would pinpoint Ocean View, the west Berkeley community where he had grown up. He was surprised, and slightly amused, by the nostalgic pull he felt. For the last ten years, he had done nothing but talk about leaving, and now he was feeling . . . what? He wasn't sure. Not sad, certainly. He had no regrets about leaving the blue-collar Irish neighborhood. Still, there was something bittersweet about the era of his life that was coming to an end with this ride across the bay.

He shrugged off the feeling and glanced toward Oakland. It was shrouded in the smoke of its shipyards and lumber mills. Adam thought again of the scene in the *Oakland Tribune* office yesterday. He had gone in to pick up his final pay and the city editor, Joe Davenport, had pressed him again about why he was quitting. Adam told him it was just for the bigger salary. He didn't have the heart to tell Joe the truth. Joe had, after all, taken him on at the *Tribune* six years ago when Adam was twenty, and he had taught him everything he knew about newspapers. And now Adam was repaying him by jumping across the bay to the *San Francisco Times*.

Adam shivered, watching the Oakland shoreline shrink away. I'm sorry, Joe, Adam thought, I couldn't tell you what I really thought. The truth is, I have a future—a big future. And big futures sure as hell don't happen in places like Oakland.

Adam turned and made his way through the parked cars. He stopped abruptly. Even in the sunless morning light, one car stood out, a gleaming vision of black, yellow, and chrome. It was a Wills Sainte Claire, the latest toy of rich auto enthusiasts. Adam touched the fender.

"Nice, isn't she?"

Adam looked up. A man was watching him with a bemused expression. Adam quickly took in the man's cashmere, velvet-collared coat, his bowler hat, and his walking cane.

"Yes," Adam said, taking his hand off the car. "The most beautiful machine I've ever seen."

"Could have gotten a Deusenburg," the man said, "but the Wills here has much more style, right?"

Adam nodded, trying to decide if the man was patronizing him. "A superior choice," Adam said finally, with a smile.

The man smiled back, and Adam sauntered off, thinking about the automobile. Ever since the new machines had begun appearing on the city's streets when he was a boy, he had longed to own one. He had always envied the things money could buy, but automobiles especially fired his imagination. He resolved he would someday own a machine as splendid as the Wills. And fine clothes. He was thinking now about the man's clothes. Clothes had never really mattered to Adam. The tweed suit he now wore had served his needs for years. But now, for the first time, Adam felt shabby, and he realized the old suit was far too small and out of fashion.

Adam went up to the bow, bending slightly in the wind. He gripped the rail and stared at the city spread before him.

San Francisco. Its waters marked with the crosscutting wakes of dozens of ferries. The approaching waterfront, the graceful tower of the Ferry Building extending like a welcoming salute, and beyond, the undulating sprawl of the city's pale buildings.

Adam's pulse quickened. He was by nature an emotionally reserved young man. But now he felt himself smiling, and, in a sudden, uncharacteristic burst of expectant joy, he threw back his head and laughed.

He was the first one off the ferry, and he went swiftly through the terminal, carrying his small suitcase. On Market Street, he paused, debating whether to splurge on a trolley car. He decided to walk. He needed every cent of his small savings to begin his new life. As he went up Market, his head filled with a dizzying array of images. Everywhere he looked were people, of all means and descriptions, all intent on some purposeful venture. Men in fine lounge suits with flowers in their lapels. Day laborers in dirty overalls. Chinese in both oriental and western dress. And women. Splendid women in fur-trimmed coats, their pretty faces framed by cloche hats. Everywhere he looked, Adam saw another woman more beautiful than the last. If there was one thing he coveted more than a new automobile, it was a beautiful woman. With his good looks, he had never lacked for female companionship. But these women, so richly dressed and brimming with confidence, seemed like modern, unapproachable goddesses. Each one ignored his smiles. No matter. Someday they would be smiling back.

At Union Square, Adam paused outside the entrance of a tall Gothic building and stared at the gilt letters above the door. THE SAN FRANCISCO TIMES. He glanced up at the large clock, which read nine-fourteen, and then quickly looked at his watch. He cursed under his breath. He was late after all. He quickly found his way to the third-floor city room and was directed to the office of the city editor, George Ringman. Adam anxiously waited for Ringman to finish some business with another man. The pause gave Adam a chance to look around the city room. It was lit by large, shadeless windows and crowded with plain oak desks and slat-backed chairs. Homely gooseneck lamps poked out of the piles of paper on each desk top, and telephone cords snaked over desks and up into the ceiling. Men in loosened vests and ties, the sleeves of their white shirts rolled high, were bent over black typewriters or seated in silent clusters, their pencils moving like little whirligigs as they edited copy. A cloud of pale yellow cigarette smoke hovered near the ceiling. A pang of disappointment went through Adam. The *San Francisco Times* city room looked just like the one in Oakland, just bigger. Yes, bigger, Adam thought with satisfaction.

"Bryant? Come on in."

Adam looked back to George Ringman, standing behind his desk. Adam shook Ringman's hand and took the offered chair.

"Sorry I'm late, Mr. Ringman," Adam began.

"Late? You're early. And by the way, call me George."

"But the clock outside—"

George Ringman laughed. "Jesus, that thing hasn't worked since the Bickford family built this place in eighteen sixty-five. Just like half the stuff around here."

"Well, I didn't want to be late my first day."

"Joe Davenport said you were that kind of guy. And that you were the best reporter he ever had."

"Best one he trained," Adam said with a smile. George Ringman laughed. "Mr. Ringman—George," Adam corrected himself at the man's frown. "We never discussed my exact salary. You said only that it would be generous."

"I'm starting you at fifteen hundred dollars a year," Ringman said quickly. "That's what all our young street men start at."

Adam struggled to hide his disappointment. The figure was only one hundred dollars more than he had been making at the *Oakland Tribune*. It was a livable wage, but he had expected more, much more. He looked at Ringman, who was smiling slightly.

"When do I start?" Adam said simply.

"Right now. But first you have to go upstairs and meet the owner. Old man Bickford likes to meet every new man. He's expecting you. The elevator's on the left."

As Adam rode the elevator up to the tenth floor, his disappointment over the salary hardened into anger. He was worth more than what Ringman was paying. It would not take long to prove that. But more important, it was the last time, he resolved, that anyone was going to take advantage of him.

Robert Bickford's office was a mahogany-paneled fortress guarded by a stern secretary. Bickford himself was not nearly as imposing as his surroundings. He was a short, fat man, his red face straining above the crisp collar of his immaculate white shirt and finely tailored suit. He sat behind his desk, lobbing questions at Adam about his background.

"So, you are from Berkeley," Bickford said, glancing at Adam's résumé and tossing it on the desk.

"I was born in San Francisco," Adam replied. "My parents were killed in the earthquake. I grew up in an orphanage in Berkeley."

"Terrible, terrible," Bickford mumbled.

"I was only six. I remember very little," Adam said.

"Well, thank the good lord for that, son."

Bickford launched into a rambling reminiscence about the quake, and Adam's thoughts began to drift back to his childhood. He seldom dwelled on it; there was so little he could remember clearly that it seemed pointless. Yet, occasionally, fragments would float up from his subconsciousness, and he would concentrate on them, as if to bring them somehow into focus. He thought now of his mother, of her smell, a sweet mix of yeast and the clove oil she used to erase the odors of her cleaning job. He could remember his father's loud, easy laugh, and the smell of ink, and the stains on his hands from the print shop where he worked. He could also remember their small house on Folsom Street with its olive-green prickly upholstered sofa. But no matter how hard he tried, he couldn't recall more about his parents.

The earthquake. He could remember that vividly. He had been awakened by a strange sound, something more sinister than the usual rumble of the milk wagon. He crawled out of bed and went to the window. Below, in the dim morning light, the milkman was having trouble pacifying his fretful horse. Then it came. A moan and a jolt that sent Adam flat on his face. The floor shifted beneath his stomach. He wasn't scared. It felt funny. He giggled.

Then he felt his mother scoop him up, and they were running through the dark halls. Suddenly, it wasn't funny. He could tell his mother was frightened. They ran out into the street, where people were yelling and swaying, as if caught in a macabre dance. Quick, shattering noises. A roar of sound. Trolley wires wriggling like snakes on the street, spitting blue sparks. He could remember his mother suddenly screaming and setting him down. "Stay here!" she commanded. She ran back into the house. He started after her.

Adam felt someone grab him. There was a loud crash and a great rush of dusty air. Over the retreating shoulder of the stranger who had saved him, Adam saw the house on Folsom Street fold into itself. Then it stopped. Only seconds had passed, and it was over. It was quiet, except for the bells of the city's churches, still lurching in a frantic and discordant symphony.

His mother had died in her attempt to find her husband. Their bodies were later found in the rubble. Adam was taken to a refugee station in Union Square. A woman tethered him to a clothesline of other bewildered children and led them on the march down Market Street to the ferries. Everywhere he looked he saw fire and ruins and people, their faces dazed and dirty in the harsh morning light. He was taken to a makeshift refugee shelter in Oakland, which had escaped the quake's impact. No one ever spoke to Adam about the earthquake or his parents. He was placed in the Sisters of Charity Orphan Asylum. He missed his parents terribly, but after the first year he adjusted to life in the orphanage. He was a good boy, but the nuns worried that he was too much of a loner. He had a quick mind, and they tried to encourage his education, but he was too impatient and independent to learn about the world through books. He wanted to experience it. No one was surprised when one night the fourteen-year-old Adam simply disappeared from the orphanage. The Sisters of Charity missed Adam, but they did not worry. He is a strong, smart boy, they said, he is blessed. The good lord would look after Adam Bryant.

Adam, however, wasn't going to count on that. He intended to look after himself. His years in the orphanage had left him with a rudimentary education and a vague, obligatory sense of his Catholic spirituality. But more than anything, they instilled in him the burning fire of ambition. He had grown up with nothing—no family, no sense of home, nothing he could really call his own. All he had was his brain, his drive, and some dreams. He wasn't sure what he wanted to do, really. But he knew he wanted to be rich. With money at least, he reasoned, he would be protected.

He found work as a day laborer cleaning streets and then as a caulker's assistant in the shipyards, but he hated the stench of the docks. He got a cleaning job in a print shop. It was tedious work, but it triggered the residual memories of his father, and he stayed on. Eventually, he became an apprentice, then a printer. He lived alone in a boarding house in Ocean View. When he was eighteen, a man told him he could earn more as a printer for the *Oakland Tribune*. When he went for an interview, he got off on the wrong floor. He met the city editor, Joe Davenport, who offhandedly asked Adam what he really wanted to do for a living. Adam glanced out over the busy, purposeful newsroom and announced, "I'd like to be a reporter." The answer surprised Adam himself. He had been keeping a journal since his days in the orphanage, filling it with events of the day, using it unconsciously as an emotional outlet for his loneliness. But he had never thought about writing professionally. It had never occurred to him that people— that he—could get paid for doing something as pleasurable as putting words together on paper. Joe Davenport hired Adam as a copyboy. Within six months, Adam finagled his first assignment, a small fire in a hospital. Within a year, he was a full-time street reporter.

He loved the job. The newspaper struck some deep, resonant chord inside him, and he knew immediately he had found his calling. He loved going out onto the streets, hunting down the stories, then furiously phoning in the facts to the rewrite men. There were times he wished he could do the actual writing, but he quickly learned his real talent was out on the street, getting people to talk. He had matured into a handsome man—tall and dark-haired, with inquisitive blue eyes. And his quiet manner made people believe he was a good listener. They poured their hearts out to him. Especially women. He had great success with women, because they believed he was different than most men—he listened. He brought imagination and intensity to sex, but he would end an affair when he sensed a woman was trying to lure him into marriage. He wanted a family—but later. He had listened to married men at the newspaper, the ones who gathered in speakeasies before they went home, mourning their stillborn dreams. He had no intention of ending up in the same trap; he intended to be someone. Run a newspaper someday, or even own one. So women remained just a diversion. His real passion was his work. Often, when he couldn't sleep, he would go down to the composing room to watch the newspaper being made up. He would stay there for hours, the oily odors of ink and sweat heavy in his nostrils. Then he would go home, sometimes arriving at sunrise, just as the *Tribune* was being delivered to corner newsstands.

Adam looked back at Robert Bickford, wondering if the man had ever soiled his hands with ink. Probably not.

"Yes, yes . . . April eighteenth, nineteen-oh-six. A black day," Bickford was going on, still lost in his own memories of the earthquake. "My father ran the *Times* in those days. We couldn't publish, you know," Bickford said. "Had an 'extra' ready to go, but a damn fire ruined the Linotypes. . . . We lost the house on Nob Hill and had to move my family over to Oakland. We lived over there for almost eight months while we rebuilt."

Adam waited until Bickford drifted back to the present. "So why did you want to leave Oakland?" Bickford asked.

Adam paused. He could recall the exact day he had asked himself that very question. It was five years ago, January 16. Prohibition had just become law, and Adam was assigned to cover how it was creating economic chaos in the wine country and in San Francisco. It was his first trip to the city, and it instantly ignited his imagination and all his latent ambitions. Suddenly, his happy existence at the *Oakland Tribune* seemed too small. Or maybe the rest of the world was too alluringly big. Adam became obsessed with the idea of moving back across the bay.

Adam looked at Bickford. "Why did I leave Oakland?" He paused. "You lived there, sir. Why did you leave?"

Bickford stared at Adam. The impasse was interrupted by the door opening. Adam smelled the woman's perfume before he saw her. She strode across the suite to Bickford and kissed his balding head. "Hello, Daddy," she said.

"Lilith, I've told you to knock," Bickford said. "I'm busy."

The woman looked over at Adam. "Oh, sorry," she said with a smile. She was in her early twenties, tall and slim, with dark eyes. Two curlicues of black hair wound out of her green hat onto her white cheeks, and her lips were painted bright red. She wore a bottle-green suit, trimmed in mink. "I'm Lilith Bickford," she said, extending her hand to Adam.

He took it and introduced himself.

"Adam's our new street man," Bickford said. "Just starting today."

"Well, the stodgy old *Times* could use some new blood," Lilith said, rolling her eyes. "Why did you decide to come work for my father, Mr. Bryant?"

Adam considered the question before replying. The truth was, he wanted to work for San Francisco's other daily newspaper, the *Journal*. It was bigger and far superior to the *Times*. He had failed to land a job there, however. "I came here because this is an excellent newspaper," Adam said, looking at Bickford. He looked back at the woman and smiled.

Lilith Bickford stared at him, then slowly smiled. "Oh yes, the *Times* is, indeed, an excellent newspaper." Adam picked up her sarcasm and saw that Bickford was oblivious to it. "Well, Mr. Bryant," Lilith continued, "I hope you do better than those washed-up lushes down there." Bickford shot his daughter an angry look, which she ignored.

"I intend to, Miss Bickford," Adam said. "Within a year, I guarantee that I'll be the *Times*'s top reporter."

She arched her penciled eyebrow, then turned to her father. "Daddy, we have to talk."

Adam took the cue and rose. He shook Bickford's hand and said his good-byes to Lilith Bickford. She watched him walk through the doors.

"Arrogant chap," Bickford said.

Lilith Bickford walked slowly around the office, her fingers stroking the mink of her collar. "Yes," she said. "And much too handsome for his own good."

Chapter
Four

❧ Within a year, Adam made good on his promise, rising quickly to prominence among the *Times*'s moribund reporters. He was indefatigable and relentless in his pursuit of stories. When a carpenters' strike erupted into violence, the city's readers found the best accounts in the *Times*. After a small earthquake, it was Adam Bryant's colorful reporting everyone quoted over breakfast the next morning. The rival *Journal* repeatedly tried to lure him away, but he turned the offers down. He had studied the inner workings of the *Times* carefully and deduced that the quickest path to the top in San Francisco journalism was to start at the bottom-rung newspaper. He wanted an arena in which he could make his mark quickly. And that was the *Times,* rife with problems and bereft of men capable of solving them.

Adam quickly became Bickford's favorite reporter—and the object of Lilith Bickford's attention. She gave Adam every opportunity to make an advance, but he avoided her ploys. He wanted to become editor in chief of the *Times* someday, and he considered that Lilith could be a conduit to his goal but rejected the idea. He didn't particularly like Lilith. Bickford had hinted that the city editor position was coming open soon and that there were only two candidates: Adam and another man named Rogers. Rogers had more experience, but Adam knew he could do the job better. So Adam tactfully ignored Lilith, hoping she would leave him alone.

Then, one afternoon, Bickford came down to the city room to see Adam. They chatted about the day's news, but then the conversation sputtered to a stop. Adam knew Bickford had something else on his mind. Bickford pulled a cigar out of his breast pocket and carefully clipped off the end. "Say, Adam," he said, "I'd like you to come to dinner tomorrow."

"We have city elections tomorrow, sir," he said slowly. "I really should be here for the late results."

"It's Lilith's birthday," Bickford said. "I know she'd be pleased if you came." He paused. "So would I."

"I'd be honored," Adam said with a stiff smile.

"Fine." Bickford got up to leave. "Dinner's at eight."

Despite their wealth, the Bickfords were not considered to be among San Francisco's best families. They lived in Pacific Heights, where the best did dwell, but at a respectable, not stellar address, on Vallejo Street. Their mansion was small by neighborhood standards but lavishly decorated in a neo-French Colonial style. Still, it was more opulent than any home Adam had ever seen. At dinner, he sat quietly by Lilith's side, feeling . . . not ill at ease, really, but slightly uncomfortable. He had worn his new lounge suit, which had cost him two months' pay. He glanced at Bickford, focusing on his gold collar pin, and thought about the hidden safety pin holding his own collar erect. Someday, he thought, someday . . .

He watched as a maid came in and set a plate of birthday cake before each person. He picked up a dainty dessert fork, focusing on the cursive *B* monogram. A part of him was impressed by the Bickfords' finery. After all, he lived in almost monastic solitude in a boarding house near the newspaper office, having decided some time ago to save his money. But he was careful not to allow his awe to show. No, it wasn't feelings of inferiority that made him uncomfortable as he sat at the Bickfords' table. It was Lilith. She had been acting almost tauntingly possessive, as if she considered him a birthday gift delivered by Daddy.

He glanced at her. She was babbling on about the opera star Luisa Tetrazzeni, who had married a man twenty years her junior. "*Quel scandale!*" Lilith exclaimed to her mother. "But then, what can one expect of Italians, after all. . . ."

Adam accepted a cup of coffee from the maid, his gaze traveling from the stoically silent Bickford back to Lilith. He supposed that some would consider her a striking woman. But despite his healthy sexual appetite, he was not attracted to her. He found her beauty contrived, and her straight figure, so well suited for the fashions of the time, held no allure. He took a bite of the dry white cake and, with a discreet glance at Mrs. Bickford's plate, carefully set his own little fork, tines up, across his own. The room was overheated and was making him drowsy. He tried to look interested in the conversation, but his mind kept wandering. He thought about the city editor position. He had proved himself, yet Bickford was still dangling it before him like a carrot. He glanced at Lilith. Was she part of the package?

Now Lilith and her mother were talking about Rudolph Valentino's funeral, talk that then deteriorated into local gossip. Adam caught Bickford's eye and saw in the man's gaze a weary resignation. He felt a little sorry for Bickford in that second, caught as he was between two insipid women.

There was a lull as Lilith paused to drink her coffee, and Adam jumped in. "So, sir," he said to Bickford. "What did you think of the Dempsey-Tunney fight?"

Bickford brightened. "Dempsey's nose is like glass . . . couldn't hold up after he had it rebuilt for the moving pictures, you know."

Adam listened as Bickford went on about the fight, offering an occasional comment. The conversation moved on to the upcoming World Series, and Lilith and her mother sat in vanquished silence, sipping their coffee. Adam felt a slight distaste for resorting to the ingratiating ploy with Bickford, but he was beginning to accept the evening for the opportunity it was. What was wrong with ingratiating himself with the boss over dinner? It was just good business. And after all, it was he—not Rogers—who had been invited.

"What do you think, Adam?" Bickford asked. "Can the Cards finally beat the Yankees?"

"They've got the talent," Adam said, smiling.

Bickford laughed. "It'll take more than talent. It'll take plenty of luck!"

Adam felt Lilith's eyes on him. "Yes," he said. "A little bit of luck never hurts."

"Spoken like a true Irishman," Bickford said amiably. He rose, patting his belly. "A fine dinner, Catherine," he said to his wife. "How about a cigar in the library, Adam?"

"Sounds fine to me, sir."

"It's time we drop this 'sir' stuff," Bickford said. "It's Bob from now on, or better yet just plain ol' Bick."

Adam smiled and allowed himself to be led out of the dining room. "If you insist, Bick . . ."

During the next two months, Bickford invited Adam to the house often. It became increasingly clear to Adam that the promotion was forthcoming. And that Lilith was, indeed, part of the deal. He began to see her occasionally, just enough to appease everyone. Then, one afternoon, Adam was called up to Bickford's office. Lilith was sitting there.

"Bryant, do you have a dress coat?" Bickford asked.

"A dress coat?"

"I thought not," Bickford said with a grunt. "Well, here's some money. Go over to Tilton's and rent yourself a dinner jacket. You're going to cover the opening of the Mark Hopkins tonight." He smiled at Lilith then at Adam. "We'll have a grand time."

It rose nineteen stories, a brick monolith of French and Spanish architecture, on the crest of Nob Hill where the rail baron Mark Hopkins's mansion had stood before the earthquake. Every inch of it glittered with the most dazzling decor and furnishings the outrageous five-million-dollar price could buy. Yet beneath the splendor of the Mark Hopkins Hotel was a skeleton of metal braces engineered to withstand any fire or earthquake. It was an ingenious building. Steel and silk. The perfect melding of the city's gold-leaf sense of history with the most modern disaster-proof engineering.

The gala opening was the biggest social event of the season, a dinner dance for 1,500, with thousands turned away. As the opening approached, the two newspapers competed for superlatives: "A Fitting Crown for Nob Hill" . . . "New Hostelry Recalls Days of Gold."

Standing in the lobby of the new hotel, waiting for Lilith to return from the powder room, Adam found himself coming up short on adjectives. Everywhere he looked was some element designed to titillate the eye—exquisite Persian rugs, intricate chandeliers, handcarved woodwork, gilded ceilings, and murals depicting California history. The evening had been an elaborately choreographed ballet for the senses that left Adam awed. Earlier, he had sat at the Bickfords' table in the Peacock Court, trying to forget that Bickford had picked up the ten-dollar-a-plate cost. The dinner was a feast of brook trout, breast of guinea hen, Glace Prince Puckler, *mignardises* and bitter coffee Lilith called demitasse. Adam had never tasted food so wonderful in his life.

The sights and smells! As entertainment, twelve beautiful models swirled across the dance floor in the latest fashions, picked up by colored spotlights. And everywhere was the scent of perfume, projected through the ventilating system.

Now, as he waited for Lilith, Adam watched the parade of wealthy guests waltz by in a dazzling kaleidoscope of color and jewels. The sounds of laughter and music mingled with the gentle gurgling of a nearby fountain. He felt slightly dizzy, satiated with sensation. He felt . . . not quite happy, really. But good. He felt uncharacteristically charged, as if the night held out some strange promise. It felt good to move in such a grand circle. In just this one night, he had discovered a whole new world, populated by the most powerful men and most beautiful women, a world that made even the Bickfords' existence seem hopelessly bourgeois by comparison.

Lilith returned and gave him an appraising smile. "Even in that terrible suit, you are the most handsome man here."

"What is wrong with my suit?" Adam asked.

"It's rented, darling. You need custom clothes. It's the only way. You'll look better once I get you to a good tailor." She took his arm. "Let's go dance."

In the Peacock Court, Eddie Harkness's orchestra was playing the new Gershwin song, "Someone to Watch over Me." While they danced, Lilith hummed along in Adam's ear, which he found annoying. He found many things Lilith did annoying, especially her little condescending asides, such as the remark about his clothes. He disliked her assumed air of ownership of him, which lately was getting more pronounced. He had been observing her all evening as she interacted with various people, and he was beginning to understand what motivated her. Despite her vapid manner, she was, at her core, an ambitious woman. Marriage to Adam Bryant was certainly below her, yet she shrewdly understood that Adam had the potential to be the savior of the ailing *Times*. More than anything, Lilith Bickford wanted to make the leap from middle-strata society to the city's gilded upper circle. And she was quite willing to take a temporary step down to do so. In her own way, she was as covetous of success as he was. And like him, she had her own rapacious dreams.

Adam moved Lilith around the dance floor, his feeling of contentment dissipating. It was a special night, and he wished suddenly that he were dancing with someone else. Some girl who could, with the press of her body against his, stir him inside, give him that sudden flood of . . .

A woman's laugh floated above the music. It was a contralto laugh, absolutely artless in its joy. Adam glanced over Lilith's shoulder.

She was sitting at a table, one hand on her hip, the other reaching up to cup the chin of a perturbed-looking young man. She laughed again, said something to the man, and he walked away. She was very young and very beautiful.

Adam maneuvered Lilith closer to the girl's table, but the song ended. The orchestra suddenly struck up a fast tune, "Black Bottom." A few brave couples ventured out onto the floor and attempted the new dance craze, looking awkward in their evening clothes.

"Looks like fun," Adam said to Lilith. "Want to try?"

"Oh, Adam, God, no. Let's sit down."

They went back to the table. Adam turned back to watch the dancers. He heard the throaty laugh again and then saw the girl. She was dancing, holding her silver beaded gown above her knees, much to the delight of her partner. She moved gracefully across the floor, more in response to some free-form idea of ballet than the prescriptions of the faddish dance. And she laughed—at her partner's red face, at her own missteps, at the faces of everyone staring at her.

Like all the other men, Adam sat transfixed. She had cream-colored skin and flaming red hair, not cut short in a bob like most of the young girls, but restrained in a chignon at the back of her long neck. She was tall, very tall, and she had a voluptuous figure that even her fashionable gown, with its tight, boyish bodice, could not hide. Adam watched as she twirled around, holding her gown high on her long, slender legs.

"That girl is inebriated," Mrs. Bickford said.

Adam let the remark pass. Most of the guests had flasks concealed in breast pockets or handbags, some were even sipping gin from demitasse cups, but somehow he didn't think the girl was drunk. She just looked . . . very happy.

The song ended, and a slow one began. The dance floor quickly filled with couples. The girl disappeared into the crowd. Adam excused himself from the table. He walked around the perimeter of the large room, searching for the girl in the silver gown. Finally, he saw her, at the far end dancing with a different man. Adam ventured closer and leaned against a pillar, watching her. Her eyes, large and alert, flitted across the room over her partner's shoulder. She saw Adam staring at her. She stared back. He thought she smiled.

Without thinking, Adam went over and tapped the man on the shoulder. The man moved away, and Adam paused, astonished by the girl's beauty. She had pale green eyes, like light jade, and damp strands of red hair clung to her forehead.

She slowly raised her arms and smiled. "Well?" she said.

He took her into his arms and they danced. She moved with a natural, languid rhythm. He was not a graceful dancer; he had never had the chance to learn. Yet he found he could move her effortlessly, as if she were a wisp of wind. He drew her closer and became lost in the sensation of her, the gentle brush of her body against his, and her wonderful smell of nothing but skin.

She was the one who finally pulled away. The music had stopped. They stared at each other for a moment. The music began again and they danced, but this time she looked him in the eyes.

"You know, I was quite happy dancing with that other fellow before you cut in," she said.

"Then you shouldn't have smiled at me."

"I didn't."

"Shall I take you back to your table?"

She stared at him, then leaned into him, laying her cheek against his. "No," she said.

When the song ended, Adam pulled away reluctantly. "There's something I have to take care of," he said.

"Then you'll have to take me back to my table, after all." She smiled and started off the floor. Adam followed her to a table, where a finely dressed couple and an elderly woman waited. They eyed him with interest as he approached.

"Mother, Father," she began, "this is . . ." She turned to Adam. "My goodness, I don't know who you are!"

Adam saw the disapproving look pass over the man's face and the women's fixed cool expressions. He quickly introduced himself. Charles Ingram shook Adam's hand. Adam began to excuse himself. He had to get back to the Bickfords.

"You are coming back, aren't you?" the girl said. "We'd like you to join us, Adam."

Adam saw the cool expressions harden. He smiled. "Yes, I'd like that . . . ah . . ." He was going to use her first name but realized to his chagrin he did not know it.

"Elizabeth," she said, laughing.

Adam quickly made his way back to the Bickfords' table, thinking about the red-haired girl. Elizabeth . . . Elizabeth Ingram . . . he repeated her name in his head, reliving the feel of her in his arms. His stomach tightened as he suddenly realized what he was about to do. He wasn't an impulsive man; he could not think of one genuinely spontaneous act he had committed in his entire life, except the day he told Joe Davenport he wanted to be a reporter. Yet now, tonight, for the moment at least, he wanted to be a different man, to feel outside himself. He wanted to be with this woman.

The Bickfords looked up expectantly when he returned. "Where have you been?" Lilith demanded.

"Working," Adam said, sliding into his chair. He pulled a small notebook out of his jacket. "Phoning some details in." He saw Bickford smile. "Listen," Adam said, "It's getting late. And I still have work to do here. I hate to be rude, but I'm afraid the party's over for me."

Bickford nodded. "No problem, Bryant. We understand. I think Mrs. Bickford and I are ready to call it a night anyway." He rose, and held out his wife's chair.

Adam noticed Lilith made no move to leave. "You should go, too," he said, touching her arm.

"I'm not ready to leave."

"Lilith, I really have a lot to do. I have to interview the manager and the chef."

"I'll help."

"Lilith, let him do his job," Bickford interrupted. "Come on home with us."

She looked at Adam, then sighed. "All right. The evening's been a bore anyway."

He walked the family out to the lobby. Then he went quickly back to the Peacock Court and made his way to the Ingrams' table. Elizabeth was not there, but her father rose when Adam approached and coolly invited him to sit down. Adam took a chair and waited. If the icy gaze of the women was meant to intimidate him, he was not going to allow it.

"You are not from this area, are you, sir?" Adam began politely.

Ingram was surprised. "No, my wife, daughter, and I are from Atlanta. We are visiting Mrs. Carter, Elizabeth's aunt," he said, nodding to the elderly woman. He paused. "How did you know that? Surely our accents are not that pronounced."

"No, sir. But I know this city's best families."

"Oh?" said Mrs. Ingram with a slight smile.

"I'm a reporter," Adam said.

The woman's smile faded. There was a long silence.

"Interesting line of work," Ingram said finally. Another long pause. "Where did you meet Elizabeth?"

"On the dance floor," Adam said.

The aunt let out a sigh of derision. Mrs. Ingram closed her eyes. Ingram cleared his throat. "Young man," he began, "I hope you don't take offense at what I am about to say. It is no reflection on you. In fact, it is more a reflection, I fear, on my inadequacies as a father." He paused. "Elizabeth is a . . . very impetuous child. She has a habit of . . ." He looked toward his wife, who looked pained. "A habit of inappropriate behavior, and taking up with strangers—"

"Sir, I have no intention of—"

"Yes, I know," Ingram interrupted. "No one ever does."

Adam saw Elizabeth making her way back to the table.

"She is only sixteen," Ingram said.

Adam did not have time to reply. Elizabeth sat down next to him and smiled. He stared into her beautiful face, stunned. Good lord, a child! No, a woman. She's a woman. I felt it. Elizabeth's gaze traveled from Adam to her father. She grabbed Adam's hand. "Let's dance," she said, pulling him onto the dance floor.

"What was my father saying to you?" she asked.

"That you are only sixteen," Adam said.

"Warning you, in other words."

"Just being protective of you, I suspect."

"Of me! Oh, no. Of my money. You see, Mr. Bryant, my family is worth ten million dollars. And someday it will be mine." Adam stopped in midstep. Her eyes bored into his. "When I tell a man that," she said, "he always does one of two things. Runs like hell or tries to seduce me. Which will it be, Mr. Bryant?"

Adam was still struggling to regain his composure. "I think you are spoiled and should be spanked."

"And what if I liked that?"

Adam stared at her, then threw back his head and laughed. She laughed, too, and they began to dance again. When the song ended, she looked at him. "Let's go," she said.

"Where?"

"Anywhere."

She took his hand and led him to the entrance. Outside, she stood for a moment in the paved courtyard, amid the bustle of livery men helping departing guests into Cadillac sedans. The evening air was chilled and misty, but she stood bare-armed, breathing deeply, her silver gown floating around her ankles. Adam watched her, entranced.

"Oh, the cold! It feels so good! It's always so damn hot in Atlanta." She turned to Adam. "Show me San Francisco."

Adam knew he had about three dollars on him. He was still in shock over Elizabeth's admission of her wealth. How in the world was he going to dazzle a pampered heiress?

"I've never been on one of those," she said, pointing to a nearby cable car on California Street. She started off toward it and Adam had to run to keep up. She climbed onto the sideboard. The two other male passengers stared; a woman riding the sideboard was prohibited, but the brakeman took one look at Elizabeth and, with a wink at Adam, let her stay where she was. Adam followed, fishing in his pocket for the nickel fare. The car started down a steep hill.

"Your parents," Adam began, "Won't they—"

"They're used to it," she laughed.

The wind was charging up from the bay. "It's cold. Let's ride inside!" Adam said.

"No, no! This is lovely!" Elizabeth clung to the rail, her eyes wide with delight. Her gown fanned out behind her, and her red hair spilled from its chignon.

Below them, a fog was advancing over the waterfront, slowly snuffing out the glimmering lights of the bay.

"Oh, Adam, it's so beautiful," she said.

"Yes," he said. He could not take his eyes off her. From the moment he had seen her, he knew he had to meet her. It had been a purely physical reaction. But now, alternating thoughts went through his mind. The press of her body against his. And her words . . . ten million dollars.

At the line's end, she wanted to ride again. They boarded another car that took them to Chinatown, and rode another down to the North Beach Wharf and back up again, through the neighborhoods of Russian and Telegraph Hills. Standing behind Elizabeth, Adam saw that she was shivering. He folded her into his arms and she leaned back against him. He closed his eyes, losing himself in her flowing hair.

He finally looked at his watch. It was one A.M. Somehow, he had to finish his work. They got off the cable car on Market. He explained that he was a reporter and had to complete his story on the hotel opening.

"You don't seem surprised," Adam said.

"That you work for a living?" she smiled. "I may be spoiled, Mr. Bryant, but, unlike my parents, I'm not a snob."

Adam paused. He didn't want the evening to end. It had been magical, and she was an apparition that would disappear with the mist in the morning.

"Can I see where you work?"

Her question surprised him, bringing him back to earth. This woman in a dirty newspaper office? The thought was absurd, this silvery ephemeral creature entering his life where the reality was smudged newsprint, rented suits, and a bare apartment South of the Slot? Suddenly, he saw the folly of the whole evening. He was a fool. How could she ever be part of his world? He glanced at her, realizing suddenly that he wanted desperately to be a part of hers. But how could he? The distance between them was so great. For the first time, he was feeling doubt, a wavering in his one true faith—himself. It was rising like a foul taste in his throat. He grabbed Elizabeth's hand. "Come with me," he said.

In the city room, the men on the desk gawked at Elizabeth as she sat waiting for Adam to finish his story. Then, Adam led Elizabeth on a tour of the newspaper. They waited until the first edition came off the press, and Adam gave one to Elizabeth. His account of the hotel opening was the lead story. She read it carefully.

Outside, she paused. "Your story is very good," she said. "Why isn't your name on it?"

"None of the stories have names. That's just the way it's done," he said.

"Well, it should be different!" she said. "Your name should be all over this paper. Adam Bryant. In letters as big as . . ." she pointed up at the gilt letters on the Times building. "As big as that!"

He laughed. His feelings of doubt were rapidly dissipating. He would, somehow, see Elizabeth again. If he weren't sure of it in his own mind yet, he could read it in her face. He looked at his watch. It was nearly 4 A.M.

"The gala's over now," he said. "Where do I take you?"

She sighed. "To my aunt's, I guess."

Adam found a taxi and Elizabeth gave the driver directions to an address on Broadway in Pacific Heights. Elizabeth sat quietly in the crook of Adam's arm.

"Tired?"

"No," she said quickly. "I don't want the night to end."

"It's almost sunrise."

She smiled. "Then let's watch it." She glanced out the window at the mansions. "But where?"

Adam gave the driver new directions to go to the Palace of Fine Arts. The taxi left them in a small park on the eastern edge of the Presidio. In the foggy predawn light, an imposing colonnade loomed like a shadow over a duck pond. The palace was the remaining structure from the 1915 International Exposition. It was Adam's favorite place in the city, a tranquil place where the cacophony of modern life was drowned out by the echoes of the past.

They sat on the grass, saying nothing. They stared up at the colonnade, watching the architectural details emerge from the lingering mist as the sky lightened from gray to rose. It was quiet.

"You come here often, don't you," she said finally.

"How did you know?"

"Your face. It's like you're in church," she said.

He stared up at the columns. "I went to the exposition. I was only fifteen, but it left a big impression on me. The whole bayfront was filled with these wonderful buildings and sights. The city had come back from the earthquake. Everyone was so optimistic about the future. It made me think that anything was possible."

"And you still think that?"

He looked at her. "Yes, I do."

She laughed softly. "You're a dreamer."

"I guess so."

"And what do you dream of?"

He looked up at the columns, then back at her. It seemed suddenly strange to be sitting in the park with a girl he barely knew, talking of things as misty as dreams. He felt vulnerable. It was a long time before he answered.

"I dream of having power, and money," he said slowly. He paused. "And a family."

He waited for her to laugh. She just smiled gently. "How do you plan to make your dreams real?" she asked.

"Newspapers," he said. "I'll run one someday. Then own one. Then two. Then three. I'm saving money. I have ideas." He began to talk faster now, and she watched his face. "There's so much opportunity now," he went on. "This state is growing so fast. And I could open a newspaper in every city. I see a whole chain of them, strung out across California. And maybe more in other states. Powerful newspapers. But good and fair newspapers. Not like they're run now. Not newspapers controlled by politicians or criminals or rich bastards out to screw the poor. Newspapers controlled only by me."

He looked at her. "And my sons after me." He looked away, self-consciously. He couldn't understand what it was about her that compelled him to talk this way. He had never expressed such thoughts before. But then, his thoughts had never been so perfectly crystallized as they now were.

She was staring at him, her face serious, her eyes shining. "You are so sure of yourself," she whispered.

She laid back on the grass, staring up at the colonnade. It was nearly light and the fog was retreating, leaving the figures atop the columns visible. They were Grecian women, standing with their backs outward, seeming to stare down into the tops of the columns.

"What are they doing?" Elizabeth asked, pointing.

"Some people say they are crying."

"Why?"

"They are supposed to represent Art weeping at the impossibility of achieving dreams."

Elizabeth glanced at him. "A lesson in humility, perhaps, for us mere humans, Mr. Bryant?"

Adam smiled. "I like to think of them simply as beautiful women, who have some wonderful secret that I don't get. Maybe if I keep coming here, someday I'll get it."

"Do you always get what you want?" she asked.

He leaned over and looked at her. Her hair was a tangle of red against the green grass, and the pearly morning light made her skin look translucent. He kissed her gently.

"Yes," he said. "I'm a lucky man."

Chapter
Five

Adam stood outside the Tudor mansion, staring up at the windows. It was raining lightly, and his coat and hat were damp from the walk up the hill from the trolley stop. He had been standing outside the house for several minutes, working up his courage to ring the bell, thinking about last night.

He had stayed with Elizabeth in the park until nearly seven. They had talked about many things, yet nothing in particular that he could now recall. They had laughed . . . he had laughed, as he never had before, the feeling of lightness foreign to him. He remembered that feeling vividly. And he had kissed her, again and again and again.

When he had walked Elizabeth back up the hill to the mansion on Broadway, the well-kept streets of Pacific Heights had been empty except for a few domestic workers, slipping into back doors. Adam and Elizabeth had lingered on the porch, holding each other. "I want to see you again, Adam," she said. "Come back this afternoon." Then with a weary smile, she went inside. He had gone back to his room, bathed and waited. It was Sunday, his day off, and he had nothing to do. So he lay on his bed, thinking about Elizabeth . . . beautiful, rich Elizabeth. He replayed the night back in his mind, feeling the way her kiss excited him, seeing the looks of envy on the faces of all those other men at the ball. Elizabeth . . . a symbol of everything he could ever hope to have. She was a woman as far above him as those Grecian statues in the park. And yet . . . she wanted him. At three, he dressed in his best day suit and set off for Pacific Heights.

Now, as he stood outside the mansion, he felt uncertain. It had been just one night, one magical night, and he had always distrusted things he could not prescribe to logic. Now, it seemed more a foolish interlude, more a dream than reality. What am I doing here? he thought. But something made him go up the walk and ring the bell.

A maid answered, and Adam said he had come to see Miss Ingram. She ushered him in and told him to wait in the foyer. He was standing, hat in hand, staring up at a chandelier, when Elizabeth appeared at the top of the staircase. "Adam! I knew you'd come!" She came tripping down the stairs.

She was wearing a simple blue-and-white dress, sashed low on the hips, and her hair was loose, pulled back from her face. She looked sixteen . . . until she smiled slyly at him. "Come into the library," she said, pulling him along. She closed the doors behind them. Adam stood in the middle of the large, paneled room, his eyes traveling over the paintings, soft Persian rugs, and shelves of books. Elizabeth took his hat. "Why, you're all wet," she said.

"It was raining. I had to walk from the trolley."

"Come sit by the fire," she said, smiling. She led him to a sofa and sat down next to him. Adam felt suddenly awkward and tongue-tied. Why had it been so easy to talk to her last night and now . . .

"I had a wonderful time last night," she said softly, her eyes sparkling. "It was very special."

He looked at her. "Yes, it was," he said.

"I barely got a wink of sleep," she said with a small laugh. "I must look a fright."

"You look beautiful," Adam responded without thinking.

"My mother was furious. She wanted to know what the gray smudges were on my dress." She smiled mischievously. "I told her I spent the night on a park bench wrapped in newspapers."

There was another pause. Elizabeth grew serious. "At first, when I woke up this morning, I thought I had dreamed the whole thing," she said softly. Her eyes bored into his. "There's something about you. You're different than the silly boys I've met, the other men—"

"Not really," Adam said.

"But you are!" She got up suddenly. "You have dreams, plans for yourself, things you want to do. You're not just sitting in college with your nose in a book, or lolling about on a boat. The way you talked about your newspapers. It was so exciting!" She grew serious. "You're different, Adam." She paused again, a strange look in her eyes. It was a wistful look without a trace of artfulness, and it went straight to his heart. "I envy your passion," she said softly.

He was taken aback. Never would he have used that word in

regard to himself. But never before would he have consigned a word like magical to a one-night encounter. He stared at the young woman before him and wondered with vexation what it was about her that caused his emotions to be so off-balance, his thinking so . . . imprecise.

"I envy men sometimes," Elizabeth said. "Their freedom to do things, to build, to achieve." She came back and sat near Adam. "I wish I could help you build your empire."

Before Adam could reply, he heard a latch click and saw Elizabeth's eyes shift toward the door. Her eyes clouded, and he looked up and saw Charles Ingram standing by the door.

Elizabeth rose. "Father," she began. "You remember Mr. Bryant. From the party last night?"

Charles Ingram came into the room. Adam got to his feet and extended his hand. Ingram gave it a perfunctory shake and uttered a small greeting. There was a long silence as Ingram eyed Adam and Elizabeth suspiciously. "Would you mind giving us a few moments alone, Elizabeth?" he said.

Elizabeth looked at Adam but didn't move. "Elizabeth, do as I say," Ingram said softly but evenly. She frowned slightly and seemed to want to say something. But with a final look at Adam, she turned and left the room quickly.

Ingram turned to Adam. No invitation to take a chair was offered. "Are you responsible for keeping my daughter out all night?" Ingram asked.

"I was with her, yes," Adam replied.

Ingram's gaze was icy. "How old are you, sir?"

"I'm twenty-six."

"Then you surely should know better." Ingram paused. "You know, I could have charges brought against you for corrupting a minor."

Adam squared his shoulders. "Sir, if I might be so bold, Elizabeth seems old enough to—"

"Mind your words, young man."

"I was only going to say that she seems old enough to think for herself, make sound choices."

Ingram took a few steps away, and thrust his hands into his pockets, staring at the floor. He looked back at Adam and gave a long sigh. "And you, Mr. Bryant, are one of her sound choices?"

Adam said nothing.

"I think not," Ingram said. "I'll try not to insult you, Mr. Bryant. As I told you the other night, I've seen a variety of men trying to get near my daughter. And they all want only one thing."

"You know nothing about me," Adam said.

Ingram considered Adam coldly. "I haven't gotten where I am by not being a good judge of character, Mr. Bryant. I've found if you want to know a man, all you need to know is what he wants. I know that you work for a newspaper, so I can guess you make perhaps two thousand dollars per year." His eyes swept over Adam's damp suit. "Can you look me in the eye, Mr. Bryant, and tell me you wouldn't like to be rich? Can you tell me that you aren't interested in my daughter's money?"

Adam stared at him, but finally looked away.

"You may very well be a man of character," Ingram said. "But I can't take a chance. I have a fortune to protect, a daughter to protect. You have nothing to offer a girl like Elizabeth." He paused. "She's very impressionable, given to romantic whims. I must, therefore, count on you to behave as a gentleman and make no further attempts to see her."

Inside, Adam was raging with anger, but he retained his composure. "I won't be brushed off like this," he said.

Ingram sighed and moved toward his desk. He pulled out a leather book and flipped it open. "How much will it take, Mr. Bryant?" he said flatly, picking up a pen. He looked up at Adam, his expression filled with disdain and condescension.

Adam's face began to burn with humiliation. "I don't want your money," he said through clenched teeth.

Ingram gave him a final look then closed the checkbook. "In that case, we have nothing else to say." He reached over to push a table buzzer. The maid appeared at the door. "Charlotte, would you show Mr. Bryant out, please?"

Adam paused, then picked up his hat. Without looking at Ingram, he went swiftly out into the foyer and the entrance. The heavy door closed behind him with a soft finality. Adam stood on the porch for a moment, his face still burning. Then he put on his hat, turned up the collar of his coat, and stepped out into the street. He paused for a moment to look up at the upstairs windows of the mansion, then started back down the hill in the light rain.

For the next two weeks, Adam tried to get through to Elizabeth with no success. His phone calls to the house were intercepted, his letters returned unopened. When he went to the mansion, he was turned away brusquely by servants. Finally, he learned that the Ingrams had returned to Atlanta.

He thought of Elizabeth constantly, his attraction to her becoming inseparable from the acute embarrassment and anger he still felt at her father's words. His rational mind told him he was being foolish, but still, he grew obsessed with seeing her one more time. He didn't know what he wanted from Elizabeth really—perhaps only a confirmation that he was, in fact, good enough for her. He asked for some time off from work and went to Atlanta. He located the Ingram home, a red brick fortress in the country-side, surrounded by an iron fence. Again, he tried to call Elizabeth but was rebuffed by Ingram. He resorted to staying outside the gate, waiting for Elizabeth to leave. Finally, the police arrived and told him that Ingram would have him arrested on harassment charges unless Adam agreed to leave Atlanta.

Adam returned to San Francisco, mentally and physically ex-hausted. Without thinking, he went into the office, through the city room, sagging into the chair behind his desk. A few of the men stared at him in curiosity. A secretary told him that he was to report to Bickford's office. Adam pulled himself out of the chair and took the elevator upstairs.

Bickford looked up from his paper, and stared at Adam, stand-ing by the door. "Have a seat, Adam," he said slowly.

Adam sat down, straightening his tie. He had not changed his clothes after he had gotten off the train that morning. Bickford looked at Adam, his face reflecting disappointment. "I got a phone call from Atlanta this morning," he began, "from a Mr. Ingram."

Adam closed his eyes.

Bickford's face reddened slightly. "I had a hard time believing what he told me, Adam. The man told me you were harassing his sixteen-year-old daughter."

Adam looked at him. "I was in Atlanta . . . ."

Bickford cleared his throat. "Look, Adam. I can't tell you how to run your life. But when it starts affecting your work, well, that's something else." He paused. "You've been acting odd for a couple of weeks now. Does this girl have anything to do with it?"

"My work comes first with me, Bick. You know that."

"Yeah, well . . . maybe." Bickford's perturbed look was soft-ening. "You know that promotion is yours, if you want it, Adam. But when you move up into management, you must watch your conduct. I don't like my top men's names showing up on police blotters." He paused. "Lilith doesn't know about this, and I won't tell her. Don't mess this up, Adam. You've got a future here, a really great future."

Adam stared at Bickford, almost dwarfed by the large mahog-any desk. A future . . . a great future.

Bickford let out a sigh, shaking his head. He was visibly relaxed now, apparently content his chastising of Adam was over.
"This Ingram fellow . . . you should have heard him," he said.
"After he called, I had the morgue check him out. Big name in the
South, I guess. One of those moldy old families that's been hanging around since before the Civil War . . ." He glanced at Adam.
"I can understand your wanting to sow some wild oats before you
settle down. But what in the world were you doing chasing his
daughter?"

"It was just one night, Bick," Adam said absently.

Bickford's mouth compressed into a grim line. "A man should
never try to play above himself, son. If you reach too high, you set
yourself up for a fall. Just be cautious, work hard, make a good
marriage . . . that's how you get ahead."

Adam didn't look up.

"You have a great future here, Adam," Bickford went on.
"This promotion is just the first step. You're young. You've got
so much ahead of you. But me . . . I'm not so young." There was
a different tone in Bickford's voice that made Adam look up. "I
always wanted a son," Bickford said, "someone to carry on after
me. What do daughters bring you . . . just heartaches. I love
Lilith, but she certainly couldn't run this newspaper after me." He
paused again. "But you could. I've known that from the first day
I met you. Your future is here, Adam, with the *Times*. If you want
it."

"I know, Bick. And I do want it."

Bickford's secretary knocked and leaned in to announce that
Bickford had someone waiting outside. Adam got up to leave.
"You look terrible," Bickford said. "Take the rest of the day off.
You can start fresh tomorrow . . . as city editor."

Adam hid his surprise. "Thanks, Bick," he said finally. "You
won't regret it. I'll work hard."

"I know you will," Bickford said.

Adam paused in the lobby long enough to pick up a copy of that
afternoon's *Times*. Outside, he paused. It was a chilly but sunny
day, and Union Square was filled with people—shoppers taking
advantage of the post-Christmas sales, men filing purposefully in
and out of the office buildings. He stood there, not knowing where
he wanted to go. He didn't want to go back to the boarding house,
and he felt no compulsion to linger over a drink in some speak-
easy. He folded the *Times* under his arm and set off to catch a
trolley. He rode it down across town to the marina and then
walked over to the Palace of Fine Arts. He found a bench near the

duck pond, and sat down. He sat there, watching the red-cheeked children play under the watchful gaze of mothers and nannies. He glanced down to the *Times*, still folded on his lap, and he thought of his promotion. He knew he should be elated about it. But instead, he felt a weariness that seemed to come from somewhere deep inside him. He glanced up at the colonnades, to the mysterious Grecian statues, perched so high above, their faces turned forever away from him.

He looked back to the newspaper in his hands. He unfolded it and idly scanned the headlines and then noticed the date. December 31, 1926. He hadn't even realized it was New Year's Eve. Tomorrow, he would go into the office and begin his new job as city editor. A new year would begin. His future would begin. He folded the paper and set it aside, fighting the urge to look up at the statues.

Chapter
Six

Adam sat at the dining room table, the newspaper spread out before him, staring out the window. From his vantage point in his Pacific Heights home, the bay was blue and the sky cloudless. A beautiful morning, filled with promise. He picked up the front page and began to read. There was no promise in the *Times*'s pages, just despair. The Depression was deepening, and life everywhere around the bay was tense. The city's neighborhoods were deteriorating, and out in the farming areas, homeless migrants congregated in shanty towns called "Hoovervilles." No promise at all.

No, that wasn't quite true, he told himself. There was a story about President Hoover approving legislation to build bridges across the bay, a longtime dream of city officials. That was promise. But it wasn't enough. Adam glanced at the date at the top of the page. January 1, 1930. A new decade had begun. A time to look ahead and hope for better things. Not a time to look back.

He looked at his watch. He had to leave soon, yet he felt sluggish. He was glad he had not drunk a lot at the New Year's party last night. He glanced at the other end of the mahogany table, where the breakfast setting sat untouched. The maid came in, offering more coffee, but Adam dismissed her. He stared at the newspaper, thinking about the disparity between the despondent life reflected on its pages and that of his own. He was now editor in chief of the *Times*. He was a success. And he was a man of some means now, with a large home on lofty Vallejo Street and a bright future.

"What time is it?"

Adam looked up. Lilith stood by the door. Her hair was combed and a violet silk robe was sashed around her slim figure, but her face had a gray pallor.

"Just after seven," Adam replied.

"I couldn't sleep." Lilith sat down at the table. The maid poured coffee for her.

"You have a hangover," Adam said. He picked up the newspaper. "You shouldn't have drunk so much last night. You can't handle it."

Lilith sighed in annoyance. "If you're going to start lecturing me again, can't you have the decency to wait until after I've had some coffee?"

There was no reply from behind the newspaper. Finally he folded it and rose.

"Where are you going?" Lilith demanded.

"I have to go out."

"You never stay and have breakfast with me," she said peevishly. "It's seven o'clock in the morning on New Year's Day. Where in the hell are you—" She paused. "Oh, God, not that stupid club thing again, Adam."

"I have to go. I'm picking up your father on the way."

Lilith laughed. "But Adam, it's so ridiculous! Every year, grown men getting together to act like children. You and my father . . . you'd think this was some big family tradition or something."

Adam paused, an idea forming in his head. Family tradition! Why hadn't he thought of it before? He called for the maid. "Annie," he said when the girl appeared. "Get the baby ready. I'm taking him out."

Lilith almost dropped her coffee cup. "What do you think you're doing?" she asked.

"You're right," he said, his excitement rising. "It *is* a family tradition, and Ian is going to become a part of it."

Lilith shot to her feet. "You're not taking that baby to this idiotic ritual! I won't allow it!"

"He's my son," Adam said.

Annie returned holding a wicker carrier. Adam took it and started toward the door. Lilith ran after him. "For god's sake, Adam," she said. "He's only two months old!"

Adam smiled. "I'll take care of him." He hurried down to the car, put the basket in the backseat, and drove off. He knew Lilith would eventually calm down. God, drinking always left her so foul tempered. Thankfully, she didn't drink often. In the two and a half years they had been married, in fact, he seldom had found her truly disagreeable to live with. Her imperious moods and her social climbing schemes sometimes irritated him, but living with Lilith was generally an untroubled existence. He had his work. She had her home and clubs. Now there was the baby. It was a comfortable life.

Robert Bickford was waiting outside his own home when Adam pulled up. Bickford jumped into the car with an eagerness that belied his age and weight.

"Ready for the ol' Hike 'n' Dip?" Bickford asked. He was smiling. The man truly savored this annual event, even more so in recent years when Adam had started joining him.

Adam glanced at Bickford. A heart attack last year had left him in weakened health. "You feeling up to this, Bick?"

"Sure. Haven't missed one in thirty-one years!"

"We've got a new member to initiate today," Adam said with a smile. He cocked his head toward the basket.

Bickford's face lit up when he saw the baby. "What a grand idea, Adam! Three generations sharing the tradition!" Bickford was beaming. He loved having a grandson. "You know," he said softly. "With you running the paper now, it's almost like you're my son, Adam. I'm a happy man."

Adam glanced at the old man. Over the years, his feelings toward him had softened. It wasn't affection he felt toward him so much as charity. Bickford had struggled all his life in the shadow of his brilliant father, Edward Bickford, and he had been unable to move the *Times* ahead. Bickford's wife Catherine had died last year, ending their joyless marriage. His health was failing him. He had no sons. He was living out the remainder of his life finding little comforts wherever he could. And if Adam—and now Ian— were his comforts, who was Adam to take that away?

"Me, too, Bick," Adam said quietly.

Adam steered the car down the coast road toward the country club, thinking about Lilith. Despite the comfort of their life together, there was not a day that went by when he wished he wasn't married to her. He could have not gone through with it; he could have ignored the deal that had always been implicit in Bickford's promises. But he had willingly struck the Faustian bargain— control of the *Times* in exchange for marriage. He had made the decision clear-eyed, and he had learned to live with it.

But . . . there was scarcely a day that went by when he did not think of Elizabeth, and think of what his life would have been like with her.

He tried not to, but something would always remind him. A

silver flash of a window reflecting the sun. The clanking rumble of cable cars, a carved jade cat in a window in Chinatown. Someone laughing. Someone singing. Anyone with red hair. At first, it had made him sick, this constant, desperate longing. He saw her face everywhere he went. And at night, when he craved the black relief of sleep, she would appear to torture him in his dreams. Then, slowly, the obsession hardened into a dull ache that occasionally, when he was absorbed in work, subsided, but never totally went away.

It was about a year and a half after he had last seen Elizabeth, while he was routinely reading the *Times*, that he saw the announcement of her marriage. It was just a small story, buried in the society pages. Elizabeth Ingram, heiress to the Ingram fortune, had married Willis Foster Reed, a millionaire real estate developer and oil entrepreneur. The bride was eighteen. The groom was fifty-one. The story detailed the lavish wedding and told how Reed had given his bride a block of oil stock, a certified check for $1 million, a $10,000 diamond necklace, and had built her an Italianate mansion on a cliff overlooking the Hudson River. Adam had reread the story several times. He hadn't realized until that moment that deep inside him, a heartbeat of his fantasies about Elizabeth had endured. Now, with the announcement, any dreams he had harbored about her dissipated, like a final sad sigh.

Soon after, Adam and Lilith were married. He didn't love Lilith, but he had to keep going forward. His only real opportunity, the one for which he had prepared so carefully, was embodied in Lilith. She would someday inherit the *San Francisco Times*. She had ambitions of her own, and they centered on him. It was a joyless but just arrangement.

He drove on, watching a gull hover over the ocean in the overwhelming empty expanse of blue sky.

"I saw the new circulation figures yesterday," Bickford said, interrupting Adam's thoughts. "The country's going to hell in a hand basket, but we're doing okay. Thanks to you."

"We're in this together, Bick."

Adam drove on, glad to focus his thoughts on the newspaper. He thought with satisfaction about how much progress he had been able to make in the last three years. During the flush years just before the crash, he had improved the *Times*'s finances, and the newspaper had even begun to prosper. Adam convinced Bickford to pour most of the capital right back into the paper for badly needed improvements. Lilith had protested, saying they should be able to enjoy their newfound fortunes, but Bickford, well aware of his daughter's spendthrift tendencies, backed Adam. Bickford bought new presses for the photographs and rotogravure color Adam planned to use, and he authorized modest salary increases.

Then, two months ago, the crash had come, and overnight everything changed. The bottom fell out of advertising, with revenue dropping 45 percent. But circulation remained steady. Even in the worst of times, people still needed newspapers. While Bickford and Lilith fretted constantly about the Depression, Adam kept a cool head. His plan was to keep the *Times* on a steady keel during the financial storm, poised for new growth when recovery began. He worked long hours, often not even returning home. Across the country, weak newspapers watched their small-profit margins evaporate, and some important newspapers perished. But the *Times* held steady.

So did Adam's own finances. His natural frugality had given them a small cushion, and he forced Lilith to pare down. He had never invested in the stock market, so the crash left him almost untouched. For the last four years, he had been pouring every extra dollar into land in Napa Valley. Ten years of Prohibition had killed the wine industry, and the fallow vineyards were ridiculously cheap. Adam knew Prohibition would someday end, so he kept buying, slowly, acre by acre. When opportunity came, he would be ready.

He also wanted the *Times* to be ready to move ahead, so he worked to improve it editorially. The job had proven formidable. Under Bickford's laissez-faire ownership, the *Times* had stumbled along for decades, retaining the worst elements of yellow journalism but with none of its vitality.

When Bickford's father Edward had run the *Times* at the turn of the century, it had been a feisty newspaper, filled with sensational crime stories, sob-sister columns dispensing advice to girls and lovers, sports, society news, articles about psychics, comics, and the occasional "arts" review, emphasizing descriptions of actresses' legs. The paper featured huge, screaming headlines and faked photographs. Like the owners of other yellow journalism newspapers, Edward Bickford also liked to stage campaigns for the human underdog on his pages. When a headless torso was found in the bay, the *Times* inflated the story into a gothic horror tale, a running daily serial of lurid details. Bickford offered a $1,000 reward to the reader who could identify the corpse. When the murderers were finally found—the victim's wife and her lover—Bickford wrote a front-page editorial hailing the *Times* as "a detective force at least as formidable as that maintained by this city's taxpayers." The next day, the newspaper began running a new slogan on its masthead: The *Times* Is on Your Side! For three weeks, the *Times*'s circulation soared.

But by the time Edward Bickford died, yellow journalism had begun to decline. Newspapers across the country began to clean up their pages, led by the example of a young editor in New York who wanted his struggling newspaper to be a sharp contrast to the yellow papers. As a slogan for his *New York Times*, Adolph Ochs chose: "It Does Not Soil the Breakfast Cloth," later changed to "All the News That's Fit to Print."

Slowly, other newspapers across the country began to follow suit. But the *San Francisco Times* did not. When Robert Bickford took over, he timidly kept to the approach as outlined by his father. By the 1920s, the *Times*'s circulation had stagnated, and it survived as the quirky, blue-collar afternoon alternative to the bigger, establishment morning newspaper, the *San Francisco Journal*.

As Adam made his way up the ranks through the *Times*, he came to understand the Bay Area market and *Times* as no editor since Edward Bickford had. As soon as he was named editor, Adam began to change the *Times*'s image. He cleaned up the latent sensationalism and stressed the need for detailed, hard reporting. He fired deadwood editors and hired young men he could train himself. As budget permitted, he sent reporters to cover nationally important stories, such as the stock market crash aftermath in New York and the swearing in of President Hoover. He began writing thoughtful editorials that bore his distinctive democratic bent.

He kept the newspaper's slogan "The *Times* Is on Your Side" because he envisioned a newspaper that would echo the average person's needs and ideas. It would be a paper that did not indulge the reader's basest instincts, but one that would reflect his highest ideals.

Bickford watched the changes with some dismay, but Adam soothed his concerns. "The *Times* should be something people can believe in," he said. "People need that, especially now."

Adam steered the car around a gentle curve in the coast road. His thoughts wandered toward a momentary and soothing nothingness. He glanced over at the ocean. The sun glinted off the water in silver shards. Elizabeth. She was suddenly there again, filling his mind. He couldn't escape her. The moment his thoughts emptied, she was there to fill them.

"Adam, are you all right?" Bickford asked.

Adam looked over and smiled. "I'm fine."

"Well, pay attention, I have something to tell you." Bickford paused. "I've had a new will made up—"

Adam glanced quickly at the old man. "Hey, no talk about that today, huh?"

"We have to. It's important." Bickford turned to Adam. "I've been thinking about this a lot lately. About the newspaper. I want it to go on, Adam, after I'm gone."

"Bick—"

"Let me finish. You know what I think of you, and what you've done with the paper. Well, I know that you'd make sure it doesn't die, that it will . . . What I'm saying is that I've decided to leave you a majority share of the newspaper."

Adam was so surprised he nearly drove off the road.

"I know what you're thinking," Bickford went on before Adam could speak. "What about Lilith? Well, I love my daughter, but frankly, she hasn't got a brain in her head when it comes to money. I can't trust her with the *Times*. She'd milk it to death." Bickford paused. "So I'm leaving her a forty-nine percent interest and you a fifty-one percent interest."

Adam stared at the blue sky. He had never expected such a move from Bickford. "I-I don't know what to say, Bick," he finally stammered. "It's truly generous. Thank you."

Bickford smiled. "Well, it's not entirely unselfish. This way, you get control of the *Times*, but it still stays in the family. You and Lilith . . . running things together."

Adam drove on, gripping the steering wheel. He hadn't realized until then that he had been harboring a secret dream—about divorcing Lilith. Now, with stunning clarity, he recognized it for the fantasy it was. As much as he often regretted his marriage, he knew divorce was not workable. Lilith would never consent to it. Besides, in some ways, his marriage was liberating. It provided a convenient framework for his life, freeing him to funnel his passion into his work. Divorce was just not feasible, especially now, in light of Bickford's bequest.

At the country club, he let himself be pulled into the socializing to take his mind off his dispirited thoughts. The presence of Ian, now lying awake but quiet in the basket, lent him a special cachet with the other men. Bringing a son into the Olympic Club was an exceptional event.

When Bickford had proposed two years ago that Adam join the exclusive men's club, Adam had declined. He had always thought such clubs were for stuffy old men, those somber, three-piece-suited souls he saw trudging up the steps of the Pacific Union Club on Nob Hill. Bickford took Adam to a few functions, and Adam was slowly drawn into the Olympic Club's easy, rather democratic style. He joined soon after, becoming a regular at the club's downtown headquarters. He grew to like the club's quiet, masculine elegance. The mahogany-paneled rooms filled with hunting prints. The long, chandeliered dining room. The big, dark bar where deals were quietly closed over surreptitious scotch. He especially liked the swimming pool, where he would do laps to work out the day's tensions, beneath a beautiful stained-glass dome and under the watchful eyes of carved gargoyles.

Lilith resented Adam spending what little free time he had at the Olympic Club. But Adam didn't care. He was meeting the right men. And being a member had restored that camaraderie he had lost after leaving the newspaper in Oakland. The club was the only thing that forced him to occasionally emerge from the introspective niche into which he had been retreating lately.

No, not the only thing. Now there was his son.

Adam took the baby out of the basket, holding him tenderly for the other men to admire.

"A fine boy, Adam," someone said. "A future Olympian, of course."

Adam smiled. "That's why he's here today."

The thirty-seventh annual Hike 'n' Dip, at the club's oceanside annex, was about to begin. It was a sunny, unseasonably warm day, and everyone was standing outside wearing bathing suits, laughing, and kidding. A dog barked and jumped with excitement. The old tradition called for a sprint across the dunes to the ocean and a plunge into the water—to wash away the old year and begin the new. The charge began, and the cheering rose. Adam cupped Ian's dark head and held the baby's naked body tight against his chest, letting the other men race past. The baby was awake but quiet. Adam walked to the ocean and waded in up to his waist. All around him, the water churned with howling Olympians.

"To the future, my son," Adam said softly.

The baby looked up at him, dark eyes wide with trust. Adam carefully dipped the baby's feet into the water.

Ian Thomas Bryant began to scream.

Chapter
Seven

Adam closed the ledger with a small smile of satisfaction. The *Times*'s advertising revenue figures showed a substantial increase for the first four months of 1937. Now, after all the lean years, things were on the upswing.

He glanced at that day's proof of the *Times* front page on his desk. May 27, 1937. "Western World Jams City to Celebrate Amazing Span" read the banner headline across the front page. Adam rubbed his hand across his eyes. He had been up most of the night, catching a short nap on the sofa in his office. He was in the midst of sensitive union negotiations. But of more immediate concern was one of the biggest news events of the year—the opening of the Golden Gate Bridge. Adam himself had personally supervised the coverage, so enthralled was he with the event. He reread the lead story: "A necklace of unsurpassed beauty will be placed about the lovely throat of San Francisco today. It is the Golden Gate Bridge. It is the bridge that sings. It is given to the people who willed it to exist; given to them after years of struggle, years of doubt, years of labor. . . ."

But the bridge was more than that, Adam thought. It was a symbol of a hopeful new era, coming after seven years of crushing Depression. A symbol of a grand dream realized.

That was what he found so compelling about the bridge—its metaphoric connection to his own life. Though many people's lives and dreams were still as barren as the country's dusty heartland, his own dreams were flourishing. He had survived, even prospered, during the last seven and a half years. Four years ago, after the repeal of Prohibition, Adam had sold nearly all of his Napa Valley land, realizing a sizable profit. In a rare sentimental gesture, he had saved one large vineyard, which he had bought from a German immigrant winemaker who had been wiped out during Prohibition. Adam had allowed the man and his wife to live for nothing in the house that they had built on the property.

He turned his attention back to the latest story about the Depression. The country was slowly climbing out of the mire, but homeless families were still living in tar-paper shacks and foraging in San Francisco's dumps. He sighed. He knew that the world outside his own privileged sphere was still filled with despair, and he was not immune to feelings of guilt. He assuaged them with regular donations to the city's charities and had done what he could to help his own employees. Four years ago, when the *Times*'s shrinking profit margin was dictating layoffs, he had found ways to keep men on the payroll. No one who worked for Adam Bryant suffered.

Unlike so many businesses, the newspaper industry had weathered the bad years. Nationwide, newspaper circulation had even risen slightly during the thirties. After all, at two cents, a newspaper was still one of the few bargains to be had. The *Times* had more than held its own. It was growing now at a faster rate than the rival *Journal*.

Adam glanced up at a photograph framed on the wall and smiled slightly. He had had the photograph framed because he thought it summed up why the *Times* would someday overtake the *Journal*. The picture was taken back in 1934, during President Roosevelt's National Recovery Act program. It showed 7,000 children in Seals Stadium, forming the initials "NRA" and a giant eagle, the program's symbol. Both newspapers had printed the picture, but Adam took it a step further, printing the names of all the children. He wrote an editorial, calling them "The New American patriots." The *Times* had to do an extra press run to accommodate demand.

Adam leaned back in his chair, running his hand wearily over his eyes. He thought suddenly of Bickford. He had died three years ago, leaving Adam the promised 51 percent majority interest. As ineffectual as he had been in running the *Times*, Bick had become the closest thing Adam had ever known to a paternal figure. There were moments when Adam genuinely missed the old man, missed having someone who shared his pride in the *Times*'s progress, missed having someone occasionally say, "Well done, Adam, well done."

His thoughts switched to Lilith. Their marriage had never been happy, but at least it had been civil. After Bickford's death, however, that began to change. Bickford's will had come as a complete surprise to Lilith, and she felt betrayed by her father. For three years now, she had been taking out her bitterness on Adam. She questioned every expenditure Adam made for the *Times* that she imagined was eating into the profits. Their arguments became more frequent and more furious. Bickford's will, which he had hoped would unite Lilith and Adam forever in mutual service of the *Times*, had left instead a legacy of increasing rancor.

Adam thought back to two years ago, when he had bought a struggling newspaper in Sacramento, using the profits from his Napa land. He had been so excited; it was the first step in his dream to acquire a chain of newspapers, and he was proud that he had done it only with money he himself had made. It was the first time he had really felt the loss of Bickford's death; he wanted to share the fine moment. Finally, he told Lilith, hoping she might at least appreciate the financial potential of his plan, perhaps begin to understand why he was doing it. But she angrily accused him of diverting profits from the *Times* to further his own fortune and ridiculed his plan as foolhardy. After that, Adam never again tried to talk to Lilith about his dream.

Soon after, he sent her to Paris for an extended vacation. During her absence, he spent most of his time in Sacramento, leaving Ian in his governess's care. For four months, he was blissfully free of distraction, concentrating all his energies on work. Lilith came home with a new spring wardrobe and a new attitude of calculated indifference. An uneasy calm settled in, as if both she and Adam, too weary to continue the war, had called a truce and agreed to coexist. Lilith left Adam alone to his work. His side of the bargain was an occasional public appearance to maintain Lilith's social pride. Only his closest editors knew that, more often than not, Adam Bryant spent the night on the sofa in his office instead of going home.

Adam glanced over at the sofa and then down at his pants, which were creased from his fitful nap. He rubbed his palm across his stubbly jaw and glanced at his watch. No time to go home; he'd have to clean up here. He turned to go into the adjoining bathroom, and someone rapped on the door.

One of Adam's editors poked his head in. "We're all through with the tour, boss," he said. He ushered in a dark-haired boy. "Thought I'd better bring him back here."

"Fine, thanks, Hank," Adam said. "I appreciate your taking the time to watch him while I finished up."

"Anytime." The man left, closing the door behind him. Ian stood waiting, staring up at Adam. Lilith had dropped him off earlier, and Adam had intended to show the boy around the news-

paper. But pressing last-minute business had forced Adam to en-
list the help of his editor. Adam looked at the boy, feeling a bit
guilty. At seven and a half, Ian was tall for his age. His face, a
combination of Lilith's dark coloring and Adam's handsome features, was almost too beautiful for a boy, Adam had always
thought, and he worried that Lilith's preoccupation with the boy's
clothes rendered him effeminate-looking. Today, though, Ian
looked different. He wore a smart gray suit, shiny shoes, and a
neat, striped tie. His hair was newly cut in the new short style that
young boys were starting to wear. Ian looked older—suddenly
older. In fact, except for his knee-length pants, Ian looked unnerv-
ingly like a miniature adult. And any urge Adam had to smile was
vanquished by Ian's dark eyes, staring up at him ever so gravely.

"Sit down, Ian," Adam said, motioning toward the sofa. Ian
did so, his eyes traveling slowly across the office. Adam began to
straighten his desk. "So," he said, smiling finally. "How'd the
tour go? Did Hank show you the presses?"

"Yes," Ian said, his eyes still wandering.

"What did you think? Pretty impressive, huh?"

"I guess so," Ian said with a shrug. "Awful dirty." His eyes
finally returned to Adam. "Is this your office?"

"Yes. It used to belong to your grandfather. You were in here
once before, you know. Your mother brought you in to see your
grandfather when you were a baby."

"I don't remember," Ian said, his gaze wandering again.

"No, I suppose you wouldn't."

There was a silence. Ian was staring at Adam, as if waiting for
something. Adam cleared his throat. "I'm sorry I couldn't give
you that tour myself, son," he said. "I've been trying to get my
work done so we could go to the bridge opening this morning."

"That's okay." A flicker of disappointment crossed the boy's
face, which he quickly hid by seeming to study his shining shoes.
He began to kick his feet out rhythmically, and the miniature man
image evaporated.

"I have to get cleaned up," Adam said. "Why don't you come
in and keep me company." Ian climbed off the sofa and followed
him into the adjoining bathroom. Adam stripped to his undershirt,
and began to wash his face and hands at the marble sink. Ian stood
nearby, watching the ink-tinged water from Adam's hands spiral
down the drain. His eyes traveled from Adam's powerful bare
arms, down to his suspenders hanging slack at his pants waist.
Adam began to shave, and Ian's dark eyes followed every move
intently.

"Does that hurt?" he asked softly after a while.

"Only if I slip and cut myself," Adam said, flicking the cream into the sink. He turned to smile at Ian, but the boy regarded him solemnly. Finally, Ian went to a window and stared out, his fingers drumming restlessly on the glass.

As he finished shaving, Adam watched Ian's reflection in the mirror. He could tell Ian had a keen intelligence, yet he seemed so easily distracted and bored. And he had a self-possession and coldness that was downright disarming in one so young. What distressed Adam the most, however, was that this attitude extended to him. He didn't want Ian to grow up to be emotionally weak, but he was hurt by his son's aloofness. Yet he had no idea how to counteract it. He was always intending to spend more time with the boy, but something always seemed to come up at work. Adam had learned to justify his long hours by telling himself he was working to give Ian the luxuries that he had never had as a boy. Indeed, Ian had every toy, everything a youngster could possibly want. Adam also told himself that his long hours were necessary because he was building something important—an empire perhaps—to hand over to his son someday. In his own mind, Adam conjured up many justifications for the emotional chasm between himself and Ian . . . the boy's natural moodiness, work above all, even that Lilith was trying to turn Ian against him. What he couldn't see, however, was the sad legacy of his own childhood. He had always been proud of the fact that he was a self-made man, learning by imitating others. He had learned how to write by reading the best authors. He had learned how to be a good reporter from observing experienced men. He had learned style and manners by emulating the rich. But what he had never learned was how to be a father. How could he, when he had never had a father himself?

Adam dried his face with a towel and went to the closet, pulling out a fresh white shirt and a newly pressed suit from the small wardrobe he kept at hand. He returned to the mirror to do his tie, watching Ian from the corner of his eye as the boy wandered listlessly back to the outer office.

He thought, not for the first time, how different it might have been if Ian had a brother. Knowing the loneliness and self-absorption that came from being an only child and orphan, Adam had wanted a large family and expected that Lilith would comply. But after Ian's birth, she announced that she wanted no more children. "I'm not some brood mare," she told Adam. "I won't ruin my figure just so you can prove your virility. Besides, large families are vulgar.'' Adam swallowed his disappointment, and the issue of children became just another brick in their wall of estrangement.

Adam came out of the bathroom and smiled at Ian. "So, what do you think of the place where your father works?"

Ian was standing at Adam's desk, rearranging the pens and pencils in the holder. "It's okay, I guess," he said.

Adam paused. "Think you'd like to work here someday?"

Ian looked up at him. "Sure. As long as I don't have to be down with those dirty presses." He smiled slightly, and his face was transformed. "I'd like to work up here in this office. With you, Father."

Adam came over and ruffled Ian's hair. It was an awkward gesture, and Ian pulled back slightly. At that moment, the door opened, and Lilith came in. "Lilith," Adam said, surprised. "I thought you were going to wait at home for me to pick you up."

She was dressed in a suit by Coco Chanel, a boyish design that she couldn't carry off without looking hard. "Frankly, I didn't trust you to remember," she replied. "I don't want to be late for the ceremonies. Are you ready to leave?"

Adam began to gather some papers off his desk and put them in his briefcase. "In a few minutes. I have some—"

"Adam, I told you I don't want to be late—"

"I know, Lilith, I know."

"You promised when you left last night, you wouldn't let work get in the way. You said—"

"Dammit, Lilith!" He threw a newspaper on the desk. "I'm up to my ass with this union contract! It's important—"

"It's always important! Well, I'm important, too, Adam! You keep forgetting that!"

They glared at each other. Adam glanced down at Ian, whose dark eyes were fiercely bright, as if he were fighting back tears. Adam smiled at Ian in an effort to ease the tension. "You ready to go see the new bridge, sport?"

Ian was determined not to cry. "Can we take a trolley?" he asked softly.

Adam glanced at Lilith. "Your mother doesn't like you riding on trolleys. The car'll get us there quicker."

They rode across town in silence, the car making slow progress in the crowded streets. The entire city was caught up in the frenzy of celebration. The new Golden Gate Bridge was scheduled to open for vehicles tomorrow, but today it belonged to pedestrians only. It had opened at six that morning, and tens of thousands of people had already made the two-mile round-trip walk. The streets were filled with revelers, many dressed in Indian or cowboy costumes, and out-of-state license plates seemed to outnumber the familiar black-and-gold ones. At cafés and bars along Market and Powell, lines snaked out into the streets. On every corner, pitchmen hawked silly souvenirs—commemorative medals for a quarter, caballero hats, giant balloons.

Ian pressed his face against the car window, his eyes wide. Adam watched him in the rearview mirror. He felt guilty that Ian had witnessed another fight between him and Lilith. Adam stopped the car for a traffic signal, and a group of happy celebrants ran by, laughing and holding balloons. Then a man in a worn suit started across, walking slowly with his head bowed. He had a young man's face, but with ancient, lifeless eyes. Adam had seen the man's expression on so many faces during the Depression, and the complete, utter emptiness of it never failed to unnerve him. Adam stared at the man until Lilith finally told him the light had changed.

Seeing the man triggered something in Adam. Even amid the party atmosphere, disillusionment was inescapable. He felt it in his own life. His marriage had turned into an absurd drama, and with each passing day, he was finding it harder to convince himself that he could continue to live a life of neat accommodation, a life devoid of happiness and . . . passion. That was the only word for it, really. Passion. As much satisfaction as the newspaper gave him, he still felt an emptiness, as if he were only half alive.

He and Lilith were held together only by Ian and her preciously maintained social facade. They had separate bedrooms now, and Adam was glad she made no demands. He had begun to suspect lately that Lilith had taken a lover. It was an accepted practice among her crowd, as long as it was discreet. At social functions, Adam surveyed the rapier-eyed young men, trying to figure out which one was sleeping with Lilith. He didn't really care. He was just curious.

His own sexual needs were met at Sally Stanford's bordello. There was no passion in what he did, just the quick-burn pleasure of sheer physical release. He never asked for the same woman twice. Sally, thinking he simply craved variety, kept him accommodated with an eclectic stream of women. Adam refused her choice only once, when she sent to his room a tall, cream-skinned redhead. If Lilith knew about the prostitutes, she never said a word. Many of her friends' husbands were on Sally's client list, so Lilith knew the proper code of conduct. *I don't care what you do* in private, was the unspoken rule, but in public, you are my husband.

A facade of fidelity, discretion, and the occasional public appearance. It seemed a small price to pay, so Adam played along. He didn't enjoy going to social events, but he found they were very helpful in cementing business contacts. And the idea of Ian someday moving in society's highest circles appealed to him. He had never forgotten the humiliation of that day in Charles Ingram's library, and he didn't want Ian to ever suffer in the same way.

But, five years ago, his disinterest evaporated with one event. It was the opening of the new opera house. Adam had begrudgingly taken his seat next to Lilith in the grand new house, dreading the dreary evening. Lilith complained bitterly that they had been issued seats in a marginal orchestra section, and peered covetously up at the box seats. Then, the performance of *La Tosca* began, and Adam, who had never heard live music before, became enthralled, hearing in Puccini's music something that spoke to his soul as nothing ever had. A week later he surprised Lilith by announcing he had purchased a lifetime box subscription. He began collecting recordings, becoming fixated on Puccini, often playing recordings in his office late at night. When Sally Stanford's women failed, the music was able to dull the ache of his emptiness.

As he drove to the bridge, Adam began to hum a segment of Cavaradossi's "Eluceum le stelle" from the third act of *La Tosca*. The mournful aria had been swirling through his head lately, a whispered background song for his frame of mind.

As they approached the Presidio, traffic choked to a stop. Thousands of people had abandoned cars and trolleys and were walking to the bridge. "This is incredible," Adam said, staring out the windshield. He parked the car. "We'll have to walk."

"I can't walk that far in these shoes," Lilith said.

"I told you to dress sensibly."

"We have seats in the reviewing stand. I couldn't go looking like some housewife."

Adam was already out the door with Ian. "Lilith, you can stay here if you want. We're walking." Pouting, Lilith joined them, tottering along in her new platform shoes.

Suddenly Adam stopped, transfixed by the scene before him. Hundreds of thousands of people were milling on the bridge, a long crescent of cement that curved out across the water. And there above them all, two towering orange spans rose up through

the wispy morning fog, framed against the green hills of Marin.
Adam stood, mesmerized, holding Ian's hand. "Look, Ian. . . ."

Lilith caught up to them. Adam turned to her, smiling. "God,
Lilith, have you ever seen anything so beautiful?"

"It's lovely," she said flatly. She clutched her turbaned head
against the breeze. "I can't stand all these people. Let's go get our
seats." She went off with Ian. With a last look at the bridge,
Adam followed.

The parade was five miles long, snaking through the city and
ending at the viewing stand at Crissy Field. Ian sat on Adam's
shoulders, entranced by the march of bagpipers, cowboys, mum-
mers, mounted police, and motorcyclists. A stagecoach went by,
followed by people dressed as cavemen, decks of cards, pencils,
and paint tubes. A silent group in white passed by, all members of
Blindcraft, paying homage to the new marvel they could not see.
Overhead, a squadron of silver-winged airplanes swooped over
the soaring, fog-tipped towers of the bridge. Then a slight figure
stepped out of a black limousine, and thousands of people—in the
stands, balancing on soapboxes, hanging from streetlights, roared.
It was Joseph Strauss, engineer of the bridge that everyone said
couldn't be built.

Lilith tugged on Adam's arm. "I see Enid," she shouted over
the din. "I'm going over to talk to her. Do you think you can keep
an eye on Ian?" Adam nodded and watched her wend her way up
the grandstand. Finally, the last of the parade divisions went by,
and it was over. The police nudged people back from the parade
line and the crowd began to disperse.

"Did you enjoy it?" Adam asked Ian.

"Yes . . . especially the motorcycles." The boy's face was
more animated than usual. "Can we go walk across?"

"Well, I don't know. . . ." Adam had to get back to work
soon, but he saw a light in the boy's eyes. "I guess we can,"
Adam said with a smile. "Let's go find your mother." They
walked along, Adam scanning the grandstand crowd for Lilith.
Then suddenly he froze.

"Elizabeth," he whispered.

She was standing in the front row at the far end of the grandstand, and he could see her clearly. She was wearing a conserv-
ative black dress, holding her hat, and her hair was like a blazing
red beacon in the sunshine.

Without taking his eyes off her, Adam took Ian's hand, and he
made his way toward her. When he finally reached her, all he
could do was stand there, staring up at her. Around him, the

restless crowd pressed close. With a flourish of cymbals, a band began to play. Adam heard none of it. He didn't feel Ian, tugging on his hand. He could see only Elizabeth, standing there above him, only a few feet away.

The music ended. Suddenly, as if she sensed the weight of Adam's gaze, Elizabeth looked down. She saw him immediately. A look of shock crossed her face. It gave way quickly to an odd expression of joy and then sadness. He saw her mouth his name, and he pushed his way to her. She bent down. For a moment neither of them could say anything.

"Elizabeth . . . how . . . why . . ."

"I never thought I'd see you again," she said.

"I knew I would see you again," he said quickly, without thinking. "I didn't know when, but I just knew."

All around them, people were moving toward the bridge, a tide that threatened to carry Adam off in its wake. He gripped the railing. Elizabeth laughed nervously. "Oh, Adam, this is so . . . I don't know what to say!"

She noticed Ian, standing behind Adam, staring at her. "Is this your boy?" she asked softly.

Adam realized suddenly he had forgotten about Ian. He pushed him forward. "Yes, this is Ian," Adam said proudly. "Ian, this is . . . a friend of mine. Her name is Elizabeth."

Her smile was wistful. "You said you wanted a son." There was an awkward pause. "Is your wife here, too?" Elizabeth finally asked.

"Yes, somewhere."

They stared at each other. People were pushing forward, trying to leave the stands. She began to search the crowd, as if looking for someone. She seemed disoriented.

"Are you here with someone?" Adam finally said. It was no time for small talk, yet he was afraid she might vanish somehow if he didn't keep her here.

"Yes, my aunt . . . I seem to have lost her."

Adam reached up and grabbed her hand. "Come with us."

"What? Where?"

"Across the bridge. Let's walk across the bridge."

"Oh, Adam, I can't."

His grip tightened. "Come with us."

She stared down at him for a long moment. Suddenly, she smiled, and the melancholy dissolved from her face. Then, she laughed, the same magical, deep laugh Adam remembered. "Oh, what the hell," she said. "Help me down from here!"

Adam hoisted Ian onto his shoulders and the three of them joined the human mass that was moving slowly toward the towering orange spans. A stiff wind was blowing up from the ocean as the crowd trekked north. Adam and Elizabeth walked along silently, side by side.

Adam didn't know what to say. He felt out of sync with the buoyant crowd around him. He watched as an exuberant young man whooped with delight and tossed his beer bottle over the rail. It plummeted down, curving in the wind, missing a boat by inches. The man started to climb over the railing and was pulled back by his girlfriend.

Adam looked up at the fog pressing close, and then he looked down, over the railing, down to the green waters. He felt dizzy with wind and space. He was a mountaintop, close to the clouds, miles from earth. A man teetered by on stilts. Two girls whizzed by on roller skates. Elizabeth laughed and grabbed Adam's arm. Her touch made him pull in his breath. It brought him immediately back to earth.

"How far across is it?" she asked.

"We can go back," Adam said quickly.

"No! No! It's wonderful out here." She wove her arm through Adam's, and they walked on.

Adam had millions of things he wanted to ask, things he wanted to say, but he didn't know where to start. So many years had passed—had it been only eleven? It seemed much longer—and he was different now, not the same earnest young man who had sat at her feet and confessed his dreams. Not the same man who had been told by Charles Ingram that he had nothing to offer. He glanced at Elizabeth. And she was different, too. Still so beautiful, but subdued somehow, even sad. Perhaps, he thought, it was only the black dress she wore. It was not a good color for her. She belonged in pinks, and whites . . . and silver.

As they neared the Marin side, the curbs became lined with people eating box lunches. Up in the hills, Adam could see picnickers. Finally, they reached the northern end. Adam found a spot on the grass and left Ian and Elizabeth, returning with sandwiches from a lunchwagon. Ian sat in stony silence slightly away from Adam and Elizabeth. He nibbled on his sandwich, glancing at Elizabeth and Adam, who sat with their shoes off, barely touching their food.

"How long are you here?" Adam asked finally.

"A week or two," she answered. "My father thought the change of scenery would do me good."

Adam stared at her, realizing suddenly she was very pale. "Have you been ill?" he asked.

She smiled strangely. "You might say that." She paused. "I'm in mourning. My husband died three weeks ago."

Adam was stunned. He had heard nothing about Willis Foster Reed's death. Surely it had been noted in the newspapers. How had he missed it? He seldom had time to read every item in the news these days, and his ongoing battle with the pressmen's union lately demanded all his attention. He had missed the story. Willis Foster Reed was dead.

Adam glanced at Elizabeth. The words "I'm sorry" formed in his head, but he couldn't say them. It wasn't true. He wasn't sorry. He was . . . astonished, confused. Elizabeth was free. She was free, and she was sitting here beside him.

"Why did you marry him, Elizabeth?" The words were out before he could think.

She looked at him, her green eyes turning strangely opaque. "I had no choice, really," she said softly.

"Yes, you did. There was me. There was us." The words spilled out without thought.

"Oh, Adam. That was only one night . . . a long time ago. . . ."

The sad finality in her voice made him fall silent for a long time. "It could have been us, Elizabeth," he said finally. "We could have been together." He paused. "I was in love with you. I wanted to marry you."

Her eyes grew wide with astonishment. Then, abruptly, she looked away. After a moment, her eyes brimmed with tears. "Then why didn't you fight for me?" she whispered.

For a moment, Adam was too stunned to say anything. "Fight for you?" he repeated. "I did! I tried to reach you. I tried for so long to reach you, Elizabeth. I called you. I went to your aunt's house. I followed you to Atlanta. Your father threatened to have me arrested if I didn't leave you alone. I wrote you letters, dozens of letters. You never answered any of them."

She turned back to him. "I never got them, Adam," she said softly. She looked out over the crowd, still coming across the bridge toward them. It was a long time before she spoke. "When I didn't hear from you," she said, "I started to think that my father was right. That you were like all the others, that you were only after my money."

Adam's eyes dropped to the ground. He plucked a handful of grass and watched the blades sift through his fingers and drift away on the wind. When he looked up, he saw that Elizabeth was crying.

"Why are you crying?" he asked softly.

"Because it might have been different," she said. "If I had just known that you really cared, if I hadn't listened to my father, it might have turned out different."

In all the moments he had dreamed of her, he had never been able to imagine her crying. It was unsettling. His own emotions were a tumultuous mix—joy over seeing her again, sadness over the lost years, and a piercing pang of guilt. The money—it *had* been a factor then. He had never been able to separate what he felt for Elizabeth from the fact that she was wealthy. And even now, as he looked at her, he couldn't separate it. Her incredible beauty still stirred him physically as no other woman ever had, and even in mourning, she radiated a vitality that he found irresistible. But still, in the back of his mind, was the money.

He stared at her—Elizabeth, still the symbol of everything he wanted. "It wasn't the money," he said. "It was you, Elizabeth. Just you."

She looked at him, her eyes cautious, waiting. "I should have trusted you," she said softly. She pulled a handkerchief from her sleeve and wiped her eyes. "I was so young," she said with a sigh. "My father always said I was just a wild thing, with no sense. He wanted me to get married. 'But you must marry a rich man, someone who doesn't need your money,' he said, 'for your own protection.' " She frowned slightly. "He kept after me, threatening to send me off to some women's college. Finally, I couldn't stand it anymore. I had to get out. So I did what my father told me to do—I protected myself. I married Willis. Needless to say, my father was very pleased with my choice."

He stared at her. The wind whipped her red hair into a fan around her profile. "Were you happy with him?" he asked.

She absently brushed the hair from her eyes. "Protection can be very expensive," she said softly. She stared vacantly out at the bay. The light had left her eyes.

"I love you," Adam said suddenly. "I never stopped loving you."

She turned to him. "You have a son and a wife. It's too late, Adam."

He stared into her green eyes. "No," he said. "I gave up once. I won't give up again."

Chapter
Eight

❦ Adam drove slowly along Mission Street, searching for the address. He found the number on a door sandwiched between a rundown dry-goods store and a butcher shop. He got out of the yellow Cadillac and looked up at the second floor window with its neatly painted letters: J. HILLMAN, ATTORNEY AT LAW. Upstairs, he looked for a secretary, but there was no one in the bare anteroom. An interior door opened, and a young man with glasses looked out.

"Mr. Bryant?" he asked politely. Adam nodded. "Please, come in."

Adam went into the office. In contrast to the outside office, this one was crammed with books. It was clean but dimly lit by an old overhead fixture. The young man extended his hand to Adam. "I'm Josh Hillman," he said.

Adam shook his hand and took the chair he offered. He took quick stock of Hillman: about thirty, with a thatch of sandy brown hair atop an earnest face. His serious brown eyes were trained on Adam, also taking stock. Adam saw them flick over his expensive clothes and back to his face.

"I was very surprised when you called me yesterday," Hillman began. He smiled self-effacingly. "It's not every day I get a call from someone like you, someone so well-known."

"I appreciate your being able to fit me in."

"That is no problem, I assure you." Hillman sat down behind his desk. "What is it I can do for you, Mr. Bryant?"

"I need a lawyer. A good one."

"I would imagine a man like you would have a squadron of them to help you run that newspaper of yours."

"What I need help with has nothing to do with the *Times*," Adam said. "It's a personal matter."

Hillman leaned back in his chair, regarding Adam carefully. "A personal matter," he said slowly, "one requiring the utmost discretion. Something a little too touchy perhaps for the corporate boys."

"Yes," Adam said simply.

Hillman stared steadfastly at Adam, unintimidated. "Well, besides the fact that I'm a nobody, Mr. Bryant, why me? Did you just pull my name out of the phone book?"

"I remembered a case you handled a few years ago. You defended a longshoreman who was accused of attacking a cop during the Battle of Rincon Hill strike. I remembered your defense . . . brilliant . . . but I couldn't remember your name, so I had the clips pulled from the morgue."

"I lost that case," Hillman said.

"Everyone wanted the unions broken. You were fighting public sentiment, as well as some very powerful people."

"Nonetheless, I lost."

"It was an impressive defeat. Especially considering you were, what, twenty-seven at the time?"

"Twenty-eight. A year out of law school." Hillman's smile faded, and there was a long pause. "What do you want from me, Mr. Bryant?" he asked quietly.

"As I said, I need a good lawyer," Adam answered. "But also someone discreet. You're right that this is something I can't allow my usual attorneys to handle." His eyes locked on the young man's. "I don't know you, but when it comes to people, I rely on my instincts until I'm proven wrong. I feel like I can trust you, Mr. Hillman."

Hillman folded his hands in front of his face. "Go on."

"I want a divorce," Adam said. "I know my wife won't agree to it. I want to force the issue, whatever it takes."

Hillman considered this for a moment. "Why do you want the divorce?" he asked.

"So I can marry someone else," Adam said. He told Josh Hillman briefly about Elizabeth. "I don't take this lightly," Adam said. "I have a son to consider, and I want custody because I believe his mother is turning him against me. And I'm Catholic, so I do not like the idea of excommunication. But I will do what I have to to get this divorce."

Over the bridge of his hands, Josh stared at the man across from him, locking in on the coolness of his blue eyes. Bryant radiated such power, but it was a hard power with no warmth. This was a man, he decided suddenly, that he could respect, maybe even come to like, but never be close to. His thoughts went to the task Bryant was asking him to do. He had always avoided domestic cases, and a contested divorce could be an ugly matter. As for custody, the courts never went against the mother unless she could be proven unfit. Josh knew something about Bryant's background. He had heard how he had wrested control of the *Times* away from his wife—the legal will notwithstanding. All things considered, this case could make for a truly gruesome public spectacle.

He really didn't need the hassle right now. He was struggling to build his practice, taking on cases that appealed to his idealistic nature, trying to develop his reputation as a crusader for the common man shut out by the legal system. He didn't lack for clients. The problem was, he was finding, the common man was commonly broke, so Josh often offered his services pro bono. It had been going on like this for four years now, and he was still heavily in debt from his law school loans. He could barely afford the rent on the office, the phone company was on his back, and he couldn't even begin to think about paying a secretary. It was simply becoming too much, and he was beginning to doubt his abilities. He had gone to law school burning with an idealistic intensity, but the constant financial pressure had caused the flame to burn low.

He sometimes felt guilty about his preoccupation with money. His parents, after all, were German Jews who had settled in New York with virtually nothing. They had moved to the west and opened a small tailor shop on Sutter Street, creating a comfortable but hardly commodious life. He was oldest of four children, the only one to go to college. When he decided on law, everyone said he was destined to do some good in the world. And he had. But still, he wished sometimes it were not always such a struggle.

He glanced at the photograph on his desk of his wife Anna. He didn't long for money for himself. He wanted it for her. She deserved it after supporting him throughout law school. And a family, he wanted to give her that. She had been patient, waiting years to start a family, and now she was pregnant with their first child. He didn't know how they were going to pay the hospital bill.

"I know this isn't your usual line of work," Adam said, interrupting his thoughts. "But I'll make it worth your while. I intend to be a very important man in this city someday, an important man in the state, perhaps in the country. I will accomplish this through my newspaper, and the others that I will someday own." He paused. "If you help me with this one matter, Mr. Hillman, I

promise you that you can be right by my side, as far as you want
to go.''

Bryant said all this matter-of-factly, and Josh stared into his
cool blue eyes, not doubting for a second that he would do as he
said. And he was extending his hand, offering to pull Josh along.
In that instant, Josh felt himself being drawn in by Adam Bryant's
aura of power, and he had a strange sense that his life was never
going to be the same.

Josh held out his hand. ''You've got yourself an attorney, Mr.
Bryant,'' he said.

Adam reached across the desk and shook Josh's hand. ''Good,''
he said simply. Adam leaned back in his chair. ''What do you
know about newspapers, Mr. Hillman?''

''Only what I read.''

''What about the *Times*? Do you read it?''

''More often than I used to.''

''What do you think of it?''

Josh held Adam's eyes, considering his answer carefully.
''When I was growing up, it was fish wrap. But it's changed.'' He
paused. ''Now . . . there's a certain intelligence behind it.''

Adam's mouth turned up in a slow smile. He rose, putting on
his coat. He went to the door and turned around, holding his hat.
''That is only the beginning, Mr. Hillman,'' he said.

The performance of *La Boheme* was magnificent, but Adam
barely paid attention. His mind was racing ahead, his nerves were
wire taut. It had been a week since his meeting with Josh Hillman,
and the young lawyer had put together everything he needed to
proceed with the divorce, including information that could, if
necessary, cast shadows on Lilith's character. However, Josh had
advised Adam to try to convince Lilith to settle; going to court
meant an ugly, protracted battle that could affect his own reputation and Ian's stability. Adam, realizing he was right, had agreed
to talk to Lilith.

After the opera, when he and Lilith got home, Adam went
straight to the library. He took off his tie and poured a brandy. He
waited a half hour, giving Lilith time to prepare for bed, then went
up to her room. Lilith was brushing her hair at her dressing table,
wearing only a black silk slip.

''I thought you went to bed,'' she said.

''I was waiting to see you.''

She stared at him. ''I didn't think you knew where my bedroom
was these days.''

He stood by the bed. "We have to talk, Lilith."

She began to slowly brush her hair. "I didn't think you even liked doing that anymore."

"I want a divorce."

The brush stopped in midair. Then it resumed.

"Lilith, did you hear me?"

The brush strokes grew more forceful.

"I want a divorce."

She didn't turn around, but continued to drag the brush through her short, dark hair with quick, violent strokes.

"Our marriage is a joke, Lilith. We don't love each other anymore—"

She swung around suddenly and hurled the brush at him. It missed and smashed into a porcelain lamp, shattering it. "You don't love *me*! That's what you mean!" she yelled.

"Lilith—"

"You've never loved me!" She began to cry, great gasping sobs that made her bare shoulders shudder. "You never, not for one moment, loved me. Don't you think I've known that?"

Adam watched her, stunned by her outburst.

"You don't care about my feelings, about what's important to me," she went on. "You never have!"

Adam had anticipated every reaction except tears. He stood, unable to move toward her to offer comfort. "I never meant to hurt you, Lilith," he said.

"Then why in the hell did you marry me?" she asked bitterly.

He said nothing. She picked up a handkerchief and blotted her eyes. "You married me to get the newspaper," she said flatly. "You made some sort of deal with my father, didn't you. That's all it ever was to you . . . just a deal."

There was nothing he could say in his own defense. She was right.

She looked up at him, her face pale, her eyes black smudges. "I could always tell," she said. "The way you looked through me, never at me. The way you touched me, never with warmth, never because you really wanted to. The way you made love to me. It was a duty to you, wasn't it. And you always held something back. Like you were waiting for something, someone better."

She buried her face in her hands. "God, Adam, don't you know what it's been like? You're so . . . cruel sometimes, so ungiving. You never loved me. Not for one single moment."

He had never seen Lilith this way, so vulnerable. It didn't touch him so much as make him feel sad. All these years, he had assumed she was content with their arrangement. Now, for the first time he saw the pain in her eyes, and a reflection of his own years of emptiness. Theirs had not been a marriage in any sense. It had been a sad, terrible match. Now there was nothing left to do but end it.

Lilith turned back to the mirror. He watched her reflection in the mirror as she struggled to compose herself. "I won't give you a divorce, Adam," she said.

The vulnerable Lilith was gone as quickly as she had come, making it suddenly easier for Adam to go on. "Lilith, what's the point of going on like this," he said.

"What's the point?" She spun around. "The point, my darling husband, is that we are married. That may not mean anything to you anymore, but it means everything to me. I will not become some sad, pathetic divorcée for everyone to pity. I care about what people think of me!"

That was the response Adam had been counting on. It was his only way out. "Lilith, I intend to get this divorce," he said slowly. "If you force me to, I will take you to court and say you have been unfaithful to me."

She laughed hoarsely. "Oh, Adam, that's ridiculous! Everyone in town knows you've been going to Sally Stanford's for years. We're both guilty on that count."

"But there's one difference between you and me, Lilith," he said. "I don't care who knows it. I don't care who knows that I fuck whores. And that my wife fucks everyone from Italian gigolos to Japanese gardeners. And that she had a little ménage à trois with her girlfriend and a famous opera star last month in an opium house on Grant Street."

Lilith's face went white.

"I don't care who knows any of it," Adam said. "But you do and I know that you do. If you don't give me a divorce, I'll drag you into court and lay out all the ugly details of our marriage for everyone to see. You know how this town loves dirt. It'll be the best-read story in the newspaper."

She stared at him. "You bastard," she muttered.

"Don't make me do it, Lilith," he said. "I don't want to hurt you any more than I already have."

Lilith continued to stare at him, but after a moment, she seemed to be searching his face intently. Adam could almost see her mind working, analyzing her position, looking for his weaknesses, sizing up her chances. She gave him a strange look. "I was going to ask you if there was another woman," she said tonelessly. "Then

I realized how absurd that is. There's no room in your life for anyone but you. You're a robot. You have nothing to offer a woman." She gave him a final, spiteful look. "Get out of my room," she said.

"There's one more thing," Adam said. "I want Ian."

She laughed. "You've got to be kidding! What do you want with him!"

"He's my son."

"Oh, you noticed?"

Adam took a breath. "I don't like what you're doing to him. You're turning him against me, Lilith. I won't have it."

"So, you've decided to try out for Father of the Year all of a sudden? For god's sake, Adam, if you cared at all about Ian's feelings, you wouldn't put him through a custody fight. Why don't you think of him instead of your own ego for once." She turned back to her mirror. "You stole the newspaper from me, Adam," she said, as she calmly applied cream to her face. "And someday, someway, I intend to get it back. But you might as well forget Ian. You lost him years ago."

Adam watched Lilith. He knew now she would agree to the divorce, but her words about Ian cut into him. If he wanted him now, he would have to endure a custody battle and all its sordid fallout. Josh was right; the courts would never grant him custody, and putting Ian through it would only alienate him further. He stared at Lilith's back, at the rippling movements of her thin shoulder blades. Suddenly, all he really wanted was to be free of her forever.

"I'll be staying at the club," he said quietly. "I'll have the divorce papers delivered to you tomorrow." He left Lilith's bedroom, closing the door behind him.

It was dusk, and the grounds of the Palace of Fine Arts were deserted. Adam sat on a bench alone, near the pond. He pulled his coat collar up against the cold wind that was blowing up from the bay, his eyes trained on the street. He had just come from Josh Hillman's office. Lilith's lawyers had delivered the divorce papers, signed. It had been only eight days since he last saw Elizabeth on the bridge. He shivered and glanced at his watch. When he looked up, he saw her coming toward him, and he jumped to his feet.

"I'm sorry I'm late," she said, out of breath. "It was hard for me to get away when you called. Then I couldn't get a cab and had to have my aunt's driver bring me here. I gave him fifty dollars to shut him up.'' She smiled. ''I hope it was enough.'' Her smile faded as she noticed Adam's somber expression. ''What is it, Adam? Why did you want to see me?''

She was swathed in a silver fox coat, a white scarf wrapped around her hair. Her cheeks were red from the cold, and her lips were parted expectantly. She had never looked so beautiful, and he had never felt so unsure of himself. What if, after all this, she didn't want him after all?

''Adam? What is it?'' she asked. ''You look so strange.''

He took her by the shoulders. ''Marry me, Elizabeth.''

Her eyes grew wide. He was acutely aware of the silence, growing unbearably longer with each second she hesitated. He searched her face for a clue to her thoughts. There was a glimmer of the same wariness he had seen in her eyes that day on the bridge, when she said she thought he had wanted her for her money. He grasped her hands. They were icy cold.

''Marry me,'' he whispered urgently.

''But, Adam—'' she said softly.

''I'm getting a divorce. I love you, Elizabeth. Marry me, please.''

The details of her face were growing blurred in the fast fading light, but her eyes were locked on his. Suddenly, he felt her fingers curl tightly around his.

''Yes,'' she whispered. She smiled, and it grew into a laugh. ''Yes,'' she repeated. She threw her arms around his neck and kissed him. He clasped her to him, burying his face in the soft warmth of her fur and neck.

Finally, she pulled away, her expression serious. ''I have to go home to Atlanta. I have to tell my parents.''

His fingers tightened around hers. ''When will you be back?''

''As soon as I can.'' She glanced at the waiting car. ''I have to go, Adam,'' she said. He wouldn't release her hand. ''Don't worry,'' she said softly. ''It will work out. It will be different this time. I'm not sixteen. I'm twenty-seven. My father can't tell me what to do anymore. This time, I won't listen to him. This time, I'll listen to my heart.''

She leaned into him. ''Oh, what a wonderful life we're going to have together,'' she whispered against his cheek. ''I'll share your dreams. I'll make you so happy. We'll have children . . . so many children. I love you, Adam.''

She pulled away and, with a final smile, ran across the lawn. He stood watching the car's lights creep up the hill until they were gone. He sat down on the bench and looked up at the Grecian statues on the colonnades, but they were lost in the dark. He shivered, from the cold and from an intoxicating sense of victory. He closed his eyes, taking a deep breath of the cold, tangy air, feeling his body tingle with a sense of anticipation that he had not known since his first day in the city. He opened his eyes and looked out at the lights glimmering on the East Bay. His life, he knew with breathless certainty, was never going to be the same.

Chapter
Nine

Adam and Elizabeth were married a month later.

It was a small ceremony, held in the rustic sanctuary of the Swedenborgian Church in Pacific Heights. Elizabeth's sister flew in from Atlanta to be the maid of honor, but her parents refused to come. Adam, realizing he did not really feel close to any man, at the last minute asked Josh Hillman to be his best man. There was no one else in the small, candlelit church to hear the tender ceremony.

Elizabeth wanted a honeymoon in Paris, but Adam felt it was unwise because of the growing threat of war in Europe. He also couldn't afford to be away from the newspaper long because union negotiations had broken down and a strike seemed imminent. They decided on a week in New York.

They arrived at the Waldorf-Astoria in late afternoon on a balmy day that promised summer. In their suite, Elizabeth went immediately to the window and gazed down on the busy street below. "I like this city," she said. "There's so much to do here, so much to see."

"We've been married less than a day," Adam said with a smile, "and you're bored with me already."

Elizabeth came to him and slipped her arms around his waist. "I will never be bored with you," she said.

He kissed her, almost formally. She gave him an inquisitive half smile and kissed him back, a deep kiss that left him stirred. She brought up her left hand to examine the thin gold band. "I like the way this feels," she said.

"I'm sorry it couldn't have been a diamond," Adam said. "I'm sorry we couldn't go to Paris."

She saw the self-consciousness in his eyes that he was trying to hide. "Oh, Adam," she said softly. "I don't care. We're finally together. That's all that matters."

He stared at the face before him, the one that had haunted his dreams for so many years. She looked the same, but different somehow. The girl of eleven years ago was gone, replaced by a woman now. The events of the last month had happened so fast that they seemed almost surreal. But now, seeing Elizabeth before him, everything was very real. He took her face in his hands and kissed her longingly.

When she pulled back, she was breathless. "We should take off our coats at least," she whispered, smiling. She drew the drapes, muting the dusky light. She kept her eyes on him as she began to undo the buttons of her suit coat. Adam's hands moved mechanically toward his own clothes, his eyes on hers. He looked away for a moment to slip off his belt. When he looked up again, his fingers froze.

She was standing by the window in her slip, her hair freed from its coil at her neck. The white satin pulled across her hips, outlining the soft curve of her pelvis, and across the tips of her breasts. Adam stared at her, mesmerized, as he felt himself growing hard. He had known she was beautiful, but not like this. He had relied on his dreamy memory of a girl. This was a woman before him . . . his wife.

He shrugged out of the rest of his clothes and went to her. At the first press of her body, he felt he would explode. He fought back the urge, drawing on a mental trick he had learned from one of Sally Stanford's prostitutes, and guided her down on the bed. He had always been vaguely ashamed about going to prostitutes, but he knew he had learned much about pleasing women from them, things he could now bring to Elizabeth. He didn't expect much sophistication from her. She had been a sheltered teenager, and what could she have gained from a marriage to an old man like Willis Reed? They hadn't even had children. He was fully prepared to be the patient teacher. But at this moment, delirious with the feel of her flesh against his, he was fighting for control. He had to hold back. He had to perform.

He was losing himself in her body, kissing her, feeling her, trying to be gentle. Finally, when he could stand it no longer, he positioned himself above her. Her eyes stared up at him, clear and steady. Slowly, he inserted himself inside her, and immediately had to shut his eyes. Stop, stop, wait, wait, he repeated to himself desperately. Then, the wave reared, and he began to move inside her, helpless.

Suddenly, he felt her inner muscles grow tight, then tighter, her wet warmth gripping him. Stunned, he could only stop, and the wave subsided.

"Wait for me," she whispered.

Her arms were draped gently across his back. But inside, she was holding him fiercely, with no apparent effort. She lay there quietly, looking up at him. He was totally in her control. It was the most incredibly erotic sensation he had ever experienced.

"Oh my god," he whispered hoarsely.

Her lips turned up in a small smile, and she closed her eyes in pleasure. She released him, then tightened, repeating the exquisite pulsing rhythm for several minutes. Then she let go and began to move her hips rhythmically, her breath coming in short gasps. She raised her legs to take him deeper, pulling his back, as her climax tore through her body. With a final quivering thrust and cry, he collapsed.

He was breathing hard and his buttocks hurt from where her fingers had dug into his skin. But he was completely, gloriously spent, bathed in sensation and sweat.

"I wanted to make it good for you," he whispered against her neck.

"You did," she murmured.

They lay there, entwined, as the room grew dark. After a while, Adam moved to his side so he could see Elizabeth's face. Her eyes were closed, her red hair fanned out on the pillow, a half smile on her lips, one hand draped languidly across her breast. She looked so blatantly sensual, and the way she had moved, and held him like that—where had she learned such things? She was obviously not the innocent he had assumed. His ego was slightly bruised, and he felt vaguely disconcerted, unable to reconcile the fact that this woman he had held up as some ideal goddess, had sexually beguiled, even *manipulated*, him as no prostitute ever had. Who is this woman? he thought, staring at her.

She opened her eyes, smiling sleepily. "Hello, husband," she said softly.

He thought of the statues in the park, the Grecian women with their hidden faces. He stared into Elizabeth's eyes.

"Hello, wife," he said.

The next five days flew by. They returned home to take up residence in a suite at the Mark Hopkins until they could find a house. Elizabeth said she didn't mind, but Adam did. He had lost the house on Vallejo to Lilith in the divorce, and the rest of his finances had been greatly limited. He had retained majority ownership in the *Times* and the paper in Sacramento, but Lilith had extracted high alimony payments, her lawyer claiming she was entitled to be supported in the style equal to her social position.

The irony of his situation was not lost on Adam. Here he was, just married to the widow of one of the country's wealthiest men, and a woman who would one day inherit her own family fortune, yet he was so financially strapped himself that he could not afford to buy her a new home.

Elizabeth had inherited $100 million from Reed, but it was tied up in stock holdings, set up in a trust, directed by a board of executives from her late husband's company. The revelation had come as somewhat of a disappointment to Adam. He certainly hadn't expected to plunder Elizabeth's fortune, but he had expected to have some access to it eventually. As it was cunningly set up, however, Elizabeth could sell small blocks of stock and spend the capital as she wished, but Adam could lay no direct claim to it. She could buy whatever she wanted. But nothing could be in his name. Someday she would also inherit money from her father. But Charles Ingram, Adam was sure, would do whatever was necessary short of disowning his daughter, to prevent Adam from using Elizabeth's inheritance for his own means.

So money was, for Adam at least, an unspoken issue. To have all that money so close yet so far was unbearable. Especially since he was so eager to get on with building his newspaper empire. He had plans . . . such big plans. But no big money of his own to back them up.

He often thought about bringing it up to Elizabeth, asking if she could sell some stock. But however he framed the question in his mind, it sounded like a confirmation of what Charles Ingram had said: that Adam was nothing but a fortune hunter. Even now, after nearly twelve years, he still smarted whenever he remembered Ingram's dismissal that day when he came to see Elizabeth in the mansion on Broadway: "You have nothing to offer my daughter." As it was now, Elizabeth believed that Adam loved her only for herself. It was, he reminded himself, the reason she married him. She trusted him. How could he possibly ask her for money?

They settled into a comfortable but uneventful existence first at the Mark Hopkins, then a month later at a rented home on Jackson Street. It was a commodious, cheerful Victorian, but on a less desirable fringe of Pacific Heights. Elizabeth did not seem to care about her newly scaled-down life-style. The only discontent she expressed, however, was over her inability to conceive. After five months, she still had not become pregnant.

She wanted children so badly. She wanted them partly to make up for the fact that Adam had lost Ian in the divorce. Just as Josh Hillman had predicted, the court granted Lilith custody, giving Adam visiting privileges and a hefty schedule of support payments. Adam took the loss of Ian as a personal defeat. Lilith, he was convinced, now considered Ian as part of a vindictive trade-off because of Elizabeth. Soon after Adam returned from his honeymoon, Lilith had called. She ranted that his remarriage was an insult to her, that it made her look foolish to her friends. "You never had any sense of propriety," she told him. "This will ruin any chances you ever had of being somebody in this town. And Ian's, too."

"She can't control me or the newspaper anymore," Adam told Elizabeth, "so she will control Ian, and turn him even further against me."

"He's your son, Adam," Elizabeth said. "I'm sure he still loves you."

But Adam's fears were confirmed when Ian finally came for his first visitation. He was withdrawn and silent, greeting Elizabeth with cold good manners and pointed indifference. Adam had arranged to have the day off and they went to see the popular new film *Snow White and the Seven Dwarfs*, which the eight-year-old Ian pronounced "a baby movie." By the end of the weekend, Adam returned Ian to the house on Vallejo, feeling defeated.

"Lilith's right," he told Elizabeth. "He's lost to me."

"Oh, Adam, it's not true," she said. "He's probably just very hurt and confused by the divorce."

Adam frowned. "I don't like the way he treated you."

"He's just a boy, Adam. Don't be so hard on him."

But he couldn't be placated. After a moment, he took her in his arms. "Let's have a baby," he said.

"We've certainly been trying," she said ruefully.

"I want children," Adam said. "A house full of them."

"Yes, I know . . . sons," she said. "And maybe a daughter to keep me company, hmm?"

Later, they lay quietly in each other's arms in bed after making love. Adam stared at the ceiling, lost in his thoughts. As always, Elizabeth had surprised him with her passion and skill, and he found her so exciting. Part of it sprung from his own feeling of possession, of finally having this exquisite woman. But it also arose out of Elizabeth's adventurous spirit toward sex. He found himself wondering more and more about Willis Reed and what kind of marriage they had had. "Elizabeth, are you awake?" he whispered.

"Barely," she answered lazily.

He propped himself up on one elbow to look at her. "Why didn't you have children with Reed?" he asked.

She looked at him for a moment. "You're worried that I can't, aren't you," she whispered. "I know I can, Adam. I just know it. And we will."

Adam leaned back against the headboard. He had not been thinking about infertility but of her lovemaking skills. His question was just a roundabout way of broaching the subject of sex without seeming uncouth, or worse, threatened.

Elizabeth saw the look on his face, and she sighed heavily. She sat up in the bed, facing him. Her expression was suddenly dispirited. "I should tell you something about Willis and me," she said softly without looking at Adam. She took a deep breath. "It's not that I can't have babies. It's just . . . Willis never made love to me. Not once in ten years."

Adam looked at her in astonishment, but she wouldn't meet his eyes. She sat naked, slightly stoop shouldered, her eyes on the bed. "He was . . . a strange man," she whispered. "He stayed in the city and came up to the house only on the weekends. I was alone there all the time." She paused again, her voice faltering. "On Saturday night, always at nine, he'd come up to my room. He'd sit in a chair near the bed and then order me to . . . take my clothes off, lie down, and touch myself. He sat there and watched; then, after a while, he would get up and leave."

She looked up finally at Adam, her eyes glistening. Adam was stunned. "Wh-why did you do it?" he stammered finally.

She closed her eyes. "I don't know. I was only seventeen, and I had some stupid notion that it was my duty as a wife or something." Her mouth twisted bitterly. "I owe that to my mother. I never once saw her show any affection to my father, but she still felt qualified to give me quite a little speech about a wife's duty before I got married."

She wiped her hand across her eyes. "After a few months, though, I couldn't stand it anymore. I refused, and he didn't press it. He just left me up there in that god-awful house. I was going crazy all alone. I couldn't go home, so I started running off to the city by myself, staying in hotels just to get away."

Adam reached out and gathered her into his arms. He held her silently for a long time. "I've had lovers, Adam," she said. She pulled away and looked at him. "No one I cared about, nothing that lasted long." She paused, her face reddening slightly. "I had to tell you, Adam. Please don't hate me for it. I was lonely, and needed someone to make me feel . . . clean and normal."

Conflicting emotions careened through Adam as he stared at Elizabeth. A stab of jealousy toward the faceless lovers came and went, and he quickly fought back the distasteful feeling that his ownership somehow had been violated. But the pain in Elizabeth's eyes quickly drew him away from the thought, leaving him with only a strong protective urge. And rage toward Willis Reed.

"It doesn't matter," he said, holding her. "Forget about Reed. You're with me now." He held her for a long time, until he could hear her breathing become deep and even.

"Why do people do it," she murmured, before she slipped into sleep, "why do people marry the wrong person?"

"They have their reasons," Adam answered vacantly. "Reasons that always seem right at the time."

Six months after their marriage, a handsome cotton rag envelope arrived addressed to Mr. and Mrs. Adam Bryant. Elizabeth opened it and asked Adam, "Who is Enid Atherton?"

"Queen of the social butterflies," Adam muttered. "She probably wants a donation for one of her charities."

"Actually, she wants us," Elizabeth said. "It's an invitation to a post-opera party."

Adam read the invitation. "Well, I'll be damned," he said with a smirk.

"Let's go, Adam," Elizabeth said.

"You can't be serious."

She put her arms around him. "Please," she said. "I'd like an excuse to dress up for you." Adam had planned to take Elizabeth to the opera opening, but the last thing he wanted to do was go to a party afterward. But he saw the eager look in Elizabeth's eyes and felt guilty. He had been spending so much time at work, and she was surely restless, cooped up in the house alone most of the day. It would be good for her to get out and meet people. People . . . the right people. He stared at Enid's name on the invitation, feeling a small surge of satisfaction. "Of course we'll go," he said. "And I want you to buy a new dress. I will be with the most beautiful woman in the world, and I want everyone to see her."

At the opera, Adam sat proudly at Elizabeth's side in his box. People stared up and whispered, and he tilted his chin higher. He was well aware that, right from the start, his marriage to Elizabeth had created a furor, generating columns of type in Eastern newspapers. One New York tabloid headlined it "Mrs. Reed's Gold-Rushed Romance." Most accounts in the East had politely referred to Adam as the owner of the *San Francisco Times*. But the implication was clear that the twenty-seven-year-old heiress had married beneath her.

But until now, Adam had been unaware that he also had become a curiosity in his own town, especially among the social elite. His divorce from Lilith and quick remarriage to an alluring rich woman had given him an air of notoriety. There were a few people who dismissed him as a parvenu. But most were intrigued, even a bit proud, of the handsome San Franciscan who had risen from nothing to capture Elizabeth Ingram Reed, the flower of one of the Old South's most illustrious clans. San Franciscans, unlike easterners, had a healthy respect for epic romances and mavericks, and Adam suddenly found his life and himself recast in those roles.

After the opera, when he and Elizabeth entered Enid Atherton's drawing room, all eyes focused on them. Adam felt a wave of unease. He recognized a few people who Lilith had played up to for so many years, people who had always snubbed him. They were staring now at him . . . and Elizabeth. He felt her fingers tighten on his arm.

"Courage," she whispered, and led the way into the room. He watched her as she began to easily work through the crowd, smiling warmly, introducing herself and Adam. He held back, taking his cues from her, amazed by her performance. She drew appreciative stares from all the men and envy from the women. She was wearing a fluid white satin gown by the French designer Vionnet, a spectacular dress that subtly reflected every undulation of her body. It was provocative among all the demure silks and correct brocades. She wore her hair pulled up and no jewelry. No other woman looked so elegant.

Soon, Enid Atherton came up to introduce herself. The woman was about forty, with hard gray eyes that missed nothing. She was the city's biggest arts patron, the woman who controlled entry into the city's elite inner circle. She leveled her steely eyes at Elizabeth and smiled.

"I know your aunt, and I've wanted to meet you for some time, my dear," Enid said. "I should have extended an invitation sooner."

"We're delighted to be here," Elizabeth said, as if she were a supplicant demurring to royalty.

"Did you enjoy the performance tonight?" Enid asked.

"Very much." Elizabeth took Adam's arm. "But I know so little about opera, really. My husband is teaching me. He lives for it, I think."

Enid gave Adam a stare. "Yes, he must, to have gotten a lifetime box." She smiled. "Perhaps we can convince you to become a patron now, too, Mr. Bryant. Art, after all, does not come cheap."

Adam smiled. "Nothing does that's worth having."

Enid's smile widened. "Then I'll have one of my guild people contact you." She looked at Elizabeth. "Perhaps you might join the guild, dear. We'd love to have you." She glanced around. "I must see to my other guests. Enjoy yourself, you two." And she waltzed off with a rustle of satin and click of pearls.

"Did I just spend money?" Adam whispered, with a grin.

"Think of it as an investment in your future," Elizabeth replied, laughing.

Throughout the rest of the evening, Adam watched as Elizabeth proceeded to charm every man and, eventually, most of the women. She spoke French to a baroness, talked about the resignation of Anthony Eden with a British diplomat, and exchanged ribald stories with the director of the opera. Adam was astonished by her effortless social grace, a skill born of years of breeding, schooling, and practice. He had married, he told himself proudly, a true lady.

After Enid's party, other invitations quickly followed. Adam found he had entrée to people and places he had never had when he had been married to Lilith. He knew the invitations came because hostesses wanted to put the glamorous couple on display. We're salon circus freaks, he told Elizabeth. But secretly, he enjoyed the attention. He liked mingling with the wealthy and famous in grand homes. He liked the splendid food and wine. But most of all, he liked showing off his beautiful wife.

People were attracted to Elizabeth, responding to her uncomplicated, open nature, her kindness, good humor, and insatiable joie de vivre. As the year swept by, she seemed to flower even more. Everyone seemed to draw an energy from her. Even Adam felt it. He was changing, in ways too subtle for him to notice. Slowly, he was emerging from inside himself. Being with Elizabeth was like being swept up in a wild fiesta. All his life, he had been content to be a mere spectator. Now, he longed to be a celebrant.

A little more than a year after their marriage, they found themselves at another affair given by Enid. This time, Adam moved through the crowd with smooth confidence. He looked around the room of well-dressed people, caught Elizabeth's eye, and smiled. For the first time in his life, he didn't feel like the outsider. He felt like he belonged.

"So, Bryant, what do you think? Are we going to find ourselves in another war?"

Adam turned his attention back to the small circle of men. "I think it's a real possibility," he said. "Washington has recalled our envoys from Berlin."

"I think we should stay out of it," one man proclaimed. "Let the Jews fight their own battles."

"But the Nazis are getting a bit out of hand," another said. "Last month, when they smashed all those windows . . . what'd they call it? . . . Crystal . . ."

"Kristallnacht," Adam offered. "More than ninety people killed, most of them Jews."

"They brought it on themselves," the first man said with a wave of his hand. "That Jew kid killed a German politician, for chrissake. And we're the ones who're going to have to send our kids over to fight their battle!"

Adam stared at the man in distaste, refusing to take the conversational bait. After a few heated minutes, talk returned to the mundane details of business as the men went on about their banks, companies, and financial portfolios.

"Say, Bryant, the old *Times* looks pretty healthy these days," one of the men remarked amiably. "Pretty fat with ads."

"I certainly give it enough money every week," said another man, who owned a chain of department stores.

"Circulation's growing steadily," Adam said.

"You know, Bryant, you should think about expanding, like that fellow Hearst down in L.A. Buy a couple other little rags somewhere. A man can't make his mark these days thinking small. You've certainly got access to the capital."

"It's a thought," Adam said tersely.

The man went on to talk about how he had commandeered his own store into a chain. But Adam was not listening. He had not missed the man's reference to Elizabeth's fortune, nor the condescension implied in his advice. Slowly, Adam's good spirits began to dissipate as he looked at the older men's expressions of self-satisfaction. They don't consider me in their league, he thought. They tolerate me not for my successes but because of my marriage. After a moment, he excused himself and went out onto the terrace.

He leaned against a pillar, alone in the dark for a long time. The man's remarks about thinking small had brought home a sore point. He wanted badly to buy another newspaper, to move ahead with his plan. But the only way he could do it was with Elizabeth's money. I have to ask her, he thought. I have to, dammit.

He heard a laugh and recognized it as Elizabeth's. He saw her coming out onto the terrace with two older women, and drew back into the shadows, not wanting to face her.

One of the women, a dour matron, was talking about marriage, and she seemed determined to despoil Elizabeth's good humor. "It's so important to marry the right person," the woman was saying.

"Yes, indeed," Elizabeth replied.

"One can't be too careful these days," the woman went on, "about finding a man of distinction and good standing. One wouldn't want to be taken advantage of, I would think."

"No, indeed," Elizabeth said

The old woman leveled her gaze at Elizabeth. "Perhaps you can help with something, my dear. I've heard some people say that your marriage is not a very brilliant match for you." She smiled. "What in the world should I tell them?"

Elizabeth looked the woman in the eye and smiled back. "Tell them that it is a match of the heart. How can anything be more brilliant than that?"

Adam stood in the shadows for a long time, until after Elizabeth and the women had gone back inside. Conflicting emotions coursed through him. He felt angry and humiliated over the woman's insult. Like the man's remark earlier, it stirred in him a passion to fight to prove his worthiness. But there was another emotion churning inside him, a dirty little feeling of shame, illuminated clearly now by the light of Elizabeth's stunning retort to the woman. He felt suddenly small and unworthy. He loved Elizabeth, but it was partly for what she could do for him—for her wealth, her position, for what she could help him become. But she loved him purely for what he was, right now.

He moved out from behind the pillar and stood there, staring at the brightly lit room beyond the terrace doors. He spotted Elizabeth but could not move to go in. So he remained outside, watching her through the glass.

Chapter Ten

It was Christmas Eve, and the office was dark and quiet. Adam was the only one left in the executive suite. He had remained to go over some business after calling Elizabeth and telling her not to wait up. He picked up a memo. It was from Josh Hillman, and it detailed the dismissal of a minor libel suit against the *Times*. Adam marked it to be filed and put it aside, thinking of what an asset Josh had become. Adam had hired him not long after the divorce, getting rid of the overpriced law firm that the Bickfords had used for decades. Josh had proven to be not only an excellent lawyer, but was also becoming a trusted general counsel.

Adam turned his attention to a thick folder that had arrived late that day. It was a research report he had ordered and as he read it, he quickly ascertained that it told him exactly what he had expected. It was about the rival *Journal*, and the news was not good.

During the past year, the *Journal* expanded its circulation to the new parts of the city in the south. Adam had had no choice but to follow course, and now the *Times* and the *Journal* were locked in a costly circulation war. To make matters worse, the Sacramento paper that Adam had bought several years before had still not turned around, and some improvements had come at the expense of the *Times*'s revenues. Adam couldn't afford to keep siphoning money from the *Times*; its profit margin had shrunk to its lowest since Bickford had run the newspaper.

Adam set the folder aside dejectedly and picked up a second one. It was a market study of two family-owned newspapers in San Diego and Seattle. Adam had ordered the study six months ago to determine the potential of the struggling newspapers. The report confirmed his hunches. The papers were poorly managed but located in growing markets. Adam knew they could be turned into gold mines—without much initial investment. It was a surer bet than Sacramento.

The two newspapers were ripe for takeovers, ideal to become the first strong links in the Bryant newspaper chain. Adam put the report down with a sigh. He had tried to borrow money from banks, using the *Times* as collateral, but its profit margin was too low. For the first time in his life, Adam felt truly discouraged. There it was—opportunity, right in front of him, a chance to realize his dream. Opportunity, and no money to take advantage of it.

He glanced at his watch. It was after eleven. He stuffed the reports in his briefcase and started for home. It had been raining, and red-and-green Christmas lights reflected off the patent-leather streets. As he drove up the hill toward Jackson Street, Adam tried to put his dispirited thoughts behind him. He was always careful not to bring the office home. Home was Elizabeth, the only thing that took his mind off everything else.

He thought of Elizabeth now—Elizabeth and all her money. He thought about how he could use it—to give her a grand house and the splendid life she deserved. And he thought about how he could use it to launch his dream.

He had been thinking about the money for weeks now, ever since Enid Atherton's party, trying to sort out his feelings. The money—her money—*did* matter, as much as he tried to pretend it didn't. It was a reality. It was part of who Elizabeth was. As much as he loved her, there were moments when he thought back to the night he first saw her, so beautiful and elusive, and he asked himself the questions. What if she had not been rich? Would she have seemed so alluring? Would I have fallen in love with her?

He pulled into the garage and let himself in the front door. Upstairs, he was surprised to see the light on in the bedroom. He opened the door softly.

Elizabeth was sitting on a window seat, staring out at the rain. She was wearing a robe of thin white silk, and her hair was arranged in a haphazard way on her head.

"I've been waiting for you," she said.

He went over and kissed her. "You shouldn't have."

"I wanted to." She slid off the window seat and Adam's eyes were drawn to her bare legs. She slipped off his jacket and loosened his tie. "Damn you, you've forgotten, haven't you," she said, smiling.

"About what?"

"It's Christmas Eve," she said. She used his tie to pull him toward her lips. She kissed him deeply, pressing her body into his. "Sometimes I think when you're in the office, you forget about the rest of the world," she said.

"Not all of it," he murmured.

"Well, you've forgotten that you always give me my gift on Christmas Eve."

He reached in his pants pocket and pulled out a small black velvet case. With a laugh, she took it and opened it. Inside was an antique jade cat. "Adam, it's beautiful," she said, turning it over in her fingers.

"It's the same color as your eyes."

"I love it," she said.

He began to unbutton his shirt. "Well, it's not a diamond necklace," he said with a small laugh.

"Adam, I said I love it." She placed it carefully on the bedside table and laid down on the bed on her stomach, staring at it. He glanced over at her, the excitement rising slowly inside him. She turned over and her robe fell slightly open.

"Are you hungry?" she asked, smiling.

He laughed. He was never quite sure if her sexuality was purely ingenuous or part of an artful plan. He was never sure of anything with her, except that she loved him. Before he could answer, she went to a small table, set with dinnerware and candles. "I knew you would probably forget to eat tonight," she said, as she lit the candles and poured two glasses of champagne. "So I had something prepared for you."

"I want only one thing right now—you."

Elizabeth looked at him for a moment, then with a smile, picked up a glass of champagne and sat down on the bed. She set the glass aside and let her robe fall to her waist. She was wearing nothing underneath it.

Adam stared at her breasts for a moment—how he loved them— so round and creamy white. He took a step toward her.

"No," Elizabeth said. "I want you to undress in front of me . . . slowly."

Adam began to take off his clothes. Elizabeth reached over, dipped two fingers in her champagne and then ran them slowly, lightly over her nipples. Adam stood before her, naked.

"I want to watch you get hard," Elizabeth said. She pushed aside the robe and ran her fingers slowly down her body, past her stomach. She spread her legs, touching the insides of her thighs, then the mound of soft, red hair. Adam watched her, stunned. He had never seen her touch herself before. He assumed it was some-

thing she would never do, considering what Reed had had her do.
Her expression, as she looked at him now, was one of complete
trust. Aroused, he took his penis in his hand. Their eyes were
locked on each other as they stroked themselves.

"I'm so wet," she whispered. "I want you now."

Adam went to her and lowered himself, easing himself inside
her. "I love being in you," he whispered.

"Go deeper."

Adam plunged and she let out a sharp cry. With each stroke
Adam withdrew almost completely and went back in as far as he
could. Their climaxes came at the same time, leaving them limp
in each other's arms.

Adam lay on top of Elizabeth, softly kissing her neck and face.
Then, as he felt himself grow soft inside her, he slowly withdrew.
He rolled to his side, drawing her into his arms. They lay there for
a while, Elizabeth lightly stroking his chest.

"Now I am hungry," Adam said.

"But not for me, now," she said, touching him playfully.

He laughed. "Maybe. But first, some food."

While he ate, she listened to him talk about Josh and the lawsuit
and the circulation war. He considered telling her about the newspapers in San Diego and Seattle but didn't. He had discovered that
she was extraordinarily intuitive about his moods, and she might
pick up on his worries about money. So he listened as she enter-
tained him with inconsequential anecdotes about her day. She was
a talented mimic and made him laugh with her imitations of Enid
and the other women of the opera guild, which she had recently
joined. But mainly, he just watched her. The graceful sweep of
her expressive hands. The shimmer of candlelight on her skin and
in her green eyes. Her mouth. Her throat. The blush that spread
down her throat and across her chest as she laughed and drank.
The press of her breasts against the silk robe. She was so full of
life, so alive.

He reached over and suddenly grabbed her hand. "I love you,
Elizabeth," he said.

At dawn, he was still awake, staring at the ceiling. He lay still,
watching the shadows leave the room. Somewhere out on the
street, he could hear a truck. He obsessively imagined it delivering
copies of the morning *Journal* to every house in the city.

"Adam, what's wrong?" Elizabeth touched his shoulder.
"You've been tossing and turning all night."

"Nothing, really. Go back to sleep."

She propped herself up on an elbow and looked at him. "I know something's bothering you. I've known it for weeks, but I thought you'd eventually tell me." She paused, waiting for him to speak. "Adam, don't shut me out. I can help you."

He looked at her for a moment then kissed her. "I don't think so," he said.

"Is it the newspaper? Is something wrong?"

"No, the *Times* is doing fine."

She paused. "Remember that first night we spent together, down in the park?"

"Of course."

"You told me about your dream, Adam. About how you wanted to build this empire of newspapers." She touched his face. "That night, I wanted to be a part of it. But how can I when you keep me shut out?" He saw the hurt in her eyes and he sighed. "Tell me," she prompted.

"There are these two newspapers," he said slowly. "In Seattle and San Diego. I'm thinking about buying them."

She smiled. "That's wonderful!"

Adam hesitated. "The problem is, I don't think I can . . . assume the financial burden right now." His eyes dropped to the bed. "I don't have the capital."

There was a long, pregnant silence. A dog barked somewhere outside. When he looked up, Elizabeth was staring at him intently, her expression somber.

He touched her cheek. "There will be other chances, other newspapers to buy in the future. When the *Times* is stronger financially, I'll be able to swing it." He kissed her. "Go back to sleep."

He swung his legs out of bed and started for the bathroom to get dressed. He wanted to get to work early.

That spring, Elizabeth became pregnant. Adam was relieved because he had grown concerned about her obsession with it and her insistence that she had failed him. As she put on weight, she would stand before the mirror admiring her changing body. Adam was caught up in her euphoria. "It's a boy," she said, placing his hand on her belly. "I can feel him. It's your son, Adam." Tears formed in her eyes, and she pressed her face into his shoulder, and he held her tightly. "I'm so happy, Adam," she said.

He liked to watch her after she fell asleep. He would lie next to her, watching the rise and fall of her rounded stomach. He was filled with awe and a terrifying happiness.

One night in June, he was awakened by a moaning sound. He

turned over. Elizabeth was gone. He was immediately wide awake. Then he saw her, standing at the door of the dressing room. In the moonlight, he could see her stricken face. She was holding her stomach.

"S-something's wrong," she stammered.

He went to her. "What—"

"I don't know, I don't know. . . ."

He grabbed her robe from the bed and saw the dark stain of blood on the sheet in the moonlight. He threw the robe over her shoulders and quickly dressed. He led her carefully down the stairs and to the car. He was calm, his mind working by rote as he drove through the deserted streets. Even the sight of Elizabeth curled into a ball on the seat next to him, her face contorted with pain, did not unnerve him. He was utterly, completely calm.

At the hospital, Elizabeth was taken into the emergency ward. Adam watched her disappear behind the doors, flanked by strangers in white. He found a chair and sat, staring at the doors, waiting. He tried to remember a prayer, but only fragments from the boyhood catechism and remembrances of lulling Latin words came to him. He closed his eyes and held his lowered head in his hands.

"Please, please, please . . ." he murmured, over and over.

After an hour, a young doctor emerged. Adam jumped to his feet.

"Your wife had a miscarriage, Mr. Bryant," he said. "She's lost a lot of blood, but she will be all right."

Adam fell back in the chair. He closed his eyes.

"We couldn't save the child," the doctor said. "I'm very sorry."

Adam slowly got to his feet. "Can I see her?"

The doctor took Adam to a room. Elizabeth was lying in bed, her eyes closed. Her hair, tangled on the pillow, was the only relief of color in the overwhelming whiteness. She opened her eyes and saw him standing over her. She turned toward a far wall. Tears formed in her eyes and fell slowly down her cheeks. "I'm sorry, Adam," she whispered. "I'm so sorry. . . ."

He took her limp hand and pressed it to his face. "It's not your fault," he said softly. "You're all right. That's all that matters. Elizabeth, look at me, please. We can try again. We can have other children—"

She pulled her hand away and covered her face, crying. The doctor standing behind Adam told him he had to leave, that he could return later. Adam bent over to kiss Elizabeth, but she still wouldn't turn to him. Reluctantly, he followed the doctor out to the hallway.

"We've given her a sedative," the doctor said. "She'll be asleep soon. There's nothing more you can do so I think you should go home and get some sleep, too." He paused. "Many women react like your wife, Mr. Bryant, but they eventually get over it. The best thing to do is to go ahead as soon as possible with another pregnancy."

"Doctor, I want to know—"

"Oh, yes, she's young, and quite capable of—"

"No, not that," Adam interrupted. "I want to know . . . what was it?"

"Excuse me?"

"What was it?" Adam asked firmly. "A boy or a girl?"

"Mr. Bryant—" The doctor hesitated. "There's no need—"

"I want to know!"

The doctor stared at him for a moment. "It was a boy."

Adam slowly drew in his breath and then let it out in a long sigh. He stared at the floor, nodding his head absently. He looked up into the blank face of the doctor. He thanked the man and started for the door.

It was almost dawn, and the cold foggy air was still and close. Nothing moved. Nothing made a sound. Adam paused outside the hospital entrance. He wasn't sure where he was going. Home. The doctor had said to go home. He glanced around, disoriented. Adam started off slowly across the lawn. He stopped suddenly.

He stood there, thinking about Elizabeth lying up there in the hospital bed, thinking about how close he had come to losing her. He realized suddenly, with a piercing ache, that he loved her more than he had ever thought possible. She was not the Elizabeth he had conjured up as a magical vision, not the Elizabeth he had married for her beauty and wealth. She was just Elizabeth. His wife, his very light. And he had almost lost her. Suddenly, nothing else mattered, least of all the money.

He stood there, heedless of the wet grass dampening his shoes and of the mist settling on his shoulders. His throat constricted with the threat of tears, but he beat them back. She was all right . . . she was all right. He walked slowly toward his car to go home.

Chapter
Eleven

Elizabeth was waiting for him at the breakfast table. "This is a nice surprise," he said. "I'd gotten used to eating alone."

"I'm turning over a new leaf," she said, smiling. "No more lazing about in bed until noon."

He watched her as she poured his coffee. She was wearing a new white dressing gown and had her hair down, which made her look very young and radiant. She did, in fact, seem changed. Since the miscarriage six months ago, Elizabeth had dwelled in an emotional limbo somewhere between a quiet normalcy and melancholy. At first, she had been so depressed that Adam sought medical help. The doctor had prescribed antidepressants and another pregnancy. The drugs helped but only to a point. A spark had gone out of her that no matter of acting on her part could hide.

But this morning, she seemed truly happy. It seemed to come spontaneously, not from her usual attempt to assuage Adam's worries. "You look beautiful this morning," Adam said.

"Well, thank you. An old lady appreciates hearing such things. Even from her husband."

"You're not old," he said, smiling.

"I'm thirty! That's old."

"Then what does that make me?"

"Next week you'll turn forty . . . absolutely ancient."

He laughed and reached for the newspaper, but in addition to the usual morning *Journal*, there were two others—copies of the *Seattle Dispatch* and *San Diego News*.

"What's this?" Adam asked, unfolding the Seattle paper. A letter dropped onto his plate. He looked at Elizabeth, who was smiling enigmatically. He opened the letter and read it.

"This is a letter of purchase," he said incredulously.

"Happy birthday," Elizabeth said softly.

Adam stared at her, dumbfounded. He unfolded the second newspaper and another letter fell out. It was a repeat of the first. Both letters stated that the newspapers had been purchased the week before by Elizabeth Bryant and that Adam Bryant was empowered to act autonomously on her behalf as publisher.

"Elizabeth . . ."

"I know . . . it's a bit of a shock. But I wanted it to be a surprise, Adam. Josh helped me get it all straight legally. I swore him to secrecy. I wish they could have been bought in your name, but I couldn't get around Willis's damn trust." She looked at him anxiously. "You are surprised, aren't you?"

"That isn't the word for it."

"Adam, what's wrong?"

He stared at her. "Whatever made you do this, Elizabeth?

"I did it because I know how much you wanted those papers. It's your dream." She took his hand. "I did it because I love you, Adam. And I knew you would have never asked me yourself for the money."

He dropped his eyes to her hand grasping his own. After a moment, he wound his fingers through hers. Finally, he looked up. "It's not just my dream anymore," he said. "It's ours."

"There's something else," she said softly. "I'm pregnant."

He slowly rose and went to her side. She bent her head back toward him, and he kissed her. "That's the best present you could have given me," he said.

The doctor ordered Elizabeth to remain in bed during her pregnancy. She chafed under the inactivity but did as she was told. She wanted nothing to jeopardize the birth. Adam spent the next few months commuting between Seattle and San Diego. The two papers required virtually all his time and energy, and he was able to make only occasional stops at home to check in on Elizabeth and the *Times*.

As his research had predicted, the new papers were positioned to be stable moneymakers. Adam spent two months observing the operations and then quickly made the necessary personnel changes. He brought in his best young editor to run the Seattle paper. In San Diego, where decades of family ownership had created an inbred banality, Adam was forced to fire nearly all the top management. With the force of Elizabeth's money behind him now, he was easily able to hire experienced editors from other newspapers. It was exhausting but exhilarating work. Adam's mind was operating at a frenzied pace, filled with plans and ideas. The *Times* also began to move forward. Elizabeth gave him enough money to fund expansion to keep pace with the *Journal* and more. Adam was proud of the coverage his war correspondents sent back for the newly created Bryant News Service. For the first time in years, Adam felt as if he were moving forward. Elizabeth teased him that he loved the newspapers more than her. They're the most precious things in the world to you, like jewels, she said.

It was June 1941, and he was in Seattle when he got the call from Josh. Elizabeth had been taken to the hospital for delivery two weeks early. Adam caught the first plane back to San Francisco, arriving at the hospital late at night. Elizabeth was still in labor. Adam sat, terrified, for three more hours, trying desperately not to think about the last time he had been in the same room, waiting.

Finally, a nurse approached. "Your wife had a very difficult birth," she said, "but she is resting now." Adam waited. "Congratulations, Mr. Bryant," the nurse added. "You're the father of a beautiful little girl."

Adam had to reach out to the chair to steady himself. He thanked the nurse and went in to see Elizabeth. Her eyes were closed, and she looked so still and white that Adam was momentarily afraid some terrible trick had been played on him and that she was dead. He approached the bed and looked down at her. Finally, she opened her eyes.

"You're here," she said weakly. "I'm glad."

"I'm here." He sat on the edge of the bed. He brushed the hair from her forehead. "I love you," he whispered.

She smiled. "I know." She was struggling to stay awake. "You look terrible," she said. "You aren't eating or sleeping right, are you?"

"No, maybe I should come home."

"Good. I need you to come home." She closed her eyes and it was a moment before she opened them.

"It's a girl," she murmured.

"I know."

Elizabeth was soon asleep. Adam stayed for a while, then finally left. Out in the hall, he slumped against the wall, giving in to his fatigue. He saw Josh coming toward him. The lawyer looked concerned when he saw Adam's slack face.

"Is there something wrong?" he asked quickly, looking at Elizabeth's door.

"No, no, everything's fine, Josh. I'm just tired. Thanks for being here with her. . . ."

Josh smiled. "Say, have you seen the baby yet? I was just down at the nursery. Come on, I'll take you there."

Adam followed Josh down the hall to a large window. Inside, there were a dozen bassinets tended by two nurses. Even through the glass, Adam could hear the squalling.

"That's the one, third from the left," Josh said.

Adam looked to where Josh was pointing. Inside the bassinet was a churning baby in a tangle of pink blanket. It had a bright red face, and it was flailing around so much it had kicked one plump leg free of the blanket.

"She's beautiful, Adam," Josh said, smiling.

Adam laughed at Josh's utterly romantic observation. There was no way the little creature was remotely beautiful. It was a scrunched-faced, howling thing, just like all the others in the nursery.

"She sure looks to be a fighter," Josh said.

Adam continued to stare at the baby.

"Well, how does it feel to have a daughter?" Josh asked.

Adam glanced at Josh then turned back to the window. He pressed his forehead to the glass and stared at his daughter for a long time.

He smiled slightly. "She has red hair," he said.

Adam stayed at home to make sure Elizabeth adjusted well to the new baby. He found he didn't have to worry. The nanny he hired was kind and proficient. Elizabeth was happy, and even in her weakened condition she spent hours with the infant. Elizabeth decided to name the baby Kellen, in honor of her favorite grandmother's maiden name. "I know it's a bit unusual," she said. "But I have a feeling she's going to deserve something distinctive." She told Adam to pick a middle name. He chose Elizabeth.

After a few weeks, Adam began anew his commute between San Diego and Seattle. Now that his path seemed clear, he was driven to make progress as quickly as possible. He had spent the Depression and many years after watching other men amass fortunes and power by linking newspapers into chains, men like Frank Gannett, E. W. Scripps and James Cox. John Knight had strung together papers in Miami, Detroit, and Akron before he was thirty-nine. With just a grammar school education, Samuel Newhouse was making his first newspaper investments by age twenty-five. Like all the men, Adam understood that newspapering had entered a new era, and that it would be governed by the same law of economics as any business: small competitors had to give way to big. And he had every intention of being one of the biggest. He was also looking into buying a radio station in Oakland. There was money to be made in radio, and Adam also wanted to be in a position to take advantage of what a few visionaries were predicting would be the next boom medium, something called television.

He told Elizabeth about his plan. She immediately bought the station. "If nothing else," she told him, "it will keep you closer to home."

Not long after Kellen's birth, Charles Ingram died suddenly. His death threw Elizabeth into a minor depression, and she told Adam she felt guilty that she hadn't been able to end the estrangement that her marriage had created. "I wish he could have known you as I do," she told Adam. "I wish he had at least consented to see his granddaughter."

Elizabeth went to Atlanta for the funeral and stayed with her mother and sister for a week. She returned home in a better frame of mind, less bitter. She talked about going back when Kellen was old enough to travel, so her mother could see the baby. "My mother and I have old wounds that still need healing," she said. "I'd like you to come back with me when I go."

"We'll see," Adam replied. But he knew that he would never be accepted into that forbidding brick mansion.

Soon after Elizabeth's return from Atlanta, her father's will was unearthed. He had divided his estate, totalling nearly $30 million, equally between his wife and daughters. Only Elizabeth's share was tied up in a trust, to be administered by the family lawyer. Again, Elizabeth could use the trust payments for whatever she wanted, but Adam could not touch the money.

"He's still trying to run my life, even from his grave," Elizabeth said. "I'm sorry, Adam. I'd hoped it would have been able to be our money."

"I don't care, Elizabeth," Adam said. But deep down, he did. His dream was on its way, and he had at his disposal more money than he had ever thought possible. But it was not his money, and it never would be. His newspapers were owned by his wife. He would just have to live with that somehow.

After Kellen's birth, the house on Jackson Street seemed suddenly too small. The baby and the nanny had already taxed things, but whenever Ian came to visit, the tension was almost palpable. "It's time we had our own home, Adam," Elizabeth told him one night.

"We're doing all right," Adam said, though he knew she was right. He had been reluctant to think about moving because he knew it could be done only if Elizabeth paid for it. He had taken pride in the fact that he had managed to pay for the house so far.

"But I have my father's money now. Let's use it!" Elizabeth smiled. "Let's use it to create the grandest house this city has ever seen!"

Adam's desire to see Elizabeth happy was doing battle with his ego. Finally, he relented. "All right," he said. "Let's find a new house."

It took Elizabeth only two weeks to find their new home. It was an old mansion on the corner of Divisadero and Broadway, high on a hill, with a panoramic view of the Golden Gate Bridge. The nineteenth-century house, designed by the eminent San Francisco architect Edward Swain, was solidly built, with thirty rooms spread over four stories. Like so many of the city's grand old houses, it had been designed for rich visual effects, symbolizing the newly won wealth of the original owner, a merchant who had amassed his wealth in the aftermath of the gold rush. The house was filled with hand-carved mahogany and birch, intricate oak parquet floors, and marble fireplaces. It still had its original Otis hydraulic cage elevator and an electric converter that was once used to draw house power from the streetcar system. Even some gaslight fixtures were still in place.

The house had been vacant for years, having passed from the owner to his heirs, who disliked its old style. It needed complete refurbishing, but Elizabeth had fallen in love with its eccentric charm and could not be deterred.

The first time Elizabeth brought Adam to see the house, he was so stunned he could say nothing. He walked into the foyer and stood at the bottom of the broad, carved staircase and stared. With its preponderance of paneling and its large windows draped with dust cloths, it seemed dark and forbidding. He went into the living room, staring at the massive marble-and-wood fireplace, with its carvings of cherubs, shells, and bears romping around a Medusa head. He wandered into the adjoining dining room with its huge window that overlooked the bay, and then into a small room tucked alongside. It was a smoking room, done in a whimsical oriental style, complete with a Turkish liquor cabinet. He went slowly and silently through each room, with Elizabeth trailing behind, pausing in a room off the foyer that was empty except for walls of bookcases. The circuit complete, he returned to the staircase. He noticed, for the first time, that there were strange little faces carved in the balustrade, set at even intervals up the staircase. The bottom face was set in a grimace, and the others were gradated expressions leading up to the topmost face, which was creased up in a big smile.

He had not said a word during his entire tour, but now, as he stared as the silly carved faces, his own mouth pulled up in a small smile.

"Does that mean we take it?" Elizabeth asked with a tentative smile.

"Only if I can have that study as my own room," he said. "If I'm going to live in a place like this, I'll need a place to retreat to."

Elizabeth paid for it in cash—just under a half a million dollars. In a delighted frenzy, she then set out to make it a showcase. She kept the mansion's turn-of-the-century style but meticulously modernized all the rooms and the ornate brass elevator. She fashioned an elaborate music room just off the living room and kept the oriental smoking room, saying she liked the gracious old custom of men retiring for brandy and cigars. The only room she allowed Adam to have any say in at all was his study. He chose some comfortable, good antiques and, to Elizabeth's chagrin, brought home a monstrous oak desk from the office.

When the mansion was finished, even Adam had to admit it was the most exquisite home he had ever seen. The formidable gloom was gone, replaced by a warm ambiance, a sense of humor, and an almost bittersweet mood of bygone splendor. The old house on Divisadero, so long just a neglected relic of the city's past, had been magnificently reclaimed.

Elizabeth hired a full staff of servants, including a Japanese gardener, who immediately set out to restore the mansion's grounds to their former beauty. Soon, Elizabeth's hallmark, artfully arranged vases of fresh flowers, began to appear in the rooms. Though he initially felt overwhelmed by the house's splendor, gradually Adam came to feel at home.

Elizabeth had hoped Ian would, too. She had taken special care in decorating the room he occupied during his weekly visits. But he didn't notice. In fact, his behavior toward Elizabeth remained aloof, much to Adam's annoyance. He was the only dark spot in the otherwise joyful house, and though Elizabeth still tried to befriend the boy, Adam finally gave up trying to penetrate his wall of indifference.

Then, unexpectedly, Ian struck up a friendship with the daughter of the gardener. Chimmoko, two years older than Ian, was a quiet, pretty girl. Adam watched Ian's growing infatuation with concern, but Elizabeth suggested it was good for Ian to finally have a friend.

Just before Thanksgiving, the Bryants held their first party. It was meant as a housewarming, a dinner party for fifty people. Everyone who was invited came, even Enid Atherton. Elizabeth somehow corralled opera star Marian Anderson as a dinner guest and, to Adam's delight, the beautiful contralto sang after dinner. Everyone talked about how lovely the house was. An account of the evening appeared the next day in the *Times*.

The house and the party had an energizing effect on Elizabeth. Any doubts or vestiges of pride Adam had about using her money to acquire it had dissipated. He didn't care what anyone thought about him. Elizabeth was happy, and she was already trying to get pregnant again. He was proceeding full force with his newspapers. Even Ian, with Chimmoko as his friend, seemed more content. Life in the house on Divisadero was calm, grand, and filled with promise.

It was a few weeks before Christmas. Adam was sitting in his office, looking at a picture of Elizabeth he kept on his desk. He still had not decided what to get her as a present. She had so much. She could buy for herself whatever she wanted. But it was their fourth wedding anniversary, and he wanted to get her something special.

The phone rang. It was Josh. "I'm down in the newsroom," he said. "Get down here right away."

Adam went quickly downstairs. Nearly everyone was crowded around a radio in the editor's office. No one looked up as he went in. They were intent on the broadcast.

"We repeat . . . Japanese planes have bombed Pearl Harbor," the voice on the radio announced. "The full extent of the damage is still unknown. Witnesses claim that ships have been sunk and thousands are feared dead. . . ." Everyone listened in stunned silence. Adam could hear the teletype machines clattering in the background. The next day, President Roosevelt declared war on Japan. Thousands of San Franciscans flocked to Ocean Beach to stand on the dunes, staring out at the western sky, searching for enemy planes. Suddenly, everything was in turmoil as an atmosphere of fear gripped the city. Adam spent long days and nights at the newspaper, working with his editors to mobilize the staff.

A week later, Lilith called Adam and asked to see him. Adam was surprised; he had not talked to Lilith in at least a year. The last he had heard of her was that she was involved with a European count of somewhat dubious lineage. She said she had to see Adam immediately, something to do with Ian. She came to the office that afternoon.

"I need a favor from you, Adam," she said, taking a seat across from his desk. "I know you don't care about me, but I'm hoping you'll help me on this."

"What is it, Lilith. Do you need more money?"

She laughed. "Yes, I do. Not that you'd give it to me. Though you certainly can afford it, thanks to that woman." He let the remark pass. "I need you to take Ian," Lilith said.

"What?"

"Just for a while. I have to go to New York. Antoine has family in Italy, and he's going to try to get them out."

Adam looked at her. "You want to run off with your boyfriend, and Ian is in the way, right?"

Lilith stood up and began to put her gloves on. "Spare me the lecture. Do you want him or not?"

Adam stared at her for a moment. "I'll take him."

A chauffeur deposited Ian and his luggage in the foyer of the house on Divisadero late that night. The boy, now twelve and already tall, stood resolutely, trying hard to look nonchalant. Adam hugged him, but the boy pulled away. "I'm too old for that, Father," he said.

Ian allowed Elizabeth to lead him up to his new room. "Give him time," she told Adam later. "He's probably feeling a little abandoned right now."

Abandoned? Adam tried to draw on his own childhood memories. Abandoned . . . he could understand that. Hadn't he felt the same thing when his parents were killed? No, it wasn't the same, he decided. Ian had a father, someone who loved him. Adam just had to find a way to prove it. He knew he had lost something with the boy. But now, events had conspired to bring Ian to him, and Adam thought that, perhaps, he had been given a second chance.

Christmas was a strange affair. Adam watched happily as Elizabeth opened gifts for baby Kellen. But Ian sat quietly, surrounded by the expensive gifts that Adam had bought on one night's flurry of shopping. At one point Ian wandered over to the mantel and began to stroke a bronze of a horse.

"Do you like horses?" Adam asked.

"Yes. They are powerful and beautiful," Ian answered.

"Would you like to have one?"

Ian looked up at Adam and for a moment, his eyes came alive. "A real horse?"

"Yes, a real one."

Later, when he was alone with Elizabeth, he told her of his plan to get Ian a horse. "You're spoiling him, Adam," Elizabeth said, nestling into his arms. They were sitting in the library before the fire.

"He needs spoiling now. I want to give him the best."

"I think he needs you . . . not more gifts," Elizabeth said gently.

"I've been with him as much as possible," Adam said, a bit defensively. "You know how busy I've been lately. It's all I can do to find time for you." He kissed her. "Merry Christmas, by the way," he said softly.

"You've done it again. You've forgotten my gift."

"Wrong. I wanted to wait until we were alone." He got up and retrieved a package from under the tree and placed it in her lap. She smiled and eagerly tore off the paper. It was an old cigar box. She looked at him, puzzled, then opened the lid. A photograph sat on a pile of tissue paper. "Why, Adam, this is you," she said. "When was it taken?"

"About fifteen years ago. The day I came to San Francisco. A friend of mine was seeing me off on the ferry. He took it and sent it to me."

"You look so young and serious," she said, laughing. "But why are you giving it to me?"

"Because that day, I thought my life was beginning. I was wrong. It began when I met you."

She kissed him. "You are such a romantic at heart, you know. You try so hard not to let anyone see it, but you are."

"Maybe you're the only one who can see it." She started to set the box aside. "Look under the tissue," Adam said.

She pulled the paper aside, and her eyes widened. Nestled in the box were three uncut stones, one red, one green, one clear. "Adam—"

"The ruby is for San Diego. The emerald is for Seattle. The diamond is for San Francisco." He watched her face. "You're the one who called them my jewels."

"They're beautiful," she said finally. "But how—"

"Now, a lady should never ask how much something costs, or where the man got the money. She should just graciously accept the gift and the love that goes with it."

Her eyes filled with tears, and she put her arms around his neck.

"You sold the last of your land in Napa, didn't you," she whispered.

"All but a hundred acres. I would have sold it, too, but I couldn't bring myself to kick out the old fellow who's still living in the house there."

She kissed him. "That doesn't sound like a ruthless businessman speaking." She picked up the old photograph. "Where is this solemn fellow, the one who was so ready to set the world on fire, damned be anyone who gets in his way?"

Adam knew she was teasing, but he felt vulnerable just the same. She was the only person who could make him feel that way. "He's still here, inside me, somewhere," he said.

Chapter
Twelve

Like the gold rush had done a century before, the war turned life in the Bay Area upside down. Overnight, San Francisco was transformed from a sophisticated, comfortable city into a giant quasi-military camp. Tens of thousands of servicemen took up residence in makeshift camps. Thousands more, en route to the Pacific, filled the bars, raced up and down the hills in Jeeps, and lingered on Eddy Street, sizing up the "sea gulls," as the prostitutes were called.

Some of the changes were small. Pictures of FDR and General Dwight D. Eisenhower were tacked up above diner grills. The hotels were jammed with VIPs. Men patrolled the streets in Civil Defense uniforms. Blackout exercises began. And in the lounge on the top of the Mark Hopkins, the bartenders gave away drinks to departing servicemen who sat in the "weeper's corner" comforting girlfriends and wives.

But most of the changes were monumental. It was a boom time as hundreds of thousands of workers jammed the city. Along the East Bay, shipyards geared up to meet the war demand, churning out Liberty ships built by the newly recruited work force of farmhands, retirees, teenagers, blacks, and women. The population surge overwhelmed schools, hospitals, and jails. Temporary housing was slapped up on the East Bay waterfront and a complete new town, Marin City, was created to house workers. Ferries reappeared on the bay, bringing in workers. Everything was pushed to the limit as the rest of the world elbowed its way into the city's comfortable sphere of self-possession. Some people sensed, a bit sadly, that nothing would ever be the same again.

For Adam, the war brought the same dichotomy of boom and bane. Sales of the *Times* soared, but like everyone, Adam was plagued by labor shortages. When some of his men left to join the war effort, Adam was finally forced to hire women. Adam watched their work warily; he just could not get used to the idea of "paper dolls" in his own newsroom.

But he didn't have time to dwell on it. He was still shuttling between the flourishing San Diego and Seattle papers. His main connection to the *Times* was the editorial he still managed to write every day. The editorials had always been his special love, and in his clear, democratic voice he spoke out against myriad injustices of the war. But one event finally challenged even Adam's humanistic beliefs. Early in 1942, Roosevelt ordered all Japanese living on the West Coast to be transported to internment camps. Some saw it as validation of the vicious stereotypes that had become ingrained into Bay life. But most justified it as a cautious move in the fearful atmosphere of war. Adam wrote an editorial saying San Francisco was a potential enemy target and that relocation was an unfortunate but necessary move.

The day after it was printed, the Japanese man who worked as Elizabeth's gardener resigned. He and his wife and daughter had been ordered to go to the temporary camp at the Tanforan Race Track in San Bruno, just south of the city.

That night, at the dinner table, Ian sat in stony silence. Adam and Elizabeth watched him carefully.

"Ian, you should eat something," Elizabeth said gently. "You haven't eaten all day."

"I'm not hungry," Ian muttered.

Adam glanced at Elizabeth. "Ian, I know you're upset," he began softly. "I know that Chimmoko was your friend."

Ian looked up suddenly. "Where did she go?"

Adam paused, trying to decide how to tell the boy. "She went with her family to a camp. It was for her own protection, Ian. We are at war with Japan, and many people are afraid of the Japanese right now." Ian was on the verge of tears. "She'll be safe there," Adam said softly.

Ian threw his napkin on the table and ran from the table. Adam heard his bedroom door slam shut.

"You should go to him," Elizabeth said softly.

"There's nothing more I can tell him," Adam said. "Besides, you know how moody he is, Elizabeth. He'll be fine in the morning. I'll talk to him when I get home tomorrow."

The next day, Elizabeth called Adam at work and told him to hurry home. Adam rushed home and found Ian huddled on his bed. He was filthy and had been crying.

"I can't get anything out of him," Elizabeth whispered to Adam. "He ran away this morning and was gone all day."

Adam sat down on the bed. "What happened?" he asked.

The boy stared at Adam. "I went there," he said.

"Where?"

"The camp."

"You went to the internment camp?" Adam asked in astonishment. "How did you get there? How did you find it?"

"I asked people. I took a bus."

"Why, Ian? Why did you go down there?"

"To find Chimmoko."

"Ian, son—"

"You lied to me," Ian said. "You said she would be safe there." His eyes brimmed with tears. "I read what you wrote in the newspaper. You said the camp was something good."

"Ian, please—"

"You lied! It's not good! There's a big fence. She's in a stall with her mother and father. A horse's stall. That's where they have to live. With dirty hay and shit!"

"Ian!" Adam reached for him, but Ian recoiled.

"You lied! You lied! Leave me alone! Leave me alone!" He huddled in the corner, crying.

Adam stared at him helplessly. Slowly, he stood up. He went to the door, glanced once at Elizabeth, then walked woodenly out of the room.

The war dragged on, and Adam charted its progress on the pages of his newspapers, as reported by his now far-flung staff of reporters. His newspapers continued to prosper, although shortages and transportation and labor problems mounted. By 1943, everything was scarce—gasoline, coffee, even shoes. Adam didn't care about rationing; he and Elizabeth had everything they needed. But he knew there was one thing he could not live without—paper. Supplies were running low, especially because he had been printing so many extras. He knew that soon newsprint would be like gold.

He asked Elizabeth to buy a Canadian paper mill. A year later, when the blitzkrieg in Norway cut off the Scandinavian supply, newsprint's price rose to fifty dollars a ton, and newspapers were crippled by shortages. Many papers resorted to rationing, cutting out valuable advertising, leaving out the comics, even freezing circulation. For one week, the *New Orleans Item* left out all ads. And the *Philadelphia Record* was finally forced to print on brown wrapping paper. Because of Adam's foresight in buying the mill, the *Times* was spared. He generously sold or loaned newsprint to other newspapers. Adam watched as the rival *San Francisco Journal* shrank in size. Finally, one afternoon Howard Capen appeared in his office. He got right to the point. He wanted to buy newsprint at whatever price Adam wanted. Adam refused.

Like many people, Adam made money during the war. Advertising and circulation were breaking records. He was able to raise the paper's price to five cents. He was quick to donate space to the good causes of bond drives and rationing programs. But he wanted to do more, something for the servicemen overseas to lessen their loneliness. He decided to publish a "pony edition." It was a pocket-sized replica of the *Times* printed on lightweight paper. Every afternoon, it came stuffed inside the regular newspaper, with the suggestion that the "pony" be mailed to loved ones overseas. The minipaper was immensely popular, and the *Times* circulation—and reputation—continued to grow.

By 1945, the *Times*'s excellent war coverage and its liberal editorial stance had placed Adam firmly in the Democrats' favor, and Adam found himself cast by city leaders in the role of public-spirited humanitarian. There were even mumblings that he should run for public office. "With your looks and politics, you could be a senator," one of his club cronies told him. "Hell, maybe even president." Adam found the idea intriguing, but he quickly discounted it. Despite his recent successes, he was still far from achieving his dream. He still did not rank among the top newspaper chain owners in the country. So all his energies went to his newspapers, as he scouted new purchase opportunities.

By the age of forty-five, Adam was at the zenith of his powers. Never in his life had he felt so confident, and it radiated from him like a beacon. Thanks to Elizabeth, her elegant dinner parties and their donations to the opera, his reputation now glistened with respectability. As if in confirmation, a national women's magazine decided to do a feature on the Bryants.

Adam found the article ironic. It painted a portrait of family bliss, yet it was far from the truth in regard to Ian. Since Chimmoko had left, Ian had become severely withdrawn, not hiding the fact that he somehow blamed Adam for Chimmoko's disappearance. Ian began to have trouble in school. All the tests confirmed that he was a smart boy, but his teachers said he was lazy and antisocial. He had not had a close friend since Chimmoko. Ian's behavior toward Elizabeth and his half sister Kellen grew worse. Adam didn't notice it at first because he often did not return home until after the children were in bed. But one night, he came home early, hoping to spend a quiet evening with Elizabeth.

All during dinner, Ian was sullen, and Adam watched in silence as Elizabeth tried to draw Ian into conversation.

"Tomorrow's Saturday," Elizabeth said, as dessert was served. "Perhaps you could take your father to the stables, Ian. Maybe he'd like to go riding with you." Elizabeth looked at Adam hopefully.

"I don't know," Adam said slowly. "I have to be in Seattle Sunday for that board meeting."

"That's right!" Ian said. "He has to work! He always has to work. He has to go write his fucking editorials!"

Elizabeth reddened. "Ian, you shouldn't use that language or tone of voice when talking to your father."

Ian turned to her, his dark eyes hard. "Quit trying to tell me what to do!" he snapped. "You're not my fucking mother! Quit trying to be my mother!"

"Apologize this instant to Elizabeth!" Adam demanded. Ian just stared at the tablecloth. "Now!" Adam bellowed.

Ian muttered an apology without looking up.

"Go to your room," Adam said, his voice low as he tried to control his temper. Ian stomped out of the room.

"Adam—" Elizabeth began.

"That's the last straw, Elizabeth. I won't have him treating you like that! I won't tolerate—"

There was a scream from the foyer and Elizabeth, recognizing Kellen's voice, jumped to her feet and ran out. When Adam caught up, he saw her cradling the crying Kellen at the foot of the staircase while the nanny hovered nearby.

"I'm so sorry, Mrs. Bryant," the nanny stammered. "I didn't see him coming in time! I was bringing Kellen in to say good night and the lad went by us like the wind, knocking right into her, then he tore up the stairs. I'm so sorry. . . ."

"It's all right, Hildie," Elizabeth said. "It wasn't your fault. You go on up. I'll put Kellen to bed."

Hildie left, and Adam watched Elizabeth comfort Kellen, trying to control himself. "I can't take his attitude anymore, Elizabeth," Adam said through clenched teeth. "The boy needs to be disciplined. I'm going to look into sending him to a military school."

Elizabeth looked at him over Kellen's head. "Don't send him away, Adam. That's the last thing he needs right now. He needs you. Can't you see that?"

Adam was taken aback by her accusatory tone. "Elizabeth, you know what it's like at work now. I don't have time to take an extra breath! Besides, he's not a child anymore, he's nearly fifteen! For god's sake, I was on my own when I was his age!''

"He needs his father, Adam," she said.

Adam threw up his hands in exasperation. "I try! I spend time with him! He doesn't even care anymore! He doesn't care that I work hard so he can have what I didn't! I don't want him to ever have to struggle like I did or have people look down on him, goddamn it!''

Elizabeth looked up at him sharply. "Please, not in front of the baby." She dabbed at Kellen's eyes with the hem of her dress. "I understand what you're saying, Adam, but Ian doesn't. All he knows is that you're not here.''

Adam ran his hand over his face, then dropped his arms to his sides in frustration. He hated himself for arguing with Elizabeth. These were the first sharp words they had ever spoken to each other.

Elizabeth rose, taking Kellen's hand. "Why don't we go on up to bed, hmm?''

"No!" Kellen said. "I don't want to go up there. I want to stay down here with you and Daddy." She tried to make her face into a defiant frown, but her chin was quivering.

"Ever since that bad thunderstorm last week, she's been a handful to get to bed," she said to Adam under her breath. She gave him a conciliatory smile. "I'll just be a minute or two, and then we can have our coffee together." She paused. "I'm sorry. I don't mean to tell you how to raise your son.''

Adam gave her a wry half smile. "I'm sorry I lost my temper," he said. He leaned down to give Kellen a good-night hug, then started toward the dining room. But Elizabeth's soft voice made him pause and look back. She was standing at the bottom of the staircase holding Kellen's hand, trying to coax Kellen upstairs.

"I'll tell you a story in bed," Elizabeth said.

"Tell it to me down here," Kellen said.

Elizabeth paused thoughtfully. "Once upon a time," she began, "there was a little girl who was always afraid to go upstairs to bed." She pointed to the small carved frowning face at the bottom of the balustrade. "Every night, she'd make her face into a big frown just like this, just like that one on your face right now.''

Kellen suppressed a giggle, determined to be stubborn.

"Then one day," Elizabeth went on, "an evil fairy froze her face in a frown and turned her into wood, trapping her inside the staircase.'' Kellen looked up at Elizabeth and down at the carved face.

"The little girl cried so much that finally a good fairy heard her,'' Elizabeth went on. "She told the little girl that she could break the spell by being brave and climbing the stairs. But she also had to smile because smiles are very powerful weapons against evil spells.''

Kellen was listening, enthralled. So was Adam.

"The little girl tried to smile,'' Elizabeth said, "but it was hard because she was so scared. But finally, a tiny smile snuck out, and she began to float up the stairs.''

Now, Elizabeth was gently leading Kellen up the stairs, pointing out the little carved faces as she went. "The bigger her smile became, the farther up the stairs she floated,'' Elizabeth said. "Until she smiled as big as she could. And there she was, at the top of the stairs, free at last from the evil spell!''

Elizabeth and Kellen were now standing on the landing. Kellen was staring at the topmost carved face, which was turned up in a toothy grin. She wrapped her arms around Elizabeth's legs. "Oh, Mommy, that's silly,'' she giggled.

"Yes, it is,'' Elizabeth said, laughing. She glanced down and saw Adam staring up. Kellen looked down, too. "Good night, Daddy,'' she said. "I'm going to bed now, by myself.''

"Good night, Lil'bit,'' he said softly. He watched them, in wonderment, until they were out of his sight.

During the next few months, Ian seemed to calm down, and Adam put aside his plan for a military school. But just before Ian's sixteenth birthday, Adam received a call from the man who ran the stable where Ian's horse was boarded. Ian had been seen mistreating the horse, and Ian would not be allowed in the stable again. Adam sold the horse and ordered Ian to stay in the house.

"I don't know what to do with him, Josh,'' Adam said. They were sitting in Adam's office. It was early evening, and outside the August sky was metamorphosing into a blazing sunset. Adam morosely studied the sky for a moment.

"Maybe he's just trying to get attention,'' Josh said.

"For chrissake, Josh, he's not a baby anymore. I refuse to treat him like one.'' Adam leaned back in his chair. "How come your kid never gives you any trouble?''

Josh smiled. "Stephen's only seven. Give him time.''

"I've got to find a way to get through to him. Lilith is coming home soon. He'll be legally old enough to decide who he wants to live with." Adam stared at Josh. "Despite his behavior, I just can't let him go back to her."

"Maybe Ian needs something to keep him steady. Maybe he needs to work."

Adam smiled ruefully.

"What's so funny?"

"I've spent my life working my ass off so my kids wouldn't need a thing. And you're telling me Ian should get a job." Adam stared out the window. "I don't want him to have to struggle. I want him to have a head start."

Josh rose. "I've got to get home." He paused at the door. "What I said about a job, what I mean is that maybe Ian just needs something to really care about."

Adam nodded absently. "Yeah, maybe. See you tomorrow."

A week later, the war ended. The city went wild in a frenzy of celebration. People wandered the streets, singing and hugging. Car horns blared. Bells pealed. In the *Times* newsroom, Adam drank a paper cup of champagne with his staff. Then everyone went back to work, covering the story. By night, the story had developed a sinister angle. Mobs of drunken men were roaming Market Street. Fighting broke out. Windows were smashed, and stores were looted.

Adam read the reports as they came in, and an editorial began to form in his head. The city had endured such unrestrained growth and problems during the war that the top had finally blown off. The mob's anger was a twisted emotional expression of gratitude for victory and peace, and a deeper violent release of all the tensions everyone felt. As the violence grew through the night, reports of raping filtered in. Local and military police were called out. Around midnight, Elizabeth called Adam, sounding distraught. Ian had been arrested.

Adam drove quickly to the police station. He was told that Ian had been apprehended as part of a gang of men. When it was discovered Ian was a minor, the police had called the Bryant home. The sergeant on duty watched disdainfully as Adam signed for Ian's release. "I can't charge him with anything, Mr. Bryant," he said. "But you should know this was a bad bunch your son was with—older men, including two men we booked on rape charges. You'd best keep an eye on the company your son keeps."

Adam drew in a breath when he saw Ian emerge—dirty, bruised, and in handcuffs. They were silent as they rode home in the car. Adam clenched the steering wheel, trying to control his surge of anger and disappointment. Finally, he pulled the car to a screeching halt and turned toward Ian.

"What in the hell is the matter with you!" he said. "Why did you do this?"

Ian stared out the windshield.

"Answer me!" Adam shouted.

Ian flinched but did not turn toward Adam. "I don't know," he said, his voice flat.

Adam stared at Ian's profile, then turned away. His grip on the wheel remained tight. His mind was spinning. He felt an urge to strike Ian rise inside him, anything to get a response. Appalled at his own anger, he shut his eyes for a moment. When he opened them he felt only slightly calmer.

"Did you rape anyone?" he asked.

"No. I just watched."

Adam glanced over at Ian, still staring straight ahead.

"I don't understand," Adam said, almost in a whisper. "Maybe you can help me. Make me understand what you are doing. I give you everything. I give you the best! How do you repay me? You go out and—"

Ian turned toward him. "I didn't do anything to you! That's all you care about! How it looks to everyone for your precious son to get thrown in jail! It sure puts a dent in your plan to be a big shot, huh? Well, I don't care about any of that shit! I don't care about anything!"

Adam could only stare at Ian. Then he started the car and began to drive slowly home. The crushing sensation in his chest was suffocating. He glanced over at Ian. The muscles of his handsome face were clenched in agitation, and his dark eyes were glittering. How did he get so angry, Adam thought despondently, how did he get so . . . empty?

The ache in his chest was the pain of sad realization. His son was not simply mean-spirited or apathetic. He was emotionless. He had no passion. He really didn't care about anything, not even himself. Adam thought back to his talk with Josh. What had he said? That Ian needed something to care about? But what? Nothing seemed to move him.

Adam pulled into the garage. He watched in hopelessness as Ian got out of the car and, without a word or look at Adam, lumbered up the stairs.

The next morning, Adam woke Ian early and told him to put on a suit and tie. Sullenly, Ian did as he was told. He didn't say a word as he rode with Adam to the *Times* building. He didn't speak as Adam led him up to the newsroom. Ian simply walked by Adam's side, his bruised face inscrutable. Just inside the newsroom, they paused. Faces looked up at them with intense curiosity. Adam scanned the busy newsroom. Ian stood, hands in his pockets, staring at the linoleum.

Adam turned to Ian. "This is where you'll start."

Ian looked up in surprise. "Start what?"

"To learn."

A woman brushed by them and looked back over her shoulder. Ian tried to hide his embarrassment.

"Ian, listen to me," Adam said. "This place is very important to me. I built it. I care about it. It is my . . . my passion." He paused, feeling awkward. "I want you to care about it, too. You're going to run it someday. I'd always hoped you would."

Ian looked out over the large room. It bustled with seemingly random activity and was filled with strange faces and an odd, dry smell of smoke, dust, ink, and paper. Slowly, from somewhere in his memory, a picture of himself as a boy sitting in a similar office with Adam drifted up to his consciousness. Watching his father shave, a parade at the bridge. He couldn't remember much else, other than a vague feeling of security.

He turned to Adam. "I'll try," he said.

Ian worked in the newsroom for the next year as a copyboy. He did not like running errands for the people who worked for his father, and the dinginess of the place offended his senses. But there were things he did like. He liked the near-military energy of the city room, and he liked it when the power brokers and politicians came in, kowtowing to his father. For the first time, he began to see Adam in a different light, the reflective light of power. He began to envision himself in the same role. Encouraged by Ian's apparent interest, Adam created an editorial aide position for Ian so he could observe the news-gathering process. When Lilith finally returned from New York, Ian shocked her by announcing he wanted to remain living with Adam.

For the next three years, Ian spent time in advertising, circulation, and other departments, trying to learn the business. He was a half-hearted student, but clever at feigning interest when he recognized how much it pleased Adam. It wasn't the business itself that intrigued him; it was the power he seemed to be automatically accorded by all around him as the son of Adam Bryant.

On Ian's eighteenth birthday, Adam named him associate publisher. It was, everyone in the newsroom knew, a figurehead position, but Ian took his new title seriously. He carried out Adam's orders briskly, with the air of a newly christened lieutenant. Adam's editors bristled at Ian's superior air, but they tolerated him as a harmless dilettante. Ian still had a bad temper, directing it mainly at servants and an occasional low-rung newspaper employee. But to Adam, he seemed to be, if not happy, at least occupied. Adam was so pleased with Ian's transformation that he turned a blind eye to the fact that Ian did not, in his heart, share Adam's passion for the newspaper itself. He wanted, more than anything, to believe his son could someday run the Bryant newspapers. He was convinced that the ambition and fire that burned so bright in himself would someday spark in his son.

After Ian graduated from high school, he surprised Adam by declaring that he wanted to go to college to study business administration. Adam pulled every political string to get Ian enrolled in Princeton's freshman class of 1949. With Ian gone, the house on Divisadero Street seemed drained of the tension that had gripped it for years. Elizabeth, who had been plagued with sporadic migraines and depression, seemed rejuvenated.

The war years had been such a hectic time, but the four Bryant newspapers were flourishing, and for the first time since his marriage to Elizabeth, Adam was beginning to move forward on the impetus of money he generated, not just money Elizabeth gave him. Everything was still in her name—and always would be. But Adam allowed himself a feeling of pride. He was finally, truly, a man of means.

"Perhaps you can slow down now and enjoy yourself," Elizabeth told him one night at dinner.

He heard the hint buried in her voice and felt a stab of guilt for all the nights during the last four years he had come home from the office too late to do more than slip into bed beside his wife's sleeping body. He looked at her across the table. He had planned to tell her about a newspaper in Oregon he was thinking about buying. She had always been excited to share in his dreams. But tonight, he saw a loneliness in her eyes that had never been there before, and he decided it should wait.

"I think," he said, "that it's time for a second honeymoon. How about Paris this time?"

Two weeks later, they left for Paris, taking a suite at the Ritz. The weather was cold and drizzly, but the ambiance in the city was warm, a residual aura of the post-war celebration. The Parisians' faith in the future seemed to parallel Adam's confidence in his own. Everything was going so well for him and Elizabeth now.

The newspapers, Ian, they had all come together. Only one thing could make it better. They both still wanted more children, especially Elizabeth. But even that did not really diminish his contentment.

Or the love he felt for Elizabeth. Alone with her, away from all other distractions, he realized anew why he loved her so much. She was like a bright light that warmed him and illuminated the dark corners of his soul. In Paris, he had a lightness of spirit he had not felt before in all his life.

Elizabeth's love for Paris was contagious, and she happily took Adam to her favorite places. They went to the opera and to a club crowded with Parisians who had come to hear "Le Jazz" of Louis Armstrong. When it was too cold to venture out, they stayed in the suite and made love. Elizabeth half joked about how the air was so conducive to conceiving babies. They celebrated Christmas Eve by ordering a dinner from room service and exchanging gifts.

The day after Christmas, a fog enveloped the city, gently blurring the gray facades of the old buildings. They walked hand in hand along the Seine, past the shuttered booths of the *bouquinistes*. They stopped for coffee at a café, where the empty terrace was heated by large bracieri, filled with coals. They sat at the table saying nothing, content in each other's company.

"I love this city in winter. It is like being inside a gray pearl," Elizabeth said, looking out at the fog. "My parents brought me here for the first time in winter, when I was thirteen. I wanted to live here someday."

"Why didn't you?" Adam asked.

"I got married."

Adam watched the wistful smile fade from her lips. He decided he would not ask her the question that had formed in his mind, if she regretted the turns her life had taken.

"Oh, well. It wasn't meant to be," she said suddenly, as if reading his mind. "Maybe that's why I like San Francisco so much. It reminds me of Paris a little."

"But you could have had the real thing," Adam said.

She smiled. "I do." She pulled the collar of her fox coat up around her neck.

"Are you too cold?" Adam asked. "We could go back to the hotel."

"No, I'm fine."

He realized suddenly that she looked tired. He always took her energy for granted, and it was odd seeing her look wan. The skin under her eyes had a slight blue cast. She had been trying so hard to make the city come alive for him, he thought, and she had simply run herself down. He picked up her gloved hand and pressed it to his lips, shutting his eyes. When he opened them, she was looking at him, smiling. "I love you," he said softly.

"And after another twelve years of marriage, when I'm old and fat . . . will you still love me as much?"

"Yes."

She kissed him. Her lips were cold. She laid her head against his shoulder. Her hair was soft on his cheek, and he brought a hand up to cradle her head. She was quiet for a long time.

"This fog reminds me of home," she said finally.

This time, Adam clearly heard the fatigue in her voice. She began to shiver, and he pulled her tight into his arms.

"Let's go home," he said suddenly.

"Yes," she whispered.

"Tomorrow." He stroked her hair and stared out at the bare trees lining the boulevard, standing like gaunt sentries in the fog.

Chapter
Thirteen

Kellen ran, her legs churning over the grassy hills. She ran up one slope and down another, her hair streaming behind her like a tattered red banner. At the crest of a hill, she stopped. She began to paw the ground like a horse, her breath making clouds in the cold air.

Another girl ran up the hill and drew to a stop at Kellen's side. The girls made snorting and whinnying noises.

"I'm chestnut colored and my name is Charger," the other girl said.

"I'm all black with a white mark on my forehead," Kellen said. "My name is Diamond, and I'm faster than anything."

Kellen bolted down the hill, driven by the sea wind and an impatience inside her that she didn't understand. I'm strong and beautiful, she thought, and no horse can beat me. She ran until her head throbbed and her sides ached. She fell down on the grass. Her friend caught up and plopped down beside her. They lay there, staring up at the blue sky.

"I hate being ten," the other girl said.

"You're not. You're only nine."

"Nine and three-quarters."

Kellen sucked on a blade of grass. "Well, I'm ten. Soon I'll be thirteen, then sixteen. I can't wait to be sixteen. Then I can go wherever I want."

"Where?"

Kellen sat us and gazed out over the green meadow of Golden Gate Park. "I don't know. Somewhere." She heard someone calling her name and saw her governess Hildie motioning for her to come back. "I gotta go," Kellen said. Kellen ran to the car, arriving out of breath, her clothes grass-stained.

"Look at you. You're a wild thing," Hildie said, picking the leaves out of Kellen's tangled hair.

"Why do we have to go home so early?" Kellen asked.

"You have a date with your father tonight, remember? And it's going to take hours just to get this hair combed."

As they rode home, Kellen thought about the party that night. It was the annual father-daughter dinner at the Olympic Club, her first one. She hated the thought of getting into the dress her mother had bought for her, a stiff white organza thing that scratched her neck. But she was looking forward to spending the evening with her father. Finally, one whole night when she could have him all to herself! He hardly ever had much time for her. Oh, he'd hug her, and ask her how school was going, and look at the pictures she drew. But tonight, for one whole night, he was hers.

She took her bath and allowed Hildie to smooth her unruly red curls into a ponytail. She was slipping the white dress over her head when her mother came into the bedroom.

"Oh, you look so pretty," Elizabeth said softly.

Kellen heaved a sigh. "It's too . . . I look like a baby."

Elizabeth pulled the satin belt a little tighter, realizing suddenly that her daughter was just beginning to develop a figure. "You know, I think you are right," Elizabeth said softly. She undid the ponytail and brushed Kellen's long hair down over her shoulders. "Maybe you are too old for ponytails, too. What do you think?"

Kellen glanced in the mirror and smiled. "Better," she said. She hugged her mother, and her body, wrapped in the satin robe, seemed to give. She had lost weight, and Kellen was worried because she seemed sad lately. Kellen was sure it was because she wanted to have a baby boy and couldn't. She had heard her mother and father talking about it last night. She had stood outside their bedroom door, fascinated by their intimate talk. Her mother had cried.

Kellen stared at her reflection. "I wish I was a boy."

Elizabeth laughed. "Why?"

"I don't know. Things would be different."

"Well, you're right about that. But you are a girl, a very beautiful one."

"I'm not beautiful. You are. I'm ugly looking."

Elizabeth smoothed Kellen's hair. "No, you're not. Why don't you ask your date. He's waiting downstairs."

Kellen kissed her mother's cheek, and dashed to the top of the stairs. She saw her father standing below, so tall and handsome in his tuxedo, and her heart beat faster in happiness. She held her head up the way she had been taught to in ballet classes and walked slowly down the staircase.

Adam watched her, his smile growing wider. "You look so pretty, Lil'bit," he said, using the nickname he had called her since she was a toddler.

"Daddy, I told you not to call me that!" Kellen said, rolling her eyes.

"Oh, sorry. I guess you are getting too old for that." He glanced up at Elizabeth, who stood at the top of the stairs. "We won't be too late," he said.

"I'll wait up," Elizabeth said. "I love you both."

At the club, Kellen was so happy she barely ate. When the orchestra began to play, Adam led her onto the dance floor. She remembered her ballroom dancing lessons and counted in her head, trying hard to be graceful.

"You dance very well," Adam said.

"That's because you lead so divinely, sir," Kellen said, mimicking the demeanor she had been taught in class.

The tone in her voice caught Adam off guard and for a moment she seemed to him much older. But then she giggled, and the image evaporated. "I remember when you were little you stood on my feet when we danced," he said. "Want to try?"

"Daddy!"

"Too old for that, too, huh?"

He looked down at her. He had always been aware that his daughter was pretty. Her face was lovely, almost cherubic, except for her cunning green eyes. She was, he knew proudly, going to be beautiful. There were moments when he saw the hints, moments like now when her resemblance to Elizabeth was startling. He let his thoughts stay with Elizabeth for the moment. She just hadn't been herself lately. She had been mildly depressed and seemed to tire so easily. She had been this way for nearly two years now. Adam had forced her to see a doctor, who pronounced her healthy but slightly anemic, like many fashionable women who watched their weight. He privately suggested to Adam that rich, idle women like Elizabeth sometimes were simply bored or lonely. Adam found the idea absurd. Elizabeth was involved in dozens of clubs and activities, and their social life was too busy, if anything. But there was something implicit in the doctor's words that bothered him: that perhaps Adam was neglecting her. She had always been so understanding about his work, never seeming to mind his late hours or frequent trips to the other newspapers. Just the same, Adam felt guilty. He decided to give Elizabeth a surprise. He bought a home on the ocean just north of Carmel. It was a modern architectural wonder of glass and wood, set on a cove amid a grove of wind-swept cypress trees. It was the antithesis of the mansion on Divisadero, a cozy retreat.

Elizabeth loved the beach house. She and Adam spent a week there alone, then they returned to the city because Adam had to go to Las Vegas to meet the owner of the paper there he was considering buying. When he left, Elizabeth was in good spirits. But within a month, her depression returned.

Finally, Adam decided he had figured out the cause. It was so simple but so frustrating, because there was nothing he could do about it. Elizabeth was depressed because they had been unable to have more children. She had always joked about it in the past. But in the last year there had been just a growing despondency, and oblique remarks about how she had let Adam down. In his heart, Adam did want more children, but he would never tell Elizabeth that now. So he did what he could to reassure Elizabeth, resigning himself to the fact that Kellen was to be their only child.

Now, as he danced with Kellen, he glanced down at her shining red hair with a combination of bewilderment, love, and blighted hope. A daughter, he thought, and no other sons. He sighed inwardly. What did it matter, he thought. Ian may prove capable after all, and I'll be able to hand the newspapers over to him someday. He glanced down again at Kellen, who was looking at her feet, a small frown of concentration knitting her brow. The sight touched Adam. She was such a joy, and he did love her. But sometimes he just didn't know how to act around a little girl . . . a daughter. Like tonight. It was the first time he had spent a whole evening alone with her, and he felt awkward. Luckily, Kellen was loquacious enough for both of them, and she was so happy to be with Adam that she was oblivious to his discomfort.

Kellen stepped on his toe. "Oh, Daddy! I'm sorry!" she said with a giggle. "I do that in class all the time because most of the time I lead."

"But why?"

"Because Miss Brady doesn't have enough boys to go around and I'm so tall that she makes me fill in." She smiled. "At least I won't sit around at parties. I can always dance with girls."

Adam smiled. "You'll be too busy with the boys for that, I suspect."

"Boys," Kellen sniffed. "Who needs them."

Adam tried not to smile.

"I bet you wish I was a boy," Kellen said.

He hid his surprise by not meeting her eyes. "That's not true."

"If I was a boy, I could come to this place with you any time I wanted, like Ian does." It was not a petulant plea for attention. She was serious, and it made Adam feel ashamed of his earlier thoughts. He tilted her chin up. "Kellen, listen to me. You're my daughter, and you're very special to me."

"Do you think I'm pretty?" she asked.

"Very."

"As pretty as Mother?"

He looked down at Kellen's face. "Yes," he said softly. The music crooned on, and he guided her around the room, awash in pastel and ribbons. He watched his club cronies waltz their little ladies around, wondering if they found their daughters as mysteriously intimidating as he did his own.

It was about ten when they arrived home. Adam made sure Kellen was in bed and then went to his own room. The bedside light was on and Elizabeth was propped up on pillows, her eyes closed. He began to undress and the sound of the closet door awakened her. "Go back to sleep," he whispered.

"I was waiting for you," she said softly. "How did it go?"

Adam pulled off his tie with a wry smile. "I'm afraid I'm not very good with her, Elizabeth. You know, as bad as it was with Ian when he was young, at least around him I didn't feel . . ." He stopped, at a loss.

"Uncomfortable?" Elizabeth smiled. "She's just a little girl, Adam. She won't bite you."

He slipped into bed, and Elizabeth fit herself into the crook of his shoulder. "I'm not so sure," he mused. "She's got some strange ideas. She said she wants to be a boy."

"Yes, I know."

They lay quietly for a moment. "You can't imagine what this night meant to her, Adam," Elizabeth said. "She loves you so much. She worships you, really." Adam reached over and turned out the light. "Adam, I'd like you to do something for me if you can," Elizabeth said softly.

"Anything."

"She looks up to you so. There are things you could teach her."

"What can I possibly do that you don't do already better, Elizabeth? You're teaching her how to be a lady. What's more important than that?" He paused. "You should have seen her tonight. The way she looked and handled herself around people.

A real little lady. I didn't realize how grown up she is. Made me quite proud."

"But there are things," Elizabeth said, "that I can't give her that you can, Adam." She propped herself on one elbow to look at him. "Make time for her. Make her feel like she's something important in your life. And that she's . . . worthwhile. Daughters need that sort of thing from fathers."

Elizabeth's expression was serious. He was not sure what she was asking of him. That he spend more time with Kellen, probably, and not make the same mistakes he had with Ian. It was so hard, especially now with the Las Vegas deal looming. Maybe the three of them could go down to the house in Carmel. Next month, he could probably arrange a long weekend.

"You're right, Elizabeth," he said. "I'll try to make more time." He pulled her close and, feeling a stir of arousal, lightly cupped one of Elizabeth's breasts. Her body gave the slightest tensing motion, and Adam knew what it was. Whenever they began to make love lately, there was always that moment of dreaded anticipation. As good as their lovemaking was, it had ceased to be a pleasure in itself and now was always colored with the question of conception. But then he felt Elizabeth relax. They made love slowly and silently. It was still exciting, but an energy was missing, just as it was from Elizabeth herself. When it was over, he sensed a need in her left unfulfilled. There would be no more babies, he knew sadly. He had to help Elizabeth face that.

In the summer of 1951, Adam closed the deal on the purchase of the *Las Vegas Record*. Now there were five newspapers in the Bryant chain, spread over three states. With the exception of the *San Francisco Times* and the paper in Sacramento, all were solely owned by Elizabeth Ingram Bryant. But it was Adam's guidance that had turned them all into stable moneymakers and the *San Francisco Times* into one of the country's most influential newspapers. Across the country, it was becoming known that Adam was a force to be reckoned with, and he was elected to head several major publishers' organizations. When William Randolph Hearst died and control of his empire was dispersed among his five sons, it was Adam Bryant who most said was heir apparent to the title of most powerful newspaper owner in the country.

At Thanksgiving, as the year 1951 wound down, Adam sat at the dining room table in the house on Divisadero, his head bowed to lead grace. He recited the prayer of thanks, and when he looked up, he felt a surge of gratitude. He was, indeed, a very lucky man. He allowed himself a feeling of pride as his eyes took in his surroundings. The beautiful dining room, its picture window yielding a breathtaking view of the Golden Gate Bridge in the twilight. The table laden with candelabra and a feast of food. On his left was his son, Ian, soon to be graduated from Princeton, a fact that in itself made Adam proud, considering his own education had stopped at fourteen. On his right was his daughter, Kellen, already showing promise of becoming a beautiful young woman. And at the other end of the table, his wife, Elizabeth, ravishing in green velvet, wearing a necklace made from the three jewels he had given her on their fourth anniversary.

"Before we start, I have some news," Adam said. He smiled at Elizabeth. "President Truman has offered me an ambassadorship to France."

There was stunned silence.

"Adam, that's . . ." Elizabeth's voice trailed off.

"Unbelievable?" Adam finished.

Ian was looking at him as if he were crazy.

"What's an anbassership?" Kellen said.

"Ambassadorship," Elizabeth corrected softly. "It's a job where a man represents his country in a foreign country." She glanced at Adam. "It's a very important job, an honor."

"Does this mean we have to move?" Kellen asked.

"No, Lil'bit, it doesn't." He looked back at Elizabeth. "I turned it down."

Elizabeth's face was blank, but then a small smile tipped her lips.

Ian let out a breath and picked up his wine. "Well, thank god for your good sense, Father," he said. He frowned. "The idea of living with all those unwashed Frogs—"

Adam shook his head. "Ian, France is a wonderful country. You'd do well to visit there."

"Why?" Ian said imperiously. "As long as they keep sending over their wine, I see no reason to go there."

Adam glanced at Elizabeth in shared dismay, but they let the remark pass. Ian, it was apparent, was becoming a snob. He further annoyed Adam by leaving early, saying he had a date. But the rest of the dinner continued without incident. Afterward, Adam and Elizabeth sat in the living room before the fire with their coffee.

"You're glad I turned it down, aren't you," Adam said.

Elizabeth paused. "Yes."

"But why? I'd have thought you'd jump at the chance to live in Paris."

She shook her head slowly. "You could never leave your newspapers, Adam. I could never allow you to." She looked around the room. "Besides, this is my home. I could never leave it." She smiled, her eyes lit by the fire. "I'm so proud of you, Adam. You've done all you set out to do."

"You made it possible."

"Money is just money, Adam. It takes more than that to make dreams real."

"I don't mean the money," he said. "I mean by your belief in me. I'd be nowhere without that."

Elizabeth embraced him, then pulled away. "I've got to go say good night to Kellen. I'll be down in a few minutes."

Kellen was sitting up in bed, waiting when Elizabeth came in. "Why didn't Daddy take that new job?" she asked.

Elizabeth began to tuck her in. "Because he likes his own job more. Running newspapers is just as important as being an ambassador."

"Maybe I'll be an ambassador when I grow up." Kellen frowned. "No, I think I'll do what Daddy does—go to an office."

"I thought you wanted to be a veterinarian."

She looked at Elizabeth hopefully. "I could do both."

Elizabeth sat on the edge of the bed. "That would be rather hard. It might be better if you chose one."

"You're right." Kellen nodded her head solemnly. "Maybe I should just be a newspaper magnet."

Elizabeth laughed. "Where did you hear that word?"

"I heard someone call Daddy that once. What does Daddy do, exactly?"

"Well, he watches over all his newspapers in the chain."

Kellen smiled broadly. "That's what I thought! A magnet that holds the chain together!"

Elizabeth pulled the covers over Kellen. "It's magnate, by the way. But you've got the idea."

Kellen slid down in the bed. "Mummy, can a girl be a magnet . . . magnate . . . or just boys?"

"Well, I've never heard of a girl doing it, but that's no reason why you couldn't. Girls can work just like boys."

"How come you don't?"

Elizabeth brushed the hair back from Kellen's forehead. "I stay here with you. I like that better." She paused. "But when I was your age, I dreamed about doing things, too. I wanted to go to Paris and be a dress designer.''

"Like how you draw clothes for my paper dolls?''

Elizabeth smiled. "Something like that.''

"Why didn't you?''

"When I was your age, girls didn't do things like that.'' She rose, switching off the lamp. "Come on, it's past your bedtime.''

"Mommy?''

Elizabeth paused just inside the door. "Yes?''

"Do you think I could really be a magnate?''

"I don't think there's anything you couldn't be, sweetheart,'' she said softly. "Sleep tight . . .''

"Don't let the bedbugs bite,'' Kellen answered.

Adam decided he wanted to throw a New Year's Eve party. It was a payback, he told Elizabeth, to all his political and club cronies and important advertisers, and a chance to return social obligations he had been too busy for in the past year. "It's been a hell of a good year for us, Elizabeth,'' he said. "Let's really celebrate with a bash.'' He didn't tell her he also hoped planning a party would buoy up her spirits, as it always had in the past.

As usual, she did a stunning job. The house was ablaze with holiday decorations, the dining room given over to a giant buffet. The beautiful old Kashan rug in the foyer was rolled up and everyone danced under the chandelier to tunes played by a small jazz quartet. Everyone important in town came, and a few famous faces dotted the crowd. Adam was so festive that many of his friends commented on it. But none so succinctly as Josh.

"I've known you for almost fifteen years,'' Josh said. "And I never thought I'd be able to say this. You've changed, Adam. You're a different man.''

"I'm a happy man, Josh,'' Adam replied.

Just before midnight, Kellen was awakened by the noise. She crept out to sit at the top of the staircase, watching the scene below with wide eyes. The big house had never seemed so happy to her. It was filled with the sweet smells of food, the sound of laughter, music, and champagne corks. When the clock struck midnight, she watched as Adam took Elizabeth in his arms under the chandelier and kissed her in a whirlwind of confetti and balloons. Then, with a yawn, Kellen went back to her room and fell asleep, her heart bursting with happiness.

Hours later, after the last guests had gone, Adam lay on the bed, watching Elizabeth as she combed out her hair. He was heady with champagne and the success of the evening. He went to Elizabeth, filling his hands with her heavy, soft hair, arching her neck back so he could kiss her.

"I love you so much," he whispered.

She kissed him softly. When he pulled away to look at her face, he paused. Her just-cleaned face had a waxy pallor, and there were deep circles under her eyes. She had disguised it earlier with makeup.

Adam stepped back to look at her better. "Elizabeth, are you all right?" he asked quietly.

"I'm just tired, Adam," she whispered. "So very tired."

The party had taken too much out of her, he thought, berating himself for putting her through it. "Let's go to bed," he said. She allowed him to tuck her in, like a child, and by the time he slipped in beside her, she was asleep. He turned out the light and lay there in the dark. It was quiet except for an occasional car horn or the laugh of a late reveler in the street. When the gray light began to creep around the edges of the drapes, he was still awake, lying there, listening to her breathing and feeling a small pit of fear growing in his stomach.

Chapter
Fourteen

After the New Year's party, Adam began to pay closer attention to Elizabeth's behavior. For a week, she stayed in bed, too tired to get up. The doctor said Elizabeth had a virus and prescribed antibiotics and massive doses of vitamins. But after a month, Elizabeth was no better. The doctor then suggested Elizabeth go into the hospital for tests. Adam agreed with great reluctance; after what she had gone through with the miscarriage and Kellen's difficult birth, the mere idea of putting Elizabeth in a hospital made his blood run cold. The tests revealed nothing extraordinary, other than the previously diagnosed anemia. Elizabeth was sent home with antidepressants and a strict diet.

The drugs seemed to help Elizabeth's mood somewhat, but by spring, Adam noticed an alarming change in her behavior. She seemed at times disoriented, and she was beginning to forget things easily—where she had left her keys, that someone was coming to dinner, where Kellen had gone for the day. The doctor prescribed a stronger antidepressant. When she showed no improvement, Adam angrily dismissed the doctor and found another. The new doctor said her depression was a reaction to an old, undiagnosed bout with hepatitis, and he gave her new medications. Elizabeth did not respond and, in fact, grew worse. Her appetite waned; she developed insomnia and began to have crying spells. And still she talked, almost obsessively now, about not being able to have children.

In fearful frustration, Adam finally sought the help of a psychiatrist. He told Adam Elizabeth's obsession with pregnancy was the cause of all her ills, and prescribed yet more antidepressants and a new antianxiety drug. Elizabeth improved slightly, and Adam grew hopeful. She allowed a few close friends to visit and one night, even went to the opera with Adam, though they had to leave at intermission. She even felt well enough occasionally to come down to dinner. One night, Elizabeth was sitting at the table in a blue silk dressing gown, her hair pinned up but her face wan. Kellen, delighted her mother was there, chatted away to keep spirits high. She began to talk about weddings, and Elizabeth sat quietly, half listening.

"Mommy, what was your wedding to Daddy like?" Kellen asked.

Elizabeth's pale face was a blank, and Adam held his breath, curbing his urge to prompt her memory. Then, she smiled slightly. "Oh, it was beautiful," she said softly. She glanced down the table at Adam then back at Kellen.

"We got married in this little church, not too far from here," Elizabeth said. "Just a small sanctuary, with beams across the ceiling and wooden pews. The pastor was an old man, with a funny little beard." She looked at Adam, and her eyes came to life. "Do you remember him, Adam?"

"Yes," Adam said softly. "Very well."

"I wore a dress made of cream-colored lace," Elizabeth went on dreamily. "And a matching hat with a veil. Your father wore a blue suit and had a red rosebud in his lapel. It kept falling off. . . ."

Kellen was listening intently, her eyes on Elizabeth.

"There were candles," Elizabeth said. "It seemed like hundreds of candles. And it was raining. A sweet, soft rain that smelled like eucalyptus trees." She smiled, and for a moment, she seemed like her former self. "I can remember it all so clearly, like it was yesterday. But it wasn't, of course. It was . . ." She paused, and very slowly her smile faded and the light left her eyes. "It was . . ." she repeated in a whisper. Her face crumpled suddenly in despair. "It was . . ."

Kellen looked at Adam. He felt frozen to his chair as the awful seconds ticked by. Tears began to fall down Elizabeth's face. "I can't remember," she said, her voice breaking. "I can't remember. I can't remember when it was!"

Kellen's face was white with alarm. Adam jumped up and went to Elizabeth. She gripped his arm. "I can't remember," she repeated. Adam pressed her head against his chest, holding her while she cried.

"It was the summer of nineteen thirty-seven, Elizabeth," he said, the words coming out in a choke. "July ninth."

After a moment, Elizabeth's crying abated into soft sobs. Adam helped her out of the chair and led her upstairs. Kellen sat at the table alone, staring at the flickering candles, too stunned and too scared to move.

One by one, Elizabeth stopped doing the things she loved. She stopped accepting visitors. She no longer went out of the house at all. She lost interest in the garden and stopped arranging vases of flowers. She was disinterested in sex. Finally, Adam stopped approaching her. He continued his frustrating search for answers, bringing in doctor after doctor to examine her. With great apprehension, he even took her back to the hospital, but after a battery of painful tests that left Elizabeth exhausted, doctors still could find no physical cause. "Please take me home, Adam," Elizabeth pleaded. Seeing the fear in her eyes, Adam agreed. He read whatever he could find on depression, and he became convinced that he had allowed Elizabeth to unwittingly fall into a habit of drug abuse that was now affecting her mind. He found another psychiatrist who prescribed a different set of drugs that he claimed were the latest medical advance, and he assured Adam that the depression could probably be broken through medication and patience.

"And if it can't?" Adam countered.

"Then your wife will have to be committed," the doctor answered.

For the first time in his life, Adam was afraid. The thought of losing Elizabeth left him numb with terror. But he forced himself to remain positive. He resolved that Elizabeth would never be shut away somewhere. He hired a team of private nurses to monitor Elizabeth's medication, and he drastically curtailed his work hours.

But as summer approached, Elizabeth's condition began to deteriorate at an alarming rate. Adam watched in helpless horror as his wife slipped away from reality and into a world of confusion and physical instability. It came to the point where Adam did not know what to expect. One moment she was withdrawn, the next she was temperamental. Most of the time, however, she hovered in a drugged state of apathy. Finally, Adam had a neurological specialist flown in from Europe. The doctor examined Elizabeth, then met with Adam in his study.

"I've never seen anything like it," the doctor told Adam. "Your wife seems to have all the symptoms of senility."

"That's impossible," Adam said. "She's not even forty-two years old." After he had recovered from his horror, he added, "So what can be done to help her?"

The doctor shook his head. "To my knowledge, nothing, Mr.

Bryant. We just don't know enough about how the mind works
. . . or why it suddenly stops working.''

Adam stared at the man silently, then looked away.

The doctor began to write out a prescription. "She could become violent,'' he said. "I suggest you have these sedatives on
hand just in case.'' He held out the form, but Adam did not take
it, so he set it on the desk between them.

Adam looked up vacantly, suddenly grasping the doctor's
words. "Violent?'' he whispered in disbelief. His face collapsed
in despair and incomprehension. "There's got to be something
. . . more that I can do,'' he said.

The doctor paused, choosing his words. "It will get worse, Mr.
Bryant. You should think about a hospital—''

Adam's eyes hardened. "A hospital? You mean have her committed? I won't do that! Never!''

The doctor stared at the man sitting before him with compassion. Adam was pale and unshaven; there were hollows under his
eyes from the strain. The doctor stood, picking up his bag. "I'll
let myself out, Mr. Bryant,'' he said. He picked up the prescription form. "I'll have this filled and delivered.'' He left the house,
leaving Adam sitting alone in the study, staring at the walls.

In the next week, Elizabeth began to grow agitated. But
Adam could not bring himself to give her the sedatives. To do
so, he thought, would be a final admission of defeat. He recognized she was growing worse every day, but a part of him
clung to the belief that somehow, through the sheer force of his
love, he could pull her back from the brink of total collapse. He
was consumed with a silent, raging sense of impotency. For the
first time in his life, he had encountered something he could not
overcome.

One night, Adam awoke to see Elizabeth standing over him in
the dark holding a pair of scissors. He managed to get the scissors
away from her and get her back to bed. He found the sedatives the
doctor had sent and gave her one. The next day, he moved to
another bedroom. After that, he had to use the sedatives to keep
Elizabeth pacified. She lived in a narcotic stupor most of the time,
a series of nurses looking to her grooming needs. Adam went to
the newspaper office as little as possible, trusting Josh to act as
liaison to his editors. He spent all his time sitting by her bedside,
holding her hand, talking gently to her, still trying to break through
the fog that was growing more dense around her every day. He
fought with his guilt, blaming himself for all the times he had not
been there for her. But he knew that guilt would not help Elizabeth

now. The only thing that mattered was that he be there for her. In his anguish, he did not see that someone else needed him even more.

Kellen sat on the bottom step of the staircase, staring at the reflections of her patent leather shoes. She had just come from her mother's room, but the nurse had sent her away, just as she always did recently. Kellen had not been allowed to see her mother for a month, and no one would tell her why.

Kellen jammed her fists into her eyes, fighting back tears. She knew something was terribly wrong with her mother, but no one would talk about it. "Just be a good, brave little girl," Hildie told her brusquely, with tearful eyes. "That's the best thing you can do for your mother now."

So she tried. But it was so hard. If she could see her mother, maybe she could help her somehow. Bring her soup or read her a story. She was sure she could make her feel better. If only she could see her.

Suddenly, the doorbell rang, and she jumped up to answer it, glad to see anyone who might be there. She opened the door, and her face fell slightly when she saw Josh, who had come over from the office with papers for Adam to sign.

"Oh, come on in, Mr. Hillman," she said. Then she smiled as she saw someone else coming up the walk. "Stephen!" she called out and ran to greet him.

"Hey, Squirt," Stephen said. "How you doing?"

"I'm so glad you came over!" she said.

"I thought maybe you could use some help with your homework," Stephen said.

She took his hand and pulled him through the door. "I sure can! Come on up to my room."

"Is it all right, Dad?" Stephen asked Josh.

"Go ahead. I'll come get you in an hour or so," Josh answered, heading for the study.

Kellen followed Stephen up the staircase. At fourteen, Stephen was a quiet boy, with a mop of sandy brown hair and serious hazel eyes. He had befriended Kellen when she was just six, treating her like a younger sister, helping her with her schoolwork, playing games with her, teaching her to ride. "How's your mother?" Stephen asked, when they were in Kellen's room.

Kellen shrugged and looked away quickly. "I dunno," she mumbled. "They won't let me even see her anymore."

Stephen sat down on the bed, not knowing what to say in

comfort. "Okay, so what will it be today," he said to change the subject. "Arithmetic? Science?"

Kellen picked up a schoolbook and plopped down on the bed next to Stephen. "Geography," she said.

"What about that essay you had to write?"

"Finished it. I don't need any help with English."

Stephen began to leaf through the textbook she had given him. "So why geography then? You having trouble?"

"No, I just feel like it today," she said with a sigh. She crossed her legs under her, resting her hands under her chin. "I like to read about places that are far away. I like to imagine I'm there."

"Where?"

"Anywhere," she said quietly. "Anywhere but here."

Stephen could feel her pain, and he wished there was something he could do. But he didn't know what. As an only child, he had never had the advantage of the emotional interplay between siblings, and his demeanor had always been more adult than childlike. Expressing things wasn't easy for him. "Everything's going to be all right, Kellen," he said, hoping somehow it was enough. "I just know it will."

She looked up at him with despondent, hopeful eyes.

"You can always come and talk to me if you need to," he added. "You know, if you need someone."

Her eyes overflowed, and she wrapped her arms around his waist, burying her face in his sweater, crying. The geography book fell to the floor, and Stephen just sat there stunned, feeling terrible but unsure what to say or do. Finally, he just brought up one arm and patted her with what he hoped was reassurance. He had seen her cry before, when she skinned her knee or fell off a horse, but never like this. It made him want to cry. But he didn't. He was fourteen, after all, and something more was surely expected from him. He had to be strong for her right now.

"Don't worry, Kellen," he repeated. "It'll be all right.

Down in the study, Adam and Josh sat across from each other in silence. Josh closed the folder of papers, unable to get Adam to concentrate on them. He reached across the desk to turn on a lamp. The light made Adam blink, and Josh could see clearly now how drawn with grief his friend's face was.

"I have some bad news," Josh said. Adam stared out the window. "Hank turned in his resignation this morning." Josh waited for a response. "Adam, did you hear what I said?"

"Sure, sure . . . Hank quit."

Adam's eyes were bloodshot from lack of sleep, and he was unshaven. Josh took a deep breath. "Adam, you can't go on like this," he said. "You're killing yourself." Adam didn't respond. "Well, if you don't care about yourself, then you should care about what's happening to your newspapers. Things are falling apart."

"The newspapers will survive—"

"Not without you. For eight months now, you've been sitting in this house—"

"The papers will survive!" Adam said loudly.

Josh sighed. "I'm sorry, Adam. I know what you've been going through." He paused. "I'm worried about you. You're taking too much on your own shoulders. You've done all you can."

Adam stared out the window. "No, there's got to be something I can do. . . ."

"It's in God's hands," Josh said.

"God's hands . . ." Adam repeated bitterly. He turned to Josh, his face slack. "God abandoned her. But I won't. I won't just sit by and—" His voice broke slightly. "And watch her mind slip away."

Josh dropped his eyes to his hands, clenching the folder of papers in his lap.

"She was . . ." Adam said, his voice a pleading whisper. "She had . . . emotions, intelligence." He turned back to face Josh. "She had such life in her, Josh. And now it's gone."

Josh looked away, unable to meet Adam's brimming eyes. "Elizabeth needs more help than you can give her," he said. "She needs to be in a hospital."

"No," Adam said harshly. "I won't have her locked away like some animal."

"Adam, you've got to listen—"

"No! No hospital!"

"Adam—"

"Leave me alone!" Adam shouted. He ran his hands over his eyes. "Please, Josh," he added quietly. "Maybe you better leave."

Josh rose and set some documents in front of Adam on the desk. "I'll come back for these tomorrow." He went to the door and turned back to Adam, who was staring at nothing.

"If there's anything I can do to help, Adam—anything—just call me." Josh closed the door quietly behind him.

Adam sat motionless in the study. He sat there for several

hours, alone with his thoughts. Someone finally opened the door.

"Daddy?"

He looked up and his eyes focused on Kellen, silhouetted in the light from the hallway. She came tentatively into the room. "What are you doing?"

"Working."

She came over to the desk and stood there, staring at him. "You missed dinner again," she said.

"I'm not hungry, Lil'bit—"

"It's Mother, isn't it."

Adam looked up at her. From the cloudiness of his mind came the realization that he had barely seen Kellen in the past week. He saw now that she looked exactly how he felt right now—very frightened. "Yes," he said softly. "She's very sick."

Kellen stared at her father for a long time. She had never seen him look so tired and sad. She thought about what Hildie had said about being brave, and what Stephen had said about being there to help her. She wanted to do the same for her father. "She'll get better, won't she?" she asked.

Adam knew she deserved to hear the truth. The truth, which he finally had to bring himself to face somehow. He tried to speak, but the words stuck in his throat. He couldn't even bring himself to nod. It took every fiber of his strength not to cry.

Kellen searched his face, and she touched his sleeve. "Don't worry, Daddy," she said softly. "It'll be all right. . . ."

Adam pulled her into his arms, burying his face in her soft hair. He held her tight for a long time, then pulled away, almost brusquely. "It's late," he said. "You should be in bed. Come on, I'll take you up."

Upstairs, Adam waited patiently outside the door, honoring her request for privacy, until she had gotten ready for bed. Then he tucked the blanket around her, his motions made mechanical by his crushing weariness. She lay there, clutching her stuffed sock monkey.

"Good night, Lil'bit," he said, reaching for the light.

"Leave it on," she said quickly. "Just for tonight."

He nodded woodenly, closing her door. He went down the hallway, his footsteps heavy. He started to go to his own room, but then turned and paused just outside the closed door of Elizabeth's room. The nurse, seeing him from the open door of her own room across the hall, went to him.

"She's been asleep all day, Mr. Bryant," she reported. "She

didn't even wake up long enough for me to give her her medication."

Adam nodded absently. "I'm just going to say good night to her," he said. He went into the bedroom, closing the door behind him. As usual, Elizabeth was lying in the bed, propped up by pillows, her eyes closed, her hands clasped together and folded over her chest. Adam sat down on the side of the bed and gazed at her face. He had given up expecting a response; he just wanted to sit there and look at her. Even now, in her depleted health, she still looked beautiful, he thought. Her face was too thin and gray, but her long red hair, maintained carefully by the nurses, was as glorious as it had always been. He reached up to stroke it.

Elizabeth's brow furrowed, and her eyes fluttered open. It didn't surprise him. She would often wake up, but her eyes always had a faraway look, as if she were struggling to figure out who the stranger was sitting by her side. She stared at him now, but Adam realized slowly that her eyes looked different somehow. The opaqueness was gone. Her eyes searched his face, and she frowned slightly. Her fingers were moving, and Adam saw that she was clutching the little jade cat that usually sat on her bedside table. Her eyes, so clear and green, stared at him beseechingly. Her lips trembled as she struggled to speak.

"I'm scared," she whispered. "Hold me."

There were tears in her eyes, and Adam saw in them, in one precious moment of lucidity, a reflection of his wife. He drew her into his arms.

"Hold me," she whispered. "Hold me."

Chapter
Fifteen

It had been an aberration. That one moment of lucidity was gone as quickly as it had come, and Elizabeth then slipped back into her twilight world. During the next three days, she awoke only once and began to call out unintelligible words and nonsensical sentences. Adam stood outside her closed door with his eyes closed, listening to her rantings and the gentle ministrations of the nurse.

The nurse came out, closing the door behind her. "Mr. Bryant," she said. "I'm going to have to switch her to an I.V. for the sedatives. She won't take pills any longer."

"She's not in pain, is she?" Adam asked. The nurse shook her head. "Then do what you must," Adam said vacantly. "I just don't want her to suffer."

"She'll be fine for a while," the nurse said. "So I'll take my dinner break now. I'll look in on her in an hour."

Adam went downstairs. He paused in the foyer when he saw Kellen, sitting on the sofa in her white bathrobe, clutching her monkey, staring at nothing. He was exhausted, and his first instinct was to call Hildie to take her up to bed, but he knew he had waited far too long to face Kellen. He went over and sat down next to her. Her face was tear-streaked, but her eyes were dry. "Are you all right, Lil'bit?" he asked. She just sat there, numbly, without looking at him. "I think we should have a talk," Adam said.

"About Mother," Kellen said flatly.

"Yes."

Finally, Kellen turned to meet his eyes. "She's going to die, isn't she."

Adam felt the last breath of energy leave his body. He nodded numbly.

Kellen stared at him, unblinking. "Why can't I see her?" she asked.

"Kellen, she—"

There was a sound in the foyer, and they both turned. Elizabeth was standing at the foot of the stairs, holding on to the balustrade to steady herself, her bare feet visible beneath her white night-gown. Her hair was a tangle around her white face, and her eyes were wide with fright as they darted around the room. She seemed to be desperately looking for something, and finally, her gaze fell beseechingly on Adam and Kellen, who both sat in frozen shock.

"Elizabeth," Adam whispered, rising.

She stared at him uncomprehendingly. Her mouth moved, as if she wanted to say something, but she couldn't. Tears began to fall down her cheeks. "I'm scared," she whispered.

Before Adam could move, Kellen swept by him and went to Elizabeth's side. Elizabeth stared at her blankly, but Kellen didn't seem to notice that her mother didn't recognize her.

"I'll help you back upstairs, Mommy," she said.

Elizabeth pulled back slightly, but Kellen took her hand. "Once there was a little girl who was afraid to go to bed," Kellen said softly, pointing to the carved frowning face in the balustrade. "And her face looked like this. An evil fairy came along one day and turned her into wood."

Elizabeth's eyes were still wide with fear, but she was listening to Kellen's small voice. Adam hung back, waiting.

"But then the good fairy came along and told the girl she could break the spell if she'd smile and be brave. . . ."

Somehow, Kellen had turned Elizabeth around and was very slowly leading her by the hand back up the stairs. "So the girl smiled, and she started floating up the stairs. . . ."

They had reached the first landing, and Adam stood below, unable to move. Finally, the nurse appeared and helped Kellen take Elizabeth up the rest of the way. Adam watched them until the three of them were nothing but slowly retreating white blurs, misshapen by his tears.

It was late the same night when Josh rang the bell of the mansion. No one answered, but the door was unlocked, so he let himself in. The foyer was dark, as was the rest of the house, and it was eerily quiet. The study door was ajar and Josh went to it, pushing it open. The room was dark, except for the moonlight streaming through one window near the desk. He saw someone sitting behind it.

"Adam?"

"Come in, Josh," a voice answered, flat and lifeless.

Josh went slowly to the desk. He paused, staring at Adam's motionless form slumped in the chair. He reached over to switch on the lamp.

"No, leave it off, please."

"I got here as soon as I could," he said, sitting down. "Where is everyone?"

"I dismissed the nurse and the rest of staff for the night. Kellen's spending the night at a friend's."

Josh waited, but Adam did not move. "What is it, Adam? Is it Elizabeth? What's wrong?"

Adam looked up, his eyes glistening in the moonlight. "I need your help," he said.

Elizabeth died the next morning, two days before her forty-second birthday. Adam made quick arrangements for a simple funeral. Kellen sat by Adam's side during the service, clinging to Hildie's hand. Ian came home for two days, then returned to college. In the *Times*, there was a small, sedate obituary that Adam had ordered be underplayed. In contrast, the *Journal* ran a large, prominent story, playing to the gossip that had surrounded Elizabeth's illness for the past six months. The life and death of Elizabeth Ingram Bryant was a story tailor-made to inflame the imaginations of readers, rich and poor. It had all the elements—money, glamour, madness, and mystery. Adam read the *Journal* story with a strange dispassion that concerned Josh. "That ought to sell a few papers for that bastard Capen," he said.

Josh watched Adam carefully, looking for signs of a breakdown, but there were none. Adam was calm and dry-eyed throughout the funeral and its aftermath. It worried Josh at first, but then he realized that Adam was just reverting to his natural introversion as a defense mechanism, handling his grief as he did most things, in a private and orderly manner. But he had changed, as if a light had been extinguished inside him, and it was reflected in his appearance. His face had grown sharp from his loss of weight, and a new, short beard intensified the look of severity. His entire manner seemed stiffly precarious, like an oak tree after a storm, still upright but with its roots unloosed and exposed.

Adam spoke to Josh about Elizabeth only once. A week after the funeral, he called Josh to the study and handed him a cigar box. "I bought this two months ago," Adam said, "for her birthday. Just put it away somewhere, Josh."

Puzzled, Josh opened the box and saw a large, unset sapphire lying atop some old photographs. The three-jeweled necklace that Elizabeth had so loved was also in the box, and Josh understood that the sapphire was meant to represent Adam's fourth newspaper. Josh put the box in a bank vault.

A week later, Adam hired a housekeeper to oversee the staff. She was a cool, efficient woman who immediately set out to restore the order that had been lost during Elizabeth's illness. Dinners were again served at seven, with candles and silver service. Flowers reappeared throughout the house. The staff was snapped out of its lethargy. A forced sense of normalcy returned to the house on Divisadero.

To impose order on his own life, Adam turned to the newspapers. He didn't want to go back to the office yet, so Josh brought his work to him, encouraged by the fact that he was showing interest again in the neglected newspapers. But he wished Adam would do the same for Kellen. Elizabeth's death had left the child floundering. She had been brave during the funeral, but now she felt abandoned, and no amount of comfort from either Stephen or Hildie could fill the gap. Only Adam could, but in his pain, he was unable to give his daughter the comfort and love she so desperately needed. Josh attributed it to Adam's need to put Elizabeth's death behind him as quickly as possible, and Adam was expecting Kellen to do the same, seeming to forget she was only eleven. Josh asked Stephen to keep an eye on Kellen.

Stephen took his new responsibility seriously, listening to her when she needed to talk, holding her hand when she cried. They talked often about death, about why people had to die, where they went afterward. Stephen had always put his trust in books, so he looked there for his answers as to how to comfort Kellen. He had recently been reading about the mystic cabalistic Jews, whose writings taught about reincarnation, and he suggested to Kellen, in the simplest terms, that Elizabeth's spirit could live again someday. Kellen, too young to recognize this was at odds with her Catholic instruction, was comforted. She still mourned for her mother, but slowly she began to come to grips with her death. But she still harbored an anger toward her father.

"I hate him," Kellen told Stephen one day, about two months after the funeral.

Stephen knew she was just hurt because Adam was ignoring her. "You don't really hate him," he said gently. "He's your father."

Kellen's eyes filled with tears. "Why is he acting like this,

Stephen? Why can't he be like he used to? Why can't everything
be like it used to?''

But for all he had read in books, Stephen had no answers for
that.

Three months after Elizabeth's death, another story about her
appeared in the *Journal*. It began: "Socialite Elizabeth Ingram
Bryant died under mysterious circumstances involving her husband, Adam Bryant, publisher of the *San Francisco Times*, the
Journal has learned exclusively."

The story quoted some of Elizabeth's friends who said they had
noticed changes in Elizabeth's behavior and that she had been
taking drugs. One unnamed source suggested that the Bryants
were having marital problems. Most damning, however, was the
quote by an unnamed doctor who said he believed Mrs. Bryant's
severe depression resulted from an untreated infection and spec-
ulated that Adam's refusal to keep his wife in the hospital had
jeopardized her health and chance for recovery. The doctor did not
explicitly call Adam responsible for Elizabeth's death, but the
implication was there.

The story also pointed out that most of the Bryant newspapers
and properties were owned solely by Elizabeth, and even quoted
Charles Ingram's lawyer, explaining how the trusts of Elizabeth's
two inheritances had been set up to prevent Adam from accessing
her fortune.

Enraged, Adam called Josh. "I want that fucking bastard Capen
sued. This is nothing but conjecture and gossip. Not one source in
this story is named. No one had the guts to go on record."

"It sounds like they've stayed just this side of libel," Josh
answered. "You might be best to ignore it. People forget easily.
You won't have to worry about it in the long run."

"I don't care about me!" Adam said. "I don't want her dragged
down like this."

"I'll file the suit," Josh answered.

Two days later, another story appeared in the *Journal*. This
time, a source did go on record: Elizabeth's attending nurse said
that, on the night before Elizabeth died, Adam had acted strangely
and had ordered her to leave the house just before midnight. The
police quickly launched an investigation, and the body was ex-
humed, despite Josh's legal attempts to stop it. The results of the
autopsy were dutifully reported in the *Journal*. Elizabeth Bryant
had died of heart failure, probably brought on by a potent mixture
of several narcotics. Adam endured a police investigation. He

would face a manslaughter charge if he could be implicated for negligence, for allowing Elizabeth's death. But the conclusion was that the drug overdose was probably accidental, given the great number of conflicting diagnoses and treatments Elizabeth had received. Adam was not charged, but the episode left him devastated. To escape the publicity, he went down to the house in Carmel alone. While there, he received a call from Josh.

"It's not over," Josh told him. "The *Journal*'s got a copy of the codicil."

"But how?"

"I don't know . . . someone in my office, maybe. All I know is their reporter just called me and asked if I'd comment on Elizabeth's will."

"I'll be back as soon as I can." Adam hung up the phone. He stared out at the beach where he and Elizabeth had walked together. He knew that tomorrow morning there would be another story in the *Journal* that would refuel the fire of gossip. It would say that three weeks before her death, Elizabeth Bryant had signed a codicil to her original will, which had been drawn up by her father before his own death. The codicil, prepared by Josh Hillman, named Adam Bryant sole beneficiary of her fortune and her newspaper holdings, to the exclusion of Elizabeth's sister. Through a legal loophole, it also circumvented the wishes of the trustees who had overseen the holdings Elizabeth had inherited from Willis Foster Reed. The codicil left Adam the sole heir of a fortune estimated at $200 million.

Adam hurried back to the city. The next day, the story appeared as expected. It traced Adam's life from his penniless childhood to his rise through the *Times* via marriage to Lilith Bickford. It described his hasty divorce and remarriage to an heiress and her purchase on his behalf of four newspapers and other holdings. It recounted her illness and death, noting that she had changed her will only weeks before her death. The story, Josh told Adam, was not actually libelous. But it cleverly implied that Adam Bryant had somehow, by design or negligence, engineered his own wife's death.

The publicity began anew, but this time it grew beyond the front page of the *Journal* or the tasteful obits that had run in Atlanta and New York. Phone calls from newspapers all over the world flooded the house. Reporters and photographers camped outside the door. Adam refused to comment and ordered his own newspapers to ignore the story. Ian returned home unexpectedly, saying the publicity in the East made his life impossible. At school,

Kellen was taunted by classmates who called her father a murderer. Adam pulled her out of school and sent her to stay with Josh and Anna.

Two months dragged by, and very slowly, the furor began to die down. The phone calls trickled to a few and then finally stopped as other stories grabbed the headlines: Eisenhower was nominated for president. The Americans outscored the Soviets at the Helsinki Olympics. And in southern California, the second biggest earthquake in the state's history killed eleven people. The story of Elizabeth and Adam Bryant, inflated to Wagnerian proportions by the press to titillate readers, had finally ceased to be news.

In October, Adam returned to the office for the first time since Elizabeth's death. He walked through the newsroom, head high, and paused by the city desk to make a brief announcement. Everyone eyed him curiously. The publisher they remembered was a gregarious man who would come down to the newsroom with his shirt sleeves rolled up when a good story was breaking, or swoop in late at night in a tuxedo with Elizabeth at his side to check on a story. This was not the same man. This thin man in a gray suit, a salt-and-pepper beard blunting his unsmiling face, was a stranger.

"I wanted to tell you all how good is it to be back," Adam said. "I know my absence had created some difficulties for you." He paused. "It's been a difficult time all around. But the *Times* is a great newspaper. It will always be, thanks to the hard work and devotion of people like you." He surveyed the room, thanked his employees, and went upstairs to his office.

Adam resumed his role as head of the Times Corporation with fierce energy. He was making up for the months he had neglected the newspapers, monitoring costs and overseeing the hiring of key personnel. He was looking for another newspaper to buy. But his manner had turned brusque. He was impatient, even intolerant if business did not progress on schedule. At home, it was the same. Adam stayed in his study, working, and treated the servants with indifference. When Ian announced he was returning to school, Adam managed only a cool good-bye. And he continued to ignore Kellen. Hildie confided to Josh that Kellen was having behavior problems in school and that Adam refused to listen. "You've got to talk to him, Mr. Hillman," she said. "She needs him so much right now." But when Josh broached the subject with Adam, he was rebuffed. Josh persisted, and finally Adam exploded.

"Goddamn it, Josh!" Adam said. "I can't run this corporation and play nursemaid to a willful preteen girl!"

"Adam, listen—"

"I've been working my ass off to get things running smoothly again at the paper. And I've almost got this guy up in Oregon where I want him on the price of his newspaper. I've got to go up there again this week." Adam shook his head in irritation. "Not now, Josh, please. I've got too much on my mind."

"Kellen's having problems at school, Adam," Josh said. "Her grades have slipped. She's getting into fights."

"It's that school," Adam answered. "All she needs is a structured atmosphere, away from here."

"Away?"

"She's had her head filled with all those stories. It's no wonder she's having problems." Adam paused. "She'd do better in a boarding school."

"Adam, for god's sake, don't send her away," Josh pleaded. "She doesn't need that. She needs—"

"It's my decision, and I've made it. It's for the best, Josh," Adam said brusquely. He began to sort through some papers. Josh waited, helplessly. Adam looked up. "If there's nothing else, Josh, I'm really busy right now."

Josh rose. "No, there's nothing else," he said quietly.

A week later, Kellen stood in the foyer, dressed in a new coat and hat, staring at the car that would take her to Monterey, where Adam had enrolled her in the Santa Catalina School for Girls. Stephen and Josh stood at her side and they all watched in silence as the chauffeur loaded the suitcases into the trunk. Hildie came down the staircase, carrying her purse and the stuffed monkey. She held it out to Kellen, but the young girl wouldn't take it. With a doleful look at Josh, Hildie went out to the car to give Kellen time to say her good-byes. Kellen stood there stoically. She had done all her crying three days ago when Hildie had first told her she was being sent away. Those were not the words Hildie had used; she told Kellen she was going off to a fine school to get the best education—just like Ian did at Princeton. But Kellen knew the truth. Her father didn't want any part of her. He had not even bothered to tell her himself—he had just gone off to Oregon and had come back just last night. He was sending her away, punishing her, and she didn't know why.

Josh stepped forward to give her a hug. "Thanksgiving's only a month away. We'll see you then," he said. He moved away so she could be alone with Stephen.

"You better write to me, squirt," Stephen said. Kellen stared at the car, her chin trembling. "Listen," Stephen said, smiling. "Pretty soon I'll have my driver's permit. I can drive down to visit—with my dad, of course."

He awkwardly kissed her cheek. "It won't be that bad," he said quietly. "Call me, if you need to."

At that moment, the door of the study opened, and Adam appeared in the doorway. Kellen stared at him, her eyes hard as she fought back tears, determined not to cry. Adam came over to her. With a look at the others, he picked up the small travel satchel Hildie had prepared. He touched Kellen's shoulder, but she shrugged off his hand and walked slowly out the door. He followed her out to the car, handing the bag to the chauffeur.

Kellen stared at the car for a moment, then turned quickly to look up at Adam. Suddenly, she couldn't hold back the tears anymore, and they fell down her cheeks.

"Daddy . . ." she said pleadingly.

He stared at her. Then he leaned over and kissed her cheek. "Be a good girl, Kellen," he said.

He straightened and took a step back. She waited, but it was clear that he had nothing more to say. She got into the car beside Hildie, and the door closed with a soft thud. The car pulled away, and she turned to look out the rear window. Through her tears, she saw Adam standing there, alone in front of the big white house. He stood there unmoving, until the car turned down the hill and he disappeared.

Chapter
Sixteen

With Kellen gone, Adam withdrew even more into himself. His world shrank down to his office at the newspaper and his study at home, with an occasional trip to the Olympic Club to swim mindlessly in the large pool. Kellen never called him, and at Thanksgiving and Christmas and Easter, she didn't come home, choosing instead to stay at school. Two days after Passover ended, Josh came to the house for dinner. He sat at the table, watching Adam's wan face. Neither man spoke, and the candles cast long shadows in the large, empty dining room. Josh sensed that Adam wanted to talk about something.

"What's bothering you?" he finally asked.

Adam looked up. "Nothing really. Just that asshole in Portland trying to squeeze me for an extra million on his shitty rag. But I'll pay it. It's a good market. . . ."

Josh waited. He knew how hard it was for Adam to talk. "It's something else," Josh said. "Is it Kellen? Is she having problems at the new school?"

"Nope. Nothing but great reports from the nuns. She's a smart kid." He sipped his coffee and smiled ironically. "She must really like that school," he said. "She didn't want to come home for any of the holidays, you know."

Josh decided to plunge in. "Listen, there's something you ought to know. Kellen is very angry with you. She's been writing these long letters to Stephen . . ."

"Angry? Why? For putting her in school? It's one of the best in the country."

"She's angry because you shut her out of your life." Josh paused, waiting for Adam's usual quick rise of anger, but it didn't come. Instead, Adam stared at the tablecloth in silence. "Why did you send her away, Adam?" Josh asked.

Another silence. Then Adam ran his hand slowly over his eyes. "I couldn't stand to look at her, Josh," he finally said in a whisper. He shut his eyes. "She reminds me so much of Elizabeth."

Josh heard the catch in Adam's voice and saw he was struggling to stay in control. He had never seen Adam cry, not once since Elizabeth's death. He knew that he wouldn't be allowed to see it now. "You hurt her," Josh said finally. "She told Stephen she feels abandoned, 'like an orphan' was how she put it. She said that she feels she lost not only her mother but you, too."

Adam just looked at Josh, despair written all over his face. "Jesus, what have I done," he said. He looked away, his eyes traveling over the dining room. "This house is so empty, Josh. It's driving me crazy. I sit here sometimes alone at night and hear and see things that aren't there."

"Bring Kellen home," Josh said. "She needs you, Adam. And you need her."

Adam closed his eyes. He was remembering suddenly a request Elizabeth had made of him not long before she got sick. Make time for Kellen, she had said, she needs you. He had not given the words much thought at the time, but now he saw clearly what Elizabeth meant. Slowly, he nodded his head in assent. "Next week, as soon as this Portland thing's finished. I'll have time for her then. I'll *make* time."

Josh picked up the coffee service and poured himself and Adam another cup. Adam seemed lost in his thoughts. "You haven't been yourself, Adam." Josh paused, picking his way carefully now, knowing he was treading on tender ground. "You should make time for yourself, too," he said. "You need something in your life besides the newspapers. You need to be with people again. You need a social life."

Adam shook his head slowly. "I don't need anything like that anymore, Josh."

"You're drying up inside."

"What are you trying to tell me? That I should go out and get laid, for chrissake?"

Josh sighed. "It might not be a bad idea."

"Back off, Josh." But then he sighed, not wanting to be angry with Josh. "It'll be different with Kellen here."

Josh shook his head. "No, it won't. You can't expect Kellen to fill in for everything you lost with Elizabeth." He leaned across the table. "Adam, I tell you this because I'm your friend. Elizabeth is gone. She's been gone almost a year now. And she was sick for a long time before that. But you're still here. And you've got to start living again."

"Get to your point, Josh."

"My point is that Elizabeth wouldn't have wanted you to be like this. She was a woman of great passion. She loved life, and she taught you to do the same. She put fire and light in you. But you've let it die out. You've turned your back on the greatest gift she left you."

Adam stared at Josh. "Are you done?" he asked finally.

Josh sat back in his chair. "Adam—"

"It's getting late, Josh." Josh recognized the tone of dismissal. He had pushed far enough for one night. He rose slowly. "It was an excellent dinner, Adam. I'll see you at the office Monday. I'll show myself out."

"Josh?"

Josh looked back.

Adam paused. "Thanks for coming."

Adam waited until he heard the front door close, then went to his study. He sat motionless at his desk, and finally reached into a drawer and pulled out a silver picture frame. It was a photograph of Elizabeth taken when she was thirty-five, in the fullest bloom of her beauty. He stared at it for a long time, then set it down on the corner of his desk. It was the first time since the funeral he had looked at her picture. Now, he stared at her smiling face, expecting some flood of emotion to engulf him. But nothing came. The emptiness surprised and saddened him. After all these months of protecting himself against Elizabeth's memory, now, when he tried to confront it, he felt nothing. Maybe Josh is right, he thought. I can't feel anything anymore. But he knew that wasn't true. He felt suddenly an overwhelming loneliness. It had been building for months, and now, suddenly, he ached for the nearness of another human being. He put Elizabeth's picture back in the drawer.

He left the house and drove aimlessly around the city. After an hour, he pulled up to a stone mansion on Pine Street. He rang the bell, and a doorman appeared. "Mr. Bryant to see Miss Stanford, please," Adam said.

Adam was ushered into an alcove, then he followed a maid up a winding staircase into a large room with a glass ceiling and a fountain, its waters illuminated by colored lights. Behind it, on a raised dais, was a sunken marble bath. Adam had heard about the tub, that it belonged to Anna Held, the Ziegfeld beauty who had milk brought to her room every day to bathe in. Seeing the mythical tub made Adam shake his head. The room's gaudy Victorian splendor was oddly sad.

"Adam, what a surprise." Adam turned at the sound of the voice. Sally Stanford glided toward him, smiling.

"You look wonderful," he said, kissing her. "So does your new place."

"Oh, I've been here for years. You, however, have been away a long time. I was sorry to hear about your wife."

Adam smiled politely. He was standing in one of the world's most celebrated houses of prostitution, a house that had hosted some of the most famous men in the world. He knew that Sally could be counted on for complete discretion. But he suddenly felt vulnerable.

"Would you like a drink?" Sally asked, sensing his discomfort.

"Perhaps later."

"I've changed things since we last saw each other, Adam. I have many lovely rooms, each decorated in a different mood."

"I trust your judgment."

She smiled. "And I never disappointed you. Claire will show you to your room. It's good to see you again, Adam."

The maid led Adam to a softly lit bedroom furnished with Victorian antiques. A fire crackled in the marble fireplace, and a selection of liquor and crystal sat on a sideboard. Adam poured a brandy, took off his coat and tie, and sat down on the bed. After a few minutes, the door opened and a young woman stood there. She was medium height, with long blond hair. She was wearing a pink silk robe.

"I'm Marie," she said "And you are . . . ?"

For a moment he thought of giving the woman a false name. "Adam," he said.

She came into the room and sat down beside him on the bed. She was pretty, about twenty-five, with pale blue eyes and a small, heart-shaped face. "And what do you do, Adam?"

He stared at her. She didn't know who he was. The anonymity made him relax slightly. "I work for a newspaper," he said.

She glanced at his custom-made suit and at his shoes and watch, the quality not escaping her eye. She also saw the gold wedding band he still wore. Adam noticed her looking at it. "I'm married," he lied.

She smiled. "Most are," she said. She reached up to unbutton Adam's shirt, and instinctively, he pulled back. "You're tense," she said softly. She began to gently massage his shoulders. "I can feel how tight you are."

Adam closed his eyes. Her fingers probing his muscles felt good. He could smell her perfume, a heavy, oriental musk that didn't suit her porcelain looks.

"Whatever it is," she whispered, "I can make it go away."

She leaned into him, and he could feel her breasts press against his back and her long hair brush his neck. Her hands moved lower down his sides and slowly over his thighs. He could feel himself growing hard. A jolt of guilt went through him as he thought of Elizabeth, but he thrust it aside.

He turned quickly and pushed Marie down on the bed. He stripped off his clothes and untied her robe. In his urgency, he barely noticed her body, slender and white. He lowered himself and entered her quickly and brusquely, losing himself in the sensation of his flesh against hers, soft and warm and yielding. It felt strange and wonderful. He thrust against her, thinking nothing, feeling everything. And when he came, he cried out and grasped her to him in a violent embrace.

He lay there for a moment, his face buried in her hair. He had come to this place a dead man, but his own body told him he wasn't. Elizabeth was gone but he was alive, and he had to go on. The realization made him ache both with relief and unbearable sorrow.

He began to cry. Silent streams of tears fell down his cheeks. They grew into sobs, and he let them come. His tears fell on Marie's bare neck. Without a word, she wrapped her arms across his back and rocked him gently.

A week later, Adam sent for Kellen. He was standing outside the house waiting for her when she arrived. The car pulled up, and the chauffeur opened the door. Kellen stepped out, wearing the same hat and coat, carrying her stuffed monkey.

She stood there, staring at Adam with wary eyes, her lips compressed in a thin line.

Adam stared at her, seeing Elizabeth, feeling his hurt all over again, but knowing now how desperately he needed Kellen near him.

He bent down and held out his arms. She rushed into them. "Forgive me, Lil'bit," he whispered.

Adam was in his office when the call came in from Sally Stanford. "I wouldn't call you at the office," she said, "but this is important. You'll have to come over right away."

"Impossible."

"It's Marie. Please get here as soon as you can."

The line went dead. Adam hung up the phone slowly. He couldn't believe it—Marie was back. She had been gone for almost a year and now, suddenly, she was back. Adam sank back in his chair, stunned. When Marie had left suddenly last June without a warning, Adam had been surprised, even annoyed. He had been seeing the young woman often since that first night and had thought they had at least established enough of a relationship to merit a good-bye. He had given her many gifts and money, and he had paid Sally good money to secure Marie's exclusivity. It was not that he particularly cared for her. In fact, he found her incessant chatter about wanting to be an actress tedious. But he knew that on some level he needed her. Ever since that first night, she had been there for his sexual and emotional needs. It had been a healing experience, and after she left, he had felt no need for another woman. But now, she was back. At the house, Sally greeted him, looking troubled.

"Where is she?" Adam demanded.

"She was here this morning while I was out," Sally paused. "She picked up some things, and now it looks like she's disappeared again."

"Well, why did you call me to come over?"

"I think you'd better come up to her room." Something in the tone of Sally's voice made Adam follow her up to the bedroom where he had spent so many hours. Marie's musky perfume still hung in the air.

"She left you something," Sally said, pointing to a small cardboard box on the bed.

Adam went to the bed and peered inside the box. Nestled amid some towels was a naked, sleeping baby.

Adam turned back toward Sally "Is this your idea of a joke?"

"I didn't have anything to do with it," Sally countered. "The cleaning girl found it with this letter addressed to you." She held out an envelope.

Adam took it tentatively and opened it. The letter inside was written in an inflated, flowery hand.

Adam,

I'm sorry I couldn't tell you about this but I didn't know how. I didn't plan for this to happen but it did. I can't raise him by myself because then I will never realize my ambition to be a great actress. I know you'll give him the best.

                                        Marie.
p.s. I know what you're thinking but it really is your son.

Adam slowly folded the letter and put it inside his suit coat. He turned back to Sally. "This is preposterous," he said softly. He turned to leave.

"Adam, wait," Sally said. "You can't leave me with this mess to clean up."

"Call the cops."

"Yeah, right. And tell them to just come on over and pick up a little bundle at Sally's place. . . . Adam, you owe me better than this."

"How do I know it's even mine?"

"You paid me a lot of money to make sure Marie saw no one else. I keep my promises to my clients."

Adam paused at the door. "Have it delivered to my house," he said.

Adam was never quite sure what it was that changed his mind about the baby. But once it was delivered to his home, he couldn't bring himself to make the call to the authorities. Perhaps it was because he knew the child would be placed in an orphanage. He reminded himself that he was nearly fifty-three years old, a widower with no intention of ever remarrying, a man whose obsession with his business had already bruised Ian and Kellen. But he knew also that the baby was his son and his responsibility. He knew, too, that Elizabeth would not have wanted him to turn his back on a child.

Adam turned to Hildie, who asked Adam no questions, other than what the child's name was. Adam stared at the woman blankly, realizing the child had no name. "It's Tyler," Adam said, suddenly remembering Marie's last name.

"Tyler Bryant," Hildie said. "A big, important name for such a little tyke."

Explaining the baby to Kellen was difficult. The night the baby was delivered to the house, Kellen was intensely curious. Adam, not knowing what to tell her, said only that they were going to take care of the baby for a while. Kellen's curiosity quickly developed into a playful, almost maternal infatuation as she helped Hildie care for Tyler.

After a week, Josh convinced Adam he had to either give the baby up or legally adopt him. Adam told Josh he didn't care what people thought, but Josh reminded him he had Kellen to think about. Adam told him to go ahead with the adoption. Adam had no contact with the child, entrusting Tyler's care to Hildie. On rare occasions, Adam would venture into the nursery, stare down at the pale, blond sleeping baby, and struggle to feel some sort of connection. But he felt only a sense of obligation.

Soon after Tyler's arrival, Ian graduated from Princeton and came home. Adam had waited to tell him about Tyler, guessing that Ian would be aghast. Ian didn't disappoint him.

"Good lord, Father," Ian said. "Are you crazy?"

They were sitting in the study, and Adam stared at his grown son, a handsome young man sprawled elegantly on a sofa, his long legs propped impudently on a coffee table.

"A man must take responsibility for his actions, Ian," Adam answered quietly. "That is all I am doing."

"But how do you know it's really yours? All you have is this whore's word."

"It's mine," Adam said evenly. "I know it is."

Ian shook his head derisively. "What a homecoming," he muttered. "I come home, ready to take my place in the business, and now I have another scandal to deal with."

Ian's callous reference to Elizabeth's death left Adam speechless.

Ian rose. "Well, I'm going out for a while," he said. "I have some old friends to look up."

"Ian," Adam said sharply. "If you're going to live in this house again, you'll abide by my rules. The first one is that I want you to be discreet about the baby. I don't want anyone to know the truth about this yet."

"You can't keep something like this a secret," Ian said.

"I have to," Adam said, "until I can find a way to explain it to Kellen."

Two weeks later, Kellen came into Adam's study while he was working. She stood directly in front of his desk. He saw that she had been crying.

"Is it true that Tyler is my brother?" she asked.

Adam confronted the piercing stare of her green eyes. "Who told you that?" he asked softly.

"A boy at school. He called Tyler a bad word . . . a bastard."

Adam sighed. "Come here," he said. Kellen came around and stood by his chair. He took her hand. "It's true, Tyler is your brother," he said. "I'm his father." Kellen frowned slightly. Adam could see her mind working.

"Mother always wanted to have a baby boy . . . but she didn't," she said finally.

"No, she didn't."

Kellen stared at Adam for a long time. "You're too young to

understand," he said finally, unable to stand the accusatory look in her eyes. "Someday I'll explain it to you. But for now, I need you to do something. I need you to be good to your brother. Can you do that for me?"

Kellen was silent. "I'll try," she murmured.

He tried to gather her in a hug, but she pulled away. He released her and watched her walk slowly out of the study.

After that day, Kellen was never as affectionate to Tyler as she had been before. She tried to hide it, but Adam saw her indifference. He knew that Kellen was a loving child, but he sensed that the attention she gave Tyler came out of the promise between father and daughter, not from the heart.

Ian treated the baby the same as he always had Kellen, as if neither existed. Kellen had long ago transferred any affection she might have for an older brother over to Stephen. It seemed strange to Adam that the house, which had felt so deserted after Elizabeth's death, seemed at times just as empty now despite all its inhabitants. It was like a family of strangers, connected to each other, but strangers nonetheless. But this *is* a family, Adam told himself defiantly, *my* family. These are my children—Ian, Kellen, and Tyler, each from different mothers, but sharing my blood. They will learn to be a family. We will . . . all of us.

Chapter
Seventeen

The sun was hot, and Kellen shut her eyes in pleasure, feeling its warmth on her face. The grass was soft and fragrant, and it tickled her neck. She felt lazy and inexplicably happy.

"You're going to get freckles if you stay in the sun," Stephen said.

She glanced over at him, sitting against a tree with a book in his lap. They had come down to the grounds of the Palace of Fine Arts to study on the lawn, but the magnificent spring day made it difficult to concentrate.

"I don't care," she said. "It feels so good to be away from the house. Tyler was driving me crazy."

"He's only four. All kids are like that at four."

Kellen stretched languidly, and Stephen's eyes were drawn to the outline of her breasts, pressing against the black leotard she wore under her skirt. Kellen was now almost eighteen and though she was apparently oblivious to her own body, Stephen was not. It seemed to him at times that she had grown up so fast. One day she had been climbing trees with him. And now, suddenly, she was . . . almost a woman. It was disconcerting. He had fantasies about her now that left him excited and frustrated. It was more than disconcerting. It was agonizing. "You'll flunk if you don't study," he said.

"No, I won't. I have a *B* going into the final." She smiled. "And old man Isaacs has a crush on me."

"Everything comes so easy to you, doesn't it."

Kellen rolled over onto her stomach. "That's not true. I worked hard all year. Now, I just want to finish school and get away!"

"You can't. You're going to college. If you study."

"Big deal, across the bay to Berkeley. I want to go to Paris and really study."

"Study what?"

"Life and people." She smiled. " 'The only people for me are the mad ones, who burn like fabulous roman candles exploding like spiders across the stars.' "

"Is that more of your poetry?"

"Oh, Stephen . . . It's from *On the Road* by Jack Kerouac. Didn't you read the copy I gave you?"

"No."

"God, Stephen, sometimes you are so—"

"What? Dull, boring?" He smiled. "One of us has to be."

She smiled back. She liked the way he looked today. He was wearing his hair a little longer. It was a warm brown, like his eyes. She had decided when she was only seven that Stephen Hillman was the most handsome boy she knew. She had always been so proud and grateful to be his friend. Soon, he would graduate from Stanford's journalism school and begin to work in her father's newsroom. And, to her growing frustration, he still thought of her as a friend.

"You're not dull," she said. "But you are too serious sometimes. You need to loosen up and not think so much."

"Like you?"

She sat up suddenly and grabbed a book. "I'm going to read you something," she said. "It's a poem called *Marriage*. Maybe you'll understand what I'm talking about."

"Should I get married? Should I be good?
Astound the girl next door with my velvet suit and faustus hood?
Don't take her to movies but to cemeteries
tell all about werewolf bathtubs and forked clarinets
then desire her and kiss her and all the preliminaries
and she going just so far and I understanding why
not getting angry saying You must feel! It's beautiful to feel! . . .

She set the book down, beaming. "Isn't it great?"

"Is that another one of those beatnik things?" he asked. "You've been hanging around that dump down on Columbus again, haven't you?"

"City Lights isn't a dump, it's a bookstore," she said defensively. "And this is a great poem by a great artist."

Stephen grabbed the book and stared at the picture on the back of a tousled-haired young man. "You like it because you think he's cute,'' he said peevishly. ''Well, maybe I do think too much. But sometimes you don't think at all.''

She smiled. ''Know what I think right now? I think you're afraid. . . .''

''Of what?''

''Of doing what you really want to . . . what you really feel like doing.''

Stephen stared at her. She was sitting with her legs folded under her, her hands on her hips. The sun filtered through the trees, dappling her skin and red hair with light. He leaned over suddenly and kissed her. Her lips were soft and yielding, and, after a second, she returned his kiss. Then she slowly pulled away and smiled. ''See, it's beautiful not to think,'' she said.

He laughed to cover his nervousness. ''You are a brat.''

She stood up, gathering her books. ''Yeah, that's what Daddy tells me. Speaking of Daddy, we're having lunch together, and I'm late. Will you drop me off?''

As they drove toward downtown, Stephen found himself stealing glances at Kellen. She was wearing sunglasses, her hair streaming behind her in the wind. Her bohemian dress was only her latest fashion affectation. Usually, she wore something old and bizarre, gleaned from her excursions to thrift stores. One day, it was a Victorian petticoat, the next day a man's bowler hat. But at least this outfit seemed to suit her somehow. It made her look older, a little enigmatic, which was, he knew, precisely the effect she wanted. He had known her since he was a boy, yet now he felt off balance with her. He was not inexperienced with girls; he had slept with several at college. But he had been unprepared for the way her kiss had stirred him.

He let her off at Union Square, and she blew him a kiss. He drove slowly away, watching her in his rearview mirror.

Inside the Times building, Kellen took the elevator to the top floor, greeted Adam's secretary, Adele, with a smile, and swept into his office. Adam was on the phone and motioned for her to sit down. Kellen sank into an armchair and half listened to his conversation.

''I told you last week how I felt about that guy, Ted.''

Kellen recognized the tone in Adam's voice. It was slow, deliberate, and subtly patronizing. It was how he sounded when he was sick of dealing with a dull-witted person or someone who had made the mistake of testing his patience. A door near Adam's desk opened and Ian came in with a folder in his hand. He stared at Kellen's black leotard, tights, and skirt.

"Nice outfit," he said. "Who died?"

She ignored him.

"You'd think with all the allowance you get you'd dress like a lady instead of running around like one of those pseudointellectual creeps," Ian said.

"What would you know about intellect?" Kellen snapped. "Those country club twits you hang around with have the collective I.Q. of a box of rocks."

Adam hung up the phone before Ian could reply. "Goddamn that Whittaker," he said angrily. "I've had it with him."

"He's senile. I told you that when you bought the paper," Ian said. "What's he done now?"

"Remember that columnist I told him to fire? Well, he didn't do it. Now I've got the Portland mayor threatening a libel suit over something he wrote about his goddamn wife!"

Kellen watched Adam. She had heard stories about Whittaker before. He was the eighty-five-year-old executive editor of Adam's Portland newspaper, the last of his family to remain on the newspaper after Adam bought it. She had met him once, when he came to dinner. He had told her, with great pride, of how the Whittaker family had founded and run the paper for four generations, until financial problems forced him to sell it to Adam for his chain. Adam had kept the old man on as a figurehead to preserve the paper's community image.

"He's got to go," Adam said suddenly. "I'll go up there next week and take care of it myself."

"You're firing him?" Kellen asked, "just like that?"

Adam and Ian stared at her. "Kellen, honey," Adam said, "you don't understand."

"But he's a nice man," she said. "And he's so old, Daddy. It seems so hard . . . couldn't you just—"

"It is hard," Ian interrupted. "It's business."

"Let's forget it," Adam said, wanting to stave off another fight between the two. He opened the folder Ian had brought in. "What's this?"

"The latest circulation figures from San Mateo County," Ian said. "You aren't going to like them. We picked up some in Daly City and Pacifica but we're making no progress anywhere else. The farther south down the peninsula you go, the worse the figures get." Ian paused. "Father, I really think it's a mistake to try to expand the *Times*'s circulation right now. It's getting expensive. And besides, those people down there just don't want a San Francisco import."

Adam glanced down the rows of figures. They were discouraging, but he knew the market was there. He knew that people were moving away from the city and that communities were springing up, like patches of fungus, down the peninsula. Just south of San Francisco, endless blocks of identical homes built five feet apart were being sold for $6,000 apiece. Beyond that, farmlands were being subdivided into whole communities, the orchards paved over to make way for shopping malls and parking lots. New freeways were creating links between San Francisco and these new quasi-villages. The postwar car mania had changed everything forever, creating a whole new social strata called suburbia. To some, it meant a whole new set of problems and the death of rural life. To Adam, it meant a gold mine, with thousands of new *Times* subscribers and advertisers to be tapped.

"It's not a mistake," Adam said to Ian. "We can get those people. That guy you hired as circulation manager just isn't cutting it."

Ian hid his irritation. "We've tried. But they read those shitty little weeklies or nothing at all. We can't get them to buy the *Times*."

"Why don't you give it away?" Kellen said suddenly.

Ian sighed in derision. Adam chuckled.

"No, listen," she added. "I've used this shampoo for years—Breck. Then one day, I got this free sample in the mail of some stuff I never heard of. Well, I tried it, and it's great. I switched shampoos. You could do the same with the paper. Give it away for a while until they're hooked on it, then they'll buy it."

Ian laughed. But Adam looked thoughtful. "You know, that's something we've never tried," he said. "Sampling—"

"You've got to be kidding!" Ian said. "Give the *Times* away! We're talking about tens of thousands of papers. We'll lose our shirt!"

"Only for a while," Adam said. "Maybe Kellen's right. Once people get hooked on the *Times*, they'll subscribe. Reading a newspaper is a habit more than anything. Let's do it." He stood up and stretched. "Ready for lunch, Kellen?"

She jumped to her feet. "You taking me to the club?"

"Not dressed like that. You'll have to settle for corned beef at Breen's. Just let me go wash off the newsprint."

Adam went into an adjoining bathroom. Ian stared at Kellen. "You think you're hot shit, don't you," he said. "Making me look like a fuck-up in front of Father."

"You don't need any help from me, Ian," Kellen said. "If you spent half the time really working that you do screwing around, you wouldn't get into these spots. But then you wouldn't have time for three-hour lunches or those nice long vacations you like." She picked up her bag. "You know, one of these days Daddy's gonna discover just what a screw-off you really are."

Before Ian could reply, Adam returned. "Ian, try to get some cost estimates on sampling together this afternoon." He and Kellen left. Ian stared at the folder in his hands for a moment, then threw it across the room.

At Breen's, Kellen sat across from Adam, eating her sandwich, waiting for the right moment to bring up the subject she wanted to talk about. She had been waiting all week for time alone with her father, and now she waited some more until their small talk turned back to the newspaper.

"That was quite an idea you had back there," Adam said to her. He chuckled and took a drink of his beer.

"I have lots of ideas," Kellen said.

"I know. You always did."

"I mean it, Daddy. I have ideas about the newspaper."

"Oh, like what?"

She knew he was just humoring her, but she pressed on. "Well, for instance, the *Times* is so . . . dull." She smiled at the look on Adam's face. "Sorry, Daddy, but it's true. It's so fat and gray and serious!"

Adam smiled indulgently. "And what would make it . . . un-dull?"

"You could get a gossip columnist."

"We get Winchell from the syndicate."

"No, I mean San Francisco gossip," Kellen said, "Like that guy Sandy Francisco writes in the *Journal*."

"Kellen, that's trash!" He stared at her. "You don't read that junk, do you?"

"Of course, Daddy. All my friends do . . . everyone does. People love to read dirt, especially about people they know. And that Sandy guy doesn't know half of what's going on because he never gets invited to the best parties!"

Adam shook his head, smiling. "Well, I'll think about it. In the meantime, finish up. I have to get back."

Kellen pushed her sandwich aside. "Daddy, there's something I want to talk to you about," she said.

"Whatever you want, it's yours."

"I want to come work on the *Times*."

Adam was reaching for his wallet to pay the bill. He paused to look at her. He tossed some money on the table. "Don't be silly, Kellen."

"I'll be eighteen next month. That's old enough to go to work."

"You don't need to work."

"But I want to, Daddy." Kellen leaned forward. "I've been taking journalism courses in school. I want to learn how the business really works."

"No, Kellen. You're going to college."

"How about just the summer?" she pleaded. "Stephen worked at the *Times* during summers when he was in school."

"That was different."

"But why? Why can't I do the same?"

Adam sighed. "Kellen, it's a hard business. You have this notion that it's fun, but it's a dirty, very unglamorous business. I don't want my daughter working for a newspaper."

"But Ian can?" Kellen asked, her voice rising. "Why is it all right for him to get his hands dirty, but I can't?"

"Ian is going to run the business someday. He has to learn it."

"Why can't I learn it, too?"

"Kellen, stop it! I don't want to hear any more about it," Adam said. Then he sighed and stood up. "Come on, I have to get back."

She rose slowly and picked up her bag. She could feel her face burning in embarrassment and wouldn't look at Adam. He took her shoulders. "Kellen, listen to me," he said softly. "I love you. Your happiness is very important to me. Trust me, you wouldn't like it. You're made for other things. Better things." She looked at him, keeping her tears in check. He kissed her forehead. "Come on, I'll drop you off."

Adam put down the *Journal* and leaned back in his chair. He had just finished reading two weeks' worth of columns by Sandy Francisco. He shook his head slowly. Francisco's column was absolute drivel, nothing but overwritten accounts of parties and fluff straight from press releases put out by ambitious businessmen and politicians. Adam stared at the *Journal*s piled near that afternoon's copy of the *Times*. The *Journal* had never quite recovered from its losses during the war. It had lost so much advertising that four copies of the *Journal* put together barely equaled the bulk of one weekend edition of the *Times*. But the *Journal* still had its loyal readers. It bothered Adam that he had pirated away the *Journal*'s advertisers and some of its best reporters, but he couldn't capture the hearts of its readers. What was it the *Journal* gave them that the *Times* did not? Surely it wasn't trash like Sandy Francisco.

Adam scanned the front page of the *Times*. Eisenhower had upped the quota of atomic fuel use. A shake-up in the Kremlin had left a man named Khrushchev in the spotlight. The only light touch was a news story about the New York Giants moving to San Francisco. He flipped through the other sections, but they were just as dry, just as serious. The *Times* was a good, serious newspaper, and Adam was proud of it. Under his guidance, it had become one of the country's most respected and powerful newspapers. An endorsement by Adam Bryant's editorial page could put a politician over the top. An article about highway needs immediately reverberated in Sacramento and Washington, D.C. Adam had also been careful to incorporate into the *Times* a sense of values—family, charity, and community commitment. In the *Times*'s name, he had contributed great amounts of his fortune to charities, schools, hospitals, and the arts. When the Stanford medical school needed a new wing, Adam donated the funds. When the San Francisco Ballet wanted to go out on its first world tour, a check from Adam sent them on their way.

The *Times*, Adam thought now, as he read it, had become exactly what he told Robert Bickford it would so many years ago—a respectable symbol of good and truth.

But it had also, somehow, lost its life along the way. And as he read over the pages, he began to realize that the *Times* had failed in its most important function—it did not capture the soul of its community. It had none of the city's quirky personality.

Kellen is right, Adam thought ruefully. The *Times* has become dull and gray. His eyes went to the photograph of Elizabeth on his desk. "Just like me," he said softly.

He returned to his reading, going carefully through the pages, reading now not for content but tone. Flat, it was all flat. But then one column in the sports section caught his eye. It was about the outdoors and was well-written, in a breezy offhand way. It had . . . a bit of style, Adam thought. He looked at the byline. C. J. Able. He had never heard of the fellow. He called the sports editor, who told him that C. J. Able was a thirty-year-old ex-bookstore clerk with a penchant for fly fishing, who had somehow talked his way into his current job on the strength of a sample column he had written on the metaphysical joys of salmon fishing in Michigan. Adam told the editor to send Able up to his office. Then he told Adele to get copies of Able's columns from the morgue.

Adam was reading the columns when Adele brought Able in. Adam looked up and saw a tall, reed-thin man wearing wire-rimmed glasses and the ugliest, most ill-fitting suit Adam had ever seen. Except maybe that one I wore my first day here, he thought. "Come in, Able. Sit down, please."

The man slid into a chair nervously.

"I've been reading your stuff," Adam said. "It's good. You get good quotes from people. That's a real art, getting people to talk."

"Thank you, Mr. Bryant."

"Call me Adam, please. And I'll call you . . ."

"C. J. is fine, sir."

Adam smiled. "I never trusted bylines with initials. I always like to know a fellow's name."

The man seemed to freeze up, then his face reddened slightly. He knew Adam was waiting. "Clark," he said firmly.

"Clark Able," Adam said with a nod. Then, slowly, very slowly, Adam's smile faded as he repeated the name to himself several times.

Able sighed. "It's all right," he said. "You can't help it. I just wish my mother could have. She saw Gable and Leslie Howard in *A Free Soul* back in thirty-one when she was pregnant. She got inspired. I got the name."

Adam smiled. "Could be worse. She could have called you Leslie." The man laughed and began to relax. "I'll get to the point, Able," Adam said. "I want to start a new column, real high profile, one that could make the person writing it one of the most important people in this town. And I think you might be the man to write it."

Able sat up straighter. "I'm interested, Mr. Bryant."

"Good." Adam glanced at his watch. "My god, it's nearly six. Let me take you to dinner, Able. How about the Big Four?" Adam pushed the phone over to the other man and rose. "Call for a table, will you? I have something to finish up."

The man blanched. "We'll never get near that place this late. You'd better call, Mr. Bryant."

"No, you do it. And use your real first name."

Able waited until Adam left the room then gingerly dialed the phone. He hung up just as Adam returned. "We all set?" Adam asked, slipping on his suit jacket.

C. J. Able stood up and smoothed his hideous maroon tie. "I got a table," he said incredulously. He grinned broadly. "No problem at all."

They took a taxi to Nob Hill and, once inside the restaurant, Adam hung back to talk to someone. Able went to the maitre d' and said, "I have a reservation. The name is Clark Able."

The maitre d' looked up, then slowly down, taking in Able's suit. "Yeah, buddy, and I'm Carole Lombard."

"No, really, I called. I reserved a table for six—"

"Nice try," the maitre d' hissed. "Now get lost."

Adam stepped forward. "How's it going, Claude?"

The maitre d' looked up and smiled broadly. "Mr. Bryant! How good to see you!" He glanced quickly to the book for Adam's name, then nervously toward the crowded dining room. "We didn't know you were coming. If you'll wait one moment, we will find a table for you!"

"I'm with Mr. Able here," Adam said. "Just show us to his table."

The maitre d' blushed and stared at Able. "Of course," he stammered. "Right this way."

"You know, Claude," Adam said as he sat down, "Mr. Able is my new columnist, and he'll be dining here often. Right now, I think he'd like a martini. You know how I like mine."

"Right away, Mr. Bryant." The maitre d' looked at Able with new respect.

"Extra dry for me, Claude," Able said.

Able leaned back in his chair, his eyes traveling around the room. It was an elegant, masculine place. The few women were bright spots of color in a sea of blue and gray suits. Able recognized only some of the faces—Mayor George Christopher, golf pro Ken Venturi and Jimmy Stewart, who was in town to film an Alfred Hitchcock movie called *Vertigo*. Able knew instinctively that the faces he didn't recognize were among the city's most powerful men.

"Don't worry," Adam said, as if reading Able's mind. "Pretty soon, you will know who all these people are, what they do, what they're hiding, and who they sleep with."

"Is that going to be my job, dishing dirt?" Able asked. He looked Adam in the eye. "I'm not another Sandy Francisco."

Adam took a drink, studying Able. "If I thought that, I wouldn't have brought you here. I want you to write a column about the people and this city, Able. For lack of a more graceful term, call it a gossip column. I know that you've lived here all your life, so I know you know this town." Adam paused. "But I want more than gossip. I want a column that's urbane but at the same time homey and parochial. I want it to be witty, intellectual, lustful and, at times, a bit bawdy. And it must have a very large heart. I want it to be as fresh and biting as stepping out into a morning fog.'' Adam paused again. ''I want it to be about this city. Do you understand?''

Able smiled slowly. ''Yes, I think so.''

''Good. If you can do that for me, I promise I can do a lot for you.'' He picked up his glass. ''To your future.''

During the next two hours, they discussed the column and the *Times.* As they were leaving, Able noticed a mural on the wall. It was a panoramic photograph of San Francisco taken in the late 1800s. ''What a strange photo,'' Able said. ''Look at the streets. They're deserted, like a ghost town.''

Adam stared at the mural but said nothing. They exited the restaurant into a heavy fog and walked slowly up the block toward the Mark Hopkins. The baritone foghorns played a doleful duet with the chimes from nearby Grace Cathedral. Just outside the courtyard of the hotel, Adam paused, staring at the entrance. A foursome of teenagers, dressed in rented tuxedos and pastel prom dresses, spilled out of a taxi. One boy paused to pick up the corsage that his date had dropped. He gently pinned it to the bodice of her white gown, and they fled giggling into the hotel lobby. Adam watched them until they were out of sight. Able waited, pulling up his collar against the chill.

''Ghosts,'' Adam said softly, as if to himself. ''There are always a lot of ghosts up here on this hill.'' After a moment, he turned to Able. ''I think I'll walk for a while,'' he said. ''Good night, Able.'' He shook Able's hand, started down the hill, and was soon lost in the fog.

Chapter
Eighteen

Kellen set the needle down on the record and the bedroom filled up with the sound of Puccini.

"What is this?" Stephen asked.

"*Madama Butterfly*," Kellen said, sitting down on the bed next to Stephen. "My father would kill me if he knew I took it from his study. Do you like it?"

"Yes, very much."

She leaned back on the pillows, raising her arms to prop up her head. "This is the love duet," she said. "It's very sad. *Très triste, très romantique . . .*"

Stephen hid his smile. "I thought you liked Elvis."

"Sometimes," she murmured. "But not always."

They were quiet, listening to the music. Kellen glanced over at Stephen. He had been in the bedroom dozens of times, yet now he was nervous, as if he expected someone to come bursting through the door. Kellen thought of telling him that he had nothing to worry about; no one was home. She had made sure of that before she invited him to her room tonight. It was part of the plan she had launched a month ago after Stephen had kissed her in the park. Since that day she had sensed a change in Stephen. He looked at her differently now, no longer as just a friend. Now he looked at her just like those other boys at school did. She had always ignored the boys. She had wanted to wait for Stephen to notice her.

She had been waiting for a long time. She had waited while her friends started dating, waited while they went steady. And when they gathered in her bedroom to smoke cigarettes and talk about boys, she listened when they talked knowingly about sex. What it was like to have a boy touch you. How he expected you to touch him. Their bold talk shocked and intrigued her. But she waited—for Stephen.

She wanted him to be the first. And now, finally, the time had come. She turned toward him. He was looking at her. Then, he leaned over and kissed her, a tentative kiss. Then again, harder. His lips felt soft and good. She felt his fingers touch her neck, then move down to the buttons of her blouse. She was dizzy with expectation as she waited for him to touch her breast. When he did, she felt as if her skin were suddenly on fire.

He pressed his body against hers, and she could feel his penis, hard against her thigh. She wondered what she was supposed to do. She thought back to what the other girls had said. Was she supposed to touch it? She did, tentatively, and he moaned and began to kiss her neck and breasts. Slowly, she became aware of the power she had. With just her touch, she could excite him so much. She began to move her own body now against his, and he responded. His hand moved down and slipped under her skirt, moving up over her bare thigh. Then, suddenly, he pulled back slightly.

"Kellen, I'm sorry—" He glanced at the closed door.

"No one's home," she whispered; her eyes shining. "I want you to, Stephen. I always wanted you to be first."

He kissed her and, as slowly as his eagerness would allow, he undressed her and then himself. He was kneeling above her on the bed, staring at her, "You're so beautiful," he whispered.

Beautiful? She had never thought she was beautiful. But something in the way he was looking at her made her feel very desirable. He lowered himself to her, trying to go slowly. She kept her eyes on his face, and when he entered her, there was a small, sharp pain. She grimaced, and he stopped.

"Do it, Stephen," she whispered. "Do it."

The small pain gave way to a full one as he pushed against her and, an instant later, she felt his body go rigid. Then, he collapsed on top of her, breathing heavily. After a moment, he slid to one side. His eyes were closed. When he opened them, he saw her staring at him.

"Kellen, I'm sorry," he said softly. "It was too fast."

She raised her head to look at him.

"I couldn't help it," he said. "If only you knew how much I've wanted you. It'll be better next time, I promise."

She waited, hoping he would kiss her as he had before. The kissing had been so good. And she liked the feel of his body against hers. The rest had been . . . well, nothing special. She felt a sticky wetness and a dull ache between her legs. She brushed her lips slowly across Stephen's, but he didn't respond. His eyes were closed.

It will get better, she thought.

The Puccini recording had ended, and the bedroom was quiet. She laid her head against Stephen's chest. She could hear his heartbeat and the soft hiss of the phonograph needle stuck in its groove.

Just as Stephen had promised, it did get better. The part before, when he touched her and kissed her tenderly, was wonderful. And the part after, when he held her, made her feel loved and secure. Still, the actual sex part, she thought, was really overrated, and she couldn't understand what her girlfriends thought was so great about it. One of them had talked rapturously about having an orgasm, how it made her feel like dying. That seemed strange, indeed. Kellen never felt anything like that. What she and Stephen did made her feel very much alive, certainly not like dying.

Kellen's bedroom was the only place they could be together. Stephen was living at home, getting adjusted to his new job at the *Times*. He was working on the city desk, on an early morning shift, so he usually came over to the house about four, and they would sneak upstairs and lock the bedroom door. Kellen didn't worry about getting caught. Only the servants were home during the day, and Adam never returned home from the office before seven. But Ian's schedule was less predictable. Several times, he had come home in the middle of the day when she and Stephen were there. Once, Ian had paused for several minutes outside Kellen's bedroom door. Kellen had waited, holding her breath.

"Why do you get so nervous about him?" Stephen asked after Ian had gone. "He doesn't know about us."

"He has a way of finding out things, and using them against you," Kellen said. "When I was thirteen, he caught me smoking a cigarette and told Daddy. I got grounded."

"Kellen, stop worrying." Stephen ran his finger lightly across her breast, making her draw in her breath. "You're not a kid anymore. . . ."

The black Ferrari roared into the driveway and screeched to a stop. The door popped open and Ian got out, then froze. There was a foot-long gash in the black paint. "Fuck," he muttered through clenched teeth. The scratch had not been there that morning when he left the office. It had to have happened when he parked the car at Joyce's apartment. He was only there an hour, just enough time for a nice "nooner"—or so he had anticipated. That bitch, he thought, gets me all hot, then she tells me she has a manicure appointment. Ian ran his finger along the scratch, deciding suddenly he would drop Joyce. He was getting bored with her. He didn't care that her father owned the biggest bank in town. She wasn't that great in the sack, and her tits were too small.

He went into the house, his foul mood rising as he thought about how badly the day had gone. First there had been that scene with Stephen in the newsroom. A reporter had done a mildly critical story about a department store that the advertising director had been trying to lure into a long-term contract. Ian had taken it upon himself to chastise the reporter, and Stephen, who had just been promoted to an assistant city editor, had stepped in to defend the story.

Ian went up the staircase, impatiently tugging at his tie. He hated the way Stephen Hillman had ingratiated himself with Adam. He figured Adam had hired Stephen as a favor to Josh, but Stephen had, in less than a year, firmly entrenched himself in Adam's favor. Stephen has a real feel for the business, Adam had told Ian recently.

Stephen had also captivated Kellen. She had always worshiped him, but lately Ian sensed that it had developed into something beyond that. And Stephen's interest in Kellen seemed suddenly more than brotherly.

The little prick, Ian thought. He waltzes into the newsroom with his J-school degree, Father gives him a quick promotion, now he's acting like he owns the place.

In his room, looking for the papers he had come home to get, he thought about his mother. After the episode with Stephen, he had gone back up to his office and found her waiting for him. He had been surprised to see her. She had been in Europe for a year and had not called or written. She got quickly to the point of her visit. She needed money. She simply wasn't able, she explained, to live on the small income that her 49 percent interest in the *Times* provided.

Ian had heard Lilith's complaint before many times. Since the breakup of her second marriage to the Italian count, Lilith was constantly strapped for money. Her income from the *Times* and what her father had left her did not support her lavish life-style. So she often was forced to ask Ian for loans. He gave her money, when he had it. His own spending habits didn't usually leave him much left over. But he was getting tired of her asking for money.

"Maybe you should just sell your share of the *Times* to Father,'' he had told her. "You know he'd buy it in a second.''

"Listen to you,'' Lilith said. "By right that newspaper belongs to me. It was my father's. And it should be yours.''

"It will be,'' Ian said, with an impatient sigh.

"The *Times* makes so much money, and he has all those other papers now,'' Lilith pouted. "I don't see why your father can't be more generous! How does he expect us to live?''

Ian was getting a headache. "I can't give you any money right now, Mother,'' he had said. "Maybe next month.''

Ian found the papers he had come for and started out the door, now thinking about his own financial problems. Thanks to some gambling debts, the new car, and the South American vacation he had taken Joyce on last month, he didn't have much cash himself. He thought about asking Adam for a raise, but he knew he wouldn't get it. The circulation drive in the suburbs didn't leave any fat in the budget right now. Ian went down the hallway, thinking about money, his mother, Stephen, the scratch in the Ferrari, and Joyce, who had fondled him to arousal, glanced at her watch, and sent him on his way with a patronizing pat on the crotch. He decided suddenly to go to the club rather than back to the office. He had had enough of the damn newspaper for one day.

Outside Kellen's room, he paused. The door was half-open, which was odd, considering she kept it locked lately. He pushed the door open, and stood there, taking in every detail with intense curiosity. He went over to the bed. A ragged stuffed monkey lay at the foot, nearly covered by the tangle of sheets and blankets. Strange, Ian thought, the maid didn't make up the bed. He turned to the closet and opened the doors. It was filled with clothes of every kind and color . . . and with Kellen's smell. He slowly drew in a breath and idly fingered the hem of a white chiffon dress.

He went to the dressing table and stared down at the jumble of perfume and makeup bottles, cast-off jewelry, and snapshots of grinning girlfriends, which were lying in a snowfall of spilled white dusting powder. He picked up a schoolbook. *American Journalism: A History 1690–1950.* He tossed it on the floor. He turned to the large bureau and stood in front of it for a moment. Then, slowly, he opened the top drawer. The contents were an intriguing tangle of soft pale things. Edges of white lace, glimpses of pink silk, filigreed little straps and tiny rosette buttons. Strange, mysterious things. And the scent . . . musky, sweet, and clean. He picked up a swatch of white. Silk panties, so soft beneath his fingertips. He brought them up to his nose. The scent was intoxicating.

Slowly, he put the panties back. He was about to close the drawer when something caught his eye, a blue plastic container, hidden under the lingerie. He pulled it out and popped it open. He held up the round rubber device and grinned. "Why, little sister," he whispered, "you've been fucking around."

He put the diaphragm back in its case and stuck it back under the lingerie. He had just closed the drawer when Kellen appeared at the door.

"What the hell are you doing in here?" she said.

Ian shrugged. "Nothing. Killing time."

She glanced at the bureau. "Get out," she said. "I don't allow anyone in my room."

"Oh, really?" Ian said, arching an eyebrow toward the rumpled bed. "Someone's been in here. Are you humping Stephen Hillman?"

Kellen's face went white. "None of your business."

Ian leaned against the bureau, smiling. "You know, Kellen, you don't have to be so secretive with me. I'm your brother. We should share things. You could tell me all about your boyfriend problems."

Kellen tossed her purse and books on the bed. "I don't want to share anything with you," she said.

"Well, you don't have a choice. We share the same father. That should count for something."

"It doesn't."

Ian laughed. "God, don't let Father hear you say that. To him, this is one big happy family. He thinks that his son, his little princess, and his little bastard should love each other . . . a regular Pacific Heights 'Adventures of Ozzie and Harriet.' And here we are. We can't stand each other. And you're fucking the hired help, a Jew, no less. We'd better not let Father know the truth. Poor, deluded schmuck."

"Stop it," Kellen said sharply. "Don't talk about Daddy like that."

"Why not?" Ian grinned. "Haven't you figured out yet, princess? Daddy isn't perfect, either. That inside that great, perfect hero who buys you clothes and a sportscar and sends you to Paris on vacation, inside that father you idolize so much is an ordinary, very selfish man."

"Shut up, Ian!"

"Oh, Kellen, grow up! Our father is a selfish man who doesn't give a fuck about anybody." Ian's voice rose. "Why do you think he stole my mother's newspaper, then divorced her? Why do you think he let your mother die, grabbed her money, and took up with that whore? He doesn't love me, or Tyler, or you for that matter. He just loves himself.''

Kellen grabbed a book and threw it at Ian. It caught him just below his eye. He raised his hand to cover the gash on his cheek-bone.

"You're crazy," he hissed, backing away toward the door. "You're crazy—just like your mother was.''

"Get out!" Kellen screamed. She lunged to the door and slammed it just as Ian got out.

She leaned against the door, trying to get her anger under control. Her eyes traveled to her bureau. She went to it and opened the top drawer. Her things, which she usually kept in such perfect order, had been rearranged. He touched them, she thought. She felt nauseated, as if his fingers were touching her skin. Then, she remembered the diaphragm and searched through the lingerie. It was still there. But it, too, had been touched.

She yanked the drawer out of the bureau and overturned its contents on the bed. Enraged, she scooped up the lingerie, carried it to the bathroom, and flung it into a trash can. She went back to get the diaphragm case. She picked it up and sank down on the bed, staring at it in her hands.

She lay back on the bed, staring at the ceiling, thinking about what Ian had said about her father letting her mother die, and about Stephen. She glanced toward the window where the sunset was coming to a murky close. What she and Stephen did was not dirty or bad. It was good and tender. She touched her fingers to her lips, trying to recapture the feeling of Stephen's kiss earlier that afternoon when they had lain naked in each other's arms in her bed. She lay there for a long time, until it was dark. Finally, she got up and went downstairs.

A light was on in the study, and she went to the door. Her father was sitting at his desk, surrounded by newspapers. A tray of uneaten food sat at his elbow and a half-smoked cigar was perched in an ashtray. He was staring at a picture frame that he held in his hand.

"You're home early," she said, coming into the room.

He looked up and took a moment to focus on her face. "I thought you had gone out," he said. "What's the matter, no big date tonight?''

She shook her head and sat down on the sofa. She thought he looked tired. "What are you doing in here all alone?" she asked.

"Thinking. Just thinking.''

"About what?"

"The past."

"About mother?"

"Yes."

Kellen watched her father's face, thinking again about what Ian had said. A question, buried deep in her psyche, suddenly pushed its way forward.

"Did you love her?" Kellen asked.

Adam stared at her. "Kellen, what a thing to ask," he said. "Of course I loved her." He saw the troubled look on her face. "What makes you think I didn't?"

She looked away. He came over to the sofa and sat down beside her. "I loved your mother with all my heart," Adam said. "We had something very special together. Very special."

Kellen looked up at him. "Did you have passion?"

The way she asked the question, with utter seriousness, surprised Adam. He started to smile, but stopped himself. He saw, in that instant, that his daughter was no longer a child and that she expected a truthful answer. He felt slightly embarrassed. He had never spoken of anything remotely intimate with Ian, let alone Kellen. He stared at her solemn face, trying to remind himself that his daughter was almost eighteen. He looked into her eyes, seeing Elizabeth.

"Yes, we did," he said.

"How did you know?"

"You don't know it. You feel it."

"It's important, isn't it," she said, "to feel it."

He paused. "People need passion in their lives. It can be someone . . . or something, like work, something you can give yourself to completely. I was very lucky. For a short time, I had your mother." He paused again. "And, now, I have the newspapers." He looked at Kellen, shaking his head slightly. "I haven't answered your question, have I."

Kellen stared at her father, thinking about what Ian had said, thinking about all the gossip she had heard about her mother's death when she was growing up. She wanted to believe what her father said. She felt the small, familiar ache that always came back to her when she thought of how much she missed her mother. Then she thought of Stephen and how it felt to lie in his arms, warm and safe. Was that passion? Was he someone she could give herself to completely?

"Maybe," Adam said, "it's just something you'll have to find out on your own."

Chapter
Nineteen

Lilith sat down, gracefully unwrapping the fur collar of her suit coat.

"You're looking well," Adam said. "Italy must agree with you."

"I haven't been back to Italy in a year," Lilith said. "I would have thought you'd know that, Adam. Doesn't that gossip columnist of yours keep you up on such things?"

"When merited . . ."

Lilith looked around the restaurant. "Well, I decided I missed this dreary little town after all. I'm back for good."

"Is that why you asked me to lunch? Just to get a mention in Able's column?"

Lilith frowned. "Can we please be civil? I asked you here to talk business." She waited until the waiter had served her grasshopper and left. She took a big drink. "I want to sell my interest in the *Times*. I presume you are still interested in buying it."

Adam took a sip of his own drink, careful to let a few moments pass before he answered. "If the price is right," he said finally.

"The price is not negotiable. I'll sell it to you for twenty-five million."

"That's ridiculous—"

"On the contrary. You'd be getting off cheap." Lilith smiled. "I did some homework on this, Adam. I know that if you put the *Times* on the market right now, you'd get about fifty-five million." Her smile widened. "So I'm willing to let the five million go by . . . we were married once, after all."

Adam stared at Lilith. For years, he had been trying to get her to sell her interest. But he had never expected her to demand the full market price, and he certainly didn't have that kind of cash available. But she wanted to sell now, and knowing Lilith, she could change her mind tomorrow. "I can't put my hands on that much cash right now, Lilith," he said.

"Let's drop the bullshit, Adam," Lilith said. "I want the money, and I know how much you want full ownership. This is my first and final price. If you want the *Times* all to yourself, you'll find the money." She smiled and opened the menu. "Shall we order?"

While they ate, Adam barely heard Lilith's small talk. His mind was working, trying to figure out how to meet Lilith's price. He thought briefly of the hundred acres he still owned in Napa, but he knew he couldn't get enough for it. The only alternative was to sell a newspaper. But he knew he couldn't do it. He had worked long and hard to create his empire, and the newspapers and news wire service were now stable, growing businesses. Besides, he thought of them also as Elizabeth's—her legacy as much as his own. The Times Corporation was one of the largest and most powerful in the country, with fourteen newspapers spread throughout the West. And he was involved in sensitive negotiations right now to purchase another newspaper in Phoenix. The thought of having to pull back on the reins now was like admitting defeat.

Adam set down his fork. He didn't feel like eating. Lilith's voice droned on in the background. As much as he craved full ownership of the *Times*, her timing could not have been worse. He thought about the report lying on his desk back at the office. It was an ambitious plan, prepared by the city editor with input from Stephen Hillman, to attack the suburban circulation problem. It called for setting up small bureaus in several communities and customizing a local news section each day so only stories affecting each community were featured. It would be as if each little suburb had its own newspaper within the *Times*. It was a brilliant but risky idea that would cost about $2.5 million to implement. Adam had already given his tentative approval. But it couldn't be done if he had to meet Lilith's demand. Adam finished his drink. Somehow, he had to get full ownership of the *Times*. It was one of the things he had to get in order.

"Lilith," he said, interrupting her chatter, "I want to make you an offer."

"Not a penny less, Adam," she said.

"I'll give you thirty million." Lilith's eyes widened. "If you'll agree," he went on, "to take five million now in cash and the rest in yearly payments of two point five million."

"No," Lilith said. "I want it all, now."

Adam motioned for the check. "Then we have nothing more to talk about," he said, rising. "Shall we go?"

Lilith didn't move. "Sit down," she said. When Adam did, she stared at him venomously. "You're a ruthless bastard," she said. "You stole that paper from my father, and now you're trying to cheat me out of what's rightfully mine."

"It's a fair offer, Lilith. Do you want it or not?"

She tossed her fur collar around her neck. "All right," she said brusquely. She left without another word.

Adam remained at the table alone. It was done. It wasn't the best solution. He would have preferred to have Lilith out of the way now. He hated the idea of mortgaging the *Times*'s future, but at least now it truly would be his. Now, finally, he could have peace of mind that the newspaper's future was secure, that he could pass on what he had built to his family. The final pieces were falling into place. He closed his eyes. He was tired. He remembered suddenly that he had a doctor's appointment that afternoon for a physical. He thought briefly about canceling it, but he had already done so four times. After a moment, he rose to go back to work.

Back at the office, he rang Ian's office and told the secretary that he wanted to see him. It was time to tell Ian about the suburban plan. Adam had kept the plan secret until now because he knew Ian's reaction would be negative. The city editor had also recommended that Stephen be named suburban news editor, and Adam knew Ian was jealous of Stephen's ability. But it was more than that. Yesterday, Ian had told Adam that Stephen and Kellen were serious. Adam had been caught off guard. He had no idea that Kellen thought of Stephen as anything but a friend.

You'd better break it up, Ian told him, unless you're ready to have a Jewish son-in-law.

Adam had been disgusted with Ian's bigotry. But it made him stop and think. He liked Stephen, but he was uncomfortable with the thought of Kellen marrying him. He had known Josh and his family for more than twenty years, and the fact that Josh was Jewish had never been an issue. But now, suddenly, it was. I'm not anti-Semitic, Adam told himself. I just want Kellen to have an untroubled life. She's been raised a Catholic, just like Elizabeth wanted. I've worked hard to cleanse my reputation, buying into the social game so her path can be smooth, so she can be the lady Elizabeth raised her to be. An intermarriage will only pull her down and bring her heartache.

Ian came in. "You wanted to see me?"

Adam told him about the suburban plan, which Ian discounted as preposterous. "Well, I'm going through with it," Adam said. "There's something else you should know. I'm buying out your mother's interest in the *Times*. It will be very expensive, and to do it *and* the suburban plan will mean some serious belt tightening on other properties."

"There's always some fat that can be trimmed," Ian said. "We could start with some newsroom layoffs in San Diego—"

"No," Adam said quickly. "No cuts in news operations."

"But the payroll is so damn high, Father."

"Ian, I've told you before. You cut the newsroom, you cut the heart. And then the rest of the paper slowly dies."

Ian sighed. "Then what do you want me to do, Father?"

"For starters, the television station in Oakland needs a firmer hand."

Ian smiled. "That should be easy."

Adam shook his head. "No, Ian, no shortcuts this time. I want you to go over there and play watchdog for a couple months at least. You might even think about staying there."

"Stay there?" Ian's smile faded. "In Oakland?"

Adam began to sign some papers. "It's not a gulag in Siberia, for chrissake."

Ian laughed. "Well, let's face it, Father, it's no Cannes either. You know what Gertrude Stein said about Oakland . . . 'There's no there there.' "

Adam looked up, unsmiling. "I know about Miss Stein's infamous remark. And if you had bothered to read it in its context, you'd know that she was just saying that a person can never go home again. I feel the same way whenever I go back there." He went back to signing papers. "You seem to like to forget that your father came from the East Bay."

"But—"

"Don't argue with me, Ian. I'm not in the mood."

Ian frowned, knowing from the tone in Adam's voice that any further discussion would be useless. "I'll be in my office if you want me," he said curtly, and left.

Adam leaned back in his chair wearily. He felt a stab of disappointment that his son was not more of a visionary. It was, he thought sadly, all the more reason to make sure everything was properly lined up. Ian would be able to run the corporation someday but only if it were first set on a sort of automatic pilot. The intercom buzzed, and Adele reminded him he had a doctor's appointment. "And Kellen's here to see you," she added.

"Tell her to come in," Adam said. He ran his hand quickly over his face, as if to erase his fatigue so Kellen would not see it. He smiled slightly when she came in, wearing not one of her strange outfits but a pretty dress. "You look very grown up and ladylike today," he said. "How about if we go to the club for dinner tonight. There's something I want to talk to you about."

"I can't," she said. "I have a date."

"With Stephen?"

"Yes. We're going to the Concordia Club." She saw the look on Adam's face. "Is there something wrong with that?"

"No," Adam said slowly. "Actually, that's what I wanted to talk to you about—Stephen. Don't you think you two are seeing too much of each other lately?"

"Daddy, I've known Stephen since I was a baby!"

"Yes, but maybe it's time for you to go out with other young men. What about that fellow you met at the club dance last summer? And that young man at school, the one from Boston . . . John McIlvaine was his name, wasn't it?"

"They were boring—"

"John seemed like nice young man, from a good family."

Kellen met Adam's eyes directly. "And Stephen isn't?"

"Stephen is a fine, talented boy. But you are too young to limit yourself."

"Daddy, quit treating me like a baby. I'll be twenty-one tomorrow."

"That's still too young to—"

"Mother was sixteen when you met her."

"Times were different then."

"What are you trying to tell me? That you don't want me to see Stephen?"

"I just don't want you to get serious with one man right now. . . . Someday you'll get married, to the right man. But now, you're too young to know what you want."

Kellen stared at her father. He was now sixty, and for the first time she noticed that he was starting to show his age. And he had become so uncompromising. It seemed lately that whatever she said made him angry. She had always been able to talk to him, but recently something had changed. He had changed.

"I'm not too young to know what I want," she said, wanting to change the subject. "In fact, that's what I came to talk to you about. I want a job. Here at the *Times*."

Adam sighed wearily. "I thought you put that crazy idea out of your head."

"It's not a crazy idea!" she said. "I've got my journalism degree now. I want to work with you."

"No, absolutely not."

"But why?"

"I told you. My daughter does not have to work for a living. I don't want you working, especially on a newspaper."

Kellen grasped the desk. "But it's what I want to do! Ever since I can remember, I wanted to be a writer."

"Then be one. Write poetry—"

"I want to write for a newspaper."

"You have no idea what it means to work on a newspaper."

"Then teach me!" Kellen felt tears threatening.

"Please, Kellen, not now!" Adam closed his eyes. After a moment, he opened them and took her hand. "You have your whole life ahead of you," he said, softly now. "You're young and beautiful, and you don't want for anything. I've spent my life working to make sure of that." He sighed. "I remember when you were born. I looked at you and thought, What in the world am I going to do with a little girl? But your mother knew what to do. She raised you to be a lady. And that's what I've tried to do, too, because I know that's what she would have wanted." He paused. "You are your mother's daughter. You have her beauty and her breeding. You are a lady, just like she was, and I expect you to act like one."

"But I want to *do* something," she whispered.

"The most important thing you can do," he said gently, "is to find the right man and mean as much to him as your mother meant to me."

Slowly, Kellen withdrew her hand from Adam's grasp. She leaned back in the chair, her energy draining away as she recognized her defeat.

Adam saw the look on her face. "You know I can't stand seeing you look like that." He smiled slightly. "Why don't you and a girlfriend go off on a little trip. Hawaii, maybe. I haven't given you a graduation present yet, have I."

"No, you haven't," she said flatly.

"Well, then you pick a place and make the arrangements. And buy all the new clothes you need. Would you like that?"

She didn't answer. Ian came into the office. "We need to go over this, Father," he said, handing Adam a document.

Adam took it and glanced at Kellen. "I'll see you at home tonight. And I want you to think about that other thing we talked about." He and Ian huddled over the paper. Kellen watched them for a moment, then left.

She walked slowly down the hallway. A man got off the elevator, and Kellen brushed by him, lost in her thoughts.

"Kellen?"

She looked up. It was Clark Able. He was dressed in a finely tailored gray flannel blazer and slacks, and an outrageous pink and charcoal silk tie, all in keeping with the dandy image he had cultivated. During the last three years, he had become a celebrity because of his gossip column, "Of Cabbages and Kings." Adam had engineered his rise within the city's social circle, and Clark was a frequent dinner guest at the house. Kellen had found in Clark a kindred free spirit, and they had become good friends.

Kellen managed a small smile. "How come you haven't been to dinner lately?" she asked.

"Your old man's been pretty busy in recent weeks. Haven't been able to get through to him."

"That makes two of us," she said, punching the elevator button.

"You know, I think your father's working too hard." Clark volunteered. "He looks tired lately." Kellen didn't say anything. "Kel, what's wrong? You know you can tell me."

For a moment, she thought about telling Clark about the conversation with her father. She needed to talk to someone. But then she decided he probably would not understand. No one could, not Clark, not even Stephen. The elevator opened, and she got in. "No, everything's perfect," she said softly. Before the elevator closed, Kellen caught it. "Clark, why don't you come over for dinner tomorrow night."

He paused. "Well, I haven't been invited. Your father—"

"Well, I'm inviting you. It's my twenty-first birthday. Josh and Stephen are coming. I'd like you to be there to help me celebrate. We'll all have a great time, just one happy family," she said with an ironic smile as the door closed.

Before dinner, everyone gathered in the living room for drinks. The day had been cold, and even a blaze in the fireplace did not seem to dispel the chill in the air. Josh, Stephen, and Clark sat talking quietly by the fire. Ian, dressed in a dinner jacket, drank his scotches too quickly, annoyed about having to obey Adam's order to stay home for dinner. Adam seemed strangely dispirited and distracted. Kellen began to wonder if Clark was right about Adam's health. Upon reflection, she realized that he had seemed depressed in recent weeks and had lost some weight. He was, she decided, working too hard.

She went over to him and sat on the edge of his chair. "I didn't thank you yet for the birthday present, Daddy," she said softly. She fingered the pearl necklace Adam had given her earlier, then kissed his cheek. She stood up and held out the folds of her gown. It was Victorian, old deep blue velvet, worn to the softness of violet petals. She had found it in an antique store and had been saving it for a special occasion. "So how do you think it looks with my new dress?" she said, smiling down at Adam.

Adam barely glanced at her. "I give you money to buy clothes and you run around in old rags. You should dress more like a lady."

Kellen's smile disappeared, and she reddened deeply. Her hand went up instinctively to the gown's provocative low neckline. She could feel everyone's eyes on her.

Kellen stared at Adam, too stunned to move. He looked away, finishing his drink in a quick gulp. He rose from the chair. "Let's go in to dinner," he said to no one in particular. He went alone toward the dining room.

Stephen came up behind Kellen. "He didn't mean it the way it sounded," he said quietly. "Something's bothering him. He was edgy all day at work."

"I know what's bothering him," Kellen said quietly. "I am. Everything I do lately seems to make him angry. It's always been like this, but before I was able to reason with him." She glanced at Stephen. "He doesn't think you're good enough for me, Stephen. He wants me to find a nice Catholic boy and stay at home and raise little red-headed leprechauns."

She swept by him angrily before he could answer. He followed her into the dining room. During dinner, the conversation was stilted and filled with pregnant pauses. Ian and Stephen got into a heated discussion about the *Times*'s problems in attracting suburban readers. Adam appeared to half listen. Occasionally, he glanced down the long table to Kellen, who was sitting in the chair Elizabeth had always occupied. Kellen was stifling her anger by drinking her wine too freely and doing some strange mockery of a social grande dame, turning to Stephen on her right and then to Clark on her left, laughing and chatting with exaggerated charm.

At eight, the governess brought Tyler in for Adam to say good night. The boy was dressed in pajamas, his freshly washed blond hair slicked to his head. He stood by Adam's chair, staring up with wide blue eyes.

"Can I stay up a little later, Father?" he asked.

"No, Tyler."

"But I want to watch the end of 'Johnny Jupiter.' "

"Go to bed, son." He inclined his head downward, and Tyler kissed Adam's cheek. The governess led the boy away.

Again, the room was quiet. Dinner was cleared and a maid brought in a birthday cake and set it before Kellen. With a smile, Kellen blew out the candles and Josh, Stephen, and Clark applauded. Ian sat on Adam's right, smoking a cigarette, watching her scornfully.

"Best wishes, Kel," Clark said, kissing her cheek.

Kellen turned to Stephen. "Happy birthday," he said softly. He started to kiss her cheek, but she turned and kissed him fully on the lips. She looked back down the table in time to see Adam staring at her.

"Well, I hope it's chocolate!" she said, turning from his stare. She cut the cake, passing plates down the table. Kellen noticed Adam was still staring at her strangely.

"Daddy, Stephen told me something really interesting about the *Times*," she said, meeting his eyes defiantly. "He said you're going to hire a European correspondent!" She laughed and turned to Clark. "My god, Clark, if you only knew! That's my dream job! I'd kill to get it!"

Kellen glanced down the table to Adam. "Of course," she said, "my father doesn't want me dirtying my hands on the *Times*. He'd rather I be like those women who put on little white gloves before they read their newspapers so the ink doesn't rub off on their precious hands."

Josh shot her a look, which she ignored.

"My father's a bit old-fashioned, Clark," she went on. "He thinks that women—excuse me, ladies—don't work."

Everyone was staring at Adam now. "Kellen, this is not the place," Adam said quietly.

She ignored him. "Clark, you know a lot about rich ladies," she said. "What is it they do, exactly?"

"Well, Kellen—"

"C'mon, Clark . . . I need some help with this. I'm officially an adult today, so it's time for me to become an official lady. Let's see . . . the ladies I know give nice little teas, but they nip scotch during the afternoon. They buy subscriptions to the opera, but they give the tickets to the boring, long ones to their hairdressers. And, of course, they all seem to have the right husbands and the wrong lovers."

Kellen glanced at Adam. "My father wants me to be a lady,

Clark," she said. "The problem is, I can't figure out just what in the hell it is that a lady does!"

Adam slammed his fist down on the table. "A lady respects her father!" Adam said. "And she does not sneak men into her bedroom behind his back!"

Kellen went white with shock. She looked at Stephen, who was stunned. Then she saw the look on Ian's face and knew in an instant he had told Adam that she and Stephen were sleeping together.

"There's nothing wrong with what Stephen and I do," she said. "We love each other. And we're going to get married."

Stephen grabbed her arm. "Kellen, stop . . ." Josh and Able sat watching in dazed silence.

"You're not marrying Stephen," Adam said, oblivious to everyone's embarrassment.

"Why not?" Kellen said. "Isn't he good enough for your precious daughter?" Her eyes flashed with anger. "What's the problem, Daddy? Isn't he rich enough?"

"Kellen!" Adam shouted.

"Oh, it's not the money? Well, what is it, then? Is it because he's Jewish, Daddy? That's it, isn't it. Maybe he doesn't quite fit in this nice-little-lady life you've laid out for me!" She rose suddenly. "Well, I can't do it!" she cried out. "I can't be what you want me to be! I'm not Mother! I'm sorry, but I'm not!"

She rose. She looked at Stephen and then at the others. "I can't stand being in this house anymore. I'm getting out."

She ran from the dining room. Stephen started to go after her, but Josh held his arm. No one said a word. Adam stared down the table at Kellen's empty place, unable to move. The house was quiet.

Slowly, Josh looked at Adam. "I think we'd better leave," he said quietly, rising.

"I'll be getting home, too," Clark said.

Adam didn't even look at them. Josh followed Stephen and Clark out of the dining room. At the last minute, he stopped at the door and glanced back.

Ian was sitting silently, his hand resting on Adam's arm. But Adam didn't seem to feel it. He sat motionless at the long empty table, staring at Kellen's chair.

Chapter
Twenty

Kellen, 1966

It was Monday, the morning after Bastille Day. The tall man in a business suit pushed his way along the crowded sidewalk of Boulevard St-Michel. The gutters were still littered with paper and bottles from the celebration of the night before, and the man marveled anew at Parisians' capacity for back-to-back revelry and work. Last night, the streets had been filled with drunken, dancing people. Now everyone was going back to work, sweeping the stoops of marchés, unfurling awnings, and carefully stacking tomatoes.

It had been a tremendous party. He had watched it from his table at a prime window of La Tour d'Argent. He had half listened to the murmurings of his business associates as he watched a young man below on the quai march through the parade brandishing a dummy's head on a spike in symbolic memory of the unfortunate Foullon who, in the revolutionary furor, had been beheaded for saying of the Parisians, "If this riffraff has no bread, they'll eat hay."

The man had smiled to himself, thinking about Foullon as he had turned his attention back to dinner. In all his years of coming to Paris, he had learned one truism: You could insult a Frenchman's wife, his honor, or his country, but you could never question his cuisine. Which is why the man had kept quiet about the pressed duck he had been treated to by his hosts. After so many rich meals, he had longed for something simpler, like the plain old fish and chips from the shop he frequented on Waterloo Road back in London. But he said nothing. And when the fireworks began, lighting up Notre Dame and eliciting polite oohs and aahs from the restaurant patrons, he found himself looking wistfully down to the people kissing in the street.

Now, at nine in the morning, he was prowling the streets of the

Latin Quarter, looking for some place that sold chips. He turned down St-Andres des Arts, a narrow side street of shops and galleries, watching the jean-clad students speed by on scooters. He wasn't that much older than most of them, yet he felt out of place. He thought that his discomfort might be caused by his current business deal. It was the first time his father had sent him to handle a deal alone, and though it was a minor business matter, the responsibility was a new and strange weight on his shoulders. It wasn't an unwelcome duty; he had been waiting for years for his father's trust. But now that he had it, it made him feel suddenly older than his thirty-three years.

The man tucked his newspaper under his arm and walked on. The street opened onto a five-cornered intersection. There were three crowded cafés, and as he approached one, he smiled. There on a table, he saw what he had come for—a plate of skinny, greasy *frites*. They weren't true chips, but they would do in a pinch. He found an unoccupied table, but a nearby group of students had appropriated the chairs. He looked around and finally saw a chair at a nearby table whose only occupant was a young red-haired woman. He went over to the table. He noticed the book she was reading, a French translation of Marshall McLuhan's *Understanding Media*.

"Mademoiselle, puis-je?" he asked, gesturing toward the empty chair. The girl lowered the book, slipped off her sunglasses and looked up at him. He was struck with the clarity of her green eyes, and by the blatantly appraising look she gave him.

"Oh, faites, faites, m'sieur," she said finally, with an elaborate gesture at the chair.

Her mildly sarcastic tone, an obvious mocking of his own polite French, did not escape him. He thanked her and carried the chair back to the empty table. After he had ordered, he glanced at the girl. The tone in her voice had irritated him. He didn't particularly like Parisian women. They were all so snippy and so damn self-assured. Even the young ones. And especially the beautiful ones. He glanced at the girl once more, then unfolded his newspaper with a snap.

Across the café, Kellen lowered the McLuhan book and, over the top of her sunglasses, stole a glance at the man in the suit. He had buried himself behind a copy of *Le Monde*. That figures, she thought. He's probably a fascist attorney, or the head of a Renault plant, or just a petty bureaucrat. No, he can't be; his suit is too good. It's Savile Row.

She stared at him. He was astonishingly handsome, with thick black hair and elegant, even features. She supposed that was why she had been a bit sharp with him. She didn't care much for men who were too good-looking; they always assumed women were ready to fall at their feet. She watched him, trying to imagine what he did for a living. Too old for a model, she thought. Too well dressed for an actor. She wondered what nationality he was; his accent hadn't given her a clue. He didn't look like a Brit, though that look he gave her was laced with that British irony she found so annoying. Too smooth for an American. Maybe he was French. . . .

The man turned and saw her looking at him. He smiled. Redfaced, she looked away quickly. After a minute, she glanced his way again, but he was absorbed in his newspaper.

Just as well, she thought. The last thing I need right now is another Frenchman complicating my life. She shut her book and picked up her copy of the *Herald-Tribune*, the English-language paper published for Americans abroad. She turned to an inside page and scanned the "People" column. It was fine, just the way she had written it. Kellen folded the paper and put it aside. She realized suddenly that next month she would celebrate her fifth anniversary working at the *Trib* and her sixth year living in Paris. The realization made her remember the letter from Stephen that was in her bag. It had arrived yesterday, but she had been in a hurry and had forgotten to read it.

She felt slightly guilty. She had not written to Stephen in more than a month. She pulled out the letter and began to read it. It was short—his letters were getting shorter every time—and he talked mainly about the newspaper. He was about to be promoted to managing editor. He signed it in his usual way: Love always. She stared at Stephen's small, careful handwriting. It was strange how far away he seemed, how far away everything about San Francisco seemed. For six years now, Paris had been her home, and she had forged a new life that had nothing to do with the one she had left behind.

But that was the way she wanted it. She had come to Paris at first as an escape, a way to put some distance between herself and her father after the ugly scene at her birthday party. After the party, she had told no one of her plans, not even Stephen. A week later, she simply got on a plane and left. She called Stephen from New York. He was upset and said he didn't understand why she had to leave.

"I have to get away for a while," she had told him.

"But what about us?" he countered.

"I love you, Stephen," she said. "But I have to be on my own for a while." It was the truth. She did love him, but she was not sure she wanted to marry him. She knew she had blurted that out just to anger her father. "Tell my father not to worry," she told Stephen. "I'll be home in a month."

But after several weeks, she felt herself being drawn into Paris. She liked the anonymity it offered her, and she decided impulsively to stay. She wrote her father a short letter explaining her decision and sent for her clothes, a few books, and a small amount of money from her bank account. Adam wrote back, saying he only wanted her to be happy and that he would send her whatever money she needed. He said that he loved her with all his heart. He regularly deposited money in an account for her in Paris. She didn't touch it.

As the years passed, she called her father occasionally, but their conversations were strained. She wrote to Stephen often at first, asking him to come to Paris for a visit, but he never seemed to have enough time to get away from the newspaper. After awhile their phone calls stopped, and now the letters were growing infrequent.

She put his latest letter in her bag and ordered another café au lait. She felt a small ache as she thought of Stephen, but she recognized that it was not a longing but a bittersweet memory of what might have been. She knew now she had made the right decision in coming to Paris.

It hadn't been easy at first. She got a job waiting tables at a café near the Sorbonne and lived in a gloomy *chambre de bonne* that she rented from an old woman and her bachelor son for forty dollars a month. Everything was fine until one night when the son tried to crawl into bed with her, explaining that his mother was sick and that he had to share Kellen's room. Kellen fled to a hotel.

But the episode proved fortuitous. There was nothing glamorous about the student life, she had decided, and she was getting bored waiting tables. Now she was forced to find a better apartment and a job to pay for it. She didn't need much money, really. Living well in Paris, she had found, was more a question of attitude than finances. She was happier sitting in the park with friends eating a fresh baguette than she ever had been in any restaurant back in San Francisco.

But she did need enough to support herself and didn't want to touch what her father sent. She was searching through the *Herald-Tribune*'s apartment ads when she was struck with the idea of applying to the newspaper for work. She went to the offices,

located in a nondescript building on rue de Berri, just off the
Champs-Elysées. The newsroom was small and dingy, filled with
scarred wooden desks, dilapidated bookcases, and scuffed Royals.
There was a sea of paper, on the desks, the walls, and the floor.
A motley collection of characters lounged around the copy desk
engaged in a loud debate over whether to use "mister" or "mon-
sieur" in a story. The air was thick with cigarette smoke and
cheerful misanthropy.

Kellen was taken to an editor, and she told him she wanted a
job. His eyes traveled from her head to her toes. "You'll make a
great Golden Girl," he said.

The Golden Girls were the young women who hawked the
Herald-Tribune on street corners wearing bright yellow sweaters
emblazoned with the paper's name in black letters. Kellen knew
that no Frenchwoman would ever stoop so low as to be a Golden
Girl, and that only the English and crazy Americans would work
for such small wages. She told the editor she wanted to be a
writer. When he asked about her experience, she lied and told him
she interned on the *San Francisco Times*. It was then that the
editor, focusing on her name, realized she might be connected to
the Bryant newspaper chain. He gave her a temporary job as
assistant to the fashion editor, who needed a backup during the
couture shows.

With a grand salary of fifty dollars a week, Kellen found an
apartment on rue de Seine for seventy-five dollars a month. It was
more an artist's atelier on the top floor, with a small fireplace and
large windows that flooded the rooms with light. Despite the fact
that she had little money, Kellen was very happy. The temporary
fashion job led to a permanent position writing features for the
"Mostly for Women" page. After a year, she was assigned to
write the "At Home Abroad" column, in which she wrote reviews
of art events or movies and scouted out restaurants and events of
interest to Americans. She branched out into writing personality
profiles, showing a knack for getting interviews no one else could.

When the man who wrote the "People" column decided to
return to the States, Kellen was given the plum job. She found she
was good at mingling at social events, mining quotes from the
celebrated or recalcitrant. She proudly wrote a letter to Clark Able
and joked that she would come back and steal his job. She didn't
tell her father about it, however, afraid that his reaction would be
just censure, not the approval she wanted. She told herself she
would someday go home with a folder of clips and prove to him
that his daughter was, indeed, a writer. Not a poet but a journalist.

But for now, the *Trib* gave what she needed—a sense of achievement and belonging. She loved the newspaper's cerebral atmosphere and clannish camaraderie, and she quickly adopted the staff's parochial, anti-American pose. It never seemed like work. The newsroom was the place to go to find a dice game or a spirited debate on Stendahl. And a steady stream of starlets, movie directors, visiting novelists, newspaper people, jockeys, and expatriates paraded through the office. It was a place populated by wonderful characters, led by editor Eric Hawkins, a softspoken Englishman whose biggest foible was his demand that desks be cleaned off at the end of the day. There was Thomas Quinn Curtiss, who reviewed film and theater and lived below the Tour d'Argent, where he was honored with a menu item called "Eggs Thomas Quinn Curtiss." And there was Art Buchwald. On her third day, Kellen came into the *Trib* newsroom to see Buchwald smashing rickety chairs and piling them in the center of the room. It was, someone explained, his way of protesting for new furniture.

Kellen looked to Buchwald for inspiration. His column "Paris After Dark" had made him a celebrity among tourists, who would wander off the Champs-Elysées and up to the office just to see him. The Parisians read him, too, finding clues to the American psyche in such columns as the one in which he tried to explain Thanksgiving, "La Fête du Merci Donnant." He epitomized the carefree heart of the *Trib*.

But like many at the *Trib*, Kellen was aware of the problems that lurked beneath the newspaper's blithe exterior. In the early sixties, President Kennedy had closed six military bases in France, and the paper lost 4,000 readers. Circulation dropped further as Americans abandoned Paris to avoid the new Gaullist hostility. The *Trib*'s advertisers defected to German publications. Just as the *Trib*'s economic base was shrinking, a new foe emerged. The *New York Times* started an international edition to compete with the *Trib*. The *Trib*'s New York office decided to bring in a new editor. Like everyone, Kellen was sorry to see Hawkins leave. Across the street in the bar of the California Hotel, where he used to stop for a drink after work, a plaque was erected in his honor. The new editor fired staffers, and professionalism became the new byword, an attitude that extended even to the bathrooms, where dim bulbs were put in to discourage reading.

By 1962 Art Buchwald had returned to the States. Many groused that things just weren't the same anymore. Kellen missed the laid-back *Trib* she had known in her first years in Paris, but her life outside the office more than compensated. Many people knew who her father was, but most didn't care, especially those in her mixed crowd of French and American friends. Her name and background were useful only when it came to her "People" column, giving her entrée to exclusive events. Her identity as the daughter of newspaper magnate Adam Bryant was like an impressive accessory that she could slip on as needed, like an Hermès scarf. The Kellen Bryant she had created bore little resemblance to the girl back in San Francisco. Steeped in the city's romanticism and surrounded by the eccentrics of the *Trib*, she saw herself as a free-thinking bohemian.

The freedom extended to sex as well. Men of all ages, types, and income were attracted to Kellen. At first, she had been bewildered by their passionate overtures; it was so different than Stephen's quiet adoration. But she quickly became intrigued with testing her sexual power.

First, there had been the French doctor. He was a skillful lover who, during their first night together, while riding home from the opera in a taxi, gave her her first orgasm. The affair lasted one exhausting month, then he announced that he was returning to his wife, whom he had never bothered to mention. There were others after that. A young communist student who liked to gather pink-and-white chestnut petals from the streets and sprinkle them over her body before he made love. An American novelist who, after two months, begged her to marry him but then left the country abruptly when he received his first advance check. And a sexually inspired, indefatigable Italian actor, whom Kellen finally sent on his way because he wanted to initiate a ménage à trois with his understudy.

Kellen finished her café au lait, smiling slightly as she thought now about her lovers. There was no one in her life right now, but she didn't care. Someone interesting always came along. That was the way it was in Paris. She glanced at her watch. She had to stop by the British embassy to pick up her invitation to the reception that evening. She thought briefly about skipping it—the British always threw the worst parties—but she knew she had to go. She would get there early, grab a few quotes, and leave. Her friend Nathalie was giving a party later, one that she didn't want to miss. Nathalie had promised "a surreal adventure" and added only to bring champagne and a flashlight.

Kellen dropped a franc onto the saucer and rose. She glanced across the café to where the strange man was sitting. He was gone. She shrugged and started off toward the metro.

* * *

Kellen arrived at the embassy later than she had planned, and the reception was already in full swing. By nine, she had almost enough material for her column. The room was very crowded and stuffy. The July night was unseasonably warm, and even the open terrace doors didn't yield much fresh air. The men in their dinner jackets looked uncomfortable, and a few of the women's perfect matte makeup jobs were beginning to shine. Her own black crepe dress was strapless, but she wished she had taken the time to pin her hair up. She took a glass of champagne from a waiter. It was cool and biting. She drank it in greedy gulps.

"Kellen! There you are!"

She turned to see the managing editor of the *Trib*, standing next to a tall man with dark hair. To her astonishment, she recognized the man as the stranger who had asked for a chair in the café that morning. In the same instant, he recognized her.

"Garrett Richardson, this is Kellen Bryant," said the editor. Kellen held out her hand, and the man took it.

"*Enchanté, mademoiselle,*" he said, smiling.

"*Enchanté, m'sieur.*" Kellen smiled back.

"My god, can we drop the French? My brain is too tired tonight," the editor said with a sigh. "Besides, Kellen's an American, Garrett." The stranger looked at Kellen with surprise. "She writes our People column," the editor went on. "So watch what you say around her. She's very good. I treat her like Casey Stengel treats his twenty-game winners."

The editor's eyes darted across the room. "You'll have to excuse me for a moment. Oh, Kellen, by the way, Garrett speaks English, too. He's British. His father is Arthur Richardson, the owner of the *London Sun*. I'm sure that will give you two something to talk about."

The editor left. Kellen glanced at Garrett Richardson. He was tall and wore a dinner jacket as if he had been born in it. His hair was black and wavy, and he wore it slightly long, over his collar. His features were sharp, with high cheekbones and a thin nose, but he had a generous mouth and dark blue eyes. Kellen decided she had never seen a more physically compelling man.

"I believe we've met already," he said. "In a café. You were reading McLuhan. I thought you were French."

"Why did you think that?" she asked.

"Because I thought you were quite pretty. And a bit rude."

Kellen stared at him. "Parisians are not all rude, Mr. Richardson. That's a tourist cliché. The people here are no ruder than in

New York, or London for that matter. I just don't like being bothered by strangers.''

"I had no intention of bothering you. I simply needed a chair.''

They were silent, both staring around the room. A waiter passed by and Garrett took two glasses of champagne. "Look, we've gotten off to a bad start,'' he said, holding out a glass to her. "I'm sorry if I seemed intrusive at the café this morning.''

He was smiling, a warm, charming smile that made him look suddenly more approachable. After a moment Kellen could not resist. She took the glass and smiled.

"To cafés,'' he said, holding up his glass. "In Paris, everything starts in a café.''

"That's another tourist cliché.''

"Well, the funny thing about clichés is that they are usually true.''

Kellen sipped her drink. The bodies in the room pressed close, and the heat was lulling. She lifted her hair off her neck. She could feel Garrett Richardson's eyes on her.

"So you write a gossip column,'' he said. "That must be very interesting.''

"It is. I meet some intriguing people.''

"Really? Anyone intriguing in this priggish bunch?''

She looked at him. Brits could be so insufferably condescending, she had found, and when you got to know them, they were timid bores. "Oh, don't let appearances fool you,'' she said. "There are some real stories in this room. See that fellow over there? He's a blacklisted Hollywood screenwriter who can't get a passport to go home. That dumpy little man over there is a novelist who really works for the CIA.'' She pointed to a distinguished-looking man wearing the Legion of Honor rosette. "And that gentleman is a diplomat who prowls the quai at night looking for young boys.'' She smiled. "Does that shock you?''

"Not particularly.''

"Oh, that's right. You're used to shocking things. Your father owns that newspaper, the *Sun*. Isn't that the one with all the scandals and nude women?''

"The *Sun* prints stories that people enjoy reading, Miss Bryant. You do the same in the States. You call them human interest stories, I believe.''

Kellen smiled. "Mr. Richardson, I'm familiar with the British tabloid press, and it's nothing like the American press. We don't pander to our readers' lowest instincts.''

Garrett smiled back. "The *Sun* is an extremely profitable enterprise because of what you call pandering. And pandering is a very subjective thing. All newspapers pander to some extent to survive. The *Herald-Tribune*, for instance, is nothing but a specious small-town newspaper transplanted to Paris that panders to Americans who need to be assured that their dollar and sports teams are doing well."

For a moment, Kellen thought of telling him that she was the daughter of Adam Bryant so he would realize she had real newspaper credentials. Anything to prick his balloon of self-righteousness. She decided against it.

"The *Trib* is a good newspaper," she said finally.

He grinned. "I didn't say it wasn't good at what it does. But one can't take it seriously."

"It's good enough to cause the *New York Times* to start a competing edition."

"Ah, yes, the battle of the boulevards . . . and neither side is winning." Garrett finished his champagne. "Perhaps you should run pics of nude women."

She looked at him and saw immediately from his smile that he was teasing her. Her eyes dropped to his left hand holding the glass and she noticed he was not wearing a wedding band. Kellen glanced around the room. She could still feel his eyes on her. There was a long silence.

"It's getting too hot in here," Garrett said suddenly. "I'm leaving. Would you like to come?"

She looked at him. "Yes," she said. She handed him her jacket. He draped it across her shoulders, lifting her hair out of the way. His fingers seemed to linger on her neck.

Outside, the air was warm, almost sultry. They walked along the rue de Faubourg St-Honore, each trying to keep the small talk going. It was near ten, and the windows of the exclusive shops were dark. As they made their way along the narrow sidewalk, Garrett's arm would occasionally brush Kellen's. Each time, it would send a small current through her. Despite the fact that she didn't particularly like Garrett Richardson, she knew that she was attracted to him. She didn't question the feeling; she had experienced it with other men whom she didn't like. But the pull was never before so strong. It was as if she had known, from the moment she saw him in the café that morning, that he would somehow fit into her life.

Even if it's only for tonight, she thought.

They came to the Place de la Concorde. "Would you like a drink?" Garrett asked.

"Yes," Kellen answered.

"We could go to my hotel. The Crillon. It's nearby."

For the first time, Kellen felt a small pang of disappointment. She had met his kind before—seduction was a drink or two in an impressive hotel, then upstairs for the quick, and inevitably unimaginative, denouement. She paused.

"No," she said. "I have a better idea."

They walked toward the river. At the quai, Kellen led Garrett down some stairs to a floating bar anchored near the bridge. It was a simple place, festooned with little white lights. They took a table outdoors.

"Are you by chance hungry?" Garrett asked. "I haven't had dinner."

"Yes, a little."

Garrett ordered a bottle of chablis, bread and oysters, the only food the bar had to offer. The waiter brought a plate of enormous oysters. She tried one. It tasted fresh and salty, like the sea.

"These are *fines de claires*," Garrett said, smiling. He ate one, closing his eyes in pleasure. "The working man's oyster. Oyster snobs won't touch them."

Kellen smiled as she watched him devour the food. "You're not a snob, I take it."

"Absolutely not. I have a real talent for the baser things in life. That's what makes me a good newspaperman." He ate another oyster. "And I have a healthy appetite."

Kellen sipped the chablis. "Your French is perfect. Where did you learn it?"

"In school and then here. My mother's family had a country place in Normandy. We came here often when I was a boy." He went on to talk sketchily about his family. Kellen had heard of his father, Arthur Richardson. She knew that he had made his large fortune through a chain of tabloid newspapers in Great Britain, the largest being the hugely popular *Sun*.

"Tell me about yourself," Garrett said as he poured out the last of the wine.

"There's not much to tell," Kellen said cautiously. "I grew up in California. San Francisco."

"I've been there," Garrett said. "A great town."

Kellen told Garrett little, and lied about her father, saying that her parents were dead. She wasn't sure why she did it. She told herself there was no point in complicating what she could see was rapidly moving toward becoming just a brief sexual encounter.

"Why are you in Paris?" he asked.

She laughed. "For excitement. For fun. For romance. All the awful clichés. Isn't that why everyone comes to Paris? I came for . . ." Lost words from the past floated to her mind. "For a life that burns like a fabulous yellow roman candle exploding like a spider across the stars. . . ."

Her thoughts drifted to Stephen, then back to the present. She glanced back at Garrett. The wine was working its way through her body, nicely blurring the edges of reality. On both sides of the river, the city was quiet. The water lapped at the sides of the barge, and every so often the trees on the far bank were illuminated by the lights of passing cars.

Garrett's eyes held hers. "This great, burning life, did you find it?" he asked.

"Yes . . . no . . . not yet," she said slowly.

He took her hand and turned it over in his own as if carefully examining each line in her palm. She was aware suddenly of the pressure of his thigh against her own. He slowly brought her palm up to his lips. When he kissed it, she shut her eyes. She knew in that instant that she wanted him more than she had ever wanted any man. It had gone beyond physical attraction into something dark and irresistible.

"It's late," he said. "We'd better go."

"Where?"

"We'll get a taxi. I'll take you home."

She knew he wanted her. She could feel it. She had a sudden feeling that, after tonight, she would never see Garrett Richardson again, and she wanted to prolong the night as long as she could.

"No. Not yet," she said. "Come with me . . . to a party."

"Where?"

Kellen rose, smiling mischievously. "I don't really know. My friend Nathalie only told me to come to the Place Denfert-Rochereau in Montparnasse. And to bring champagne and . . . oh hell, a flashlight. Where can we get one?" She saw the puzzled look on Garrett's face. "You call it a torch, I think."

"Well, I can take care of the champagne," Garrett said. He had the waiter bring a bottle.

Kellen leaned over and blew out the candle on the table. "Here, hide this in your jacket." Garrett took the candle, glanced around, and stuck it in his jacket. He was smiling and shaking his head in bewilderment.

Kellen took his hand and pulled him to his feet. "Be brave, Mr. Richardson," she said, smiling. "I promise you that this will be a night you'll never forget."

Chapter
Twenty-one

It was nearly eleven by the time Kellen found Nathalie and her crowd gathered in the dark of the Place Denfert-Rochereau. Garrett watched as Kellen was embraced by the group, a multilingual clique of fashionably dressed young people. The warm night air was filled with wine-fueled laughter and the sweet scent of marijuana. The troupe followed Nathalie down a dark and deserted side street. Kellen linked her arm through Garrett's and they trailed along. Everyone paused, and two of the men reached down and pried open a manhole cover. There were suppressed giggles as Nathalie admonished everyone to be quiet. Garrett and Kellen watched in astonishment as, one by one, the party members disappeared down the manhole.

Soon, he, Kellen, and Nathalie were left on the street. Nathalie kissed them both on the cheek and descended the iron ladder. Below, in the gloom, Garrett could see the crisscrossing rays of flashlights.

"A party . . . in a bloody sewer?" Garrett laughed.

"It's not a sewer," Kellen said. "It's the catacombs. Come on. It'll be fun."

They climbed down the ladder. Below, the air was moist and cool. It was pitch black. Garrett could hear Kellen breathing and he reached for her.

"The candle," she said.

He retrieved it and took a match from his jacket. He lit the candle, and Kellen's face appeared out of the darkness. He saw that they were in a narrow passageway. There was an old stone floor and a low, rounded ceiling. Far off, down the passageway, he could see the flickering lights and hear the laughter of the others. There was a strange smell in the air, of something timeless and sacred, like the inside of an ancient cathedral.

"Let's find the others," Kellen said. They went down the passageway. Garrett had to bend over slightly to keep from bumping his head. The passageway opened into a small, circular room. The other party goers were gathered there, passing around bottles of wine. The flashlights made crazy arcs in the dark. Someone lit several candles.

To his shock, Garrett saw that the walls of the room were constructed entirely of human skulls and bones. The bones were worn to a finely polished ochre patina and were carefully arranged in precise rows, like some bizarre, artful mosaic. "What is this place?" Garrett whispered, unable to take his eyes off the walls.

"The catacombs," Kellen said. "In the eighteenth and nineteenth centuries Paris was being rebuilt, and the cemeteries were in the way. The skeletons were brought here. It's a tourist place now during the day."

"Charming," Garrett muttered. He looked at Kellen. In the candlelight, he could see her eyes shining. "And now that we're here," he said, "what are we supposed to do?"

There was a shriek of laughter. "*Cache-cache!*" Nathalie called out, and everyone ran, whooping gleefully down the passageways that led off from the room like spokes of a wheel. The sound of laughter and retreating footsteps echoed in the empty room. Garrett turned to Kellen.

"Hide and seek?" he asked.

She nodded. "Would you like some champagne?" she asked, holding up the sweating bottle.

He eased out the cork and took a long drink. "But no games," he said, holding out the bottle to her.

She took a drink. "Then let's take a tour."

They chose a passageway. It was another dark and twisting tunnel. Kellen held the candle as they walked.

"You have some strange friends," he said.

"I suppose. But at least they're not boring." She stopped and turned to look at him. "I like exciting people."

"And what, in your mind, makes a person exciting?"

She laughed. "Oh, I don't know. You just feel it when you're around them. They have a madness to them. A sense of danger and of possibilities. They're willing to go farther and do more. They're open to more experiences. They're fearless." Garrett stared at her. "They're filled with life," she said.

"Because they party in cemeteries?"

"No, because they have lives of passion."

"It's easy to say that," Garrett said. "And quite another to have the guts to really do it."

It was her turn to stare at him. She turned and walked on slowly. Garrett followed. They came to another room, smaller than the first, but with only one wall of bones. It was marked with a stone inscription that noted the year 1804 and the name of the now lost cemetery.

Kellen turned away from the wall and set the candle on a ledge. She stared down one of the three passageways that led away toward darkness.

"They say these tunnels run for miles under most of Montparnasse," she said softly. She paused. "You could get lost in here forever."

She felt Garrett's hands on her shoulders, and she turned. His face was inches from her own, dim gold in the candlelight. He leaned forward and kissed her. Her arms went up to his neck and, instantly, his kiss became harder. His arms encircled her, and his hands pressed the small of her back, pulling her toward him. The feel of his body sent a shock wave through her, a feeling so strong that she felt momentarily weak. Her hands moved, as if she could not stop them, swiftly under his jacket and over the hard surfaces of his chest and back.

She lost all reference to time or place, sensing only being in a floating, cool dark void with his body pressed tight against her own and his lips hot and moist on her face and throat. Together, they stumbled backward and she felt a wall, sharp and cold, against her back. The dark void began to swirl. He was whispering something, but she couldn't understand. His fingers pulled at the top of her dress and when he kissed her breast, she moaned and her fingers wound through his hair. There was no thought to what they did; everything was reduced to an instinctive urgent need.

Suddenly, he pushed her dress up on her thighs. Before she could help him, she heard and felt the ripping of the silk panties giving way. Her fingers fumbled at his belt.

"Oh, god, hurry," she cried out.

The wall ground into her back as he lifted her onto his hips and entered her brusquely, his lips buried in the hollow of her neck. She felt nothing but him, filling her, and then finally, a release so sweet and complete that she cried out, and tears fell down her face.

The cavern flickered back into her consciousness. The air swirled around them, cool and moist. She opened her eyes to see a shadow of their joined bodies on a far wall. Somewhere far off, like a faint echo, she could hear someone calling her name. Different voices, calling for her, over and over. Kellen . . . Kellen . . . Where are you? . . . Kellen . . . Are you lost?

She felt Garrett's lips soft on her neck, and she clung to him.

For the next week, they didn't leave each other's side. Garrett postponed his return to London, and Kellen called in to work to say she was ill. She stayed with Garrett in his hotel room. Neither of them understood completely what was happening, and they didn't talk about it.

For seven days, they were lost in each other's bodies. They discovered they had an intuitive knowledge of each other's needs and how to fulfill them. They were both keenly aware of a force at work out of their control, that their being together had a strange inevitability.

"I feel like I have known you all my life," Garrett said. "And that I will never, ever really know you at all."

"I understand," Kellen answered.

On the eighth day, Garrett told her he had to leave. She didn't question him. They had a quiet dinner together in a restaurant on the Left Bank. He told her that some pressing business in London with his father demanded his attention.

"I don't know when I can get back to Paris," he said. "As soon as I can."

She didn't say anything. She knew in that moment that she had fallen in love with him. It was crazy. She knew so little about him. And he knew even less about her. She had never told him the truth about her background.

"I'll be here," she said.

The next morning, she saw him off at the airport then returned to her own apartment to change her clothes. She went to the *Trib* office.

The editor greeted her with a concerned look. "Kellen, where have you been?"

"At home. I told you I was very ill."

"We've been calling for three days, and there's been no answer."

"I'm sorry, I took the phone off the hook." Kellen sat down at her desk and started to go through some papers.

"There's an important message for you," the editor said. "That's why we've been trying to get you." He held out a slip of paper. "This man has been calling every day. He says he has to talk to you. It's an emergency."

Kellen took the note. On it was scribbled Josh's name and office number. Kellen stared at the paper. Josh wouldn't have called her unless it was truly important. She glanced at the clock. It was midnight in San Francisco. She quickly dialed Josh's home, and he answered immediately.

"Kellen, thank god," he said. "You got my message."

"Only that it was an emergency." She didn't like the strange flat tone in Josh's voice. "What's wrong, Josh?"

"It's your father." There was a long pause, and the line jumped with static. "He's dying, Kellen. . . . Kellen, are you still there?"

"Yes . . . Josh . . . what, how?"

"There's not much time, Kellen. Please come home. He wants you."

"I'll be there as soon as I can." She hung up the phone and sat there for a long time. Her heart was beating so hard she could hear the blood throbbing in her head. Everything around her was a blur. Finally, she rose slowly and went into the editor's office. She announced quietly, to the stunned editor, that she was resigning and returning to the States. She didn't stop to get anything in her desk or to say good-bye to anyone. She stopped at her apartment long enough to pack a few things and to drop off the keys with a neighbor.

Out on the street, she paused. Rue de Seine bustled with people, and for a moment she felt disoriented. She realized suddenly that she had only about fifty dollars' worth of francs. She walked up to Boulevard St-Michel and into a bank. It was the bank where her father had been making deposits in her name for the last five years. The account now had more than $10,000 in it. She withdrew enough money for a plane ticket. The rest, she decided, she would deal with when she returned.

At the airport, she caught the first flight to New York. As the jet lifted off, she pressed her forehead against the window and watched the lights of Paris grow dimmer. The steely reserve that had powered her actions throughout the day suddenly broke down, and she began to cry softly. She was going home. Her father was dying. She was going home.

Chapter
Twenty-two

❧ In the weeks following Adam's funeral, Kellen wandered around the house in a stupor of grief and guilt. She blamed herself for not coming home sooner to repair the emotional rent with her father. She had been selfish, too caught up in her own life in Paris. But she also blamed her father. Why hadn't he told her he was so ill? Why had he waited until it was too late? Now he was gone, so suddenly and without a chance for reconciliation. As much as she had mourned her mother, it had not been like this. Even though she had not seen her father in years, she had always somehow felt his presence. But now, she had no one. She felt utterly, painfully alone. And suddenly very fragile and very mortal.

The loneliness of the large, quiet house was oppressive. Ian was seldom home, spending most his hours at the newspaper office or at the club. Tyler was a ghostly presence, hovering in the shadows. Kellen thought often about what Adam had said about Tyler before he died—take care of your brother. But whenever she made an overture toward Tyler, he avoided her. She thought also of what Josh had told her about the newspapers. He said they were in trouble; he implied that it was her responsibility to do something about it.

Both Adam's and Josh's words sat heavily on her shoulders. How could she be expected to hold together a family of strangers? And why should she care about the newspapers after being excluded? It was all so unfair—her father's death and his final imposition of duty when all she felt like doing was running away. She thought often of Paris. The idea of returning there became her emotional salvation. That was where her life was, after all. Not here, with one brother who hated her and another who was a stranger. Not here, in the huge house with nothing but memories to fill it. Not here, with Stephen. Not after what she had felt with Garrett.

Stephen had been so kind, so ready to give solace, just as he always had been. "What will you do now?" he had asked her one night, not long after the reading of the will.

"I don't know," she answered. "Try to work some arrangement out with Ian over the newspapers. Then I'm going back to Paris. That's where my future is."

She knew he wanted to know about a different future—their own together. It was strange, his gently vigilant attitude toward her, as if they had magically picked up where they had left off six years ago. She found it comforting but suffocating at the same time.

Finally, she fled to the house in Carmel. There, the memories of her father crowded around her just as mercilessly as they had at the house on Divisadero. The horrible scene at her birthday party kept replaying in her head like a looped tape. Other painful vignettes floated up from the past—the day he sent her off to boarding school, his failure to explain Tyler's birth, his disregard when she asked him for a job at the *Times*. And most hauntingly, the worn face of the stranger staring up from his deathbed.

But after a while, the memories began to mutate, and slowly, the good replaced the bad. She remembered vividly the feel of her father's arms around her, welcoming her home from school. And their dinners at the Olympic Club, and their amiable lunches on the run in downtown bars. She could see, as if it were yesterday, her parents dancing under the chandelier. And she could remember the time when, for a too brief time, he had been a happy man, overflowing with life.

It was, finally, the good memories that dominated her thoughts as she walked alone on the beach at Carmel. The beach house itself was like a balm to her. It had been there that she and her mother and father had shared their most precious time together, just before her mother fell ill. Just the three of them, together, for three glorious days. Too brief, much too brief . . .

She paused and stared out at the ocean. The crushing feelings of loneliness and guilt had eased. Now she was left with a sense of deep remorse. In the end, she and Adam had hurt each other so much. Just before he died, Adam had been able, in his own way, to tell her he was sorry. But there had been no time for her to do the same.

Kellen's eyes dropped to the sand, to the water ebbing and flowing over her bare feet. She looked up and focused on the wood-

and-glass house. It was a brilliant clear day and the sun glinted off the glass, causing Kellen to squint as she stared at the house. Ian had said he didn't want it. That white elephant's your responsibility now, he had said.

Suddenly she knew, with a piercing clarity, that she would not return to Paris. She knew there was something she had to do. She had to go back to the newspaper. It, too, was her responsibility. And it was the only way she could prove to her father that she had loved him.

Early the next morning, she returned to the city. She dressed in a suit and went to the Times building. She paused long enough to stare up at the large clock outside and to note that it was off by three minutes. On the top floor, she stopped just outside the mahogany doors of the executive office, remembering all the times she had breezed through them on her way to see Adam. Inside, Adele was still at her post, and she smiled when she saw Kellen. The secretary was still distraught over Adam's death, and Kellen listened patiently as Adele indulged her memories. Finally, she cleared her throat and asked, "Is my brother in?"

"Yes, he is," Adele answered. Kellen started for Ian's door, but Adele interrupted politely. "He's moved," she said, almost apologetically, "into your father's office."

Kellen looked at the door to Adam's office in disbelief, then pushed it open. Inside, she stopped abruptly. Ian was sitting behind her father's desk. The sight was disorienting.

Ian looked up. "You could at least knock," he said.

"I see it didn't take you long to move in," Kellen said.

"Why not? I'm the publisher now." Ian made no move to invite her to sit down. Kellen took the chair opposite him.

"So what brings you downtown, little sister?" he asked with a smile. "Doing some shopping?"

"No, I'm here on business. For good you might say." Kellen stared at Ian, watching for his reaction. "I'm here to take my place in the family business."

Ian chuckled. "And what's that supposed to mean?"

"I'm here to take my place in the running of this newspaper. Father left half of it to me, and I intend to exercise my powers."

"As what?"

"Copublisher, of course."

Ian's smile slid away. "That's crazy. You don't know anything about running a newspaper."

"Neither do you apparently. Josh told me the company's in trouble because of the way you've been running it."

"Josh should keep his nose out of things that don't concern him." He lit a cigarette. "I thought you were going back to Paris."

"I changed my mind."

He laughed softly in derision. "Oh, Kellen, you're still such a flake. You haven't the faintest idea what you want to do with yourself."

Kellen stared at him, annoyed that he obviously found her so unthreatening. "This paper's just as much mine as it is yours, Ian. You'd better get used to the idea." She rose. "If I remember right, there's a conference room across the hall. I'll have it made into my office."

Kellen saw Ian's jaw tighten, and for the first time, she smiled. "Looks like we'll be working closely together, big brother." She started out the door.

"I will not share my title," Ian said. "I am the publisher."

She turned toward him. "So am I. That's the way Daddy wanted it. And if I have to, I'll get Josh to legally remind you of that fact."

She closed the door behind her and leaned against it, expelling a long breath. Her hands were shaking slightly, but she was filled with a heady sense of victory. She saw Adele staring at her, and she squared her shoulders.

"Adele, from now on, I will be working with my brother as copublisher," Kellen said. Adele's eyes widened. She had worked for Adam for twenty years, and seeing Kellen as something more than Mr. Bryant's little girl was a shock. "That will be my office," Kellen said, nodding toward the conference room. "We'll have to get some architects and decorators up here fast. And call Josh Hillman and ask him to come up here to see me."

Kellen started toward the conference room and paused. "Oh, one last thing. Call maintenance. The building clock is running slow. I want it fixed right away."

Josh sat at the conference table across from Kellen. Spread out in front of them were all editions of the *Times* and of the rival *Journal*.

"So what made you change your mind?" Josh asked.

Kellen poured the coffee and shrugged. "I don't know exactly. When you first mentioned that the newspapers were in trouble, I was almost glad. I was so angry about being shut out for so long that I didn't care what happened to them." She paused. "Then I realized that whatever Father's reason for keeping me out, it didn't mean he didn't love me." She blinked back tears. "He loved these newspapers, Josh. I can't just turn my back. I owe it to him."

"I'm glad," he said softly. "But you have to understand, Kellen. This isn't going to be easy."

Over the next two hours, Josh told her about the Bryant corporation. He tried to paint the picture in the broadest strokes so she could understand. But a few times, he found himself lapsing into the sophisticated financial banter he had always used with Adam; then he would see the confusion on Kellen's face. And he would smile to himself, sadly, seeing the reflections of his old friend in the daughter's eager eyes. He thought, too, about the futility of trying to teach such a naive young woman about the intricate workings of a multimillion-dollar media corporation.

He thought back to how easy it had been for Stephen. The boy had made it clear to Josh very early that he intended to be a newspaperman. Josh could remember the day clearly. Stephen was ten, and Josh had taken him along on an errand to see Adam. He tracked Adam down in the pressroom, where he was talking to a foreman about a press malfunction. Even Josh had to admit that Adam cut a dashing figure, his shirt sleeves rolled high, his arms smudged with ink, standing high on a catwalk above the massive presses. When the problem was solved, the foreman punched a few buttons, an ear-piercing bell sounded, and the presses began to roll. Stephen had stood there, wide-eyed, watching the newsprint snake slowly through the huge, black machines, gradually picking up speed until it was churning at its full, teeth-shaking force. Josh looked down at his son's face and knew that nothing, especially not the quiet sanctuary of a lawyer's office, would ever be so enthralling. Later, Adam had taken Stephen under his wing, giving him various jobs and internships.

Josh looked at Kellen, whose brow was knit into a frown as she read a report. If only, Josh thought, Adam had been able to see how much of himself was in his daughter.

But there was no point in dwelling on the past. It was up to him now to do what he could. So he pressed on. He pulled out financial and circulation reports for Kellen and outlined the backgrounds and status of all the current Bryant holdings, including the fifteen newspapers, the wire service, the Oakland television station, paper mill, and printing facilities. He told her that the profitability of the entire corporation was in jeopardy because of the financial problems of the flagship newspaper, the *San Francisco Times*. Six years ago, Josh explained, Adam had made two moves that had set

up the current problems. He told her about Adam's buy-out of
Lilith's ownership via yearly $2.5 million payments.

"But why did he do that?" Kellen asked.

"I think he suspected something was wrong with his health,"
Josh said. "He wanted to make sure his estate—especially the
Times—would be left only to his children. He wanted Lilith out of
the picture."

Josh then told her about Adam's other move, the costly suburban expansion project. The suburban editions were popular among
readers but were labor- and resource-intensive.

"With the start-up costs and Lilith's payments, the company's
finances had to be closely watched," Josh explained. "Adam
intended to keep a very tight rein on all spending until the suburban editions were self-supporting." Josh paused. "Then he got
sick."

"And he didn't tell anyone," Kellen said quietly.

"Remember the night of your twenty-first birthday?" Kellen
nodded. "He knew then he had cancer," Josh said. "He had
found out from his doctor the day before. I think that had a lot to
do with his manner that night. It wasn't anything you did, Kellen.
He was just so devastated."

"Oh, Josh, why didn't he tell me?" she murmured.

"He didn't want anyone to know. He didn't even tell me until
months later. I'm sorry, Kellen. He swore me to secrecy. I didn't
even tell Stephen."

Tears fell down Kellen's face, and she turned away to stare out
the window at the gray, cloudy sky. Josh waited for a moment
before he went on. "At first your father thought he could beat the
cancer. He kept up a strong front for as long as he could, but his
energy began to fail him and he started turning things over to Ian.
There came a point when your father seemed to accept he was
dying. It was almost easier for him after that. He was confident he
had set things up to survive after him for his family." Josh paused.
"The only thing he worried about was you."

Kellen looked away.

"His wish was to see you happily married and cared for," Josh
added.

Kellen looked at Josh. "But not to Stephen . . ."

Josh sighed. He took a sip of coffee. "It's cold," he said,
setting down the cup.

"My father's attitude didn't bother you, Josh?"

Josh took a moment before he answered. "Your father wasn't
anti-Semitic, Kellen. He was just worried about you. He knew

what problems you and Stephen would have if you married and had children." Josh paused. "I can't say I disagreed with him. I've seen what heartbreak intermarriages can bring, even when two people love each other."

"But it wasn't his place to decide for me, Josh."

"You forget, your father was a Catholic. On the surface he didn't seem very religious, but he was in his heart. About five years ago, he started going to church again. He wanted a Catholic funeral. Of course, his excommunication when he married your mother had made that impossible. . . ."

Kellen stared at Josh in disbelief.

"He changed a lot while you were away," Josh added quietly. He saw the look of guilt creep into Kellen's eyes and quickly changed the subject. "As I said, your father was confident that what he had built would continue after he died. He told me that Ian would take care of the business." Josh sighed. "But Ian just doesn't have Adam's talent or inclination. He's more interested in increasing his own personal fortune than he is in maintaining the family business interests. And I can't seem to convince him that, in the long run, they are one and the same."

Kellen looked back at Josh, her eyes vacant. Josh took a breath. "During your father's illness, Ian started financially draining the *Times*. He has been redirecting profits away from the corporation and into his own pocket. He has a pretty extravagant life-style to maintain. He's frozen budgets on some newspapers and ordered cutbacks on the *Times*, which he says is overstaffed. What's bad is that Ian is pulling back just when the *Journal* is coming alive. Last quarter, the *Journal* showed a circulation gain for the first time in ten years. Ian doesn't care, but I think he's being short-sighted. And now that Adam's gone, I think he's going to cut back the suburban operation. He and Stephen are at each other's throats about it."

Kellen ran her hand through her hair. The gesture made Josh realize he was probably overloading her with too much information too soon.

"These suburban editions," she said. "They are expensive to run, right?" Josh nodded. "Are they important?" she asked.

"Your father thought so. He was a visionary, Kellen. He could see opportunity where everyone else saw only obstacles. That's what has made the Bryant newspaper empire so great." Josh put his hand over Kellen's. "The only thing he couldn't envision was what would happen after he was gone."

"I wanted to help," Kellen said flatly. "Why couldn't he have seen that?"

"When it came to the newspapers, your father looked to the future. But with his own family, he looked to the past. And in that world, daughters had a certain traditional role to fulfill."

Kellen pulled her hand away. "I disappointed him."

Josh shook his head. "I think if he could see you now, he'd be very proud at what you're trying to do."

Kellen stared at the newspapers spread out on the conference table and at the mass of financial reports. The confidence she had felt only hours ago when she walked out of Ian's office was dissipating. The task now before her was formidable. How could she possibly learn enough to run the newspapers? And how could she learn enough to counter Ian? She thought suddenly of Ian and how he had looked sitting behind her father's desk.

"I have to do it," she said quietly. "I owe it to my father."

The next night, Kellen accepted Stephen's invitation to dinner. It was the first time they had had a chance to be alone together since Kellen's return from Carmel. They sat in a restaurant, feeling awkward. The conversation was polite and filled with strange pauses. Finally, Stephen reached over and took her hand.

"Why are we acting like this?" he asked.

"Like what?"

"Like strangers. It's me, Stephen!" He smiled and maneuvered their fingers into a grasp that ended with him tickling her palm. It was the secret handshake of their childhood. Kellen laughed, and suddenly the ice was broken.

"I missed you, Kellen."

She stared at him. He had hardly changed in six years. Still the same Stephen she had grown up loving, the same reassuring, calm Stephen. She felt the years slip away and a feeling of security washed over her. "I missed you, too, Stephen," she said softly.

Over dinner, they talked. Kellen eagerly told him about Paris and the *Trib*, but sketched over her personal life. Stephen described his routine as editor and talked eagerly about the suburban coverage. He glossed over his problems with Ian. "We have our differences," he said simply.

"Ian doesn't really care about the newspaper, not the way Daddy did," Kellen said. "Or the way I do."

Stephen looked at her strangely. "How involved with the *Times* do you intend to get?"

"I'm going to run it. The way my father wanted it run."

Stephen sat back in his chair. "Your father had very strong ideas about newspapers. He taught me all that I know. I respected him very much, and I've tried to carry on as he would have wanted."

Kellen realized she had hurt Stephen's feelings. "I know that, Stephen," she said quickly. "So did my father. That's why he made you editor. And that's why I will need your help." She paused. "You'll help me, won't you?"

After a moment, Stephen smiled. He leaned forward, took her hand, and kissed it lightly. "I'll help you," he said.

The gesture surprised Kellen. She looked into Stephen's warm brown eyes. She really had missed him, and it felt good to be with him now. The pain and confusion of Adam's death and her homecoming were easing. And her life, which had always seemed directionless, was coalescing around a purpose. For a moment, her thoughts flitted to Garrett, but she had pushed them aside. It had been fantastic, but it had been just one moment, and she wasn't going back to Paris. Her future was here now, with the newspaper. She stared into Stephen's eyes and didn't pull her hand away.

For the next month, Kellen immersed herself in trying to learn how the financial, production, advertising, marketing, and circulation divisions of the newspaper worked. She tackled the reports that Josh sent to her. At first, most of it made no sense to her, but she persevered. She pestered Josh and the division vice presidents constantly with her questions. She attended departmental meetings, where she sat quietly, drawing stares from the men. As discouraged as she was by her ignorance, she was thankful for the diversion. It prevented her from dwelling on Adam's death. It also gave her little time to think about Garrett. Those times when she did, usually at night when she was alone, it was as a vibrant but somehow distant memory. Their week together seemed like a dream now. He had entered her life in a burning flash and then was gone. She had other more important things to think about. She was convinced she would never see him again.

Then, one morning, late in September, he called. She was in her office, and though the transatlantic connection was poor, she recognized his voice immediately.

"You remember me, don't you?" he asked.

"Yes." She paused. Her heart was pounding. "How did you know to call me here?"

"I called the *Trib*. They told me who you are. Why didn't you tell me yourself when we met?"

She paused. "It didn't seem necessary," she replied, knowing how weak it sounded. "I thought it was only going to be one night."

He was silent. The line crackled with static. "I heard about your father's death," he said. "I'm sorry."

"Thank you . . ."

The line hummed, and Kellen could hear the ghostly voices of another conversation. The connection was terrible.

"I want to see you again," Garrett said.

Kellen closed her eyes. She could see his face and feel the touch of his hand on her body. "I'm not going back to Paris," she said.

"Then I'll come to you."

"When?"

"Soon. As soon as I can."

There was a loud burst of static, and she lifted the receiver away from her ear. When she tried to listen again, she realized the line was dead. He didn't call back, and she somehow didn't expect him to. But she was left with the same rush of anticipation she had felt that first night in Paris.

Chapter
Twenty-three

❦ Three weeks went by and Kellen did not hear from Garrett. How dare he, she thought, inject himself back into my life, then just leave me hanging. The phone rang, and she jumped on it. It was the comptroller, saying he was sending up some reports she had ordered. She hung up the phone and leaned back in her chair. Her desk was littered with folders and newspapers. Circulation reports. Marketing surveys. Financial statements. Union contracts. Projections of production costs for 1967. In just one month, she had learned much about the company, but her enthusiasm was buckling under the reams of information still to be digested. She picked up a report, but the figures began to run together in a blur.

"Damn," she muttered. "I can't stand this any longer. There's got to be more to it than this."

She jumped up and went to the door. "I'm going down to the newsroom," she told Adele.

Downstairs, she went through the city room toward Stephen's glass cubicle. Heads swiveled. Necks craned. Many of the employees stared because they knew who she was. Those who didn't simply gawked at the sight of a tall, beautiful redhead in a black suit making her way through the newsroom.

Stephen looked up in surprise when he saw her. He motioned her in. "What are you doing down here?" he asked.

"I'm tired of sitting upstairs reading reports," she said, sitting down. "I needed a dose of reality."

Stephen laughed. "Rapunzel descends from the tower to let down her hair. . . ."

There was a rap on the door, and two men came in. Kellen waited while they conferred with Stephen. From what she could gather, it concerned a potentially libelous quote in a story. Kellen watched Stephen carefully. She had never actually watched him at work before and now, as she listened to him referee the debate between the reporter and editor, it was as if she were seeing him in a totally new light. His pragmatism and his unflappable nature, qualities she had been so quick to make light of when she was young, now seemed like shining assets. In the context of the newsroom, Stephen was a man utterly in control and completely at ease. Stephen brought the discussion to an end, and the men left.

"Sorry," Stephen said to Kellen. "What were you saying?"

"I was saying that if I intend to really run the *Times*, then I need to understand how the editorial side works. You said you'd help me." She smiled. "So where do we start?"

"Well, what do you want to do exactly?"

"Help you run the newsroom."

Stephen smiled. "I have a managing editor for that."

Kellen frowned slightly. "Stephen, it's not like I don't have some experience. I worked in Paris and—"

"You wrote a weekly column, Kellen." He paused, seeing the defensive look creep into her eyes. "Now, don't go getting angry with me. Look at it from my perspective. If you suddenly showed up down here at my side trying to run things, how would it look?"

"I don't care how things *look*, Stephen."

"I know. You never did. But think about this. It would look like the owner's daughter suddenly decided to do a little slumming. To the staff, I'd look like a puppet and you'd look like a debutante trying out the new toy."

Kellen scowled at him. "You're treating me like a child. Just like you used to."

Stephen shrugged. "All right, it's your paper. Do what you want. But I'm going to give you some advice whether you want it or not. Don't make the same mistake Ian made. Twenty years ago, your father brought him in to learn the business. My father once told me that the employees hated Ian because he never made any honest attempt to learn. He just came in and started playing heir apparent to the throne." He nodded toward the city room. "The people out there still hate him. Even the new ones who've never even seen him.'"

Kellen stared at Stephen. She was angry and embarrassed, but she understood what he was trying to tell her. "I want to run this paper the way my father did," she said. "What do you suggest I do?"

"Learn the way everyone learns. From the bottom up. You can start on the copy desk in the morning."

"Okay, I will. What time do you want me in—eight?"

"Nope. The shift runs three A.M. to nine A.M."

Kellen stared at Stephen. He was not smiling, but she could tell he was enjoying this, as if it were a retribution for all the times she had teased him when they were growing up. He was throwing out a challenge, thinking she wouldn't be up to it. "Fine," she said.

"Good . . . Chauncy needs some help with the bulldog edition. He's the morning desk editor, over there." Stephen pointed to a man out in the newsroom. "See him."

Kellen looked out at the city room. A small, ironic smile tipped her lips. "After all these years, I'm finally going to get to work for the *Times*."

Stephen smiled. "Be here on time. Chauncy's a stickler for punctuality. He won't cut you any slack."

"I don't expect any." Kellen said good-bye and started across the newsroom for the elevator. She spotted Clark Able off in a corner and went over to his desk. He was hunched over his typewriter, pecking at the keys with two fingers. An unlit brown Gauloise cigarette was clamped between his lips, and his straight brown hair hung down over his glasses. He wore a spotless white shirt with French cuffs and small antique gold cuff links. A silk tie was knotted at his throat.

"Hi, Clark."

His head jerked up, and he squinted at her. "Kellen! Sit down. I'll be done in a minute." He tore the paper out of the typewriter with a flourish. "Elliot! To the desk!"

His young assistant sprang up from his desk, grabbed the paper, and marched off down the aisle. Clark leaned back in his chair and looked at his watch. "A new record—twenty-two minutes, forty-five seconds. I'm a genius! But tomorrow, column number two thousand five hundred forty-five will be kitty-litter liner." He sighed dramatically. "No one appreciates me, Kellen."

She glanced at the stacks of mail and phone messages on Clark's desk and at the myriad photographs on the wall of Clark posing with various celebrities. Clark had been writing his column for nearly nine years, and in that time had become the most recognizable man in San Francisco, a nattily dressed boulevardier on every socialite's A list. With his thin, professorial face and floppy hair, he was an unlikely-looking social lion, but his bonhomie charmed people. That and his column. Everyone, from the mayor to Market Street cabbies, wanted to be mentioned in "Of Cabbages and Kings." It was a jolt of fame, of course, but seeing their names in print also gave them an I.D.

badge in a city that sometimes seemed too mythical and out-sized.

"Everyone loves you, Clark," Kellen said.

"But no *one* loves me," he said, smiling.

Kellen knew that was a reference to his latest broken love affair. His girlfriend of two years had just ended the relationship and moved to New York. But Clark was incredibly resilient emotionally. He never dwelled on sad events. He had talked her through more than one bad night since Adam's death. "Well, I love you," she said.

"At least I can count on that." He picked up an ornate silver lighter and lit his cigarette. "So, what brings you down to the snake pit?"

She told him about her new job on the desk. Clark roared with laughter. "Only milkmen get up at that hour."

She smiled wanly. "In Paris, that's when I used to go to bed."

He blew a small smoke ring. "I hope you're not going to let Stephen convert you into a drone for his hive here. You're a free spirit . . . *comme moi!*"

"I won't let that happen."

"Well, neither will I." He snuffed out the cigarette in an over-flowing crystal ashtray. "Listen, I have an idea. One last blowout before you become a happy little 'do bee.' Come with me to the opera tomorrow night. There's a party after."

"Oh, I don't know, Clark. I haven't been out since the funeral."

"It will do you good!" He paused. "Besides, the Bryant box has been empty for some time now. It would be nice to have someone in it."

In her entire life, she had been to the opera only once with her father, taking her mother's place in the box when she had been too ill to attend. Kellen had vague memories of the music and of the soft black wool of Adam's tuxedo as she held his arm. "You're right," she said. "I'd love to go."

"Wonderful! I'll pick you up at seven."

The opera turned out to be a boring production of *Parsifal*. Kellen sat next to Clark, trying to concentrate on it, but she was restless, her thoughts drifting between the newspaper and Paris. Several times, Garrett slipped in, but she pushed him out of her mind. She concentrated on Stephen. Last night, they had gone to dinner, and she had impulsively suggested they stop for a drink afterward. They went up to the Top of the Mark. It was an incredibly corny thing to do, but with the city's lights spread out below, and the pianist playing softly in the background, the evening assumed a magical quality. The evening had seemed so strange, almost like a high school date. A night of hand-holding in a dark corner, Stephen's face so close, and a soft good-night kiss in the cool night air.

Sudden applause drew Kellen back to the opera. The lights were going up. It was finally over. Clark draped Kellen's stole over her shoulders. "Did you like it?" he asked as they drove to Trader Vic's.

"Not particularly," Kellen said. "It was too long."

"About three hours too long," Clark said. "I hope the party is better. I need some nuggets for Monday's column."

The party was being given by Enid Atherton for the usual opera crowd. But as always, there was a smattering of celebrities and strangers thrown in to amuse the regulars and keep conversation from being too inbred. Kellen recognized almost no one and stuck close by Clark's side. Whenever he introduced her, the reaction was the same: eyes would widen and lips would curl up in toothy smiles. The women would brush their cheeks against hers and bubble up inane versions of the same comment. I knew your mother, I knew your father. How good to see you, dear. How lovely you are. I knew you when. I remember when. Your mother . . . your father . . .

"I don't know how much longer I can stand this," Kellen whispered to Clark after an hour.

"Gear up, darling," he said. "Here comes the queen."

Enid Atherton glided over to them. "Kellen, I'm so glad you could come." She kissed the air near Kellen's cheek. "I was so sorry to hear about your father."

Then why weren't you at his funeral, Kellen thought. So many in her father's old social circle had not come. They had all slowly distanced themselves from him after the scandal over Elizabeth's death.

"He was a wonderful man," Enid went on. "He so loved the opera. . . . We'll miss him."

"Thank you," Kellen murmured.

"Of course, we'd like you to join the guild," Enid added. "Your mother was a member, you know."

Out of the corner of her eye, Kellen noticed another woman insinuating herself into their circle. It was Lilith. Kellen stared at her, taken aback by her appearance. She was thin to the point of gauntness and sported a short geometric haircut and a purple beaded minidress. She was the epitome of up-to-the-moment chic for a woman twenty years younger.

"Enid . . . lovely party," Lilith said. The women kissed. Lilith turned and gave Kellen the once-over. "Why, hello, dear. I didn't know you were an opera aficionado."

"I've just invited Kellen to join the guild," Enid said. "Won't it be nice to have a Bryant on the board again?"

Lilith smiled woodenly and stared at the low neckline of Kellen's dress. "That's a lovely dress, dear," she said. "You must have gotten it in Paris. Balenciaga, right?"

"No, it's Scherrer . . . secondhand," Kellen said with a smile. "There's this little shop in the sixteenth arrondissement where all the rich women bring their clothes for resale. You can get the best bargains there." She patted Lilith's hand. "I'll give you the address, dear."

Kellen excused herself and went off to find Clark. She had had enough of the party and wanted to go home. She made her way through the crowd, but Clark had disappeared.

"Kellen!"

Someone was calling her name. She turned but saw no one she knew. Then, suddenly, she saw Garrett emerge from the crowd. She couldn't move. He was standing before her, a brilliant smile and sparkling blue eyes. Now he was bending over. She felt his lips brush her cheek and inhaled the faint smell of his subtle clove cologne. She closed her eyes and was instantly back in Paris. He took her hand.

"It's good to see you," he said.

Good to see me, she thought, my god, is that all he can say? "Garrett," she stammered. "Wh-when did you—"

"I just got here last week."

Last week! He's been here a week, and he didn't call. "I don't . . ." She smiled slightly, trying to recover her composure. She decided to plunge in. "When you called last month, I thought you were intending—"

"Something came up," he interrupted. "I couldn't leave London."

She forced her smile wider. "I understand. Business, with the newspaper."

"Kellen, why don't we get out—"

Before he could finish, Enid came over and slid her arm through Garrett's. "Well, you finally got here!" she said. "And leave it to you to immediately find the prettiest girl." She began to introduce Kellen.

Garrett interrupted politely. "We've met," he said, looking at Kellen. "We knew each other in Paris briefly."

"Such a small world!" Enid exclaimed. "You know, Kellen, Garrett's mother is an old friend of my family's. I've been trying to lure her over for a visit for years. I've had to settle for her son." She patted Garrett's arm. "Not that you are anything one must settle for, my dear man."

Kellen watched in amazement. Enid was actually flirting. She glanced around the room. Other women were staring at Garrett with open curiosity. A few people edged into the circle, including Clark. Enid made introductions. Garrett maneuvered through the small talk with complete assurance, occasionally conferring on Kellen a private smile. She was still in shock over seeing him and still angry with him for not calling. She watched him as he deftly played the conversational lobs. The crowd was charmed. Finally, simply to get his attention, she decided to join the game.

"So, Mr. Richardson," she said. "How do you like our city so far?"

"It's very beautiful," he said, smiling at her, understanding her ploy. "The people are very friendly. I feel at home here."

Smiles of appreciation all around. "Well, this is your home in a small way," Enid interjected. She glanced around at the others, smiling conspiratorially. "Garrett actually has roots here. He's a distant descendant of William Richardson, who, you'll all remember from your history books, was one of this city's most important founders."

Oohs and aahs. Enid glowed and clutched Garrett's arm. She was obsessed with San Francisco history. The only thing she liked more than tracing the lineage of a Victorian house was tracing the lineage of its inhabitants.

"William Richardson was an English seaman," Enid went on patiently, as if explaining to schoolchildren. "In eighteen thirty-five, he opened a business in Yerba Buena. Which, as we all know, became our wonderful city." She hugged Garrett, who was enduring all this with an ironic, dignified smile. "So we can truly welcome Garrett as a true San Franciscan."

Someone actually began to applaud. Kellen glanced at Clark. He was scribbling something in his little gold notebook. "Well, Mr. Richardson," she said to Garrett. "I hope you enjoy your stay here. Good night, everyone."

She turned, grabbing Clark by the sleeve. "Let's go," she whispered.

Clark protested as she dragged him over to a corner. "What's the matter with you?" he asked.

"I just want to get out of here," she said, staring at Garrett, still ensconced in the circle.

"But I want to talk to this Richardson guy. I can get a whole item out of him. The prodigal son—"

"I'll tell you all you want to know. Let's leave."

Clark pulled free of her arm. "I thought so! You know this guy, don't you—"

"I met him in Paris—"

"And?"

"And, what?"

"Well, from the way you two were looking at each other, you'd think . . ."

Kellen frowned. "Let's go."

"Kellen!"

Garrett came up behind them. "Where are you going?"

"This is a bore," she said, "I'm leaving."

"Then so am I." Garrett glanced at Clark, who simply handed him Kellen's stole with a smile. "We will talk later," Clark intoned to Kellen, and disappeared.

Garrett placed the stole over her shoulders. Without a word she turned, and he followed her out the door. The night was cool and damp but Kellen wanted to walk. They walked slowly along for several blocks, saying nothing.

"You're angry with me," Garrett said finally.

Kellen bit her lips. She didn't want to sound possessive. The one week they had shared in Paris was just that—one week of sex. Nothing more. "I expected you . . ." she began. Finally, she stopped and faced him. "You've been here a week."

"I got here a week ago, but I had to leave right away for Los Angeles. I have some business down there."

"But you called over a month ago—"

"Something came up. I couldn't leave London. Kellen . . ."

It began to drizzle. A couple dashed by them.

"That was weeks ago," Kellen said. Suddenly the dam inside her burst. "You were in L.A., for god's sake. It's only a couple hours away. A phone call away." Her dress was getting soaked, and she pulled her stole tight around her. "And now, you just show up tonight without warning." She stared at him. "Well, go on back to L.A. Go take care of your business or what—"

He grabbed her shoulders. "I came here to see you," he said. "To see you, dammit."

He pulled her to him and kissed her. It was a hard kiss. His coat was rough and wet against her skin. She raised her arms around his neck to grasp his wet hair. The rain became harder. When she finally pulled away, she was shivering.

"This is crazy," he said. He saw a taxi sitting at the corner and whistled. "Let's go to my hotel," he said.

In his room, they stripped off their wet clothes and made love quickly and hungrily. Then again, with slow and deliberate tenderness. The mad, unexplainable intensity that they had shared in Paris was still with them, burning brighter than before. At dawn, Kellen raised her head from Garrett's chest and stared at his face. His eyes were closed. She brushed her lips across his brow, and his hand moved languidly down her back. A meager gray light filled the room and two pigeons fluttered to life outside the window.

"How long will you stay?" she asked.

His hand paused on the small of her back. "Until I get what I came here for," he said softly.

Chapter
Twenty-four

❦ The news meeting ended, and everyone scattered back to their posts. Kellen drained the last of her coffee and began to gather up her papers. She felt Stephen's eyes on her and looked up. "You look tired," he said. "You've been pushing yourself pretty hard lately."

"I'm enjoying it, Stephen. You were right. It's good for me to learn this way." She rose to leave.

"Kellen, stay for a minute," Stephen said quickly. "I want to talk to you. We haven't had much chance to lately."

Kellen sat down slowly. She suspected Stephen wanted to ask her about Garrett. Since the opera party, she and Garrett had been nearly inseparable. Stephen had not once mentioned Garrett to Kellen, but his feelings emerged as a new coolness and hints that she seemed distracted at work. For the first time in her life, she felt the bond of friendship between herself and Stephen being strained.

"I've been meaning to tell you," he said. "You've done a good job these last couple weeks. You've got good instincts. About news."

"I come by them honestly." There was a long silence.

"I've been thinking," Stephen said. "Ed's going in the hospital next week. He'll be out for a month or more. It might be good for you to fill in as city editor."

She smiled eagerly. "You think I could handle it?"

"I'd help you." He paused. "Of course, it would mean longer hours. And your full attention here. No distractions."

Her smile faded. "You'll have it," she said evenly. There was another long silence. Kellen rose suddenly. "I've got some work to do," she said. "Anything else?"

"No, nothing." She left, but Stephen remained at the table, gazing at the newspapers scattered before him. There were copies of the *Times*, marked up with red ink from the editors' critique session. He picked up the feature section, turned to Clark's column and stared again at the photograph he had noticed earlier. It was a picture of Kellen and Garrett Richardson dancing. Stephen reread the column.

"Romantics are wondering which of our fair damsels would win the attentions of English press baron Garrett Richardson. Seems the baron only has eyes for a kindred soul, newspaper heiress Kellen Bryant. Do we sense a merger in the making?"

Stephen tossed the paper aside. Maybe this city editor stint will keep her away from Garrett, he thought. It will be just like the first day she came down to my office, asking me to teach her. It'll be just the two of us, working together.

A copyboy stuck his head in the door. "Paper, Mr. Hillman?" Stephen nodded, and the first edition of the *Times* was set before him with a heavy thud. Stephen reached out and touched the paper. He loved the way the paper came off the press, neat and fresh. It was warm, with a ripe, mossy-mechanical smell of paper and still-damp ink. He thought about how pleased Kellen was about the city editor assignment, and he felt slightly guilty. But I'm not only doing it for me, he thought. It's for her own good. And for the good of the newspaper. He knew Kellen so well. She was still the impetuous girl who fell in love so easily with everything in life. The thing with Garrett would pass. But the newspaper would not. It was always going to be the one constant, enduring thing in her life. For all her attempts to learn about the *Times*, that was the one thing she still did not understand. It was, he thought, perhaps the most important thing he could teach her.

He rose, picking up the *Times*. Some things, he thought, are meant to last.

Kellen stared at her desk. It was a mess, cluttered with papers, memos, unread newspapers, and a large stack of unanswered telephone messages. She sighed, giving in to the fatigue. Every day, she spent six hours in the newsroom and then went to her office to face more work. Lately, she had been neglecting the executive side of her double schedule, and she knew there were documents that awaited her signature alongside Ian's. But she just did not have the time or energy since she started working in the newsroom . . . or since Garrett had reentered her life.

Garrett . . . in a few hours, they'd be together, alone in the house in Carmel. They had decided to go down for the weekend, to get away from everything.

She sifted through the papers, looking for the report that she had promised Ian she'd read. He had been nagging her about a big move he wanted to make, and when she insisted on knowing the background, he begrudgingly had the report prepared for her. She intended to take it with her to Carmel. Finally, she found the report in a drawer and stuffed it in her briefcase. She turned to leave and saw Ian standing in the door, watching her.

"Did you read that report yet?" he asked.

She snapped the briefcase shut and pushed her hair out of her eyes. "I'll finish it this weekend."

"I told you two days ago, I need to make a decision. The buyer wants to move on this by next week. He won't wait. And I don't think we'll find any other sucker who wants a losing proposition in Seattle."

Kellen frowned. "Buyer. For what?"

Ian shook his head disparagingly. "For the *Seattle Dispatch*."

Kellen stared at Ian in disbelief. "You want to sell one of Daddy's papers?"

Ian lit a cigarette and blew a stream of smoke up toward the ceiling. "They're not Daddy's papers anymore," he said.

Kellen picked up the briefcase and started for the door. "We're not selling any of Daddy's papers," she said.

Ian grabbed her arm. "We have to. We need the money," he said. She tried to jerk her arm away, but Ian held it firmly. Finally, he let go. "Kellen, why don't you just let me handle things," he said. "This scheme of yours to try to absorb so much so fast . . . it just won't work. You can't make up in six months what it took Father years to teach me. I know this corporation. It's got some troubles right now, but if you'd just help me, I can pull things back together." He smiled slightly. "Don't worry about the newspaper. You've got other things on your mind."

She glared at him. "You can't make a move without me," she said. "And I'll never sell one of Daddy's newspapers. So don't even bring it up again." She started to the elevator.

"Have a nice time in Carmel," Ian called out.

Kellen closed her eyes and lay still on the bed, her breath still coming in short gasps. After a few moments, she opened her eyes and saw her hand, still grasping the tangled edge of the sheet. She released it and slowly moved her hands to where Garrett's head lay, low on her bare stomach. She began to stroke his hair. He kissed the inside of her thigh. After a moment, he moved upward, his chest warm and wet against her own. He kissed her, a soft, weary kiss.

She ran her tongue over her lips. "I taste like you."

"Us," he corrected.

They lay silent for a moment, then he raised his head to look at her. "We can't keep this up," he said.

"Oh, I don't know. You've been doing a pretty good job of keeping things up."

Garrett smiled. "That's a rather saucy remark for you."

"You bring out the worst in me."

Garrett laid his head back down. "I'm exhausted."

"Just think, they'll find our bodies stuck together, see our smiling faces, and wonder how we died. That will really give Enid something to talk about."

"I have to sleep."

"And if I want you again?"

"You haven't let me sleep since we got here."

"Now you're saying I'm forcing you to do this?"

He reached down to pull the sheet over them. "Yes," he whispered against her neck. "I have absolutely no free will in this matter. I will go on making love to you forever. Until we're both dead. But now, be quiet and let me sleep."

She closed her eyes and was soon asleep. She was awakened by the glint of the late afternoon sun reflecting off the ocean, pouring in through the large bedroom windows. She glanced around and saw Garrett sitting out on the deck. She put on a robe and went outside.

"It's late," she said. "You should have wakened me."

"You needed to sleep. You won't admit it, but you're exhausted."

"Don't flatter yourself," she laughed.

"You were tired before you even saw me. I could see it in your eyes when you picked me up last night."

She sat down on the edge of his chair, and he put his arm around her. She stared out at the ocean, breathing in deeply. "Maybe," she acknowledged, "but I'm fine now. Coming here always makes me feel good." She glanced at Garrett. "Your being here with me makes it perfect."

"Are you hungry? I can manage a fried egg or something."

"No, not yet." She rose. "I'll get dressed and we'll go for a walk. It's going to be a spectacular sunset."

The Carmel house was set on several acres of cypress trees, facing a cove with a long crescent beach, guarded on either side by rock jetties. Adam had bought the house for Elizabeth because it was so insulated from the outer world. That was precisely how Kellen felt now as she walked down the beach with Garrett. Here, she could forget the problems she had been carrying with her. When she was with Garrett, nothing else seemed to matter. The sexual attraction had progressed beyond the fury of lustful discovery. Now when they made love, she felt an almost mystical bond to him.

She glanced over at him as they walked. She had become so familiar with every physical detail about him. The square jut of his jaw, the slight crook of his nose, the texture of his heavy, black hair, the quizzical knit of his brows. She knew every plane and contour of his body. His tapering waist and powerful arms. The L-shaped pink scar on his lower back from a childhood accident. The fine, hard feel of his skin.

But she knew almost nothing about what was inside him. From the start, she had taken him purely at face value, never questioning who or what he was. Lately, she had thought of trying to get below the superficiality of their relationship. But she wasn't sure she wanted to know what was there. He was still a mystery, and she knew herself well enough to know that she was intrigued by the unknown. She was balanced atop a deliciously dangerous precipice, breathing the rarified air of romance. She wasn't sure she wanted to come down.

He reached over and took her hand, and she looked at him. The muscles in her pelvis still ached with the memory of him moving inside her. Sex. It had never been so consuming with any other man. But what would happen when that waned, as she knew it had to. Would there be anything there to replace it?

They had reached the south end of the beach. They climbed up the rocks and sat down. Below, on a small spit of sand, was a mother seal and three pups. They lay basking in the last rays of the sun, while out in the water, the snouts of other seals bobbed up and down in the kelp.

Kellen smiled. "The last time I was here with my father, I asked him if I could take a seal home."

"Did you come here often with your parents?"

"No, only a couple times."

The setting sun was turning the sky into liquid pastels. "Tell me about your family," Garrett said.

She looked at him, thinking the request was just a casual conversational ploy. After all these months, their talks seldom ventured beyond surface banter and playful, sexual sparring. But now, he seemed genuinely interested. She began slowly, telling him about growing up in the big house on Divisadero, about how, for a brief time, it had been a joyful place. Her recital gained momentum, and she told him, as honestly as her pent-up emotions would allow, about her mother's death and the scandal. She told him about Tyler, and about her feelings toward Ian. And she told him about her father, and how he had built his newspaper empire. Garrett listened without interruption. She hadn't intended to tell him so much, but it had flowed from her, simply and naturally. When she was done, she found she was unable to look Garrett in the eye. She felt suddenly very naked.

She stared out over the water. The sunset had deepened into a blistering bruise of reds and purples. "Now you know all about me," she said softly.

They sat silently for a few minutes. "Let's start back," he said finally.

They went back down the beach. "I've got something to tell you," Garrett said. "I've bought a house. In Tiburon."

She looked up at him in surprise. "But why?"

"Because I like it here and have decided to stay for a while. I suppose now, if I wanted to, I could look across the bay and see that monstrous white house of yours."

Kellen walked on, stunned. "Well," she said finally. "This should make you even more popular among the socialites. The Born-and-Raised will be pleased."

He stopped and held her shoulders. "What about you? Are you pleased?"

"Of course. You're very good at pleasing me, Mr. Richardson," she said lightly.

They walked on, Kellen thinking about his puzzling move. Surely he hadn't bought a home just to be near her. He had never made even an oblique reference to their future. He had always said he intended to remain in San Francisco only until his business was finished. He said he was researching investment possibilities in North America for his father's corporation and had spent the last six months commuting to Canada. Two months ago, he had finally purchased a newspaper in Toronto and was now considering buying a printing facility and mill in Vancouver. And he still made an occasional trip to Los Angeles, though he never mentioned what that entailed.

"Well, I'm not so sure I've pleased you this weekend," he said, interrupting her thoughts. "You've seemed preoccupied about something. What's the matter?"

Somehow Garrett had sensed her anxiety about Ian wanting to sell the Seattle paper. She walked on, staring at the sand.

"You know, we made a breakthrough back there when you told me about your family," Garrett said. "Tell me what's troubling you."

She found his remark strange. Could he also possibly want to delve below the surface of their relationship? She decided to tell him about her conversation with Ian, but stopped short of revealing her concerns about the state of the entire Bryant corporation.

"Is the Seattle paper financially sound?" Garrett asked.

Ian's report came to her mind. She had spent an hour reading it last night. It detailed how the *Seattle Dispatch* was facing strong competition from another newspaper and how it was suffering a loss of market share. "I think it has a few problems," she said.

"Then it might be a good move to unload it."

She shook her head slowly. "I couldn't. It was one of my father's first newspapers."

"It sounds to me like you want to hang on to it just because of your father. You're being sentimental," he said. "There's no room for sentiment in business."

It was almost dark, and they had reached the steps leading up to the deck of the house. She started up the steps ahead of Garrett then turned to face him. "You don't understand," she said softly. "It's part of my family. I'd never sell it. No matter what happened."

He looked up at her, then out at the now-dark ocean. "It's getting cold," he said. "Let's go in, and I'll make you some dinner."

Over dinner, conversation turned to one of their favorite subjects, the differences between British and American newspapers. Garrett told witty stories about the eccentric characters of Fleet Street and the trials of his newspaper's reporter who covered the royal family.

"That's all the poor bloke does," Garrett laughed, pouring Kellen a glass of wine. "But he treats his beat with utter gravity. Once, when Princess Margaret was vacationing in Mustique with a lover, our man rented scuba gear and tried to swim up to her villa. He nearly drowned."

"But you treat the royal family as serious news," Kellen said, shaking her head.

"Unquestionably. They always sell papers. The royals, sex, and murder—in that order. A couple years ago, we paid a photographer ten thousand pounds for a picture he took of Christine Keeler in her nightgown. He climbed atop a light pole outside her apartment. Ah, the Profumo Affair. Now there was the perfect story with all the elements: a sexy prostitute, a member of Parliament, spies, suicide. We haven't had one that good in years."

"You have no scruples," she murmured, smiling at him over the rim of her glass.

"I admitted that the very first night we met."

It was quiet except for the crackling of the fire and the muffled sound of the surf. Kellen's eyes held Garrett's. "Tell me about yourself," she said suddenly.

Garrett set down his glass. "There's nothing much to tell," he said, smiling easily. "My father is Sir Arthur Richardson—"

Kellen arched an eyebrow.

"Yes, a title. It sounds nice, but it doesn't mean much. It was a gift from a grateful prime minister, who liked my father's editorial policies." Garrett paused. "Actually, my father's story is very much like that of your father's. He started as a reporter on a newspaper in Leeds and worked his way up. He bought his first newspaper at thirty and built it into a string of them. He became quite wealthy." Garrett paused. "And then quite preoccupied with all that came with that. He sent me to the right prep school and then Oxford to prepare me for my future. In April, I turned thirty-four. I'm a Fleet Street publisher's son. His only son. Someday, I'll take up where he leaves off."

"That's a résumé, not a life," Kellen said.

"So you want the details, hmm?" He leaned back in his chair, hands behind his head, grinning. "I play the piano. I'm quite good. I wanted once to be a jazz pianist. I live alone in a town house in Redcliff Gardens, and my one regret in life is that when I was a boy I never had a dog. I like historical biographies, American football, Haute Brion wine, and older women who can make me laugh."

"But I'm a younger woman," Kellen said.

"I try to keep myself open to new experiences."

Kellen shook her head. "Why do I feel like I know you so well . . . without really knowing anything about you?"

"I tend to hold people at arm's length."

"You haven't mentioned anything about being married," she said playfully. "For all I know, you could have a wife or two stuck away somewhere."

He toyed with the stem of his glass. "I was married," he said, without looking at her. "When I was twenty. She was a presenter for the BBC, an anchorwoman, you'd call it." His face was curiously neutral. "We were married for two years. We had twins . . . boys."

Kellen's imagination conjured up a portrait of a pretty young woman on a television screen and two miniature, dark-haired replicas of Garrett. She felt a pang of envy.

"She was killed in a car accident in Wales," Garrett said. "We were going on a holiday. I was delayed in London, so she went on ahead with the boys. They were killed, too. Hit by a drunken lorry driver." He paused. "They told me they were killed instantly, that no one suffered. I've never been able to figure out how in the world anyone ever knows that."

Kellen sat in silent shock. "Garrett, I'm so sorry," she said finally.

A small, distant smile came to his face, and he reached out and took her hand. "A long time ago," he said.

A log fell into the fireplace, resounding in the quiet room and making Kellen jump, but she kept her eyes on Garrett's face.

"Well, I've certainly thrown a blanket over things," he said, his smile growing warmer. "Tell me something about yourself."

"You know all there is to know. I'm an open book."

"That I'll read, and reread and read again and never understand. Tell me a dirty little secret about your past."

She sensed his need for lightness. "Well," she began, "once, in Paris, I agreed to a blind date with this British fellow, a member of Parliament no less. The man turned out to be a grade-A stuffed shirt." She playfully intertwined her fingers in Garrett's. "You know how Brits can be."

"Indeed."

"When he came to pick me up, his first words to me were that I could expect no commitment from him. He was absolutely devoted to the wife, of course."

"Of course."

"But then he asked me to change into something sexier so he could parade me in front of his friends. So I changed, put on my leather coat, and off we went. When we got to the Lipp and he offered to take my coat, I told him I had nothing on underneath it. All night, he sat there staring at me, his face beet red, sweat dripping down his face. His friends thought he was having a heart attack."

Garrett laughed. "The French have a nasty word for your kind of woman . . . *une allumeuse*."

Kellen smiled. "Now it's your turn. Tell me something no one else knows about you."

"Let's go in to the fire first." They moved to the sofa near the fire.

"True confessions," she prodded.

He hesitated. "I'm adopted," he said. "That's the secret no one is supposed to know, not even me." When he saw her puzzled expression, he decided to go on. "My parents never told me," he said. "I found out the truth by accident when I was fifteen. I found some papers in my father's desk."

"And you never asked them about it?"

"I wanted to. But as I grew older, I realized they had some peculiar need to pretend it was otherwise. My mother was very concerned with appearances. I suppose she wanted to project the image of a perfect family, and I was needed to complete the picture. Even as young as I was, I somehow understood how important it was to her." He paused. "So I acted out my part, as they did theirs. It was, for all appearances, a perfect family."

Kellen was staring at him with what he knew was compassion but what he could not help but feel as pity, something he couldn't bear. So he smiled. "What would your Born-and-Raised think," he said, "if they knew the descendant of their precious seaman, William Richardson, was actually of unknown lineage?"

"I don't care what any of them think," Kellen murmured. She settled back into the crook of his arm.

Garrett stared into the fire, wondering why in the world he had told her about his adoption. He had never revealed it to anyone. Neither had he planned to tell her about Susan and the twins. He had not intended to give her more than the usual flippant answers he gave women when they began to probe. But something had made him want to tell her about himself, and it had all simply come out. The urge, he was sure, had risen only from the alchemy of the moment, the tangy night air, the wine, the lingering sexual aura, the lulling sense of comfort.

Giving away his secret, letting a woman venture close. He had not done that since Susan's death. It had been impetuous and, for a moment, exhilarating, even liberating. But now, he felt unprotected, and the urge to withdraw was potent. He could see himself falling in love with Kellen. And couldn't afford to get too close to any woman right now. Not now, he thought. There's too much to do.

His thoughts drifted to his most recent telephone conversation with his father. It had started amiably enough, but Garrett quickly realized the call was just an excuse for his father to check up on him. Even over the telephone, Garrett had heard the impatience in his father's voice. How are things going in Toronto? What are you doing in San Francisco? And, I think you should come home for a while so we can discuss this plan of yours. He was yanking his leash, and Garrett knew he'd have to go home to defend his plan anew. The fact was, his father was sixty-four and stubbornly refused to relinquish any real power to Garrett. And he obviously still did not trust him when it came to business.

Garrett thought back to two years ago, when he had first proposed to his father that they buy the Toronto newspaper. His father dismissed the idea, but Garrett had argued that a Canadian paper would establish a North American foothold from which the Richardson Newspapers could expand. His father reluctantly allowed Garrett to proceed.

Garrett had moved ahead quickly and confidently. For years, he had been looking for an opportunity to prove himself in his own right, and he was confident North American expansion was his way. Before even approaching his father, he had studied the Canadian market and readership habits. Then, he had researched the ailing Toronto paper and determined it would be the prime place to start. It was Arthur Richardson's money that had made the Toronto purchase possible, but it was Garrett's own ideas and ambitions that had put it into action.

It was as if he had spent his life preparing for such an opportunity. He had spent his youth and postuniversity years working on his father's newspapers. He had made it a point to observe the people on the street and learn what they liked to read about. He watched them on buses and listened to them in pubs. He knew what titillated and moved them. Garrett loved the newspapers, all the more so because he believed that Arthur Richardson had ceased to appreciate them. Over the years, his father had developed a strangely schizophrenic attitude toward the newspapers. On one hand, he ruled over them like a dictator. But, influenced by his wife, he was also increasingly embarrassed that his fortune had come from such a tawdry source, an attitude he assumed Garrett would adopt. But Garrett loved the tabloids precisely because of their negative status. He loved their utter commonness and never saw the sleazy stories as prosaic pulp. To Garrett, within the tabloids pulsed the passions and lifeblood of regular, everyday people.

A college friend, a psychologist, had once told Garrett his love of the tabloids represented a symbolic rebellion against his father's gentry airs. Garrett guessed the reason probably had more to do with his deep-seated curiosity about his true parentage. Plucked out of an orphanage at age two by Arthur and Helen Richardson, he had no idea who his real parents were and never would. Helen was as colorless as crystal, and it had always been easy for Garrett to fill in the void by conjuring up dreams of his real mother. She was, he was sure, just a shop girl—young, beautiful, passionate, and desperate enough to give up her infant boy so he might have a better life. But somehow, he had never been able to imagine his real father. Unlike Helen, Arthur was too real, too big, and he overshadowed everything, even daydreams.

Which was why the North American expansion plan had to work. Garrett knew that the only way he could get out from under his father's shadow was to find his own arena. That's what North America was. A new, bigger, better arena, one that was his alone for the taking.

But now, he was being summoned home. The red brick Georgian mansion with its expanse of green lawn loomed in his mind. It was Durdans, the country home in Surrey near Epsom where he had grown up. He could picture his father, standing in the drive, and he felt the usual mix of emotions—love, loyalty, and anger. Why can't he just leave me alone to make my own way? he thought.

Kellen stirred against his arm and draped her arm across his thigh. The press of her body immediately made him forget about his father and about going home. He closed his eyes, riding alternating waves of comfort and arousal.

I'm getting in too deep, he thought. I've got to stay focused on my plan. I can't afford to get too involved with her right now.

He rested his chin on her head, and he could smell her hair. Who are you kidding? he thought. The work is an excuse to keep her at arm's length, to keep from getting too close to someone again. You're just afraid. Afraid to take a chance again. Afraid you'll lose everything all over again.

She smiled up at him. "I'm getting sleepy," she said. "It must be getting late."

"We have to go back to San Francisco in the morning."

"Let's stay one more day."

"I can't. There are some things I have to tend to. The closing on the house in Tiburon for one. Then, I have to go back to London."

She sat up and stared at him, her eyes filled with questions. "When will you be back?" she finally asked.

"As soon as I can."

She reached up to the back of his neck and pulled him down to her lips. Her tongue teased him, and the memory of her body, taking him in and holding him, so warm and moist, was overwhelming. His fingers moved past the edge of her blouse and down to her bare breast. Her skin was warm to the touch. He slid off the sofa, pulling her closer to the fire.

"We're too close," she whispered, trying to edge away.

He pinned her arms above her head and opened her blouse. "I don't care," he said.

Chapter
Twenty-five

The lane wended its way beneath a canopy of ancient trees, the light rain and a trick of the afternoon light rendering the greens more luxuriant than Garrett remembered. The lane rose gently and opened onto a grassy knoll, and suddenly, like something emerging from the mist of Brigadoon, Durdans rose before him. The two-story, seventeenth-century Georgian home stood there in all its elegant simplicity.

Garrett pulled the car to a stop in the drive and got out, standing for a moment to look at the house in which he had grown up. He had not been back to Durdans in years, even though it was only an hour's drive from his flat in London. What business he had with his father was always conducted at the office in London. And despite his mother's pleas that he visit more often, Garrett avoided the house. He had happy memories of the place from his boyhood, of riding his horse, of trying to trap foxes in the woods, of hiding in the tunnel that had been built by the house's former occupant, Charles II, as a secret route to his mistress's house nearby.

But when he was fifteen, things had changed. The day he found out he had been adopted, everything had shifted slightly, making him feel like an outsider, and he never again felt as at home at Durdans as he had before. Shortly thereafter, he was sent off to school, then university. After that, there was always some convenient excuse not to go home.

This time, however, he couldn't avoid it. His father had specifically asked him to come to Durdans instead of meeting him in the city. "Your mother wants to see you, Garrett," he had said.

Garrett stood in the drive for a moment longer, staring up at the house's parapet and the arched entranceway. Then he got his bag from the car and went in. A maid greeted him, taking his bag and raincoat and telling him his parents were in the drawing room.

Garrett glanced toward the closed doors, then paused for a moment to look around him. The entrance hall looked different, testimony to his mother's one great passion in life, redecorating. He remembered it as a constant frenzy of activity in the house. No sooner had she finished the last of the thirty rooms than she would start anew at the other end of the house. Now, the entrance hall was done in a sunny yellow, which softened the austerity of the white marble floor. The side tables held artful arrangements of spring flowers and second-century roman busts. Tasteful, so tasteful, Garrett thought.

He straightened his tie and went to the drawing room doors, pausing to take a deep breath before opening them. His father and mother were sitting in chairs across from each other before the fireplace. They both turned, and his father got to his feet and came forward, extending his arm. It was always an awkward moment, neither man knowing whether to hug or shake hands. Arthur Richardson broke the stalemate with a firm handshake and clasp on Garrett's back.

"Good to have you home, son," he said briskly. As usual, Arthur Richardson was the picture of virile health, his dark hair now almost entirely gray, but his gray-blue eyes still steely with resolve. He was as tall as Garrett but outweighed him by thirty pounds. He always dominated a room, his presence seeming to suck the life-force out of other people.

Garrett looked at his mother, who sat in a chair, her demure flowered dress blending into the chintz. She had always been a quiet woman, monochromatic in her emotions and appearance. She had learned how to live in Arthur's shadow, much as a fern survives in the shade of a giant tree. Helen—Garrett had ceased thinking of her as "Mother" when he was fifteen—had come from a good family and had taken a social step down in marrying Arthur simply because he had money. She had devoted her marriage to remaking her husband into a paragon of respectability, and to all appearances, she had succeeded. Sir Arthur Richardson, standing in his elegant drawing room, seemed every bit the country squire. Certainly not the son of a Leeds shopkeeper. And certainly not the publisher of a chain of vulgar newspapers.

Garrett bent over to kiss Helen's soft cheek. "You're looking well, Mother," he said. It was a lie. Actually, she looked much older. She had never been a beautiful or even vibrant woman, but she had always had a certain sturdiness. Her hand, as it came up to cup Garrett's cheek, was cold.

"You look thin, Garrett," she said.

"I'm fine, really," he said, taking a seat.

"It's nearly teatime." She pushed a table buzzer. "I'll have food brought in for you." The maid appeared and before Garrett could protest, a tray was brought, laden with an ornate tea service, sandwiches, and French cakes.

His mother poured his tea, and he was vaguely touched that she remembered he liked it with extra cream. He took a sandwich to appease her. It was a tiny, artistic thing of trimmed crusts, cucumber, and a sprig of dill, and he smiled slightly, thinking that if he appeared on his mother's doorstep crazed with starvation, she would give him a cucumber sandwich on a silver plate. It was her idea of sustenance, to be given out in small and proper proportions. That was, he had come to realize years ago, how she had always been with her affection to him, too. It had taken him a long time to understand that it was simply her nature and had nothing to do with her love for him. Any overt displays of emotion made her uncomfortable.

By the time he was sixteen, Garrett had come to understand what a bloodless woman Helen was. The older he grew, the more he resented her for driving the life out of Arthur, and the more he resented Arthur for allowing her to do it. He wondered constantly why Arthur had made such a passionless match. Like all teenagers, he had found the thought of his parents having sex ludicrous. He wondered why they had not had children of their own, but, of course, it wasn't something to be brought up. He sometimes thought his adoption had come about simply because Helen's need for decorum precluded something as messy as procreation.

"So tell us about what you've been doing in the States, dear," Helen said.

Garrett glanced at his father, who was standing by the fireplace, his face blank. Most likely, Helen had no idea about the expansion plan; Arthur never told her anything about the newspapers, and she never asked. Garrett told her about his travels to Toronto and California, describing in general terms his purchase of the Canadian paper. His words took on more life when he described the beauty of San Francisco, and when he mentioned his house in Tiburon, Arthur looked at him in surprise.

"You bought a place? Well, I suppose it could be a good investment," he acknowledged.

"But surely you don't intend to live there," Helen said.

"I may," Garrett said. "I like San Francisco. I feel comfortable there." He had almost said "at home" but he caught himself.

Helen gave Arthur one of her looks, her mouth straightening

into a line, a signal of disapproval that she usually reserved for Arthur himself when his behavior lapsed. "Mother," Garrett said quickly, "I see you've redone the house. Why don't you show me the other rooms?"

Helen brightened. "Why, yes, I have, dear. Come along. I'll show you." Garrett glanced over his shoulder as he was led out of the drawing room. His father had unlocked the liquor cabinet and was pouring himself a tumbler of whiskey.

After dinner, Helen excused herself and went up to bed, saying she felt tired. Garrett followed his father into the library, where his father poured himself and Garrett a drink. Garrett waited for Arthur to bring up the expansion plan, ready to spring to its defense. But Arthur merely went on with small talk about his horses. He offered Garrett a cigarette, which he refused, and lit one for himself, taking a chair behind his desk.

"I thought you quit last year," Garrett said.

"I did. Don't tell your mother."

Garrett sank into the overstuffed sofa. Like nearly everything in the house, it was an old piece, newly covered in a rose chintz. A long-forgotten memory flashed into Garrett's head, of the time when he was nine, when he accidentally cut the sofa's upholstery with his pocket knife. Helen had not scolded him, but she had whisked the sofa out of the house. It returned a week later with a new skin of chintz. That was the way it had always been. Chocolate fingerprints on glass, muddy footprints on marble—no sooner did Garrett leave a mark than it was eradicated. No traces of normal boyish activity ever lasted long in Durdans.

Garrett watched as Arthur reached over and carefully tapped the ashes into a wastecan, there being no ashtray in the room. The gesture sent a spurt of old anger and sadness through Garrett. Neither would there be any traces of Arthur in Durdans, he thought.

"So," Arthur said, "tell me about Toronto."

Garrett tensed. "The transition will be rough initially, but I'm confident things will smooth out by the end of the year." He went on to tell Arthur in detail about the purchase aftermath. Arthur listened intently, giving his usual strong opinions and suggestions. When Garrett was finished, Arthur leaned back in his chair, smiling slightly.

"You know, when you came to me with this expansion plan, I thought it was a harebrained idea," Arthur said. "I thought it was just your excuse to loll around the States for a while, to get away from the old man."

Garrett said nothing.

"But I've been giving it some thought," he went on. "If our brand of newspaper can catch hold in the States, this could be a huge moneymaker for us."

Garrett could not hide his surprise. "I'm glad you see it that way, Father."

Arthur lit another cigarette. "In fact, things are going so well I'm convinced we should step up our plans to find properties in the States."

"I'm checking out several possibilities," Garrett said. "Getting some market surveys done, demographic studies of—"

Arthur interrupted with a chuckle. "Studies are for schoolboys! Instinct is what counts! What about this chain of papers in Los Angeles?"

Garrett fought back his embarrassment. "The Rotham chain," he said slowly. "I've had several talks with the owner. He's very interested in selling, and the price is right, but—"

"What?" Arthur prodded.

"I think it's too small an operation for our needs. And the *Los Angeles Times* is solidly entrenched. We wouldn't have a chance without committing huge amounts of capital."

"Too small, you say," Arthur paused. "What about that San Francisco–based chain you told me about? That didn't sound too small."

"It's not," Garrett answered. "Fifteen dailies in four western states, and other properties. Generally healthy, but several of the papers have revenue problems, including the flagship paper in San Francisco. During the last couple years, since the father, Adam Bryant, died, the papers have been stagnant, with cutbacks compromising their ability to compete in their markets. The family has been taking money out of its investment rather than putting it back in. And the San Francisco paper is an afternoon publication. Which, in the States at least, is bucking readership trends."

Arthur was quiet for a moment. "You've spent a lot of time looking into this, I take it."

Garrett finished his scotch and set the glass down on a side table. "Two years ago, when I first started searching for buy-out properties, this was the one I thought would be the best target. I had heard that Bryant's oldest son was mismanaging the corporation and that the three children did not get along. I thought they would be open to offers."

"So you went to San Francisco to study the situation," Arthur said.

"Yes," Garrett said slowly. "To study the situation."

"So? What have you found out?"

"That I was wrong," Garrett said. "The oldest son is willing, even eager to sell. But the daughter isn't. And one cannot make a move without the other legally. The third son has no say until he's twenty-one, about eight years from now."

Arthur frowned. "You're sure about the daughter?"

"I've talked to her," Garrett said. "I think she'd let the papers go to hell before she'd sell them."

"Not a good businesswoman."

Garrett smiled slightly. "Business has nothing to do with it for Kellen. She's a very sentimental woman. She believes that the newspapers her father created should remain a family concern, regardless of the fact that her older brother is running them into the ground, and she's too inexperienced to know how to stop him." He paused. "Despite the illogic of it, part of me understands her point."

Arthur took a gulp of his drink. "Sounds to me like you're the one who's sentimental, as you say," he said.

Garrett's smile faded. "She believes that the newspapers we publish are no better than pornographic rags."

Arthur didn't blink at the insult, but Garrett saw the spots of color come to his cheeks. Arthur took another swig of whiskey. "So what do you propose to do now?" he asked.

"Keep looking for the right property," Garrett answered. "There's a daily in New York—"

"New York? Good lord, no." Arthur waved his hand in dismissal. "Too expensive, too unstable. I can't stand that city. Unpredictable, uncivilized."

Garrett waited, sensing that Arthur was edging too close to inebriation to risk an argument. There was, he had learned in recent years, no point in discussing anything with Arthur when he had had too many whiskeys.

"San Francisco," Arthur said. "That's where we must focus our energy."

"It won't do any good," Garrett said slowly.

"Everyone has a price, Garrett," Arthur said. "All you have to do is find it. Talk to the son. It sounds like he's the key. I'm sure there's a way to bring the girl down from her lofty little perch. 'Pornographic,' indeed."

Garrett was silent. Arthur yawned suddenly. "The Bryant chain is our best bet, Garrett, a ready-made little western empire. All those studies of yours say so. And so do my instincts. I want those newspapers.'' He got to his feet, a bit unsteadily. ''Well, I think I'll go on up to bed now.''

Arthur went to the door and then stopped, turning back to Garrett. ''Breakfast's at eight. Sleep well.''

Garrett looked up at him. ''Good night, Father,'' he said. Garrett remained slumped in the sofa. He heard his father's footsteps going up the stairs and the closing of a door. He was filled with a quiet, simmering anger. Right from the start, his father had dismissed the North American expansion plan. But now, he was not only endorsing it, he was all but taking it over, calling the shots and effectively reducing Garrett again to little more than a glorified minion.

This is my plan, Garrett thought, and I have to keep control of it.

He sat there for another half hour as the quiet of the house enclosed him. He leaned his head back on the sofa. The long flight to London and the drive to Epsom was finally catching up to him. He closed his eyes, blotting out his parents and his surroundings. His thoughts returned to Kellen. He could feel her, smell her, and taste her—just as he could the crisp, salty air of Carmel. Every muscle in his body ached to get back to her and California. But now there was a new conflict to deal with. He knew his father was right about the Bryant chain—it was the ideal property. But he also knew how strongly Kellen felt about not selling.

Maybe Father is right about her, too, Garrett thought, maybe she can be convinced to sell. Maybe she and I could . . .

He paused, opening his eyes. Now who's being sentimental, he thought. You're plotting out a future, and you haven't even finished the business at hand. One step at a time. Focus on the newspapers. Show Arthur you can do it. Keep to the plan. Keep to the plan.

He rubbed his eyes and got to his feet. He glanced down and noticed his glass sitting on the table in a ring of water. He looked to the desk and saw the other empty glass where his father had placed it—in a silver coaster. Garrett picked up his glass and instinctively reached out to wipe the table, but it was too late. A faint gray ring was now burned into the old mahogany.

Garrett placed the glass on the desk blotter and went upstairs to bed.

The weekend passed slowly, as time always did at Durdans. Garrett tried his best to occupy himself, but in a short time, he was restless with boredom. There was no more need for his presence;

Arthur had obviously given him his orders. By Sunday afternoon, Garrett was looking forward to the drive back to London. He had a ticket in hand for the Monday morning flight to New York.

Just after tea, Arthur surprised him by asking him if he wanted to take a walk. They left the house, striking out over the grounds and heading toward the woods. The day was chilly and gray, and Arthur was done up in a dapper tweed jacket and cap. He carried a silver-headed walking stick, which he jabbed into the soft earth at precise intervals as they walked along silently, side by side.

They entered the soft gloom of the woods, passing under the branches of the old trees and over the graves of racehorses, buried there by a former prime minister, Lord Rosebery, one of Durdans' previous owners. They stopped occasionally at one tree or another, for Arthur to point out the plaques put there by the people who had planted the trees—Queen Mary, Empress Alexandra Feodorovna of Russia, and all the other royals who had been houseguests during Durdans' illustrious history. Garrett had seen the plaques before, but he had never paid them much heed. Now, as he listened to Arthur read each one, he realized he had been wrong about his father's lack of attachment to the old house. It had been the first thing Arthur purchased when his fortune was assured. He had been barely thirty at the time, and a year later he had married Helen. Garrett glanced over at Arthur, wondering if his father harbored any regrets, wishing he felt comfortable enough to ask him.

They emerged into the open. Arthur paused and pointed the tip of his stick toward a sweeping willow tree. "That," he said, "was started from a cutting of a tree growing near Napoleon's grave at St. Helena."

"I didn't know that," Garrett said.

"There are a lot of things you don't know about this place."

They walked on, down the hill to the lane. Being outdoors had had a calming effect on Garrett. He had not walked around the grounds since he was a teenager, and now he found himself unexpectedly filled with a deep sense of nostalgia.

"This makes me think of derby day," he said quietly, glancing at Arthur. "Remember how we used to come down here and walk to the race with the crowd?"

Arthur nodded. "I carried you on my shoulders. I was afraid you'd get swept away."

They walked on. "The first time you took me to the derby, I was eight," Garrett said. "You gave me a quid to bet."

"And you got so angry because they sent you away from the

window, saying you were too young," Arthur said, with a smile.

"My horse won," Garrett said, smiling.

"Ah, you were a precocious little gambler. You had an uncanny ability to pick the winners."

They paused for a moment, and Arthur looked up at the gray sky. "It's getting late. We'd better start back," he said, turning around.

They began their walk back toward the house.

"You know, Garrett," Arthur said after a long silence. "The expansion plan. It's a damn good idea." Arthur didn't look up, and the walking stick, poking at the ground, didn't miss a beat. "I'm quite proud of you."

The words so surprised Garrett that for a moment he wasn't even sure what he had heard. In all the years he had worked at his father's side, he had seldom heard such direct praise, especially in recent years when Garrett's own struggle for power had seemed to cause Arthur to cling to his throne more tightly.

Garrett found himself staring at the stick as they walked. "Thank you, Father," he said. "I appreciate your confidence. I won't disappoint you."

They walked on for a while, saying nothing.

"How long are you staying?" Arthur asked.

"I have a flight to New York in the morning."

Arthur paused, turning to look at him. "Your mother and I would like it if you'd stay on a while, Garrett."

"I have to get back to San Francisco, Father."

Arthur looked at Garrett, then up at the house, then back to Garrett. "I understand that you've developed attachments there," he said. His fingers, grasping the walking stick, flexed. "But it's been some time since you've been at Durdans, and we . . . I was hoping we'd have some time together. Go riding, perhaps."

It was quickly growing dark, but Garrett could see the hopeful look in Arthur's eyes.

"Of course, Father," he said. "We'll go riding."

They stood looking at each other for a moment, each knowing that it would not happen. Then they turned and started up the hill and soon the house came into view, its lights warm in the gray dusk.

Chapter
Twenty-six

Looking back, no one could say when it was that the quiet neighborhood of old Victorian homes near Golden Gate Park became the mecca for a new culture. It had started slowly, with just a few little shops with strange-sounding names. A boutique called House of Richard began selling Mexican sandals and ponchos. A place called the Mnasidika stocked mod clothing. And Blind Jerry's hawked health foods. But it was a coffee shop on Hayes Street called the Blue Unicorn that, by word of mouth, became the unofficial community center. There, a person could find a good chess game, a piano to play, free secondhand clothes, or a sagging sofa for a quiet hour of reading or contemplation. The owner began to issue handbills spelling out the Unicorn's philosophy: "We have a private revolution . . . a striving for realization of one's relationship to life and other people."

Something strange was happening. When word finally made it across town to the *San Francisco Times*, a reporter was dispatched to the Unicorn. He came back overflowing with adjectives about a "bohemian culture blooming in our midst." The wire services picked up the *Times*'s story, and soon other newspapers across the country were printing stories about the little nonconformist coffeehouse. And the quiet neighborhood of old Victorian homes was never the same. By the spring of 1966, the Unicorn's bohemian-rooted philosophy had grown into a rough consensus of new subculture. And its geographic heart was the intersection of two streets whose names had become synonymous with a new life-style—Haight-Ashbury.

Haight-Ashbury had its own art, led by avant-garde theater and mime groups. It had its own music, led by the Grateful Dead, whose rambling Victorian house had become a shrine for pilgrim musicians. It had its spokemen, people like author Ken Kesey and

Timothy Leary. It had its own economy, based on drugs. It had its own fashions, slogans, language, and its own unique spirit.

Soon, thousands of young people, a motley army of dropouts and runaways, were pouring into the Haight in cars and vans, on motorcycles, and by busload from the Greyhound Terminal on Seventh Street. They were barefoot and bewildered, their clothes still fresh from stores in Kalamazoo or Cleveland. Eventually, they found their way to Hippie Hill in Golden Gate Park, or to the Diggers' Free Food truck, parked under the eucalyptus trees in the Panhandle.

The curious straights and pretenders came, too. High school students from Burlingame would park mom's stationwagon just outside the perimeters, ditch their shoes, and walk barefoot into paradise. Faces from the society pages would wander through the hip stores. And then came the tourists. Every hour, Gray Line tour buses made the journey from the downtown hotels out to the "Hashberry." It was called "The Hippie Hop," six bucks a head. Operators hyped it as "a safari through psychedelia . . . the only foreign tour within the continental United States."

It was a grand, irresistible party. No admission fee, no questions asked. And everyone was invited.

Tyler stood, leaning up against a building in front of the Psychedelic Shop, taking it all in. He had been standing in the same spot for an hour, just watching the parade. He felt so good this morning. It was a beautiful spring day, and the sun was warm on his shoulders. From somewhere nearby came the soporific sound of the new Beatles' song "Strawberry Fields." And the joint he had smoked an hour ago had left a pleasant, lingering high. He felt the back pocket of his jeans. The other joint was still there if he needed it. He hardly ever smoked the stuff, but he liked having it on hand to give away. It was a sure-fire way of making friends.

He pushed his pink-tinted wire rims up on his nose. He didn't need the glasses, but he wore them because they were part of the look. The look was important: flare-bottomed secondhand jeans, an old fatigue jacket, and beads hanging over his bare chest. He used to have a pet tarantula that he let wander over his shoulders, just to see the looks on people's faces. The spider met its untimely demise one night in the crush of a Beau Brummels concert at the Fillmore. No one ever guessed he was only thirteen. He told everyone he was sixteen, and here in the Haight, no one ever bugged him. In the Haight, everyone was gloriously free to do his own thing.

Tyler brushed his hair out of his eyes. More than once, someone had commented on his looks, his pale blue eyes, his handsome features, and his tall, slender body. But his shoulder-length corn-silk hair was his best feature. Girls envied him for it. Even guys noticed it. If you were a chick, I'd go after you myself, his friend Katz joked all the time.

Katz. He was supposed to be here by now. Last night, Tyler had given some money to him because he had claimed he could lay his hands on some LSD. Since the state had made LSD illegal last fall, it had been getting harder to come by, but Katz had said he could get some Owsley tabs, the best around. Tyler had never tried acid before, and the idea scared him, but Katz promised him it would be fine. "It'll open you to the unity of mankind, the wholeness of being," Katz had said. Katz was always sponging off people—dope, money, food—and Tyler was always there to oblige. It was a small price to pay, Tyler thought, for Katz's friendship. Katz was nineteen, with an aura of street-wise glamour. He was the lead guitarist for the Katzenjammer Kids, a local band, and was going to be the next Jerry Garcia.

Tyler sighed and turned to stare at the window of the Psychedelic Shop. In the window, a girl sat in a folding theater seat, staring off into space with her mouth slightly agape. The window was meant as a joke, a live display that was supposed to mirror the soul of the street. Tyler turned away from the girl's disconcerting eyes and scanned the street. Katz was not going to show. Tyler stuck his hands in his jacket and sauntered off toward the *Oracle* office.

The *Oracle* had been launched nine months ago as an alternative newspaper to serve the Haight community. The first issue had been a disaster, with recycled political articles about the Japanese WWII internment camps and the joys of masturbation. Through a printing trick, inks were blended together to give the paper a rainbow effect, and as each issue came off the press, it was sprayed with jasmine perfume. The *Oracle* was the poetic and philosophical voice of the Haight. Eventually, the paper hit its stride, but it was in perpetual financial crisis, sputtering along on donations by the Grateful Dead, rock impresario Bill Graham, marijuana dealers, and whoever had extra cash.

Tyler had drifted into the *Oracle* office several months ago by accident, and after hanging around the periphery, he fell into the job of running errands. It made him feel as if he were part of something big and important. It was a place to go after school, something to do. He couldn't stand going home to the big gloomy house on

Divisadero. With Kellen and Ian gone most of the time, it felt like a mausoleum. Often, he stayed instead at Katz's place, an old Victorian on Pine Street that Katz shared with fifteen other people. It had a funky ambiance, with faded leather wallpaper, window seats and stained-glass windows; and it was filled with music, dirty dishes, and strangers making love on mattresses on the floor.

Tyler pushed open the door of the *Oracle* office, and went over to Chas, the corpulent, balding man who was in charge of printing and distribution.

"Hey, man, what's up?" Tyler said.

"Oh, Tyler. How's it going?" He returned to his task of counting bundles of *Oracle*s.

"New issue?" Tyler asked. He waited, hands stuffed in his jeans, but Chas ignored him. "Any good?" Tyler ventured.

Chas grunted. Tyler reached over to pick up one of the papers. "Hey, man, you're screwing up the count," Chas said.

Tyler threw it down. He sighed and looked around for someone to talk to, someone to hang out with.

"Hey, Tyler!"

Tyler spun around. It was one of the editors, Nat Musial. "C'mere, I want to talk to you."

Other than a quick hello, Musial never bothered to talk to him. This must be about the poems I gave him, Tyler thought, with rising excitement. Musial retrieved some papers from his desk. "These are pretty good," Musial began. "A little bleak, but good. But we've got more poetry than we can handle right now." He held them out. "I wanted to make sure you got them back." Tyler took them. "No hard feelings?" Musial asked with a smile.

"No. 'Course not." Tyler turned to leave, then stopped. "Look, Nat," he began, "I really want to do something around here. I want to be a real part of the *Oracle*." Tyler paused. "If I can't write . . . well, there must be something I can do."

Musial pursed his lips. "Well, there is one thing—"

"What? Anything! You name it!"

Musial let out a small sigh. "The rent. It's overdue again. If you could cover it again until this issue gets—"

"Sure! You got it!" Tyler said with a big smile. "I'll bring it in tomorrow!"

"Thanks, man. We really appreciate it." Musial shifted from one foot to another. "Oh, by the way, if you haven't got anything to do right now, Chas could use an extra pair of hands on the street today."

Tyler nodded and started to leave. "Hey," Musial called out.

"You wanna catch Joplin at the Fillmore tonight? I can probably sneak you in."

Tyler knew Musial was only tossing him a bone to make up for the money, but it was going to be a great concert. Tyler grinned. "Yeah, thanks."

"Great. Meet me outside at nine. Thanks again, Tyler. Don't know what we'd do without you."

Tyler checked in with Chas, who gave him an armload of *Oracles*. Out on the street, Tyler halfheartedly hawked the papers to the tourists and Haight denizens, thinking about the poems stuffed in the back pocket of his jeans. They were garbage. He knew that. Musial was just bullshitting him, trying to make him feel better so he would cough up some more money. Musial was one of the few people who knew his family was rich, and this was the third time Musial had hit on him. But what did it matter? The money was nothing to him. There was plenty of it, what with the monthly $1,000 trust fund allowance. And better that it go to something worthwhile like the *Oracle*. He was glad he could help out his friends. He thought suddenly of Kellen. She had started monitoring his allowance and was getting bossy about what he did, calling to make sure he wasn't skipping school, telling him to stay away from the Haight. He didn't understand it. For years, all during the times his father was sick, no one had cared what he did. It had been a succession of nannies and governesses. And now Kellen was trying to play mother.

What a joke, he thought. She just feels sorry for me because I never had a mother in the first place.

He walked along the street, clutching the *Oracles*. He was thinking now of his mother, and as usual, he could see nothing in his mind but a maddeningly ephemeral, faceless woman. No one had ever spoken of her, certainly not his father. There were no pictures, no memories, nothing. She was like a ghost—dead, but still strangely alive. He had heard the rumors about her, had heard the word "whore" before he even understood what it meant. Two years ago, he had finally gotten up the courage to ask his father about her. His father, by then very ill with cancer, had said he would tell him about her someday. Someday . . . then it was too late. The only thing left to do was to find her himself, but he had no idea how to begin. He didn't even know her name. Finally, he found out about Sally Stanford, but when he went to the stone mansion on Pine Street, he found it had been converted into apartments. He stood on the sidewalk, staring up at the windows. Even now, once in a while, he still walked by it.

His mother. Did she have blue eyes like his? Was she fat or thin? Where did she go? Why did she abandon him? He was filled with hate and an aching, yearning need to love her.

Tyler squinted up toward the sun. No point in dwelling on it, he thought, no point at all. He was alone, but he could take care of himself all right. He didn't need anyone, especially not Kellen. There had been a short time, right after Adam died, when Kellen seemed to show an interest in him. But then she got involved with the newspaper. And now there was that English guy she hung out with. She only cared about herself.

Tyler looked up and down the street, searching for a familiar face. A motley parade trudged by, couples locked arm in arm, young men toting guitars and duffel bags on their backs, barefoot children, barking dogs. No one looked in Tyler's direction.

Well, screw her, he thought sullenly. Screw everyone.

He had a plan. In five years, when he was eighteen, he'd take off and really be free. No one, including Kellen, could tell him what to do then. He'd take some money and split. Get away and see the world. Maybe go off to India with Katz. Tyler reached into his pocket and pulled out the poems. He looked at them for a moment, then crumbled them into a wad and threw it into the gutter. He could hear someone playing a tambourine. Up past Stanyan Street, on the edge of Golden Gate Park, he could see a crowd gathering. Something was going on. Something always happened in the Haight if you waited long enough. He retrieved the joint from his pocket and lit it. The sweet smell of the grass mingled with the jasmine perfume of the *Oracle*s and, after a few minutes, Tyler was feeling fine again.

"Hey, here it is!" he called out to a passing car, holding the paper aloft. He enjoyed the look the old lady in the Buick gave him. "Get your genuine hippie souvenir!"

Yes, he was feeling fine. And tonight, he'd be feeling even better. He'd meet Katz and his friends from the *Oracle* at the Fillmore. He'd open himself to the wholeness of being. He tossed the *Oracle*s into a trash bin and went off in the direction of the music.

The editors gathered in a conference room near Stephen's office for the final news meeting of the day. Stephen took his place at the table. Kellen wasn't there, and he hid his disappointment by pretending to read the news budget.

"Okay, let's get started," said Ray, the managing editor, as the others settled in. "International?"

A thin man in glasses cleared his throat. "Well, Nasser's still threatening Israel. The War Crimes tribunal in Stockholm has found the U.S. guilty of systematic bombing of Vietnam civilians. And Russia's showing off a new atom smasher. Got good art on that." He tossed a wire photo on the table, but no one bothered to pick it up.

"National/state?" Ray said without looking up.

"We have that peace march in New York, seventy thousand people showed up," another man said. "Pretty good story from our own guy, with wire art. And a good feature from the Oakland bureau about this new Black Panther party that's forming."

Ray looked at the photos and handed them to the news editor. "Hate to put New York on the front, but this might be it," he said. "Unless local can save us." He looked up. "Who's supposed to be here from city desk? Where's Kellen?"

Blank faces and shrugs. "Let's skip to sports," Ray said with a frown.

"We got the Giants at the Stick tonight, with a side bar on how the wind's been causing more problems than usual. Also, a good featch on Mickey Mantle. He's still looking for homer number five hundred. Oh yeah . . . Muhammed Ali was indicted today in Houston for draft evasion."

"What are you guys doing with that?" Ray said. "Give it to one A."

Kellen burst into the room, muttered an apology, and slid into her seat. "We'll come back to local later," Ray said, glancing at her. "Let's go on to women's."

The young assistant from the women's page looked up. "We have a profile of that woman Elvis married last week, Priscilla Beaulieu, with some nice photos." She handed them around the table to a few lewd remarks. "And we have the Haight feature. But Kellen thinks it's worth front page."

All eyes turned to Kellen, and a few people looked determinedly bored. Many people on the staff were getting tired of the Martian Chronicles, as the ongoing coverage of the Haight scene had come to be called. The paper had been covering the story sporadically since 1965, but finally Kellen convinced Ray it was necessary to create a small task force of reporters and editors to cover the phenomenon.

Ray gave Kellen her cue: "Okay, what's new from the war zone? Gimme the news first, then the feature."

Kellen glanced at her legal pad. "Muni is thinking about rerouting the buses near the Haight because of the traffic congestion.

That old bar, the Golden Cask, just reopened as a pizza place called Lee, Sam and Dick, but the city's upset about the sign because all you can see are the initials LSD.''

"Shit. That used to be a good bar," the sports editor muttered.

"We have a bust of a Methedrine lab in Pacific Heights," Kellen went on. "Cops are worried about a new psychedelic called STP that's supposed to keep you stoned for three days. Half of the psychiatric beds at General are already filled with toxic drug reaction cases."

"Is that all?" Ray asked in a beleaguered voice.

"No, we're getting about three hundred new arrivals every day, and the Juvenile Authority is thinking of turning the gym at Polytech High School into an emergency shelter for runaways. And it was just announced that San Francisco now has the highest rate of venereal disease in the country." Kellen paused. "One last thing. The board of supervisors is meeting today to approve the mayor's resolution to officially declare hippies unwelcome in San Francisco."

"They're a little late, aren't they?" someone muttered.

"God, I'll be glad when this is all over," Ray said.

"The worst is yet to come," Kellen said. "The publicity's just begun. This week, we've got writers in town from the newsmagazines, *Playboy*, *National Review*, and the *London Observer*. That exploitation movie *The Love-Ins* is coming out soon, and Dick Clark's due in to start filming *The Love Children*.'' She paused for a breath. "And now the hippies have proclaimed this the Summer of Love. God knows how many more kids that'll attract. We may have about seventy-five thousand people living in the Haight by fall."

Everyone fell quiet. "Anything light?" Ray asked.

Kellen held out a photo. "Somebody painted this fire hydrant up on Nob Hill in psychedelic colors."

"Send the photographer back to get it in color."

"Can't," Kellen said. "Fire Department already repainted it white."

"The Maiginot Line holds," someone muttered.

Ray sighed. "Okay, use it. And put it on the wire." He grimaced. "We must feed the beast its daily meal of happy-hippie-news. Speaking of which, what's this feature you guys were talking about?"

"It's the 'I Was A Hippie' series," Kellen said. "The reporter lived there undercover for a month, but he came back the other day and said he didn't want to write an exposé. He's turned into a sympathizer. But we're working on him." She glanced at Stephen. He was smiling and shaking his head.

"Well, I guess we'll have to ride out this wretched drama," Ray said and turned to Stephen. "Any suggestions, boss?" Stephen gave some opinions on story play, and the meeting was adjourned. Kellen and Stephen walked out together.

" 'I Was A Hippie'?" Stephen said, still smiling. "Are the readers ready for that?"

"Clark wanted to do it. I told him he was too old." They went back to Stephen's office. "Mind if I hide out here for a minute?" she asked.

"You seem to like being city editor," Stephen said.

"I do," Kellen said, looking out at the city room. "It's going to be hard to go back upstairs." She paused. "I couldn't have done it without you. You taught me a lot."

Stephen thought briefly about asking her to go to dinner. "Well, it was easy," he said finally instead. "We have the same ideas about the *Times*. We work well together."

She let the comment hang in the air. "Being publisher is another game. I'm afraid of making the wrong moves."

"You've made some good ones already. You stopped Ian from selling the Seattle paper. And you've kept him off my back about the suburban operation. I appreciate that."

Kellen held Stephen's eyes for a moment, then looked away, out to the city room. She rose. "I've got to get back to work. I have to go over some budget cuts for the Seattle paper later." She smiled slightly. "I'm dreading it. It's like trying to read Greek."

"Want some help?" Stephen asked on impulse.

Her smiled widened. "Come on upstairs at six. I'll order in some Chinese."

By eight, Kellen and Stephen had finished the budget work. Kellen leaned back in her chair and stretched. "Thank god, that's done," she said. "The cuts weren't as bad as I thought they'd be. You trimmed the fat so painlessly."

"It won't be painless for the staff," Stephen said. "You really should go up there yourself to give them a vote of confidence. Your father was very good about visiting the other newspapers in the chain. Ian's never bothered. And it might help you pinpoint the problems there."

She massaged her neck. "That's a good idea. I'll go as soon as someone invents a forty-eight-hour day."

The phone rang. She knew it was probably Garrett. He was still in London and usually called her between eight and nine. She always looked forward to hearing his voice; it was a quick fix to relieve her longing. But she felt awkward with Stephen in the room. Finally, she answered the phone. She was surprised to hear Ian's voice.

"I've been trying to find you," he said tersely. "Our little brother has gone and gotten himself in trouble."

"Tyler? What's wrong?"

"Who knows? Somebody called here about fifteen minutes ago and said Tyler was freaking out. That was the term he used . . . freaking out. Said somebody better come and get him."

"Why didn't you do anything?" Kellen asked.

"I'm getting ready to go out," Ian said peevishly. "Besides, the kid's a brat. He slums around with those degenerates and then expects us to come bail him out when he gets in trouble. This will teach him a lesson."

"Where is he?"

"That Fillmore dump."

Kellen hung up and turned to Stephen, who when he saw her face, got to his feet. "I've got to go," Kellen said, going to the door. "Tyler's in trouble."

"I'll drive you," Stephen said.

At the Fillmore's entrance, Kellen pushed her way through the line, Stephen close behind. Someone said that Tyler was upstairs in a bathroom. Kellen ran up the stairs and came to an abrupt stop at the door.

Tyler was crouched in the corner of a stall, his eyes wide with terror. He was muttering to himself incoherently and swatting at his body frantically. A thin young man was trying to pull Tyler to his feet as a crowd watched in deadpan curiosity. Suddenly, Tyler let out a scream. "They're all over me! They're all over me! Get them off!"

"What, man, what—?" the thin young man asked.

"Katz! Help me! Spiders! All over me . . . get them off! Oh god, get them off!"

Kellen was immobilized by the sight. Stephen started toward Tyler, but suddenly, a burly man pushed by them and went into the stall. "What's going on?" he demanded. He stared at Tyler, now curled into a ball in the corner, whimpering. "Hey, he looks like he's underage."

"Oh no," Katz said, "he's eighteen. He'll be fine."

Suddenly, Kellen pushed forward, shoving them aside. "He's

thirteen!'' she said. "He's just thirteen!" She took Tyler by the arms. "Tyler, it's me, Kellen. What's wrong?"

When he didn't answer, Kellen looked up at the young man. "What did he take?" she demanded.

"Some acid. But I don't know how much—"

"You gave him drugs? He's a child!" she screamed at him. Kellen cradled Tyler in her arms. Suddenly, his head lolled to one side, and his eyes rolled back in his head. Stephen knelt down to take Tyler's pulse. "Someone call an ambulance!" he cried out.

At the hospital, Kellen stayed by Tyler's bed. Hours slipped by, but Tyler remained in a light coma. Stephen stayed with her through the night. At dawn, Kellen was still sitting there, just staring at Tyler. The look on her face was one of utter disconsolation.

"I know what you're thinking," Stephen said finally. "It's not your fault."

Kellen continued to stare at Tyler. After a minute, tears began to fall silently down her face. "I should have been there for him," she whispered. "I should have been there, but I was too busy. Now it's too late."

Stephen stared at Kellen, puzzled. "The doctor says he'll be okay. It's not too late." Then he understood suddenly that she had lapsed into thinking about her father's death. He pulled Kellen into his arms. "It wasn't your fault," he said softly. "It wasn't your fault."

She looked at him, her eyes filled with guilt, then back at Tyler. "I'll take care of him," she said. "I promise. . . ."

Three days later, when Tyler came out of the coma, Kellen was at his bedside. Slowly, his eyes focused on his surroundings and then on her. He looked lost.

"You're in the hospital," she said. "You took some drugs and . . . you've been here three days."

He turned his head away and shut his eyes.

"Do you remember?" she asked gently. There was a long silence, broken by the clatter of a cart in the hall.

"What are you doing here?" Tyler said in a hoarse whisper. He was staring at the wall, refusing to look at her.

There was a despair in his voice that frightened her. "I'm here because I care about you, Tyler," she said. "That's why I came and got you that night."

He stared blankly at the far wall.

"You don't believe me, I know," she said. "I've never given

you much reason to.'' She reached out and took his limp hand. ''I know how you feel—like we're strangers almost. But we—''

''Go away,'' he whispered.

She waited, hoping he would turn to face her, but he wouldn't. ''You're my brother,'' she said finally. ''You're all I've got.'' She paused. ''Please, Tyler. I love you.''

Tyler squeezed his eyes shut.

''Please . . . give me a chance to prove it,'' she said.

He still refused to turn away from the wall. But Kellen felt his fingers tighten slightly around her hand.

Chapter
Twenty-seven

After the episode at the Fillmore, Kellen made an effort to spend more time with Tyler. She realized that, after so many years, a closeness with him was too much to expect, but she hoped to at least win his trust. The overdose had frightened Tyler so greatly that he agreed to Kellen's suggestion to get counseling. And though, after a month, it was too early to tell if it was having a positive effect, Tyler at least had stopped hanging out in the Haight, and his attendance at school had improved. But still, he remained wary of Kellen's attempts at affection.

Tyler was so needy, Kellen often thought, as if he were emotionally starved. Looking back on how he was raised, it was easy to see why. Adam had given Tyler his name and affection, but he had not given the boy a real sense of love, at least not the kind she had gotten. It was as if Adam's heart had opened only for a brief time in response to Elizabeth's light, and Kellen had basked in the reflected warmth. Tyler had not been so lucky. The realization rekindled a protectiveness toward her half brother that she had not felt since the day Adam first brought him home. But she also knew that she needed Tyler as much as he needed her. He was all the family she had now except for Ian. And it was suddenly very important that she not allow the fragile bond between them to break before it had a chance to grow strong.

About a month after Tyler came home from the hospital, Kellen decided to throw a small dinner party. The excuse was her birthday, but it was actually an attempt to instill in Tyler some sense of belonging. During the party, Kellen watched Tyler carefully. There were encouraging signs, small cracks in the wall he had built around himself. But she knew it would take time and trust before he let her in. She listened as Tyler tried to talk to Stephen about rock 'n' roll. Stephen looked baffled but listened cheerfully, and Kellen's heart went out to him. He had been so helpful with Tyler, and Tyler had warmed to him, like he might have to an uncle.

Suddenly, Clark jumped to his feet, wineglass in hand. "Another toast!" he exclaimed. Everyone groaned. Clark had already made several toasts and was tipsy. "To tomorrow, the solstice. The beginning of the Summer of Love!"

Clark sat down to more groans. "I'm surrounded by Philistines," he murmured with mock dejection. "A rhapsodic revolution is happening right here in our midst, and you all are turning a deaf ear."

"We're all too old to become hippies," Josh laughed.

"It's never too late to be young!" Clark said. He looked at Stephen and Kellen for support.

"Well, I'm certainly no Peter Pan," Stephen said.

Clark turned to Tyler. "Don't listen to them, they're old. Of course, your sister used to be different. She was a real free spirit."

"I haven't changed," Kellen said, smiling.

"Then prove it," Clark said. "Let's go to the Solstice Celebration!" Kellen laughed. "I'm serious!" Clark went on. "It starts at dawn. We'll stay up, then go down to the Haight and celebrate the beginning of summer!"

"All right!" Tyler exclaimed.

Kellen looked quickly at Tyler. The last thing she wanted was a replay of the scene at the Fillmore. Tyler had promised her he would never touch drugs again, but the counselor had warned her that Tyler would try to test her authority—all teenagers did—and that by trying to become his parental figure, Kellen was particularly vulnerable. But the counselor also said that she had to show she trusted him. Kellen could see in Tyler's eyes that he knew what she was thinking. And he was expecting her to issue some heavy-handed admonition that would surely humiliate him in front of everyone. Here it is, she thought, the first test. She knew she had to be careful if she was ever going to connect with him. "Okay," she said, "but only if Stephen goes, too."

"What! Not on your life."

She touched his arm. "Come on, Stephen. It'll be fun."

He glanced at Tyler, understanding what she was doing. "All right," he said, smiling slightly.

The room erupted in conversation. No one saw Ian and Lilith standing at the door. Finally, Kellen did. "Why, Lilith, Ian," she said. "We didn't hear you come in. . . . Why don't you come in and have some cake? It's my birthday."

All eyes turned to them. Lilith's mouth was a thin line. Ian's stony expression turned into an affected smile. "We can't. I'm on my way to take Mother to the airport."

Clark, feeling no pain, smiled broadly. "Well, maybe when you get back, Ian old boy, you can join our little party. We're going down to the Haight and celebrate the Summer of Love." Off-key, he started to sing. "Be sure to wear some flowers in your hair. . . ."

Tyler laughed, and Kellen raised a napkin to her mouth to suppress a smile. Ian's dark eyes surveyed the smiling faces. "No, thank you," he said. "Good night, everyone."

He and Lilith went to the foyer. Ian paused to put on his jacket. The laughter in the dining room grew louder.

"Well, that was certainly a cozy scene," Lilith said "When did Kellen and Tyler become so buddy-buddy?"

"I don't know what you mean," Ian said flatly.

"Don't you see what's happening?"

"Let's go, Mother. It's a long drive, and I'm tired."

Lilith touched Ian's cheek. "My poor baby . . . He works so hard that he can't see anything else going on around him."

Ian sighed, pushing her hand away. "See what?"

"That Kellen and Tyler are forming an alliance. And eventually, it could work against you." Ian stared at Lilith. "I mean, Tyler's just a boy," she went on. "He can't do anything now. But when he's twenty-one . . ." Her voice trailed off. "And you know Kellen. She's obviously a bit unstable, like her mother was. She's capable of anything I'm just warning you that you should watch out."

Ian glanced back at the dining room. When he turned back to face Lilith, she was smiling. "Maybe you should start being nicer to Tyler," she said. "He needs the guidance of a big brother right now. And someday you might need him."

Ian stared at her. "You amaze me sometimes."

She turned and went to the door. "I'm only looking out for your future. I'm your mother, after all."

It was about four in the morning when Kellen, Stephen, Clark, and Tyler made their way toward Twin Peaks, the hills behind the Haight. The light was seeping over the horizon, and a cool, moist fog caressed their faces as they climbed the hill. It was quiet, except for the soft thudding sound of footsteps. Slowly, figures began to emerge from the swirling mist, and soon the grassy hillside was dotted with people, sitting quietly in small groups, wrapped in blankets. Hundreds more were still coming: men carrying flags and babies, girls in shawls with flowers in their long hair.

Kellen paused to survey the eerie scene, then Tyler tugged at her hand, pulling her upward. Near the top of the hill, they sat down. The crowd began to stir, softly chanting and singing. Someone had brought a portable phonograph and was playing the Beatles' ''Good Day Sunshine.'' No one seemed to know where the sun was supposed to come up exactly. Then, a young man in a flowing robe stood up and pointed to a soft glow, low in the opalescent sky. ''Get bright, get bright,'' he chanted softly, his face infused with a messianic light.

The crowd took up the chant, and Tyler and Clark stood up and joined in. Kellen, sitting on the grass next to Stephen, stared at them for a moment, then rose. ''Get bright,'' she said softly, looking at Tyler, ''get bright.''

Bells tinkled and smoke bombs made puffs of dull color in the grayness. A red flare arched over the sky, and the air smelled of incense and wet grass. Every sound, sight, and smell was diffused by the swirling fog, as if in some strange, atmospheric dream. Then, suddenly, it was over. The sun was a smudge of pale yellow in the swirling white void. People started back down the hill.

''That was beautiful,'' Kellen said as they walked.

''Fascinating,'' Clark said.

Stephen was silent at Kellen's side. ''Strange,'' he murmured finally.

They paused at a corner. The crowd was wandering toward Golden Gate Park. ''C'mon, let's go,'' Tyler said to Kellen.

''Where?''

''The park. The celebration's just starting.''

''Not me,'' Clark said with a sigh. ''I need some sleep. You hippies can go on without me.''

Stephen looked at Kellen and Tyler. He wanted to go home, but he could tell from their expressions they wanted to go, and he knew Kellen wanted him along for Tyler's sake. Finally, he smiled, and Kellen linked her arm through his. They said goodbye to Clark and went off to the park. Tyler and Kellen were walking along side by side, so Stephen hung back slightly, giving them time alone.

Kellen walked on in silence, her eyes taking in the strange little shops and the bizarrely dressed people.

''This makes you nervous, doesn't it,'' Tyler said.

Kellen looked at him, then nodded.

"So why'd you let me come?"

Kellen shrugged. "I didn't have a choice, really. If you want to, you'll come here behind my back. But I'm hoping you won't. I have to trust you, Tyler. And you have to trust me when I tell you I care about what happens to you."

They paused at a corner, waiting for a light to change. Tyler stood there, his hands thrust in his jean pockets. He looked at Kellen. "Don't worry," he said. "No more drugs for me. Only losers do that shit. I'm too smart."

Kellen found his false bravado poignant, but she said simply, "Anyone would have been scared by what happened."

Tyler shook his head. "It's more than that. I've been doing some thinking lately. Had a lot of time to do it in the hospital." He paused. "I've got this friend, Katz. Man, you should hear him play the guitar. . . . He could be as big as Hendrix. But he's wasted all the time." He glanced around, at nothing in particular. "I don't want to be like him," he muttered. "I want to do something with myself."

"What?" Kellen asked.

Tyler shrugged. "I dunno. I haven't figured it out yet."

"You will," Kellen answered. "I'm sure of it."

The light changed, but Tyler didn't move. He glanced over at her. "I'm glad you're here with me," he said abruptly, as if embarrassed. He quickly looked away and walked on toward the park. With a small, surprised smile, Kellen followed him.

Kellen allowed Tyler to lead her around the meadow, and she began to relax. She felt optimistic about Tyler, and the benign silliness of the festival itself was refreshing. She felt more light-hearted than she had in weeks. Garrett was still in England, ironing out an unexpected problem with one of the papers for his father. They spoke nearly every night, and she missed him. But today, for the moment at least, she felt a little less lonely. She turned and saw Stephen, lagging behind. "Come on," she said, holding out her hand.

"You two go on," Stephen said. "I'll catch up later." He watched Tyler and Kellen run off together. He was glad to see them getting along so well. Kellen seemed happier than she had in weeks. He knew she had been worried about Tyler, but he also knew it was because she missed Garrett. But today, she seemed like a carefree girl. He found himself thinking nostalgically about their childhood together, and he felt the familiar tinge of envy— that feeling he always had around her when he was growing up— of being excluded from some wonderful secret, a secret that he didn't get no matter how much he tried. He also thought about the other feeling he had always had, those times she had looked to him as the center of her world. How wonderful that had been, and how he missed it at times now.

Kellen and Tyler disappeared into a tent. When they emerged, Tyler's face was transformed into a painted psychedelic mask, and Kellen had a butterfly on her cheek.

Stephen smiled. "You look silly."

"Why, thank you," she laughed.

"And very beautiful," he added softly.

She looked at him oddly. "Let's go listen to the music."

They stood by the stage in the crush of the crowd. Someone lofted a giant canvas balloon, painted like a globe, and people laughed and swatted it into the air, yelling "Turn on the World!" Kellen and Tyler joined in the game. By the late afternoon, Stephen wanted to go home. He was tired and his head was pounding from the music, but Kellen and Tyler would not leave. Finally, the crowd began to thin, and a knot of people headed west toward the ocean. Tyler and Kellen joined them, and Stephen followed reluctantly. The crowd crossed the park and straggled across the highway to the Ocean Beach strand. People built fires and stood around chanting softly and praying.

Tyler wandered down the beach, tossing a stick into the water for a dog to retrieve. Kellen and Stephen stood alone, watching the sun set in a weary display of faded pastel. Kellen folded her arms over her chest and stared at the sun. "You look tired," she said to Stephen with a smile.

"I am. I can't keep up with you. I never could."

"I think this was good for Tyler and me," she said. "And I had fun. It felt good to have fun." The sun lit her eyes.

Stephen stared at her profile. He reached up and touched the butterfly on her cheek. She turned to look at him. He hesitated, then kissed her gently. She didn't turn away, but she didn't respond either. She seemed merely surprised.

"Marry me, Kellen," Stephen said.

She stared at him, in shock.

"I love you," he said. "I've always loved you. Marry me, Kellen. We belong together. I've always felt that."

The breeze blew strands of her hair over her face, and she brushed them away. "Oh, Stephen," she said finally. The words came out in a sigh. She turned to stare at the water.

"Marry me," he repeated.

"I can't. . . ."

"Why not? Don't you love me?"

She gently cupped his face with her hands. "I care for you so much," she said softly. "You've always been part of me. But . . ."

"But?" he urged.

"I'm . . . just not ready to get married now," she said. "Not yet . . ."

She laid her head on his shoulder, and he brought his arms up to hold her. The sun disappeared, and the air quickly grew chilly. They stood like that for a long time. Over her shoulder, Stephen could see the fires blazing down the beach. Tyler and the dog were figures in the dark. It's just not the right time, Stephen thought. She's got too much on her mind. But soon she will be ready, and I'll be here, just as I've always been. Some things are just meant to be.

Chapter
Twenty-eight

❧ A week passed, and neither Kellen or Stephen mentioned the marriage proposal. There was an uneasiness between them, which they covered up by reverting to small talk and business. Now, they sat in Stephen's office, discussing the day's news events, each pointedly polite.

A copy editor poked his head inside. "Kellen, we need you on the desk," he said. "We've got something breaking."

With a glance at Stephen, Kellen went out to the copy desk, which was obscured by a crowd of reporters and editors. Then, the crowd parted, and she saw a large cake sitting on the desk. She looked up quickly and saw everyone grinning.

Ray, the managing editor, stepped forward. "The staff wanted to do something special on your last day down here as city editor," he said.

Kellen stared at the cake. It was done in white frosting with black letters, made to look like a newspaper page. Across the top was the gothic-lettered nameplate of the *Times*, and beneath that the headline: City Editor Booted Upstairs. The baker had even attempted a likeness of her, complete with candy-red hair and green gumdrop eyes. Kellen looked up at the staff. She was so surprised by such a sentimental gesture from the normally cynical staff that her eyes brimmed with tears. "I don't know what to say," she said, smiling.

Ray handed her a knife. "Now, we'll see if you can really cut it," he said, grinning.

Everyone laughed, and Kellen cut the cake and handed out slices. She went to Stephen and handed him a paper plate filled with cake. "I suppose you knew about this," she said.

"I paid for it," Stephen smiled slightly, "out of petty cash, of course."

Kellen surveyed the city room. "I didn't think anyone really cared I was here."

"They didn't, at first. But you won their respect. Mine, too."

Someone called out Kellen's name, and a secretary motioned for her to pick up the phone. After a few clicks, Kellen heard Garrett's voice.

"Where are you? In London?" she asked, her voice rising slightly in excitement.

"New York," he said. "I just got in, and my plane to the coast leaves in fifteen minutes. I would have called you sooner to let you know I was coming, but—"

"Don't worry about it," she said softly. "Just get here."

"As soon as I can. TWA flight two oh nine."

"I'll pick you up." Kellen hung up the phone, her heart racing. She glanced at Stephen. He was watching her carefully, his face solemn. There was an awkward silence. He set his uneaten cake down on the desk.

"Come into my office," he said. "There's something I want to talk to you about."

She followed him into the office. He closed the door and sat down behind his desk. He folded his hands in front of his face, as if stalling for time to form his thoughts.

"What is it, Stephen?" she asked impatiently.

"That was Garrett, wasn't it," he said.

"Yes."

He stared at her for a moment. "There are some things you don't know about him, Kellen. Things you need to know."

She frowned, puzzled. "What are you saying, Stephen?"

"I've been trying to think of a way to tell you this." He paused. "Did he ever tell you why he's here?"

She shrugged. "Of course. He bought that paper in Toronto. He's looking at other properties . . . a mill, a printing facility—"

"He's looking for other newspapers to take over," Stephen interrupted. "Here in California."

"That's not true," Kellen said quickly. "He told me he's only interested in Canada."

Stephen shook his head. "The Toronto deal is just a jumping-off point, Kellen. Garrett Richardson is out to make a foothold in the States. Did he tell you what he's been doing down in L.A.?"

"No, not in so many words."

"He was trying to buy out the Rothman chain. He could have had it—the price was right. But he decided it was too small. He doesn't want a bunch of weeklies and suburban advertisers. He wants something big.'' Kellen was silent. ''He wants the Bryant newspapers,'' Stephen said.

''Oh, Stephen, you're crazy. He has no interest at all in this company.''

Stephen leaned forward across the desk. ''Kellen, he knows there are problems with the *Times*. He knows how it's affecting the chain. For months, he's been quietly researching the corporation and the markets. The rumor is that he's positioning himself to make an offer.''

''Why are you telling me this?'' she asked quietly. ''Why are you trying to upset me?''

''Because I don't want to see you lose these newspapers. And I know that you and he—''

''God, Stephen, if this is just because you're jealous—''

''That's not it,'' Stephen said quickly. ''You know I wouldn't lie to you. I have a friend at the *Wall Street Journal* who's been assigned to watch Richardson's moves here. This reporter knows the guy, knows his father's pattern in Britain. They look for troubled papers in good markets and, when the time is right, they move in. Then they convert the papers to sleazy tabloids. That's what Garrett's doing in Toronto. That's what he wants to do here.''

Kellen rose. ''You're being paranoid,'' she said angrily.

''And you're being naive,'' he shot back.

She went to the door. Stephen jumped up and barred her way. ''Look, if you won't believe me, call my friend.''

''If I want the truth, I'll ask Garrett.''

''You won't get it. For god's sake, Kellen, think about this for a minute. Why do you think the guy's hung around here for so long?''

She stared at him for a moment. Then she pushed his arm aside and went quickly across the newsroom to the elevator.

Several hours later, Stephen's words were still with her as she drove to the airport. She knew that Stephen wouldn't lie to her. He had always been like a big brother, standing ready to protect her. Was that all he was doing now? Or was he just jealous? Before, she never would have thought Stephen would do anything just to hurt her. But things were different now—he had proposed. With just two words, he had thrust their relationship onto a completely different plane.

She knew she had to confront Garrett. But then when she saw him and felt his arms around her, all she could think about was how much she had missed him in the last month. She would wait; surely, if it were true, Garrett would tell her himself. But he made no reference to it at all for the rest of the day and evening. And as she lay in bed next to him in the house in Tiburon, Stephen's accusations came back, hovering in the dark.

Garrett reached for her hand. "What's the matter?"

"Nothing," she said softly. She lay still until she heard his breathing deepen into sleep. She got up and went to the window. The house overlooked the bay, and across the water, she could see the curving carpet of San Francisco's lights. But the tranquilizing beauty of the view was lost to her. She glanced at the bed. A shard of moonlight illuminated Garrett's bare shoulder, leaving his face in shadows. Tomorrow, she thought. I'll ask him tomorrow.

The next morning they sat quietly on the deck having breakfast, reading the newspaper. It was a beautiful, sunny day, and a brisk breeze was blowing up from the bay.

"You know, you should start keeping some clothes here," he said. "That way maybe I could get my robe back."

"That sounds like an invitation to move in," she said, pulling the terry-cloth robe tighter.

He smiled. "I have plenty of closet space."

She sipped her coffee, trying to think of a way to bring up Stephen's accusations.

"Why don't you go home, pick up some clothes, and come back?" Garrett said suddenly. "Then we'll decide how to spend the day. How about going down to Big Sur? We could go there for the weekend."

She set down her cup, surprised. "You don't have to go anywhere? What about L.A.?"

"My business is finished there."

She got up and went to the railing and stared out at the bay. She turned back around to face him. "Garrett, why did you decide to buy this house?"

"I liked it the moment I saw it. I like being able to sit over here and look at the city." He smiled. "Makes me feel as if it's mine, like owning a great painting."

Kellen stared at him. "But why are you here?" she asked.

"I like San Francisco," he said. "I told you that before." He looked puzzled. "Kellen, what's wrong?"

She took a breath. "Are you here because you want to buy my newspapers?"

If the question surprised him, Garrett didn't show it. "Who told you that?" he asked after a moment.

"That's not important."

Garrett leaned back in his chair. He looked away, and when he didn't say anything else in explanation, she turned away again. She watched a gull hover in the air and dip down toward the water below. She turned back to face him. "Don't lie to me, Garrett," she said.

He looked up at her. "I'm here because of you," he said finally.

"And the newspapers have nothing to do with it?"

He got up and came to her, but when she took a step back from him, he stopped. "All right," he said quietly. "They did. In the beginning."

"Oh, god," she murmured.

"But you've got to believe me, Kellen. That changed."

She waited, her eyes narrowed with anger and hurt.

"When we were in Paris," he went on, "you told me nothing about your family. It was only after I tried to find you that I found out about your father's newspapers. After he died, after you left Paris, I heard that your family was having problems running things. I researched the situation and determined it would be a likely purchase candidate. I assumed your family might be willing to sell. And when I talked to your brother, he said he was interested."

"You talked to Ian? Behind my back?"

Garrett paused before answering. "Yes, we had one telephone conversation, before I set foot in San Francisco. Before you and I saw each other again. I was told he was the head of the corporation and made all decisions."

"So then you came here, figuring you could coax dumb little Kellen into selling." She laughed bitterly. "All you had to do was get her into bed, right?"

"Kellen, stop it!" Garrett said. "I won't deny that I came here prepared to buy the newspapers. But I also wanted to see you again. I didn't know then that Ian was in no position to speak for you. I didn't know then what the newspapers meant to you, how strongly you felt about not selling." He paused. "And I had no idea either that you and I would ever—"

"So what about now?" she interrupted angrily. "Why are you still here? Do you still want the newspapers?"

A sudden gust of wind sent the newspaper sections on the nearby table fluttering across the deck. Garrett looked at them and then at Kellen, standing before him, her red hair and his white robe billowing around her, her face pale with anger. The image clicked in his mind like a snapshot, as if his memory were already storing it away. In the next second, he thought of his father's demand: I want those papers; and he thought of telling Kellen about it. But he knew there was no way she would accept that. Besides, he couldn't lay the blame on his father. It had been his plan, right from the start. He had studied everything about the Bryant chain so carefully, preparing himself for what he was convinced would be an easy deal. Seeing Kellen again—he had thought of that as just a wonderful bonus, a chance to rekindle a memorable affair. But over the last few weeks, it had all changed. For all his careful planning, he had made two crucial errors. He had underestimated the depth of Kellen's feelings for the newspapers. And, more important, he had underestimated the depth of his own feelings for her. Now, as he looked at her face, so filled with distrust, he realized with a sudden, terrible clarity that he was in love with her and that she was slipping away. Any explanation would be useless, any apology feeble. Now, there was nothing to do but salvage whatever he could.

"Kellen, I want you to listen to me for a moment," he said softly. "I know what your brother has done already to this corporation. If he keeps it up, he'll ruin it. Believe me, Kellen, the only way you can preserve it is to sell it."

"Sell it? To you?" Kellen said angrily. "You expect me to hand over what my father spent his life building and watch you trash it?"

"It doesn't have to be like that. Think about this. You wouldn't have to worry about them anymore. I could turn things around. And we could—"

"No!" she said. "There's no *we* anymore!"

Garrett came toward her, holding out his arms.

"Don't touch me!" she cried out, taking a step back.

"Kellen, please—"

She backed away, toward the door. "It's over," she murmured. "It's over." She ran inside.

Garrett stood on the deck, numb. He stood there until he heard the front door slam and the sound of Kellen's car racing away. Finally, he went inside to the bedroom. He glanced around, looking for some trace of her, but there was nothing. Her hairbrush, her makeup, all the little things that had marked her presence in his house were gone. He saw his robe lying in a heap on the floor and picked it up. He brought it to his nose, trying to detect the smell of her perfume, but there was nothing.

*   *   *

During the week that followed, Kellen refused Garrett's calls, and finally they stopped. Kellen knew Garrett was still in town because Clark said he saw him at a social engagement. After two weeks, Clark told her Garrett had closed the house in Tiburon and gone to Toronto. The news left her saddened yet relieved. She was emotionally spent, as if an electric current, which had vibrated throughout her body for months, had suddenly been switched off. His departure gave it a finality. It was really over, she told herself.

Stephen kept his distance. But Ian, with his usual alacrity, zeroed in on her pain, badgering her about losing the deal. His needling came to a head one afternoon, about a month after Garrett's departure. He burst into her office and tossed a paper down on her desk.

"I need your signature on this," he said tersely.

Kellen picked it up and began to read.

"It's just a fucking petty cash voucher," he said impatiently. "Just sign it, and I'll leave you alone."

"This is for ten thousand dollars," she said. "'That's not petty cash.''

Ian shrugged. "It'll come out of the editorial budget. It'll never be missed."

"What's it for?"

"For chrissake, Kellen. I can't get anything done if you question every move I make. You've signed them before."

"I want to know what you need ten thousand dollars for," she said, her voice rising in response to his.

Ian snatched the form from her hand. "Forget it," he snapped. "I'll take care of this myself."

She was momentarily stunned by his burst of anger. "Ian," she said, "I have to know what goes on around here. You have to keep me involved."

He stared at her for a moment, and she could see something in his eyes that she had never before noticed, something she could only interpret as hatred. But it passed quickly, and he started to laugh softly. He sat down across from her, and put his long legs up on the edge of her desk.

"I have to keep you involved," he repeated. "Just listen to yourself, little sister. Listen to how absurd you sound. You want to run things around here, but you don't want any of the responsibility." He lit a cigarette, knowing how much she disliked the smoke in her office.

"Let's put this in historical perspective," he said. "First you run off to play in Europe for five years, then come back, stomp your feet, and demand to get involved with the family business. But then what happens? You play around some more down in the newsroom with Stephen. And when you get bored with him, you hop over to Richardson's bed."

"Get out of here," Kellen said.

"Not yet, little sister," he said, smiling. "So, off you go with your new playmate. But while you're out getting banged by the Brit, who do you think is sitting here every day running things, getting the work done, keeping Daddy's empire in one piece?" He tapped his chest, his smile broadening into a mocking grin. "Me. Good old Ian." He took a deep drag on his cigarette. "So don't start telling me that I need to keep you involved. That, little sister, is not my job."

Kellen flushed with anger and embarrassment. "I'm not stupid, Ian. I may not have your years of experience, but I have worked hard to learn how this corporation works."

"You don't know shit!" he shot back. He jerked to his feet and jabbed the cigarette at her face, its ashes scattering across her desk. "You fucked up the best chance we had to sell! Do you have any idea how much money Richardson was ready to give us? But you were so busy fucking him, you didn't even see that he was fucking you! You're so fucking stupid!"

The violence of his outburst caused Kellen to recoil slightly into her chair. "I told you, Ian," she said. "I'll never sell Daddy's newspapers."

"This isn't some goddamn memorial!" he shouted. "It's a business! It's worth hundreds of millions of dollars! Do you think Father cares what we do with it? He's dead, for chrissake! He's dead!"

He stared at her, trying to bring himself back under control. He began to shake his head, as if in disbelief. "That man . . ." he said, struggling to speak in a calm voice. "I can't believe he did this to me. I can't believe he gave you any say in this." He focused on her. "You don't know anything. You're . . . so . . . fucking . . . stupid."

He stormed out of the office. Kellen sat motionless, her heart hammering. She had seen Ian lose his temper many times, but the fury of this outburst scared her. She touched her burning cheek. Her face stung, as if he had struck her.

That night, she decided to go to the house in Carmel. She was afraid to be in the same house with Ian, and she needed to get away to think. She packed her bags, planning to leave early the next morning. But she woke up feeling sick to her stomach. She was standing at the washbasin, splashing cool water on her face, when suddenly she froze. She stared at her pallid face in the mirror.

My god, she thought, I'm pregnant.

She went quickly to her datebook. Her period was three weeks overdue. She called her doctor and made an appointment. Two days later, Kellen received a call from a nurse, who confirmed her suspicion. Kellen put down the phone and closed her eyes. She had suspected weeks ago that she might pregnant, and it had unleashed daydreams about a future with Garrett. But then everything changed. No future with Garrett was possible now. And the pregnancy was just a harsh reality, a reality to be dealt with somehow.

She had a choice. Friends of hers had faced the same problem and knew the right doctors. A phone call, a quick flight to Honolulu for a clandestine appointment, and it would be over. Her life could go on as before. No one would know. Not even Garrett. No one would ever know.

Kellen rose slowly and went to the window of the study. She lifted the drapes and looked out on the street. An abortion . . . how could she bring herself to do it? The dictates of her Catholic schooling reverberated in her memory, but she knew her misgivings came from something even deeper within herself. No one would ever know, she thought, except me. And I don't know if I could live with it.

She glanced at the telephone, thinking of calling Garrett. Didn't he have a right to know? No, she decided suddenly, he had no rights at all, no say in what she did. He forfeited that when he lied to her. If she did have the baby, she would have to do it alone.

Kellen looked around the study. Lately, she had taken to spending a lot of time in the room. She had changed almost nothing since her father's death. The books, the photographs, the mementos were still in place, as were the stacks of current newspapers. She played back in her mind the scene with Garrett. He was right about Ian. Given enough time, Ian would reduce everything to ruin. She couldn't turn her head from that fact. Neither could she ignore the fact that she was no closer to solving the corporation's problems than she had been that day when she confronted Ian and declared herself copublisher. What had she done to change anything? Nothing. She had spent too much time playing in the newsroom, chasing a childhood dream while the real work went undone. She had spent her time with Garrett, finding in him an escape from the problems she didn't want to face.

Publisher, she thought. After two years, I have no more right to the title than Ian does.

She sat down in the leather chair. The violent scene with Ian flashed into her mind, and she shuddered. Ian was dangerous, possibly to her and most certainly to the newspaper. How could she possibly nullify his influence? The newspapers needed real leadership. If she was going to assert her power over Ian, it had to be now. And it had to be a complete commitment.

But a child . . . wasn't that a complete commitment, too?

She thought of Tyler, and how he still carried the scars of his bastard birth. Could she put her own child up to such torment? Tyler also had suffered because Adam had not had time for him. Hadn't she even felt it herself at times? She didn't want her own child ever feeling that way. No, there was not enough of her for both a child and the newspapers. She had to make a choice.

Her eyes fell on the framed photograph on the desk of her mother and father. A surge of isolation and discouragement washed over her in a crushing wave. She had made a promise to her father that somehow had to be kept. "I can't do both," she whispered.

She would have the abortion. The decision made, she sank back in the chair. But Garrett's face kept reappearing in her mind. It was his baby. . . . She shut her eyes tight, as if to push him from her thoughts. Strange little singsong fragments ran through her mind, phrases which she finally recalled as prayers taught to her by the nuns in the boarding school. Holy Mary, mother of God, pray for our sins now and at the hour of our death. . . .

"Dear God," she whispered, "help me forget him."

She knew she was wavering. She needed to talk to someone, to hear she was doing the right thing, and there was only one person she could really count on. She picked up the phone and dialed quickly before she lost her nerve.

"Stephen?"

"Kellen?"

"I . . . Stephen . . . could you come over?"

"What is it? You sound funny. Is something wrong?"

"I have to talk to you, Stephen. It's important."

There was a pause. "I'll be right there."

Fifteen minutes later, Stephen was seated on the sofa next to her. "What is it?" he pressed. "Is it Tyler?"

She shook her head, unable to look up. Finally, she looked him straight in the eye. "I'm pregnant," she said.

He stared at her, stunned. He got up and walked slowly away from her, running a hand over his face.

"I've decided," she said quietly, "to have an abortion."

He spun around. "You've what?" He shook his head in disbelief. "For god's sake, Kellen, you can't do that! What's the matter with you?"

His reaction surprised her. She had called him seeking comfort, not condemnation. "Nothing's the matter with me," she said. "I thought about this, and I made a choice."

"Obviously, you didn't give it much thought."

"Stephen, don't do this. Don't treat me like you did when we were kids, like . . . I haven't got a brain in my head."

"Good lord, Kellen, an abortion . . ." He paced in agitation. "You don't have to do that! You could have the baby and put it up for adoption."

"No!" She shut her eyes, thinking of Garrett, knowing that if she ever saw his child, she'd want to keep it. "This is the only way, Stephen. I can't have this baby. I have too many other things I have to take care of first. There's Tyler . . . and the newspapers."

He sighed in exasperation. "Kellen, I know you. You couldn't go through with an abortion. It's not right."

She was close to tears. "I can. And I will."

Stephen shook his head. "So you've decided. Then why in the hell did you ask me to come over here?"

"I thought you'd help me! I thought—" she began to cry. "—you'd be here for me when I needed you."

He stared at her for a moment, then went over to the sofa and sat down. He took her hand. "I'm sorry," he said quietly. "I shouldn't have yelled at you like that."

She struggled to compose herself, and after a moment she was able to look up at him. Stephen saw so much written in her face, despair and confusion, but also a grim determination.

"You really intend to go through with it," he said.

"There's no other choice."

"What about Garrett?"

She looked away. "That's over," she said flatly. "You were right about him, Stephen. He just wanted the newspapers."

Her words gave him no sense of victory. He had heard in them no anger, just sadness, and he knew she was still in love with him. But he also knew that this was the chance he had been waiting so long for. With a baby . . . and us working together to save the newspapers, she'll forget about him, he thought. We can build something together. I can make her forget him.

"Kellen," he said, "you've got another choice. You could have the baby. And you could marry me."

She looked at him in stunned silence.

"I'll take care of you. And the baby," he said, his eyes locked on hers. "I'll take care of everything."

"It's Garrett's baby, Stephen," she said.

He hesitated. "I know."

She shook her head slowly. "But why would you do it?"

"Because I love you," he said quietly.

Her eyes dropped to her hands.

"We've known each other almost our entire lives," Stephen said. "We belong together." He paused. "I know that you . . . care for me," he said. "That's enough for me, for now."

She slumped slightly. "I don't know," she said softly.

He gathered her into his arms and held her. "Everything will work out, Kellen," he said. "You've always trusted me, and you can now. Just give it a chance."

She leaned against him, listening to his voice. His words and arms enfolded her like a cocoon, making her feel secure and loved. It was just as it had always been. Once again, Stephen was offering his protection—to the newspapers, to the baby, and to her. She shut her eyes. Maybe he is right, she thought. Maybe we do belong together.

Stephen's hand touched her chin, tilting her face up so she was forced to look at him. He smiled slightly. "Kellen Elizabeth Bryant . . . will you marry me?" he asked softly.

She hesitated, and then the one word emerged in a sigh. "Yes," she said.

Chapter
Twenty-nine

Stephen settled into a chair by the fireplace and unfolded the newspaper. Suddenly, a small face appeared, poking under the pages. "Daddy! You're home!" A pair of huge blue eyes stared up at him hopefully.

Stephen relented. "All right, come on up," he said, pulling the child onto his lap. "Now, how do you expect me to read?" he said with a smile.

"I'll help you," the girl said, and proceeded to call out the letters in the headlines. After a while, she tired of the game and leaned back contentedly against Stephen's chest.

Stephen tried to shift her over slightly so he could finish his reading. He noted the weight of her on his lap and realized that she was growing so fast. She was nearly seven, not a baby anymore. "You know, you're almost too big for this, princess," he said.

She looked at him evenly. "Do you want me to get down?"

"No, you can stay." He was about to bring the newspaper back up again when Kellen came into the room.

"Stephen, I didn't hear you come in," she said. She went to him, kissing him lightly. Her red hair was pulled back by a scarf and she was wearing camel slacks and a flattering sweater. She was, he thought suddenly, more beautiful than the day they had gotten married.

"You look pretty tonight," he said.

Kellen gave him a pleased little smile. "I'm getting fat. But thank you anyway." She reached over to smooth the girl's hair. "Sara, why don't you let your father be. He just got home, and he's tired. Go help your brother pick up the toys, okay?" When the girl pouted Kellen added, "You can spend all day tomorrow with Daddy when we go to the zoo."

Sara brightened, slid off Stephen's lap, and went over to the Christmas tree, where a little boy was playing.

"I can't go tomorrow," Stephen said quietly.

"Stephen, you promised her—"

"I know, but something's come up at the paper. I have to go in to work."

"You've been working every weekend for weeks," she said. "You've got to take some time off. For them, if nothing else."

Stephen didn't answer and went back to reading the paper. Kellen sighed and turned toward the children. "Well, I've got to get them in bed and get ready," she said.

Stephen looked up. "Where are you going?"

"To the office. I forgot to bring that new circulation report home, and I want to go over it before the meeting Monday."

Stephen put the paper down. "You don't need to go all the way downtown just for that. I'll have someone send it over tomorrow." He paused. "Besides, I read it earlier. It's not that important."

"Stephen, I'm not going to the meeting half-prepared."

"Maybe you should skip the meeting this week, Kellen," he said. "Ben's still running a fever. I can fill you in on what goes on."

She looked at him oddly. "I'm going to the meeting," she said. "And I'm going now to the office." She brushed a strand of hair off her face in agitation. "Besides, I need to get out of the house for a little while. I've been cooped up here all week."

"It's cold out," Stephen said.

"The fresh air will do me good."

Stephen stared at her for a moment.

"You look tired," she said, "I'll get the children to bed before I leave so they won't bother you." Stephen raised the paper again without comment. Kellen went over to the children to help them gather up their toys. Stephen dropped the paper slightly and watched the three of them. Kellen's face had set into that implacable mask that he knew signaled her stubbornness, or her displeasure with him. He hated it when this happened, this arguing without really arguing. They had never really had an overt fight during their seven-year marriage. But lately, for some reason, it seemed that even their most innocent exchanges were tinged with tension.

He let out a small sigh. He shouldn't have said anything about her going to the office. She had, after all, been at home all week with the children, nursing their colds. He watched the children.

Ben was going into his usual noisy bedtime denial, but Kellen finally just scooped him up and carted him off toward the stairs. Sara followed calmly.

Stephen felt a stab of guilt. Sara was going to be so disappointed when she found out about the zoo. He had been promising for weeks to take her, but lately it was all he could do to get home from work before they went to bed. At five, Ben didn't yet seem to notice Stephen's absence, but Sara, increasingly, did. "Just make some time for her, Stephen," Kellen often said. "She's getting to that age where a father's love is very important."

Stephen let the newspaper fall onto his lap. Kellen implied he was withholding himself from Sara, but he didn't think so. He loved her as much as he would his own child.

He stared into the fire, letting his thoughts drift back to the days surrounding Sara's birth. It had been a difficult time, more so than he had ever anticipated. He had always thought of himself as a man of reason and generous spirit, and he had really believed he could accept the child. But that first day, when he saw the infant in the nursery, all his jealousy toward Garrett Richardson resurfaced. Sara had been premature, just enough to pass as Stephen's child. But she looked like neither Stephen or Kellen. Sara Lindsay Hillman had a shock of black hair and blue eyes, distinctly dark blue, just like Garrett's. A few people commented that her coloring was a throwback to her grandfather Adam, but those who remembered Garrett suspected the truth.

Stephen steeled himself against Sara's appearance, wondering if he would think of Garrett every time he looked at her. Kellen said nothing about it, but he suspected from the way she looked at the baby that she thought the same. Finally, she had said, almost apologetically, "It would be easier if she looked like me instead, wouldn't it."

Perhaps, he thought, but he was determined to be honorable. It was the bargain he had made to marry Kellen. "It doesn't matter," he had answered. "She's our daughter."

Nothing had been easy during that first year. The suddenness of their marriage and Sara's premature birth had shocked everyone. To make matters worse, it was an intermarriage, a fact that Stephen, so stubbornly honor-bound to rescue Kellen, had chosen to disregard. Even Josh and Anna had misgivings. They loved Kellen and were sympathetic about her pregnancy. But they had always envisioned a certain life for their only son, a happy life lived within the dictates of their faith and culture. It had been hardest on his mother, who was active in her temple. Some of her friends had even gone so far as to express pity over her son's choice of a Catholic wife. And there were those, of course, who clucked over the idea of a Catholic marrying a Jew, and not even a rich one at that. But then, she was Adam Bryant's daughter, went conventional wisdom, what could one expect?

Except for the one comment about Sara's appearance, Kellen never mentioned Garrett. Finally, Stephen heard that he was living in New York. He had bought a moribund New York City newspaper, *The Tatler*, and had converted it into a sensationalist tabloid. Garrett commuted between New York, Toronto, and London, never returning to San Francisco.

But he had not sold the house in Tiburon, and Stephen thought often about what would happen if he came back. Sometimes at night, when he lay next to Kellen in bed, Stephen imagined that she still carried within her some small, sad longing. He would gather her into his arms, and she would curve her body against his and tell him that she loved him. But his doubts remained.

He knew many people suspected Garrett was Sara's father and thought he was a fool. But he loved Kellen, and after a year had passed, he grew to love Sara.

Then, two years after her birth, Kellen announced she was pregnant. Stephen was overjoyed, and the fact that the baby turned out to be a boy only intensified his happiness. The birth also seemed an atonement to Anna and Josh; they had accepted Sara, for Stephen's sake, but now they had a grandson. For Stephen, Garrett suddenly ceased to be a mysterious threat who could swoop in some day to claim Sara—and Kellen. Now, because of Ben, he and Kellen had a connection that no one could break. Stephen could still feel Garrett's ghostly presence sometimes, but it grew fainter all the time. He began to believe that Kellen felt the same.

Ben's birth seemed to change her. Some of the changes were small, like the way she dressed. But it was more fundamental than that. There was a maturity and serenity about her now. She seemed more centered than she ever had in her life, he thought, as if she had finally found in motherhood something more important than herself—or the newspapers, for that matter.

Following Sara's birth, Kellen had maintained a consistent schedule at the newspaper, working in her office for a couple hours a day to keep up on all the various aspects of the operation. But after Ben's arrival, her schedule became erratic. From birth, Ben had been plagued with chronic bronchial infections, and Kellen felt compelled to remain at home on careful watch. She had never objected. "I don't want my children raised by nannies and governesses," she told Stephen. "I want them to know I'm here."

By Ben's third birthday, his health had stabilized and so had Kellen's schedule, reduced to one day a week spent at the office, with a special trip in for the monthly vice presidents' meeting. Once, she brought up the possibility of assuming her former schedule, but Stephen gently discouraged her. "You might as well wait now until Ben's in school," he said. "He needs you at home right now, Kellen. They both do. Besides, I can act in your stead, you know that."

Kellen had acquiesced, and their life settled into a smooth routine. After a while, Kellen surprised him by joining the opera guild, where her mother had worked as a volunteer. She also took the children to church, being careful to balance this with exposure to their Jewish heritage, enlisting Anna Hillman's help for instruction. Stephen thought that her new conservatism and efforts to ingratiate herself with the social elite were a reaction against the notoriety she had endured during her own childhood. She was trying to buffer Ben and Sara against hurt, and he didn't discourage her. He saw all her changes as a natural process of maturation. Kellen had finally grown up.

He glanced up from the fire, his eyes going from the Christmas tree up to the gold menorah sitting on the mantel. Yes, it had been hard at first, he thought, and there were the recent moments of tension, but what couple didn't experience that? Everything had worked out, he thought, much better than I ever hoped.

Benjamin's shrill laugh drew his attention to the foyer. Kellen and the nanny came down the stairs with the children. Ben ran over and clambered onto Stephen's lap, holding a stuffed bear. Stephen drew Ben into a hug, tickling him into spasms of giggles.

"Hey, big man!" Stephen said, with a broad smile. "Where'd you get that dandy-looking bear?"

"Grandpa Josh," Ben answered. "I named him Fred." Ben looked up at him. With his hazel eyes and sandy-blond hair, he was the image of Stephen. "Daddy, can I have a real one?"

"A bear? No, I don't think so. Maybe a puppy. When you're old enough to take care of him."

"It's past your bedtime, Ben," Kellen said gently. "Kiss your father good night."

Ben threw his plump arms around Stephen's neck, then scrambled down. Sara hung back slightly, waiting. Finally, Stephen held out his arms. She went to him, and Stephen kissed her cheek. "Good night, princess," he said.

"Good night, Daddy," she said, looking at him solemnly.

Stephen suspected Kellen had told her that he couldn't go to the zoo, and he made a vow to himself to make it up to her. The nanny led them away, leaving Kellen and Stephen alone. The room was suddenly filled with quiet.

"They got too many gifts this year," Kellen said after a moment. "Do you think we're spoiling them?"

"You're the one who thinks they should get Christmas and Hanukkah presents," Stephen said. He took her hand and tried to draw her down into his lap. She pulled back.

"I have to go," she said.

"It's much nicer here by the fire with me," he said.

She bent down to kiss his cheek. "I won't be long." She went upstairs. A short time later, he heard her leave.

Stephen sat staring at the fire, the newspaper still lying across his knee. He still felt perplexed and slightly annoyed by her insistence on going to the office tonight. He knew it was more than just a ploy to get out of the house for a while. It was a subtle act of defiance, and it, not Stephen's broken date with Sara, was the real reason behind their guarded words of tension earlier. Last night, she had brought up the idea of going back to work full-time. Stephen had sidestepped the issue, but he knew it would soon come to a head now that Ben had started kindergarten. But the truth was he didn't want Kellen to resume a full-time schedule. And it was not really because of the children.

He stared into the fire. He wanted her to stay home because it had made things easier for him at the *Times*. It was as simple, and as selfish, as that.

His marriage had elicited predictable ribbing from cohorts and employees, jokes about marrying the boss's daughter. But beneath the kidding, he sensed people thought his marriage was just a grab for money and more power. Even his most faithful employees looked at him differently after his marriage, as if they thought that as long as Kellen was upstairs in the executive suite, he was just her puppet. She had never done anything to undermine him. But the less she was there, the more secure he felt in his authority.

He had, during the last five years, gotten used to operating independently. He was editor in chief, but his power actually had grown beyond the editorial division. Adam's patronage had always accorded him a special place in the *Times*'s hierarchy of vice presidents. In theory, all the division heads were equal, but Stephen's opinion held more sway. He was, with the exception of Ian, the single most powerful person at the *Times*. But would that change if Kellen decided to resume her place in the executive suite? And how would it affect their marriage?

He stared at the *Times* lying across his lap and thought of the circulation report that Kellen had gone to the office to retrieve. He hadn't been truthful with her when he said it was unimportant. He knew that once she read it, she would be upset with him. More important, it could be the thing to galvanize her resolve to go back to work.

The report contained the latest Audit Bureau of Circulations figures, and the news was not good. Figures showed that the *Times*'s circulation had dipped to 450,000, a loss of 2,000 subscribers in the last year. That brought the net loss over the last five years to 12,000. Now, the *Times*'s circulation was about even with the rival *Journal*'s. But the most telling figure was that the *Journal* now had an edge of 15,000 over the *Times* in the city of San Francisco itself.

The report had not come as a total surprise to Stephen, but he had been hoping the figures might signal a possible reversal in the trend. But they hadn't. In fact, when these latest ABC figures were made public, everyone—including advertisers—would know that the *Times* was no longer the dominant newspaper in San Francisco. The *Times* still had the biggest circulation in the Bay Area. It was read from Marin County in the north to San Jose in the south, but even Stephen had to admit that much of that was "ego circulation," small pockets of several thousand readers spread across suburban communities, away from San Francisco. These readers took the *Times* as a worldly adjunct to their provincial local newspapers. The *Times* tried to capitalize on its cosmopolitan image with slogans like "We Bring the World to the Bay." But advertisers in the small towns found it too expensive to buy space in the *Times* when they could get good results from local papers. The *Times* still had its empire, but it was now far-flung and increasingly expensive to maintain.

And now, the *Times* was number two in San Francisco. Five years ago, the *Journal*'s publisher, Howard Capen's son Edward, had suddenly withdrawn from the suburban fight his father had begun so many years ago with Adam Bryant. Capen concentrated all the *Journal*'s energies and monies on winning the city's readers back from the *Times*. It proved a wise move. The *Journal* was now the most widely read newspaper in the crucial "core market" of San Francisco. Editorially, it still lacked the *Times*'s depth, but Capen was becoming aggressive. Just this week, he had lured away two *Times* reporters with promises of large salary increases.

Stephen sighed. He had not told Kellen about the reporters jumping ship because he took it as a personal defeat within his own realm. But there was a new wrinkle that he knew he wouldn't be able to conceal: Capen's new target was Clark Able. Apparently, Clark had told Capen he wasn't interested. But Stephen wondered if even Clark's loyalty might be tested if the *Times*'s circulation kept shrinking. Clark's ego needed the biggest possible audience. His column was the *Times*'s most popular feature, and Stephen knew Clark's defection could mean a loss of countless readers.

His thoughts went back to Kellen. She was familiar with the *Times*'s circulation losses, of course, but Stephen had assured her the trend could be reversed. He sat there immobile, staring into the dying fire. He should have told her the truth about the report before she left. But he hadn't wanted to face her reaction at that moment. He hadn't had enough time to come to grips with his feeling of defeat. He felt like he had betrayed her trust somehow. And Adam's, too. And after years of hard work, he still didn't know how to correct the *Times*'s circulation problems. How could he face her? She had always looked up to him, believing he had the answers. But this time he had none.

He rose wearily, went to the fireplace, took the poker, and prodded the logs into a renewed blaze. He stood, staring at the fire without seeing it.

Kellen switched on a light in the office and went to her desk, tossing her coat on a sofa. The desk was as neat as she had left it last week, with only a few new documents placed in a small pile by Adele. Kellen sat down and sifted through them. There was nothing that really needed her attention. The latest copies of *Editor and Publisher* and *Columbia Journalism Review*. Some routine pressroom efficiency reports. A windy memo about a new marketing campaign. An invitation to speak on a panel from the American Association of Newspaper Publishers. She picked it up with a wry smile. She received many such invitations from newspaper organizations, composed mostly of men, which tended to book Kellen Bryant Hillman as a curiosity more than anything. She set the invitation aside and turned to her telephone messages. Only one caught her eye: Tyler had returned her call, finally agreeing to meet her for dinner Monday night.

She had not seen him for months. Ever since he had moved out of the house two years ago when he turned eighteen, Kellen had felt they were drifting apart. Part of it was natural, she knew.

Tyler was no longer a child, and now he had his own apartment on Russian Hill and his own life. But she missed him; the mansion seemed different without him.

Of course, Ian had also moved out, right after Kellen and Stephen married. Not long after that, he had married a young woman named Clarisse Cross from Philadelphia. Now, they were living in a house nearby and had a young son. Kellen had been surprised by Ian's sudden marriage and embrace of fatherhood. But Stephen said he thought it had all come at Lilith's prodding; there was no way she would stand back and watch the children of Stephen Hillman inherit the Bryant fortune. Ian had a duty to produce proper heirs . . . and fast.

Kellen glanced at the photograph on her desk of Sara and Benjamin. It was strange how often she, too, thought of the newspapers in exactly those terms now—as a legacy for Sara and Ben. The newspapers were, indeed, something precious that had been entrusted to her, and which she, in turn, would hand on to her children. Of course, it would be different than the way her father had done it. She would teach them, both Sara and Ben, how to take care of the gift.

Her eyes traveled now over the office, lingering on the plaques and awards that dated back to Adam's editorship. Even after all these years, it still surprised her sometimes that she had not been able to completely bury her resentment over being excluded from the business. The feelings were resurfacing now only because she wanted so badly to return to the office full-time, and Stephen was less than encouraging.

Things had run smoothly enough during the last five years, and she had willingly taken a step away for the sake of the children. But now, she longed to come back with the full force of her energy and creativity behind her. Why couldn't Stephen understand that? Why was he trying to subtly steer her away?

She considered the possibility that he was simply being protective of his turf. But she had learned to be careful not to usurp his authority. It hadn't been easy, especially in the first two years. Her enthusiasm and need to put her mark on the *Times* had compelled her to deluge Stephen with suggestions on how to run the editorial division. Finally, he told her she was compromising his influence, and she pulled back. She was hurt at first, but eventually she agreed that Stephen needed autonomy to be effective.

Her eyes fell now on the photograph of Stephen, and she picked up the frame, staring at his face, thinking about their marriage. During the past seven years, she had come to love him, a simple matter of extending the affection she had always felt for him into her role as wife. And he was a good father to Sara, although Kellen worried that he unconsciously favored Ben. Recently, Sara had tugged at her heart by asking, "Why does Daddy love Ben more than me?"

Kellen had answered, "He doesn't really. All daddys like their little boys." But she cautioned Stephen to be more attentive to Sara.

Their marriage had been generally untroubled, and she had been happy for the most part. But in an occasional dark moment, she wondered if her marriage had not been a sort of Faustian bargain. Stephen had offered his love and protection for her and Sara, and she had reciprocated with respectful deference in regard to his ambitions at the newspaper, giving up many of her own. But what else had she given up? She set the photograph down carefully on the edge of the desk. Passion, perhaps . . . the kind that lit a marriage from within, the kind that she suspected her own mother and father had. She knew the love that she and Stephen had was different; it was not a fire but a warm, continuous glow.

Passion . . . she had felt that only once, with Garrett. She closed her eyes, allowing herself the indulgence of thinking about him. Usually, she kept his memory locked away, safely compartmentalized so as not to mix with other orderly emotions of her daily life. But sometimes she let it out, a luxury to be savored whenever she felt the need. Sometimes, she thought of him in anger. Often, her thoughts of him took the form of sexual fantasies and vivid memories. But most often, she thought of him with just bittersweet curiosity—what he was doing at a particular moment, who he was with, what he looked like now.

But passion, she knew now, was nothing but an ephemeral thing. The feeling of champagne running through your veins was for girls and poets. She opened her eyes, tucking Garrett's memory back in its place. "And I'm neither anymore," she murmured.

She glanced at her watch. It was nearly ten, and she had to stop daydreaming and deal with the report. She found it in a drawer, flipped open to the first page, and began to read.

After a half hour, she set the report down on the desk. She sat there for a few moments, stunned. Then she reread a few key sections, trying to bring her thoughts into sharper focus. She had zeroed in on the crucial figures about the losses within the core city market. The report contained an addendum from the advertising director that pointed out what the circulation drain meant in potential lost advertising revenues. The *Times*'s influence in the city, she realized, was in a slow and apparently irreversible decline.

Her thoughts shifted to Stephen. He knew how important this is, she thought. Why didn't he tell me? She sighed in confused dismay. Maybe, she thought, I should ask myself why I didn't see this coming. But hadn't Stephen continually assured her that a reversal of the trend would come? She had trusted his judgment. How could he have been so wrong?

She had to get home to talk to Stephen. She rose, stuffed the report under her arm, and grabbed her coat.

At home, she noticed a light on in the study and went to the door. Stephen was sitting at the desk, reading. It was an odd sight; he usually conceded the study as Kellen's territory. He felt her eyes on him and looked up.

"You're home," he said. "I've been waiting." His eyes focused on the report she was still carrying. "Did you read it?" he asked.

"Yes." She came in, slipping off her coat. "It's an important report, Stephen. Why didn't you tell me?"

She stood before the desk, waiting. She noticed his hands, resting lightly on a copy of that afternoon's *Times*.

"Why?" she asked again.

He rose and went to a window, staring out. It was a while before he turned back to her. "I didn't want you to worry," he said quietly.

"Worry? But you knew I'd eventually read it." She paused. "Is this also why you suggested I should skip the vice presidents' meeting Monday? Did you think I wouldn't find out about this?"

He said nothing.

"Stephen, what's wrong?" she said slowly. "Are you afraid I'll come on too strong at the meeting Monday? You know I'm always careful about—"

"Yes, I know," he said, without looking back at her.

The slight edge to his voice surprised her. She stared at his back. "What's going on here?" she asked softly. "Talk to me, Stephen. This isn't like you. Or us. We've always been able to talk things out before."

"Well, we've never had quite this problem before," he said wryly. Finally, he turned and faced her. "The problems the report outlines are serious, Kellen. I thought things were going to stabilize. But they haven't. It's only gotten worse." He shook his head, smiling artificially. "And I'll be damned if I know how to fix it."

He went back to the desk and began to turn the pages of the newspaper slowly. "I've been sitting in here for the last two hours waiting for you to get back," he said quietly. "I started looking through some of these old copies of the *Times* you keep around, the ones from when your father was alive. I got to comparing them with the *Times* as it is now."

He didn't look up at her. "Funny how you can get so close to something you can't really see it." He turned the pages. "On first glance, the *Times* looks as healthy as ever. But then you begin to notice some differences. I remember it being a bulky thing. But it's smaller now."

She came over to the desk and looked down at the two newspapers. In her entire life, she had never once heard Stephen sound so negative. It frightened her a little. "There are some problems, Stephen, but it's as good now as it ever was," she said. "Because of you, we've won two Pulitzers in the last five years and—"

"Prizes don't mean a damn if people stop reading your paper," he interrupted. "We've lost a lot of advertising, the newshole has shrunk, we're running fewer pages." He paused. "And now, it's only going to get worse."

He closed the newspapers and looked at her. "I guess that's why I didn't tell you about what was in the report. Until it came out, I thought I could turn things around. But I was fooling myself, and you, too." His eyes held hers. "I just couldn't stand your being disappointed in me."

She stared at him. "Stephen, you shouldn't take this personally. It isn't your fault. It's just as much my—"

"How can I not take this personally?" he said. "Your father gave me this job because he trusted me. And you—" He caught himself. "And you trusted me, too, Kellen. Call it a misguided sense of honor, or maybe just plain old-fashioned ego, but I took that responsibility seriously! And I failed!"

His face was flushed with frustration and lined with fatigue. She understood now why he had been working so hard during the past year, and she was angry with herself for not shouldering more of the burden. Now, she knew with certainty that she had to go back to work full-time. More than her own satisfaction was at stake. The *Times* needed her more than ever. But she knew that right now she couldn't tell Stephen that. All her life, she had looked to him for strength and reassurance, and suddenly she had to provide those things for him. If she told him now that she was going back to work, it would only confirm his feeling that she didn't trust him. She would have to tell him of her intent, but not at this moment, when he needed her faith.

"You didn't fail, Stephen," she said softly. "You're only one person, and you can't shoulder all the blame." She smiled slightly to convey an optimism she didn't really feel. "It'll work out. We'll keep looking for answers. We'll find a way." She hesitated, then put her arms around his neck. "It will work out, Stephen. You'll see."

Stephen's eyes were locked on hers. Finally, he kissed her, slowly at first, then with more intensity. His ardor surprised her; it had been so long since he kissed her that way, and she felt herself responding. Slowly, a sense of renewed hope came over her. She would go back to the *Times*, and she and Stephen would find a way to save it.

Everything is going to work out, she thought. She pulled back and stared up into Stephen's eyes. She took his hand and led him out of the study and up the staircase.

Chapter
Thirty

The vice presidents' meeting was into its fifth hour, and the strain showed on everyone's faces. Ian, who had showed up an hour late and taken his spot at the head of the long mahogany table, did nothing to hide his irritation. Kellen sat in her place at the other end of the table. Stephen sat along the table with the six other division heads. Before each person was a copy of the blue-bound circulation report.

"Look, we can sit up here all day, and these figures will not change," said the vice president of advertising, Dennis Dingman. "If circulation doesn't start coming around, we can look forward to a drop in revenue next fiscal year of at least twenty percent. And that is the bottom line."

Harry Beebe, the vice president of circulation who had been taking the brunt of the fire all afternoon, rose slowly. "Well, my bottom line went to sleep an hour ago," he said testily. He went over to the coffeepot and poured himself a cup. "Anyone want any more?" he asked, looking around.

"If I drink any more of that stuff my kidneys will explode," mumbled Fred Chase, the rotund head of production.

"You know, Harry," Chase said. "Advertising's right. It all starts with you guys. According to these reports, we're getting a lot of cancellations because of late delivery. Maybe if you got the papers out to folks on time, we'd hang on to subscribers better."

"And maybe if you guys got the paper off the press on time, we could make our delivery schedule," Harry retorted.

"Look, don't blame us," Chase shot back. "We can't print the thing until editorial gives it to us. And they've been playing pretty loose with deadlines lately."

Kellen glanced at Stephen. "Fred, we're just trying to get the latest news in,'' he said evenly. ''We can't push the deadlines up again just to allow for press downtime.''

Ian rolled his eyes. ''We're not going to hear that one again, are we? Next you'll start in about those experimental computers again—how we can solve all our composing room problems for the paltry fee of two million.''

''It's two point five six million,'' added George Avare, the vice president of finance, ''that we don't have. For a system no one's sure will replace good, old-fashioned Linotypes.''

Stephen stared at Ian, who stared back in cool defiance. He glanced at Kellen, then at each of the others, noting their defeated and frustrated expressions. ''Look,'' he said. ''We won't get anywhere pointing fingers. This isn't a circulation problem, or production problem, or editorial problem. It's a problem we have to solve together. If we don't, we can just sit back and watch the *Times* die a slow death.''

He looked at Kellen, knowing how the words would sting. But she maintained her implacable expression. She knew just how bad things were. They had talked about it over the weekend. She told him she wanted the truth presented in its rawest terms, to her and the others.

''I had some extra materials prepared for you,'' Stephen said, holding up another report.

There a few weary sighs. Everyone was tired of reading reports.

''I hope you read it,'' Stephen went on, ''because it summarizes what I think is the real problem.'' He paused. ''We've been sitting here talking about how to fight the *Journal*. But the *Journal* isn't our real enemy. Our real problem is time. The simple fact is, the *Times* is an afternoon newspaper, and people just aren't buying afternoon papers like they used to.''

Kellen listened as Stephen reiterated the contents of his report. She had read it this morning, and for the first time she had understood why Stephen was so pessimistic. The rival morning *Journal* was succeeding because it was riding a wave of altered reading habits in the Bay Area. It had started after World War II when people's work patterns began to change, but the effect was too subtle then for anyone to really notice until it was too late. Industrial workers used to leave for work early and had no time to read a newspaper in the morning. So the afternoon newspaper of Adam Bryant's day suited their needs. But now, the economy was dominated by service workers, who went to work later and had time for a paper with morning coffee. These workers came home later and when they wanted to hear the news, they switched on the TV.

And there were the practical considerations. The Bay Area's streets and the arteries extending into the suburbs were becoming increasingly congested, and the *Times* was delivered during the busiest hours of the late afternoon. The *Journal* trucks, on the other hand, maneuvered through the empty predawn streets. Just getting the *Times* to homes had become a headache. Even Kellen had taken a few calls from readers complaining about their "useless" newspapers arriving after dinnertime, well after the six o'clock news.

"So what you're suggesting," Ian interrupted, "is that we're a victim of an industry trend. And that there is no way to make this newspaper as profitable as it used to be."

Stephen stared at him. "Yes, it's a national trend. But I don't consider it hopeless."

Stephen began to explain some tactics that other afternoon newspapers were exploring. Ian thumbed through Stephen's report morosely, pointedly ignoring him. Kellen wondered if he had come only to harass Stephen. He rarely bothered to attend the monthly meetings. In fact, since his marriage, he had kept a low profile in the *Times*'s management. She suspected it was because of Clarisse. She was a rabid social climber who loved to travel and spend money, and she and Ian had done both extravagantly since their wedding. But the recent birth of their son had curtailed their free-wheeling life. And Ian had resumed his managerial style of interfering in every aspect of the *Times*'s operation without offering any real leadership. He didn't seem so concerned about the circulation problems as he did about the flat revenues. In the past two months, he had been pressuring the vice presidents to find ways to cut back on expenses. Recently, he had convinced them to institute a hiring freeze. Kellen glanced at Stephen. At least, during the past five years, she had been a buffer between Ian's self-interest and Stephen's ambitions for the newsroom. All her years of study of the newspaper operations had given her an appreciation of how each division worked, but she knew the heart of any newspaper was the editorial division. And she was determined to stop Ian from pillaging it.

Stephen finished his summary. "I know this is not encouraging," he said. "But we can't just look for Band-Aid solutions to stop the circulation drain." He glanced discreetly at Ian. "Or to inflate revenues. Whatever we do in that regard will be chimerical." He tossed his report on the table. "The real problem will not go away."

The room was silent. The animosity between Ian and Stephen

had never been a secret, and usually the other vice presidents just did their best to keep out of the way. Ian lit a cigarette. "Well, Stephen. As usual, you've given us an eloquent presentation of the problem, but no solutions."

Stephen leaned forward slightly. "No, I don't have an easy solution to the afternoon question, Ian, although I plan to keep looking for one." He glanced at Kellen. "But I do have one idea that might help our delivery problem."

His words took Kellen by surprise. He had mentioned nothing to her about any plan. He gave her a quick conciliatory look. "It's something I've been thinking about all weekend, since the report came out. I was going to wait until I had solid figures to back me up, but maybe it's something we should talk about now." He paused. "We could build a satellite printing plant in the suburbs."

"What good would that do?" Ian asked.

"Much of our circulation is in the suburbs now," Stephen said. "And it's vital that we hold on to it. If the papers could be printed and distributed closer to their destinations, circulation in the outlying communities could be maintained. Of course, a new plant wouldn't stem the circulation drop in the city, but it would buy time until we can solve the rest of the problem."

"It certainly would help me," the production man said.

George Avare shook his head. "It would cost millions. You have any idea what real estate's doing these days outside the city? It's not cows living out there anymore."

"He's right. We can't afford it," Ian said.

Kellen cleared her throat, and everyone looked at her. "It won't cost a thing to research," she said. "George, why don't you get together with Stephen and Fred and prepare a feasibility study, with complete cost estimates. Once we have some facts, we can meet again and discuss it."

Avare glanced at Ian, then made a note to himself with a frown. Ian slowly ground his cigarette in the ashtray. His eyes traveled over each face, coming to rest on Kellen's.

"All right, we'll go through with this little exercise," he said. "But I can fill you in right now on the realities of this newspaper's situation. Our revenues are the flattest they've been in twenty years, and our expenses continue to climb. The reality is, there is no extra money for any expansion right now. And I'm certainly not about to dig into my own pockets to finance any harebrained schemes."

He leaned back in his chair. "I've been very patient about this newspaper's failure to generate more revenue. But my patience is wearing thin." He glanced at Stephen. "If what Stephen says is true about the *Times* fighting a losing battle, then I may have no choice but to try to protect my own interests and those of my family." He paused. "If things continue on their present course, I may have no alternative but to sell the corporation."

The room was suddenly silent as everyone stared at Ian in complete shock. A few eyes shifted discreetly toward Kellen. No one had mentioned selling since Garrett Richardson had made his buy-out attempt eight years ago. All the men knew that Ian could make no such move without Kellen, but they also knew that Ian was capable of trying anything. The tension among the vice presidents was almost palpable.

Ian looked around. "Well, I see that we have nothing more to say. I have a dinner engagement." He rose and walked imperiously out of the conference room.

For a moment no one said anything. Then Stephen cleared his throat. "Maybe we should call it a day," he said.

"Just a moment, Stephen," Kellen interrupted. All eyes turned to her.

"I want all of you to know," she said slowly, "that no matter what my brother says, I will never sell these newspapers. That was my position eight years ago, and that is my position now. I give you my word." She looked at each of the six men and Stephen. "We have problems right now, but I'm confident we can find the answers. We have to keep looking."

There were a few nervous exchanges of glances and a couple of weak nods of acknowledgment. Then, with a rustling of papers, everyone began to leave. Stilted good-byes were exchanged, and the vice presidents filed out, leaving Stephen and Kellen alone. They walked down the hall together for a ways without talking.

"They didn't look very confident about what I said," Kellen said finally.

"They know Ian, and they're afraid of him. You're more of an unknown to them."

"That's going to change," she said quietly. Stephen, lost in his own thoughts, let the remark pass.

They went to the elevator and were silent until the door opened onto the bright lights of the newsroom. Stephen held the door open.

"You look tired," she said. "Why don't you go home early for a change."

"As soon as I clear a few things off my desk." He smiled slightly. "You, on the other hand, look like you're off to a party."

She smiled back. "I'm meeting Tyler and Clark for dinner."

"Ah, I forgot."

Heedless of passersby, she leaned over and kissed Stephen's cheek. "I won't be late."

He seemed embarrassed, but then he had always been sensitive to such displays in front of his employees. She wondered if it would get worse once she was in the office all the time. She had to confront him with her intention soon, perhaps tomorrow. He seemed more optimistic today than he had Friday night, undoubtedly because of his idea about the new plant. Maybe now he would be more supportive of her need.

"I wish you had told me about your idea beforehand," she said. "I could have been more of a help up there."

"You were," Stephen said. "You let me have my say."

With a small smile, he let go of the elevator, and the door closed before she could reply.

Kellen paused just inside the restaurant's entrance, looking for Clark and Tyler. The Washington Square Bar and Grill was crowded, filled with smoke and the cacophony of clattering dishes and conversation. The wooden bar was nearly obscured by people waiting for tables, while above them, on the television, the Golden State Warriors were soundlessly dribbling up and down the basketball court. The burgundy walls were dotted by old photographs of cable cars, and on the coat rack, two old wooden coat hangers drooped forlornly next to a man's dusty raincoat. In the back, a man was playing languorous jazz on the battered upright piano.

A man asked Kellen if she wanted a table, and Kellen smiled, her ego slightly wounded over the fact that he didn't recognize her. Despite its homely appearance, the "Washbag" was a popular hangout for journalists and celebrities. "I'm with Clark Able," Kellen said.

The man smiled broadly at the mention of Clark's name and led her through the bar. He held back the heavy burgundy draperies that divided the bar from the main dining room, and Kellen saw Clark and Tyler at a premiere table. Clark saw her and held out a chair as heads turned in their direction. A few people stared at Kellen, knowing who she was. Others just wondered who Clark Able's latest dining companion was.

"Sorry I'm late," Kellen said. "The meeting ran long." She kissed Tyler on the cheek. "You look good."

Tyler smiled. "You, too," he said.

She noticed that Clark had replaced his old horn-rimmed glasses with snappy wire aviator frames. Coupled with his impeccably tailored glen-plaid sport coat and tan slacks, he looked wonderfully debonair. At forty-six, he had that special aura so many successful men strive for but seldom achieve—the look of being splendidly at ease with the world around him. The waiter fawned over Clark, who, with a bit of theatrical flourish, ordered wine.

"I had forgotten what a fishbowl this place is," Kellen said as she slipped out of her fur coat.

"Well, do you expect *not* to be stared at wearing half the Russian sable population on your back?" Clark said, picking up a sleeve. "Where'd you get this?"

"It was my mother's. I had it restyled," Kellen said. "I thought it was a shame to just let it sit in storage."

Clark poured her a glass of wine. "It doesn't really suit you, you know."

"What do you mean?"

"It's so . . . matronly."

"Why, thank you, Clark," she said sarcastically.

"Oh, don't get huffy. We've known each other too long. It's too late for tact."

She took a generous drink of her wine. "Sometimes a little tact would be welcome."

Clark sighed. "All right, I'm sorry. It's just that you know I hate to see you dress like this. I know you think you have some corporate image to maintain at those meetings, but it's starting to carry over into your real life. Those sweet little Ferragamo pumps, that dear little Hermès bag, that precious Chanel suit. Your hair pinned up and sprayed like Queen Elizabeth. Kel, dear, you're getting ossified—"

"Ossified?" Tyler interjected.

Kellen sighed. "Clark and I have had this conversation before. He thinks I should be wearing gold lamé jumpsuits or, better yet, streaking with him through Union Square."

"Well, you are looking a little uptight," Tyler said.

Kellen stared at him, then picked up her menu. "Let's order," she said curtly.

While they ate, the conversation caromed between art, which was Tyler's favorite topic, and French movies, which had been Clark's preferred subject ever since his first trip to the Cannes Film Festival several years ago. Kellen halfheartedly poked at her pasta and tried to keep up her end of the small talk. But her mind kept drifting back to Clark's remarks about her appearance. He hadn't meant to be cruel, but his words had hurt.

Matronly? She didn't consider it matronly. She simply considered it well dressed. Hadn't she, after all, been named to the city's best-dressed list three years running now? Matronly . . . that described old women, like Enid Atherton, in gray chiffon with billowing sleeves to hide flaccid arms and choker pearls to disguise a crepey neck. Matronly was not Kellen Bryant Hillman.

It was true she had developed a taste for finer couture clothes. She was, after all, no longer a girl who could get away with the antique thrift store finds she used to love wearing. One day about five years ago, she had gone through her closet and given away the collection of antique clothes she had accumulated over the years. Stephen had said it was just a ruse to buy a new wardrobe. But she knew he had never really cared for the old clothes. He liked her best when she dressed in understated, classic clothes.

Kellen reached up and self-consciously adjusted her pearl necklace. Yes, Stephen liked the way she looked. He had told her so tonight. Kellen took another sip of wine and was struck with a sudden curious thought. Maybe the fact that he liked her to dress a certain way had something to do with his not wanting her to go back to work full-time. He wanted her to fit into a certain traditional role, one that dovetailed neatly with his own. Another thought struck her. In a perverse sort of way, Stephen was treating her just as her father had, imposing on her the same misguided sense of feminine duty. And she had been accepting it, as if she were trying to be her mother.

She felt a chill and drew the fur up over her shoulders. She realized suddenly that it smelled slightly musty.

"You're completely wrong," Clark said. "Don't you think he's wrong, Kel?"

"Hmm?"

"About Alain Delon! Haven't you been listening? Tyler thinks he was sexier than Belmondo in *Borsalino*. My god, man, Belmondo *is* sex!"

"Sex is more than looks," Tyler countered.

"Of course it is!" Clark said. "It's chemistry! It's Seberg and Belmondo. It's Lana Turner and John Garfield. It's Lady and Tramp. Sex is the right man and woman together at the right moment!"

Kellen took another sip of wine, letting the conversation recede again. Sex . . . the right man, the right moment . . . Her mind drifted back to Friday night when she and Stephen had made love. As usual, it had been pleasantly satisfying. Certainly nothing earth-shattering, but then, it never had been between them. And what could one expect, after all, after nearly eight years? Surely she had outgrown any adolescent delusions about that. Yet, lately, sex also left her with an odd emptiness that she tried to vanquish by doing everything she could to please Stephen. But it didn't go away, and their lovemaking remained a tender ritual that gave her only the relief of physical release.

She wondered if Stephen felt the same, but he gave no indication. Perhaps it didn't matter to him. He had always been content to play ascetic to her sensualist. And there were more important things that made a marriage work.

Kellen took another sip of wine and closed her eyes. The wine had relaxed her, opening the door of her memory just wide enough for Garrett to slip through. She pushed the thought back quickly. She forced herself to pick up the thread of conversation. Now Clark and Tyler were arguing about art.

"Conceptual art is garbage," Clark said.

"You shouldn't criticize what you don't know about," Tyler replied.

"I've been to these so-called shows. One was called Newt Ascends Fred Astaire's Face. Frankly, he's had better partners. . . ."

Kellen smiled. Clark was always such a welcome diversion.

"A couple of months ago," Clark went on, "I was invited to an exhibition at the Hansen Fuller Gallery. It was this fellow just sitting on a metal stool in front of an elevator. Two days later, he finally fell off and they drew a chalk outline around his body. Then they put *that* on exhibit."

"But that's the whole point!" Tyler exclaimed. "The *act* of creation is what's important. The act of art *is* the art. The result is just . . . debris!"

Clark turned to Kellen. "So that's what's been hanging over your fireplace all these years. Your father thought he was buying a Giacometti, but it's really garbage."

Kellen laughed, but Tyler's look of frustration made her sober quickly in sympathy. "I thought you were studying painting," she said to him, to neutralize Clark's needling.

"I switched to sculpture," Tyler said tersely.

"I'd like to see your work sometime," Kellen said.

Tyler took a drink of his club soda. "Well, I don't have anything . . . personally. I belong to an art collective. We have a studio in the Embarcadero. We're called the Ant Farm."

"I had an ant farm when I was a boy," Clark offered, pouring more wine. "Very industrious little creatures. Fun to watch . . ."

"Ant Farm," Kellen repeated. "Aren't they the ones who planted all those cars in Texas?"

Tyler brightened. "Yes, they took these old Caddies and half buried them in a line. It's called Cadillac Ranch. I went out there and helped dig the holes. A great example of environmental sculpture!"

Clark sighed. "My idea of great environmental sculpture is the Golden Gate Bridge. Or the Ferry Building tower. And now that's hidden by a freeway ramp—"

"Watch out, Clark," Kellen said, smiling, "you're getting nostalgic again."

Before Clark could reply, a man came up to speak to him. Clark turned to Kellen and said that he had to talk to someone at another table for a column item. He excused himself, leaving Tyler and Kellen alone.

Tyler watched him go, shaking his head. "Brother," he murmured. "He calls you ossified? He's the one turning into a fossil."

Kellen waited a moment. "Am I?"

"What?"

"You know. Too set in my ways." She shrugged off the fur coat. "What do you think of this coat, for instance? Does it make me look too old?"

"This is a first. My sister asking me for fashion advice."

Tyler's pale eyes were lit with amusement. Now twenty, he had grown into a tall, handsome young man, with a penchant for the latest fashions. Several of her friends had asked Kellen to fix their daughters up with him. But she always declined, having learned years ago that telling Tyler what to do with his life was impossible. She realized suddenly that she actually knew very little about his life lately. She knew that he had been taking art classes at Berkeley, but she had the feeling that he was just floating, looking for something to latch on to. She felt the old tug of duty toward him.

"Well, I'm asking your opinion," she said. "Do I look matronly to you?"

He picked up her wine and took a big drink. "You look like you need to get laid," he said with a sly smile.

"Tyler!" Kellen glanced around to make sure no one heard.

He laughed. "You know, there was a time when you would have hit me for saying that. Or at least laughed."

"We're not kids anymore. Or at least I'm not," she snapped. She took the wineglass from him. "Give me that. You're still underage, you know."

Tyler shook his head disparagingly. "You'll never stop treating me like a child, will you? I'll be twenty-one soon, for god's sake. I have my own life now."

"But what kind of life is it? I worry about you."

"Well, don't."

Kellen frowned. "But I do. You never tell me anything about yourself. I worry about your finding someone you care about, finding work you care about." She paused. "Why don't you come work at the newspaper? Stephen can—"

"I've told you before I don't want to work there," Tyler interrupted.

"But you could—"

"I want my own dreams, dammit, not Father's hand-me-downs."

Kellen stared at Tyler, taken back. She touched his arm. "Tyler, I don't want to argue. I just—"

"Forget it," he said quickly. When he saw the look on her face, his eyes softened. "Trust me, Kellen. I can take care of myself."

Before either could say anything more, Clark returned to the table, apologizing for his absence. "I got a really great tip from a real estate guy," he said. "This widow up on Nob Hill just died after living in the same building for twenty-five years and left her four-bedroom penthouse to the doorman. But the doorman says it's not his style so he's put it up for sale. One point two million . . . and he's going to keep his job."

"Sounds like a lead item," Kellen smiled.

"Right," Clark said, grabbing his coat. "I'm going up there. You two don't mind, do you?" He kissed Kellen's cheek. "Dinner next week? My place?" She nodded. With a hurried good-bye, Clark was gone. Kellen and Tyler sat quietly for a moment without looking at each other.

"Well, I'd better get home," Kellen said, rising. Tyler followed. They paused just outside the door.

"I don't mean to be hard on you, Tyler," Kellen said. "It's just that I hardly see you these days." Tyler pulled up the collar of his sport coat against the cold. Kellen smiled. "Look at you. You don't even have the sense to wear a warm coat." She kissed his cheek. "Call me this week, okay?"

She was about to turn, but Tyler grabbed her arm. "Listen," he said. "Let's go have a drink. I know a nice quiet place that won't card me. There's something I want to talk to you about."

Kellen paused. "All right," she said. They took a cab across town. The bar was tucked back in an alleyway, discernible only by a discreet neon moon above the door. The interior was dark, and Tyler led Kellen to a banquette. He ordered two manhattans.

"That's a rather old-fashioned drink," Kellen said with a small smile.

"I'm an old-fashioned guy at heart," Tyler said.

When the waiter brought the drinks, Tyler quickly took a gulp of his.

"Makes me feel old seeing my little brother in a bar," Kellen said.

Tyler smiled slightly and took another huge drink.

As her eyes adjusted to the dim light, Kellen looked around the bar. It was handsomely decorated in ebony wood and art deco banquettes. A pianist was playing Gershwin at the baby grand in the corner, and the men sitting at the bar were dressed in business suits. Slowly, her eyes swept the entire crowded room. Suddenly, it hit her. There were only men. It was a gay bar.

She looked back at Tyler. "Very funny," she said. "Why did you bring me here?"

Tyler's eyes held hers. Even in the half light, she could see the strange mix of emotions in them. Great trepidation, wariness, and a sort of giddy exhilaration. "You want to know about my life," Tyler said. He paused. "Well, this is it. This is my life. I'm gay."

He said it matter-of-factly, with a smile, but she could tell he was waiting for her response. She was so stunned, she couldn't think of anything to say. Finally, she stammered, "But how—"

Tyler leaned back in his chair and laughed so loudly others looked over. "We'll leave that question for the geneticists, shrinks and priests," he said, grinning.

Kellen frowned. "I was going to ask how long."

He began to play with the drink straw. "All my life," he said. Kellen could only stare at him. "But I've known for sure since I was thirteen."

The pianist started in on "A Foggy Day." The bar seemed to Kellen suddenly oppressive. She wanted desperately to say something, something right that didn't sound reproachful, but her shock was just too great. "Why did you decide to tell me?" she asked finally.

A vulnerable look crept into Tyler's eyes. "I don't know. Tired of keeping it to myself, I guess." There was a long silence. "You're the only person I've told," he said.

Another silence, long and awkward. Kellen looked at her watch. "I have to get going," she said. "Stephen will be worried."

Tyler said nothing. He sat there, staring at her, his face now serious. "You disapprove, don't you," he said.

"It's not that. It's just that . . . " Kellen's voice trailed off. She knew that whatever she said, it would sound wrong, and Tyler would take it as a condemnation, another attempt on her part to try to interfere with his life.

"Well, don't worry," Tyler said with a smile. "I'll stay in the closet like a good boy. I won't do anything to embarrass you." Kellen started to say something, but he held up his hand. "And I'd appreciate it," he said, "if you kept this to yourself. I'm not ashamed of it, but I'm not quite ready to go public. I've seen one too many friends pay the price." He looked out over the bar. "Had one get the shit beat out of him the other day," he said softly. "Just walking down the street, minding his own business and these three guys jumped him." When he finally looked back at Kellen, he smiled, but his eyes had hardened. "So. I'll see you soon," he said curtly. "Give my best to Stephen. . . ."

Kellen sighed, knowing it was useless to get Tyler to say anything more. She put on her coat and stood up. "Why don't you come over for dinner tomorrow night?" she asked.

"Can't. I'm going away skiing for a week. Ian invited me to go with him and Clarisse to his condo in Aspen."

Kellen stared at Tyler. She was unaware that Ian and Tyler had any contact, let alone were friendly enough to vacation together. She immediately suspected Ian must have an ulterior motive but decided it was a bad time to suggest such a thing to Tyler. "Well, have a good time," she said simply. "And call me when you get back. We'll get together."

"Sure," Tyler muttered. He picked up his drink and didn't look up at her. When she got to the door, Kellen looked back to the table, but Tyler was gone.

As she rode home in a taxi, Kellen's thoughts stayed with Tyler and his incredible revelation. The only person who she knew for certain was gay was her hairstylist, and he seemed like a happy, uncomplicated man. She had never given any thought to his lifestyle, thinking of it only as a sort of strange netherworld. But now it was more than that; it was her brother's life. And she realized she knew nothing about it—or him. He was a stranger to her, all over again. She realized, with a small feeling of disgust, that she wasn't thinking so much of Tyler and his feelings as she was about herself. She was wondering what people might think if it became known. And she was playing back her childhood and Tyler's, looking for clues as to what could have influenced him. Did she somehow have a part in it? Did their father?

She remembered suddenly an article that had run recently on the front page of the *Times*. It had announced that the American Psychiatric Association no longer classified homosexuality as a mental illness. It had generated many negative letters to the editor, and Ian, who had a homophobic streak, had taken Stephen to task for giving it such prominent display. At the time, she thought the article had made sense. But now, confronted with Tyler's admission, she was wondering if there was, in fact, something wrong with him. Now, more than ever, she was worried about him. He needed someone to take care of him, and now—how in the world would he ever find someone?

The taxi pulled up to the house; she paid the driver and went in. Stephen was sitting up in bed, reading a book when she came into the bedroom. "How was dinner?" he asked.

"All right, I guess."

"You sound a little down. Is Tyler all right?"

She thought for a moment about telling Stephen. "He's fine," she said instead. She went into the dressing room, closing the door behind her. She changed and went into the bathroom. She stood for a moment before the mirror, staring at her reflection. Her makeup and hair, swept up in a French twist, were perfect as ever, but she looked tired. She leaned forward to inspect the tiny lines around her eyes. No need to worry—no wrinkles, no signs of age. But something had crept into the corners of her mouth, setting it into the beginnings of hardness. She thought again of what Clark had said about her appearance. And she thought, too, of Tyler and how he had picked up on her shock and disapproval. He had told her his greatest secret. Why hadn't she been able to give him the comfort he needed? Had she become that grim and self-centered? At one time, she might have easily dealt with Tyler's news, when she had been more open-minded.

I don't like what's happening to me, she thought, staring at her reflection. I don't want to pretend to be someone I'm not.

She washed away the makeup and brushed out her hair, which had the immediate effect of making her look younger. She paused to look at herself once more, then went into the bedroom. Stephen didn't look up from his reading as she slipped out of her robe and into bed.

"Stephen?"

"Hmmm . . ."

She turned in the bed to face him. "I want to go back to work."

"We've talked about this before," he began.

"But I'm not so sure you've really listened, Stephen."

He looked at her carefully then set aside his book, waiting.

"It's not that I don't trust you to do your job," she said. "In fact, my wanting to go back has nothing to do with you at all." She paused. "It's not just for the *Times*'s sake. It's for my sake."

She had wanted to explain this to him for so long and now struggled to find the right words. "Most of my life, I've been doing things to try to please the people who are important to me. First my father; then you." She paused. "But outside of those years I spent in Paris, I've never really lived according to my own needs." She smiled wanly. "I always talked a good game, but I never really had the guts to live my life the way I really wanted."

She looked at him, but there was nothing in his eyes that told her she was getting through to him.

"I feel like I'm drying up inside, Stephen," she said quietly. "I need something else in my life besides this house and the children. I want to go back to work."

"But you've always had the newspaper, Kellen," Stephen said.

She shook her head slowly. "Not really." She paused. "My father told me something once, something I never forgot. He said everyone needs a passion in their lives, something they believe in. That's what the *Times* should be to me. Up until now, I've only given it parts of me—in the beginning because of my own limitations, and in the last five years, because the children needed me more. But if I'm ever going to really claim it as my own, I have to give myself to it completely. Just like my father did."

His expression was noncommittal. "Ben and Sara still need you," he said.

"I know. But my duty goes beyond just being here at home for them. I have a duty to preserve these newspapers and hand them over to them someday. *We* have a duty to do that."

He remained pensive, but she could see a hint of understanding, or at least acceptance, in his eyes.

"Please try to understand," she said.

He hesitated, then sighed. "I don't completely," he said slowly, "but I want you to be happy, Kellen. And I know you haven't been lately."

She forced herself not to look away.

"If going back full-time will make you happy, then you should do it," he said. He paused. "I guess the kids will survive. Don't know if I can say the same for me, though."

She realized with relief that it was an attempt at levity. Encouraged, she smiled. "Oh, it won't be so bad. Do you remember what it was like when we worked in the newsroom together? We had a lot of fun in those days."

He gave her a begrudging smile. "Don't even think about coming down to my newsroom," he said.

"I'll stay upstairs. I promise."

Kellen slid down in the bed and fit herself into the crook of Stephen's arm. His arms went up around her. She smiled to herself, already anticipating her first real day back at the *Times*. As for how it was going to affect Stephen—well, he would eventually come to accept it.

Stephen turned out the light and his arms came back up to hold her. She exhaled deeply and closed her eyes, finally letting out the tension of the day. She knew that she and Stephen would not make love, but she didn't care. At that moment, it was good enough just as it was.

Chapter
Thirty-one

Kellen picked up the *Times* that had just been delivered to her office. Ignoring the front page, she pulled out the Lifestyle section and sighed with resignation. Well, there it is, she thought. But at least the problem is solved.

The front page of the section, which normally was filled with features, photographs, and Clark's column, was dominated by a huge advertisement for Macy's touting lingerie. Clark's column was the only editorial content, stripped down the left-hand side.

Kellen frowned. It looked wrong to see an ad on a section front, but there was no point in worrying about it anymore. She had fought to prevent it, but in the end she had conceded defeat. About a month ago, right after she had returned to the office full-time, the battle over the section front had begun. She found out that the advertising department, with Ian's blessing, had promised Macy's that they could move their ads from inside the section to the front page if they re-signed their long-term contract. Both she and Stephen were incensed—sacrificing a front page to ads was a sellout, the hallmark of a small-town newspaper. But the store had threatened to pull its ads from the *Times*, saying there was no point in advertising in two newspapers when the *Journal* had a higher city circulation. The fallout from the circulation report had begun, and if Macy's, one of the *Times*'s biggest advertisers, pulled out, others might eventually follow. Reluctantly, even Stephen came to take advertising's side. "I know it stinks," he told Kellen, "but it's a matter of survival."

Clark had taken the news as a personal insult. "That column is my life," he said. "When your father gave it to me, I don't think either of us realized how important it would become. But now that column *is* me. And this tells me that it's not important. That *I'm* not important."

Kellen knew that the *Times* had to keep Macy's under contract. But she still wanted to make a stand for Clark and the *Times*. She proposed a compromise: that the store cut its ad back to three-quarters of the page, leaving space for Clark's column. "It's the best-read thing in this city," she told Macy's representatives. "Your ads will benefit from placement near Clark." Macy's signed a new contract.

It had been her first decisive move since her return, but now, as Kellen stared at the ad, she felt no real sense of victory. During the past month, she had thrown herself into work with a renewed passion, but so far she felt as if she had made no real impact. The real problems remained untreated, eating away at the *Times*'s foundation.

Stephen's plan to build a suburban printing plant was still being researched, the final cost projections due any day. She hoped the news would be positive, not just for the *Times*'s sake but for Stephen's. In the past month, he had been tense and preoccupied, working hard preparing the research and lobbying the other vice presidents for support. The plan had become more than just a way to help the *Times*; it was now a personal crusade to reassert his influence. But she didn't dare tell Stephen this.

Kellen leaned back in her chair. Since her return she had made it a point to stay out of the newsroom. Stephen listened to her ideas, including one to start a writer-in-residence program, whereby big name authors would join the staff temporarily to write on whatever topic they wished. But there was a lingering tension between them.

Ian had not helped matters. Sensing Stephen's vulnerability, he tried to use Kellen's return to antagonize him. The first challenge had come the first week Kellen was back. Ian had appeared unexpectedly at an editorial board meeting where the top editors were picking a candidate to endorse in an important local election. Ian had lobbied strongly for the Republican, but the board, led by Stephen, outvoted him and endorsed the Democrat. The endorsement was to appear the next day. But later that night, Ian went to the office, wrote an editorial endorsing the Republican, and ordered it placed on the front page. The fearful news editor complied, but a composing room foreman called Stephen at home and tipped him off. Stephen raced down to the office, and he and Ian got into a fierce argument in the composing room. It was only when Kellen finally interceded that Ian backed down.

Kellen turned her attention back to her desk. She picked up a memo Ian had sent to her that morning. She read it, shaking her head. Ian had found a new way to get at Stephen. He wanted to hire a general manager who would report directly to him, thereby undercutting Stephen's power. She would have to veto the move, once again forced into the role as Stephen's savior, another bruise to his already tender ego.

She glanced at her watch. It was almost noon, and she considered calling Stephen to see if he wanted to go to lunch. They had not had much time for each other lately. She was surprised when her secretary buzzed her and announced Stephen was on his way up to see her.

"I was just getting ready to call you," she said with a smile when he came in. Stephen was about to reply when Ian came in without knocking.

"We're busy, Ian," Kellen said tersely. "Whatever it is, it can wait."

"Not this," he said, tossing a report on the desk. "The verdict's in on the suburban plant." He held out a copy to Stephen. "You aren't going to like this."

Stephen and Kellen began to read. "Let me save you some time," Ian said. "What your feasibility study has taken four weeks to conclude is exactly what I said in the beginning. We can't afford it." Ian smiled. "See you at the meeting Monday," he said and left.

Neither Stephen nor Kellen looked up from their reading. After a few moments, she put the report down. "He's right," she said quietly. "I never thought the estimate would come in so high . . . twelve million. . . ." She looked at Stephen, who was still reading. "Stephen, I'm sorry," she said softly. "I know what this meant to you."

He glanced up at her, then went back to the report, flipping through the pages slowly as if in disbelief.

"I wish there were some way to swing this," she said.

Stephen looked up. "There is a way," he said. "You didn't read far enough. It's mentioned on page eighteen."

"What is it?"

"Liquidate an asset or company holding."

Kellen stared at him. "You mean, sell one of the other newspapers?"

Stephen closed the report. "Yes," he said quietly.

She glanced around the room in confusion, her eyes finally coming back to him. "Stephen, I couldn't do that," she stammered.

Now he stared at her. "Kellen, we have to do something, and

we have to do it soon, or we'll never be able to fix the problem,''
he said. "You might have to sacrifice one of the other papers in
the chain to save the *Times*."

She sat there, numb. She thought suddenly of the paper mill in
Canada, but she calculated quickly that selling off the chain's paper
source would be a foolish move. Paper was the single biggest expense for the corporation and having its own mill had kept that expense in line. She thought also of the television station in Oakland,
but she knew Ian would never consent to its sale. The station was
a low-cost moneymaker that Ian had always considered his personal
cash cow. Stephen was right; the only way to get enough capital to
finance the plant was through selling a newspaper.

Her eyes went to the stack of newspapers on a nearby credenza.
Every day, copies of each of the fifteen papers in the chain were
sent to her. She scarcely ever had time to glance at them, but she
always knew the papers were there, and their presence fortified
her. They represented a continuum to the past, to her father.

Stephen saw her looking at the newspapers. "Kellen, you can't
afford to be sentimental," he said softly.

"Sentimental?" she said. "I'm not being sentimental. I just
can't stand the thought of losing one of those papers." She picked
up the Lifestyle section. "It would be like accepting this ad,
Stephen. It's a small thing, but it still hurts the paper. You have
to draw the line somewhere. Selling one newspaper might seem
like a good sacrifice, but it's a loss we can never make back. Once
a newspaper is gone, it's gone forever." She shook her head. "I
can't do it."

"Kellen," he said patiently, "you know you let your heart rule
your head. Well, you can't this time."

"No," she said quickly. "Sometimes you have to use both. I
can't tear apart what it took my father all his life to build."

Stephen looked at her for a moment, then ran a hand over his
eyes. He got up slowly. "All right, Kellen," he said. "I don't
want to fight you on this. Or your father either." He turned to
leave.

"Stephen—" she called out.

He turned, waiting for her to say something.

"We'll find another way," she said.

He nodded slowly. "I'll see you at home tonight," he said and
left the office, closing the door behind him.

Kellen sat there, stunned. Not so much by the results of the
study as by Stephen's reaction to it. His willingness to sacrifice
one of the newspapers for his plan was troubling. And that he

would expect her to simply accept his idea as the only possible solution was unbelievable. And his words about her using her heart and not her head. After all this time, did he still see her as a girl, incapable of making an intelligent decision without his guidance?

He's just under strain, she thought. Just like I am.

The intercom buzzed, and Adele announced that Tyler was waiting to see her. Kellen frowned slightly. Tyler never came to the office. She hadn't seen or talked to him in a month, not since the night he told her about his homosexuality.

He came in, glancing around the office. "I've never been here before," he said, sitting down.

"It's not for want of an invitation."

There was an awkward silence. They had left each other on an unresolved note, and now neither knew how to go forward. Tyler smiled to break the ice. "You hire a decorator for this place or is this just your own good taste?"

"A little of both," she said, smiling.

He waited, but she seemed distracted, as if she wanted to get rid of him.

"Tyler," she began, "I'm a little busy right now. . . . What did you want to see me about?"

"I just came to ask a favor." He held out a piece of paper. "I'm wondering if you could help us out with this. You know, bend Stephen's arm, maybe get an article written."

She read the press release. It was about an event the Ant Farm was staging, something called Media Burn. "I try to make it a point not to tell Stephen what to put in the paper," Kellen said. "You could just ask him yourself."

"Well, I thought I'd go right to the top," he said, smiling slightly.

There was another awkward pause. Finally, Kellen picked up the press release. "All right, I'll make sure the right person gets it, okay?" she said.

Tyler nodded, then rose abruptly. "Well, got to get going," he said. "Got an important appointment across town."

She smiled. "Good luck with your show."

He paused at the door. "Would you like to come?" he asked. "It's going to be quite an event. It's tomorrow morning at eight at Cow Palace."

"I can't," she said. "I have a breakfast meeting."

He smiled, but it was forced. "Next time, maybe." He left the office.

She leaned back in her chair with a sigh. She felt bad for not giving Tyler more of her time. She sensed he had wanted to bridge the schism between them. But she hadn't felt up to it at the moment, not after the episode with Stephen. Besides, she knew she still wasn't ready to give Tyler the acceptance he obviously wanted. The shock was still too new. She scribbled a note atop the press release, routing it to Clark. She really didn't have time to go to the event, but maybe Clark could give it a mention. It was the least she could do for her brother, for now.

It was eight in the morning, and a fog still hung over the parking lot of the Cow Palace, shrouding the activities of the people gathered there in a mysterious air. It was a small group, and they went about their task with a quiet, cheerful sense of purpose. Soon, their work was completed and everyone stepped back to admire the results—a wall of forty-two television sets, stacked up in a twenty-foot pyramid, their screens looking like blank, trustful eyes.

Tyler and another member of the Ant Farm crew stepped forward with metal cans and began to douse the pyramid in kerosene. Nearby, a man in a business suit was standing behind a podium rigged from another TV set, testing the microphone. And several hundred yards in front of the pyramid stood a long, white 1959 Cadillac. Facing the TV screens, with its tail fins and towering airfoil, it looked like a menacing giant shark waiting to attack. The last ingredient came into place as the reporters, photographers, and cameramen straggled in from their cars and vans. Battery packs were turned on, notebooks flipped open.

Media Burn was about to begin.

Tyler stood off to one side, watching the show. He was searching for someone to share the moment with, but everyone looked too busy. He knew Kellen wouldn't come, but he felt a little hurt just the same. His trip to her office yesterday had been an excuse to initiate contact, but she had seemed uncomfortable, just as she had that night in the bar. He had told her about his homosexuality because he thought she was the one person he could trust to understand. But even she had let him down.

The businessman on the podium, identified only as the "Artist President," began to speak, and Tyler turned to listen. With his shock of hair, Brahmin accent, and studied mannerisms, the man looked like an ersatz John Kennedy. He implored onlookers to experience a "cathartic explosion" and "free themselves at last from the addiction of television. . . ."

Tyler spotted Clark Able in the crowd and went over to greet him. "So what do you think?" Tyler asked.

Clark jerked a thumb toward the speaker. "I think that guy does a terrible Vaughn Meader."

"This is a serious event, Clark," Tyler said. "It's a brilliant synthesis of two icons of American culture—television and cars." He gestured toward the network news cameras. "And don't you love the irony? The media that's destroying our minds is covering its own symbolic destruction?"

Clark grunted and turned his attention back to the Artist President, who was finishing with a flourish: "The world may never understand what was done here today, but the image created here shall never be forgotten."

"We shall see . . . in another twenty years," Clark mumbled.

The focus turned to the Cadillac. Two men in astronautlike suits slid into the car and someone torched the gas-soaked TV sets, which quickly ignited into a wall of orange flames. Ant Farm members wandered around, recording everything on video cameras. The car gunned its engine and took off. It plunged through the blazing televisions in a spray of flames and wood veneer as everyone cheered wildly. Then it pulled to a stop and the drivers jumped out, clasping their hands over their heads like they'd just finished the victory lap at Indy. The cameramen switched off their lights, and the reporters began to drift toward their cars.

"Now I know why they called it Media Burn," Clark said. "We're the ones who got burned—for wasting our time."

"Well, why'd you come then?" Tyler asked.

"Slow news day," Clark said with a shrug, wandering slowly off. "And I owed Kellen a favor."

Tyler stood alone, watching two men put out the blaze. He stared at the smoldering pile of wrecked TVs, feeling a sudden, small letdown. He knew he should offer to help clean up the mess, but he just didn't feel like it. He stuck his hands in his pockets and sauntered off toward his car.

"Tyler! Wait up!"

He turned and saw two men coming toward him. One man he recognized as Alan, one of the Ant Farm's minor players. The other, a tall man in jeans and a sweater, Tyler didn't know. Alan caught up. "Heading out so soon?"

"Yeah, I've got an important appointment," Tyler lied.

"Well, it can wait." Alan turned to the other man. "I just wanted to make sure Mike here got to meet you." Tyler looked at

Alan in surprise. "This is Mike Bierce," Alan said. "He's an artist. Just moved out from Detroit."

Mike Bierce extended his hand, and Tyler shook it. Bierce was wearing faded, worn jeans and a plain collegiate-looking sweater, which had a hole near the elbow. He had a sharp, intense face and looked to be about thirty.

"Tyler Bryant's a true art aficionado," Alan said. "One of the Farm's biggest supporters."

"I sculpt," Tyler added quickly.

Mike Bierce smiled. "So do I. Had a one-man show at Wayne State, and used to teach part-time. But I decided the academic rut was not for me, so I came out here. To get the creative juices flowing again."

Tyler stared at Mike Bierce, realizing suddenly he found his rough-edged looks attractive. Bierce's gray eyes stared back, unwavering. A silent, subtle signal had been passed.

"Mike's having some problems getting settled," Alan said. "I told him you might be able to help him. Help him find a studio, maybe with your connections, get some gallery to take a look. . . . Every great artist needs a patron, right?"

Tyler glanced sharply at Alan. So that was it. Another hit for money. He looked at Mike Bierce, whose face was expressionless, except for the eyes that were now considering him with open curiosity. The pull was becoming stronger. "Well, maybe I can help out," Tyler said. "Let's get together over dinner tonight and talk about it."

Alan ambled off, leaving Tyler alone with Bierce. Bierce offered a warm smile. "It's tough meeting people in this town," he said. "I don't make friends very easily."

Tyler felt his muscles untighten, almost as if by magic. Suddenly he had a sense of comfort and safety, the kind that came only when he knew he was with someone who understood. He smiled back at Bierce. For the moment, at least, he didn't feel like the outsider. For the moment, he could be himself.

Tyler smiled. "I know exactly how you feel," he said.

Chapter
Thirty-two

Kellen sat at her dressing table, finishing her hair. "Stephen, you'd better hurry," she called out. "We're already an hour late."

"I don't see why I have to go to this," he said, putting on his tie as he came out of the bathroom.

"It's for Tyler's sake," she replied. "He asked me to invite you, and I didn't want to disappoint him. How often does someone open his own art gallery?"

She turned her attention back to the mirror. An art gallery! She still couldn't believe it. She had been so surprised last week when Tyler called to tell her about it. She had not talked to him in two months, not since the day he had come to her office. She figured he was upset because she had brushed him off, but when he had called, he was friendly and excited about the gallery. He told her he had a partner, a brilliant young sculptor named Michael Bierce.

"I wonder where he got the money?" Stephen said.

"His trust fund payments are pretty generous," Kellen said. "And I'm sure his partner put up something." She noticed Stephen struggling to do his bow tie. "Let me," she said, and he relented.

"Black tie," he muttered. "Just to go stare at some sculpture. Is Tyler any good?"

"I don't know. I've never seen his work," Kellen answered. She finished the tie. "Thanks for coming with me."

He smiled slightly. "We'd better get going. The sooner we get there, the sooner we can leave."

They drove down toward Fisherman's Wharf, to the foot of Hyde Street near the cable car turnaround in Victorian Park. Stylish silver lettering on the window of the brick storefront announced the Landon Gallery. Kellen noted that Tyler had chosen to use his middle name instead of Bryant.

Inside, the room was crowded, the people fighting for space with the sculptures—colossal-sized bronzes of nude men. There was soft jazz playing, barely audible over the loud buzz of conversation. Kellen paused at the door, looking for Tyler. The gallery was tastefully done in soft cream and mauve, with gray carpeting and flattering indirect lighting with spotlights over each sculpture. She turned her attention to the nearest bronze. The ten-foot figure was poised, as if hurling an imaginary spear, its muscles overdefined to the point of grotesqueness, its teeth bared in an agonized grimace. The sheer size of it was oppressive, and its expression was so unnerving that Kellen had to look away. There were six others in similar poses stationed around the room, and nothing else.

Kellen searched again for Tyler, finally spotting him in a far corner. She and Stephen made their way over.

Tyler's face lit up when he saw her. "Kellen! I didn't think you were coming."

She kissed his cheek. "I told you I would," she said.

"Sorry we're late," Stephen said. "It's my fault."

Tyler was holding a glass of champagne, his face flushed with excitement. "So, what do you think of the place?"

"It's beautiful, Tyler," Kellen said. "Who did your decorating?"

"I did! I hired people to do the work, of course, but I thought of everything." He nodded toward the sculpture. "The lights really set Mike's work off nicely, don't you think?"

"Where's your stuff?" Stephen asked.

Tyler shrugged. "Didn't get anything finished in time." He smiled. "Besides, Mike's the real talent. I'm the brains behind him."

Kellen and Stephen exchanged a subtle look that was lost on Tyler. "I want you to meet him," Tyler said. "Wait here." He took off through the crowd and returned with a tall man in a tweed jacket. Tyler introduced Mike Bierce and passed out glasses of champagne.

Kellen sipped hers as she listened to Bierce talk, with much bravado, about his sculpture. She watched Tyler, who was in turn watching Bierce worshipfully. She wondered if Tyler and Bierce were lovers, but she quickly put the idea out of her head. Seeing Tyler now with this strange man made accepting his homosexuality somehow even more difficult.

"There's the critic from *Art Digest*," Tyler said suddenly. "Come on, Mike, I'll introduce you. Excuse us."

Kellen and Stephen stood there, staring up at one of the bronzes. "This is creepy stuff," Stephen said finally.

Kellen watched Tyler across the room, standing in a semicircle of people, next to Bierce. He was laughing and talking animatedly. She had never seen him looking so happy.

"Whatever you do," she said, "don't tell Tyler that. He needs a success right now."

Stephen shrugged. "Well, I'm no expert on this modern stuff. It's probably a lot better than I think." He put down his champagne glass. "I'm going to get a scotch and water," he said, looking to the bar. "You want something else?"

Kellen shook her head and watched Stephen make his way through the crowd. She turned toward the nearest sculpture and circled it slowly. Stephen was right. There was something disturbingly macabre about the bronzes. She didn't like them either, though she couldn't really say why. They were like Bierce himself. There was something about him she didn't like, but she couldn't worry about it. Tyler was a grown man, and he could take care of himself. She had to start accepting that fact—as well as his life-style.

"I've never seen such garbage."

"It's strictly derivative."

Two men were standing nearby, staring up at one of the bronzes. Kellen recognized them as the art critics for the *Times* and the *Journal*. She moved slightly so she could eavesdrop.

"So what are you going to write about this?" the *Times* critic asked the other.

"That the guy's a no-talent who certainly doesn't deserve his own gallery showing. Looks like he found a good thing, and now he's sucking it dry, so to speak."

Both men laughed. "You're sick, Harris, you know that?" the *Times* critic said.

"I have no qualms about slamming people who really deserve it. Especially some rich little gaybo who thinks he can buy success for his boyfriend."

"At least you can call it like you see it," the *Times* critic said. "I don't have that luxury. Tyler Bryant decided to open a gallery, and I damn well better say something nice about it."

"You get pressure from the family?"

The man shrugged. "I can't take the chance these days. Ian Bryant's a real screwball. Interferes in everything, always sending down memos to the editors about coverage on his sacred cows." The critic sighed. "At least when the old man was around, you could always count on the paper having stability and integrity. Now, the daughter's back upstairs, and who knows what she's gonna do, or how much say she has over her husband. We're a bunch of nervous cats that don't know which way to jump." He shrugged. "So I pull my punches. I'm too old to start biting the hand that feeds me."

Kellen eased away from the two men. She had always suspected that some people in the newsroom felt the way the critic did, but his words still stung. But it was Tyler she was really concerned about. She saw him in the crowd, and her heart went out to him. Her instincts about Bierce's art were right, and the gallery was not going to be a hit. As for the *Journal* critic's innuendo about Tyler's sexuality, she was disgusted with its cruelty. What gave him the right to judge Tyler? Tyler had hurt no one.

She watched Tyler, standing alone near the bar. He was riding so high, and she didn't want to see him get hurt. She went across the room to him. He was struggling to open a bottle of champagne. "Need some help?" she asked.

The cork gave way with a loud pop, and Tyler laughed. "No, I'm doing fine!" He began to fill some glasses.

"Tyler, there's something I want to say to you."

He held out a glass. "First, a toast. To me," he said with a broad smile.

Kellen clinked her glass against his. "To you," she said softly. She set the glass aside. "Tyler, remember that night you took me to that bar?"

"Of course."

She paused. The words came haltingly. "I may not understand what you're doing. . . . I can't even pretend I'm comfortable with it. But I want you to know I love you."

Tyler's face was expressionless. "That's a good start."

"I just want you to be happy, Tyler."

"But I *am* happy," he said. "I finally feel like I'm doing something, Kellen. Something of my own. It feels good." He paused. "How about you. Are you happy?"

The question caught her off guard. She thought about it for a moment but found she couldn't think of an answer that didn't sound falsely upbeat. Before she could answer, she saw Ian coming across the room. Lilith and Clarisse were trailing behind. At the same moment, Stephen came up to Kellen's side. "What are they doing here?" Stephen whispered.

"I invited them," Tyler said. "But I never thought they'd show up."

Ian approached with a grin and thumped Tyler on the back. "Tyler, old man. Looks like you have a success on your hands here."

"Thanks, Ian . . . Hello, Lilith, Clarisse . . ."

Lilith gave him a tight smile. Clarisse was preoccupied with checking out the crowd. Ian glanced at Kellen and Stephen; his eyes then traveled around the room, taking in the people and the strange sculptures. "Quite a night for the Bryant family," he said to Kellen. "We should be proud of our little brother here."

"I'm not so little anymore, Ian," Tyler said.

"No, I suppose not," Ian said. "Soon, you'll be twenty-one, and your name will go on the *Times*'s masthead, right below mine and Kellen's." He smiled at Kellen. "Hard to believe, isn't it. The three of us, running the paper together. Just like Father wanted."

Ian turned to Stephen. "We have a vice presidents' meeting next week, don't we?" he said. "Should I expect any surprises from editorial? Or should I ask Kellen?" Ian could not resist a smirking smile.

"No, nothing," Stephen said tersely.

Tyler picked up on the tension and quickly offered a tray of fluted glasses. "How about some champagne?"

For a moment everyone just stood there, holding their glasses, staring at one other, saying nothing. It was a bizarre moment, a ridiculous frozen tableau.

"Well, someone make a toast, for heaven's sake," Clarisse said.

"But not to the gallery," Tyler said. "If I hear one more of those, I'll start thinking jinx."

There was a long pause. Kellen cleared her throat. "The *San Francisco Times* turns one hundred next month," she said. Everyone looked at her in surprise, except Clarisse, who looked just bored. "So I'll make a toast," Kellen said. She raised her glass slightly. "To my father."

Lilith raised her glass higher. "To *my* father."

For a moment, no one took a drink. Then finally, Tyler did, and everyone followed. Ian drained his glass with a quick gulp and set it down. "Well, Tyler, we have to be going," he said. "We're on our way to the club for dinner, but we just wanted to stop by. Are you ready, Mother? Clarisse?"

"I'm famished," Clarisse said and started toward the door without saying good-bye. Lilith brushed Tyler's cheek with her own. "A marvelous opening, dear. Good night . . ." With a final look at Kellen, she swept off toward the door.

Ian shook Tyler's hand and was gone. Kellen, Stephen, and Tyler stood there for a moment, without saying a word. Stephen finally let out a long breath, so empty sounding that she turned to look at him. He looked tired.

"I think I'd better get going, too," she said to Tyler.

They said their good nights and left the gallery. Stephen was very quiet on the drive home. At home, Stephen went right up to the bedroom, but Kellen detoured to the children's rooms. Benjamin was sleeping soundly, and she bent low to kiss his warm cheek. In Sara's room, Kellen stood over the bed, staring down at her daughter's face. Her brows were knit in a small frown, as if she were in the middle of a bad dream. Kellen gently caressed her forehead until the small lines of tension were gone. Kellen continued to stare at Sara, thinking how much the child reminded her of Garrett. Sometimes, it pained her even to look at her own daughter, so strong was the resemblance to Garrett becoming with each passing day. Finally, she crept out of the room.

Stephen was lying in bed, arms raised up to cradle his head, staring at the ceiling. He didn't even look at her when she came in. She undressed and slipped into bed beside him.

"Stephen, don't let Ian get to you," she said softly. "That's what he does . . . plays these little mind games."

He said nothing for a moment, then leaned over and kissed her. "Good night, Kellen," he said. He turned away from her.

She switched off the light and lay there, listening to Stephen's even breathing. It mixed with the foghorns and familiar soft noises of the house as it settled into night. Usually, the sounds lulled her to sleep. But tonight, she could find no comfort in them.

It was nearly one in the morning, and Tyler was pacing the floor of his apartment, still riding an adrenaline high. He had left the gallery only a half hour ago, after ushering out the last guests. He was so euphoric that he didn't even mind when Mike announced he wanted to go home alone to his studio to do some work. Mike often worked best during the early morning hours. But now, Tyler couldn't sleep. He wanted to do something special for Mike. But what? He had already done so much—bought him the studio in the Embarcadero and supported him so he could concentrate on his art. And he had given him the gallery showing that would launch his career. What else was left? Tyler realized suddenly he could invite Mike to move in with him. He had always been wary about making commitments to other lovers. But now, well, things were different. Mike was different.

Tyler picked up the phone and dialed the studio, but the line was busy. It usually was; Mike often took the phone off the hook when he worked. Tyler grabbed his coat and started for the door. Then he paused and went to his desk. He found an extra apartment key and stuck it in his pocket.

He pulled up in front of the warehouse near the docks. A light was on in the studio, on the top floor. To surprise Mike, he decided to bypass the creaky freight elevator in favor of the stairs, taking them two at a time. His heart was beating from exertion and excitement as he paused outside the studio. He opened the door and went in. The dark loft was as messy as usual, and a towering, half-finished bronze dominated the clutter. Mike was nowhere to be seen. Tyler glanced to the far corner, where a partition hid Mike's bed. Tyler quietly picked his way through the discarded clothes, pizza boxes, chicken bones, and barbells on the floor. His fingers found the key in his pocket, and he held it tight.

He heard Mike's low laugh. Then another laugh he didn't recognize. Tyler froze, flattening himself against the wall.

"I could get used to that." A man's voice, a strange voice.

"I'll bet." Tyler shut his eyes at the sound of Mike's voice. There was a rustle of sheets.

"What about Tyler?" the other man said. "What's with you two?"

"He pays the bills. That's all."

"He doesn't think so."

"I know," Mike said. "He's like a goddamn puppy dog sometimes." There was the sound of someone turning over in the bed and then the light was switched off, leaving the loft dark except for the white glare of the streetlight just outside the window.

"Don't worry." Mike said. "He's nothing to me. Now that the gallery's open, and I'm getting some exposure, I can back off from him."

"What about this place?"

"The deed's in my name, free and clear. The kid gave it to me." There was a silence. "I don't need him anymore."

Tyler's head was spinning, and the blood from his hammering heart pounded against his temples. He stared down at the floor to steady himself. The streetlight had created a black-and-white shadow pattern on the floor, and Tyler stared at it, thinking suddenly how beautiful it looked. He felt nauseous—but unable to move away from the wall—and he felt something wet on his face and realized with disgust that he was crying. He waited, his ears attuned to sounds, but he could hear only Mike's breathing. Fi-

nally, with great effort, he pushed himself forward and silently
made his way back across the loft's debris and out the door.

Ian went to the door of the bedroom, glancing back to the bed
where Clarisse lay sleeping soundly. He pulled the belt of his robe
tighter and went out of the room and down the stairs. He heard a
clock strike three. Damn Clarisse. She never had trouble sleeping
after they fought. Tonight, the bickering had started right after
they left Tyler's gallery. Finally, thankfully, Clarisse had gone to
bed. An argument always seemed to give her more impetus to
sleep, whereas it inevitably left him keyed up.

Ian went down to the living room and over to the bar. He poured
a neat scotch and took it over to the picture window. He drank it
slowly as he stared out at the lights in the bay below. He looked
to his left, toward the Golden Gate Bridge, but the view was
obstructed by the jutting balcony of the house next door. It had
just been built by a man who had made his fortune via a string of
auto dealerships down on Van Ness. The house was a pink, modern monstrosity, as sprawling and florid as its owner, and it looked
out of place among the tasteful old homes on Vallejo Street. It was
twice the size of Ian's. And it was blocking his view.

Ian turned away, finishing the scotch. He poured himself another and plunked down on the curving white sofa. The pink house
had been, from the start, a major catalyst in his fights with
Clarisse. From the moment construction began on the house, she
had started bitching about it, and the nearer it came to completion,
the more she bugged him about moving. Of course, the pink house
was merely an excuse. Clarisse had been nagging him for years
about the sorry state of their own existence. The fifteen-room
house on Vallejo was too small, too old, too dowdy, she said.
Why can't we move to a better address? And the real stinger: Why
aren't we living in your family's mansion instead of your sister?

It didn't seem to matter to her that they had four other homes:
the condo in Aspen, the apartment in New York City, the pied-
à-terre in Paris, and a hilltop retreat near Hana on the island of
Maui. Actually, the last one he had bought for himself. Clarisse,
who hated hot weather, never went there. Which was fine with
Ian, who recently had started an affair with a secretary he met in
Honolulu. But more than anything, he preferred being there alone.
The remote area of the island was the one place in the world he felt
truly comfortable.

"Ian, why aren't you in bed?"

Ian didn't bother to turn around at the sound of Lilith's voice.

"I can't sleep," he said, staring out the window, sipping the scotch.

He watched her as she sat down in a chair across from him. She was wearing an elegant silk robe and her hair, thanks to the constant attention of her stylist, was almost as dark as it had ever been. Now seventy-three, she was also still as thin as ever, but her insistence on a perpetual tan and three facelifts had given her skin the translucent look of old parchment.

"Would you like a drink, Mother?" he asked, going to the bar.

"You know I can't."

A year ago, Lilith had suffered a heart attack. It had been a mild episode, and the doctors all told Ian she had recovered completely and would probably outlive them all. But Lilith had used her protracted convalescence as an excuse to move in with Ian. Her presence in the house had exacerbated the strain between him and Clarisse, but he couldn't bring himself to ask her to leave. His mother was old, he thought, and lonely.

The house was filled with tension. Clarisse and Lilith were constantly sniping at each other. Ian couldn't understand it, really, because Lilith had been so impressed with Clarisse when Ian first brought her home, and the two women were actually so much alike. They were both selfish, snobbish spendthrifts, whose preoccupation with status had narrowed their lives to social events and frequent trips abroad to whatever location was deemed "en vogue" by *European Travel and Life*.

It bothered Ian immensely that he had allowed Lilith to pressure him into the marriage. It bothered him even more that he had married a woman so much like his mother, as if he were some absurd case study out of a college psychology textbook. But what bothered him most was the fact that he was so apparently impotent to change his life. He had too many responsibilities now. He had a son and another child on the way. He had to run the newspaper chain and make money, always make more money.

Ian topped off his drink and returned to the sofa. Good lord, his annual income from the newspapers was more than $3 million—and it never seemed to be enough. Of course, it would soon be diminished when Tyler came of age. Then whatever revenue the Bryant newspaper chain made would be split three ways. There never seemed to be anything left over, especially for his own needs. He had paid too much for the property and house in Hawaii. And he paid all his mistress's bills. But they were the only things he seemed to care about anymore.

No, that wasn't true. He cared about his son, Robert, although he had trouble showing it. He was an undemonstrative father, finding he had no idea how to show affection. But that wasn't so important, he thought, as long as the boy felt secure.

Soon, Robert would be six. Clarisse, who had begun charting Robert's social course before he was born, had already enrolled him in the Town School. More than thirty years ago, Ian's own application to the exclusive primary school had been rejected until Adam pulled political strings to get him admitted. The same thing happened when Ian tried to get into the University School. But now, Robert Bryant was already assured a place in both, although Clarisse was leaning toward sending the boy to boarding school, probably Cate in Santa Barbara. Boarding school, she claimed, prepared a child to perform. In addition, Robert would be subjected to all the obligatory rites of initiation—sailing and riding lessons, invitations to the right parties, and trips abroad to the cultural capitals. And when he turned eighteen, a spot awaited him in the 1987 freshman class at Princeton, thanks to Ian's alumni donations.

Ian often thought that Clarisse and Lilith were trying to climb up the social ranks on Robert's back, much as his own parents had tried to do with him. But he knew it couldn't really be avoided; Robert had to be assured the best. And Clarisse, whose own insufferable family made up in pre-Revolutionary lineage what it lacked in cash, told him that it took more than years to convert new money to old.

Money . . . it was going to take a lot of money to give Robert what he deserved. And now, Clarisse was pregnant again. She had informed Ian she wanted at least five children. It was the only thing she and Lilith seemed to agree on—the need for Ian to produce a large family. A long line of Bryants to stretch into the future. A long, never-ending line of responsibilities and expenses. . . .

"Ian, you aren't ill, are you?" Lilith asked.

He glanced at her. "No, Mother. I'm just tired." His mind began to drift, and he saw himself standing atop the cliff in Hana, overlooking the beach, breathing in the ripe, humid air.

After a moment, Lilith got up and went to the window. "Well, the damn thing's finished, isn't it," she said with a grunt. "They'll probably move in soon. Dreadful people . . ."

Ian was lost in his reverie and ignored her.

She turned to face him. "We must move," she said. "And I know the perfect place. The Critchon house on Broadway is coming on the market soon. The asking price is ten million. Can you imagine? And it needs so much work.'' She paused. ''I'm sure we could get it for eight. Did you hear me, Ian?''

''We can't afford it.''

She sighed heavily. ''But we can't stay in this place. It's too small. When the baby comes, we'll have to get a nanny. Robert's governess has no experience with infants.''

Ian closed his eyes.

''You know I'd give you some of my money, Ian,'' Lilith said softly. ''But it's tied up. If I liquidated now, I'd lose everything.''

Ian looked at Lilith. He had no idea how much money she had of her own. Adam's payments to buy out her share of the *Times* had ended years ago. She was stubborn about maintaining her own finances and refused to disclose anything to Ian. She said she had a banker who managed her investments, but Ian guessed that she had simply squandered most of her money. Perhaps it was more than loneliness that had driven her into his house.

''I know we need a bigger house, Mother,'' he said wearily. ''But we haven't got the cash right now.''

''We could have it . . . in a moment, you know,'' she said.

He closed his eyes. ''How?'' he asked, more to humor her than anything.

''Sell the company,'' she said.

He looked at her.

''The newspapers, the station in Oakland, the printing facilities, the mills,'' she said. ''Sell it all.''

He shook his head slowly. ''Don't you think I've thought of that? The company is financially unstable right now, and no buyer's going to pay enough to make it worth our while.'' He smiled wanly. ''You forget, whatever we'd make, we'd have to split. And the pie's got three slices now. . . .''

Lilith came over and sat down on the sofa. ''Garrett Richardson would buy it,'' she said.

Ian laughed. ''Over Kellen's dead body.''

''Well, as you said, there are three slices now. She's only got one. One slice, one vote.''

''So what? What makes you think Tyler would side with me against her?''

Lilith shrugged. ''He might. God knows we've invested enough time with him in the last couple of years. I think he could be convinced that his big brother knows what's best. And from what I can tell, he could care less about the newspapers themselves. He'd just as soon be rid of them.''

Ian bit his lip. ''I don't know, Mother,'' he said slowly. ''I agree we should sell, but I hate giving up something that . . ." He paused. "Something we could hand on to Robert someday."

Lilith sighed in exasperation. "But we don't have to really give it up. Perhaps Richardson can be persuaded to keep a Bryant as publisher in name. Of course, that duty would fall to you . . . and eventually to Robert. We would have the money, and the family connection could go on." She smiled. "And you could stop worrying about it and get some sleep."

He stared at Lilith. "You've thought this all through, haven't you."

"Yes. I'm convinced it's the best way. We might sacrifice complete ownership, but look what we'd gain. It would force Kellen out of the picture permanently. Her husband and children would have no part in it. It would be only you and Robert."

Ian stared at the glass in his hands. He raised it slowly and drained the last of the scotch. He looked at Lilith. "I'll call Richardson as soon as I get into the office."

Lilith smiled. "Good. Now, why don't you get some sleep. You look so tired, dear."

Ian rose, setting the empty glass on a table. He paused, then bent over to kiss Lilith's cool cheek. "Good night, Mother," he said.

Lilith sat on the sofa, listening to Ian's footsteps as he trudged up the stairs. She sat there for the next hour, staring out the window, watching the predawn sky turn gray. When the jutting edge of the ugly pink house next door finally took shape in the morning light, she got up and went to bed. She fell quickly into a blissful and dreamless sleep.

Chapter
Thirty-three

✳ The cab made its way down Fifth Avenue from Central Park, its progress slowed by afternoon traffic and a raging thunderstorm. Ian stared out the window at all the people hidden under umbrellas, scuttling along the sidewalk like shiny black beetles.

Around 40th Street, the marble facades of the fashionable stores gave way to the seedy storefronts of the garment district. Then, abruptly, fortunes changed again, and the sedate gray apartment buildings of Washington Square appeared, their awnings reaching out to the curbside like arms ready to enfold the privileged.

The cab jogged around the Square, down McDougal Street, and into the rabbit warren of the Village. Ian glanced uneasily at the boutiques and ethnic restaurants. He had been to New York often enough, but he seldom strayed below Central Park. The abrupt juxtaposition of the city's poor and rich neighborhoods made him uncomfortable, as if he were crossing foreign borders without knowing where he was going. When the cab turned east, toward more dingy buildings, Ian tapped the plastic divider to get the driver's attention. "Say, if I want a tour, I'll take the Gray Line," he said, with what he hoped sounded like the authority of a native.

"You said South Street, buddy. This is the shortest way this time of day. Or maybe you wanna walk."

Ian leaned back in the seat. He hated New York. He hated everything about it, the gray weather, the gray people, the gray buildings, the feelings of claustrophobia he got every time he had to come here. Though his apartment was up on the East Side, out of harm's way, he regretted having allowed Clarisse to talk him into buying it. She said she enjoyed coming to the city for cultural events, but she never used the apartment for anything more than a closet for her shopping excursions.

The cab turned south onto the Bowery, and Ian became still in the middle of the seat, his body drawing inward imperceptibly, away from the sordid sights. The driver was taking his time. Ian glanced at his watch but was prevented from saying anything by the thought of being shoved out onto one of the desolate street corners. Finally, the cab came to a stop. "This is it," the driver said. "Seven fifty."

Ian paid him and the cab sped off in the rain. Ian looked up at the ugly, squat building and then down at the only entrance, a steel door with a buzzer. There was no sign, nothing to identify the place as a newspaper office. A man in ink-stained overalls came out of the door, and Ian grabbed it.

He was in a grimy vestibule, and the glare of the fluorescent lights off the glossy yellow walls was blinding. He went to a window, and a woman directed him to an elevator.

Ian rode the elevator to the third floor. It opened onto a newsroom, or at least some hellish, parallel-universe version of one. The small room was crammed with mismatched, beat-up desks, chairs, and file cabinets, and it smelled of dust, oil, and bodies. Ian stood there, the smells triggering a flashback memory of the first time his father had taken him in to see the *Times* newsroom. He felt the same revulsion and fascination now that he had then.

He approached the nearest man. "Could you direct me to Mr. Richardson's office, please?" Without looking up, the man pointed to the corner.

A secretary ushered Ian into Garrett's office. Ian had expected to see an office that proclaimed executive status, a counterpoint to the dinginess outside. But Richardson's office was small, unadorned, and outfitted with functional furniture. It was, however, thankfully, clean.

Richardson came out from behind his desk, hand extended. "You made it," he said. "The traffic's bad this time of day."

Ian shook his hand, taking stock of Richardson's appearance— a plain white shirt, its sleeves rolled, and no tie—and allowed himself a feeling of superiority about his own custom-tailored gray suit and Burberry trenchcoat. He realized suddenly he had been nervous about this meeting, but seeing Garrett in his plebeian element had tipped the scales back in his favor.

"I'm sorry I'm late," Ian said easily. He took off his coat and sat down in the chair Garrett offered.

"It's just as well," Garrett said. "A big story broke, and I was tied up in the newsroom."

"Oh? What happened?" Ian could care less about the news, but Richardson obviously wanted to tell his story.

"A group of Japanese tourists was walking across the Brooklyn Bridge this morning. One fellow stopped to take photos of his friends, and a cable snapped and killed him." Garrett paused. "A freak accident, poor bloke."

He held out a tabloid. It was that day's *New York Tatler*. The photograph showed a sheeted body, dwarfed by the towering stone spans. The huge headline said SNAP ZAPS JAP.

"That's quite a headline," Ian said.

"Too much so, I fear," Garrett said. "I had them change it to KILLER BRIDGE. I encourage creativity among my people, but sometimes they get a little overzealous."

Ian nodded, as if in understanding. Garrett leaned back in his chair and folded his hands in front of his face. "So, Mr. Bryant," he said. "You said you wanted to talk to me and you've come a long ways to do it. What can I help you with?"

"I'm here to find a buyer for my newspapers," Ian said.

"And you think I might be interested?"

"You were once."

"But that was eight years ago, Mr. Bryant. Surely you've had other offers since."

"Nothing that would have made it worthwhile."

Garrett paused. "More like no one's interested anymore."

Ian just looked at Garrett.

Garrett smiled slightly. "That's really why you're here, isn't it, Mr. Bryant. You've stayed a little too long at the party. And now I'm the only boy left to take you home."

"It is still a good opportunity for the right person," Ian said curtly.

"But I have the *Tatler* now. Why in the world would I be interested in your newspapers?"

Ian hesitated. He was prepared; if nothing else, that was what he was good at. "Because you haven't been able to do what you set out to do—make the *Tatler* the most widely read paper in New York. Its circulation has stagnated at six hundred and twenty-eight thousand. That's still way behind the *New York Times*'s eight hundred and fifty-eight thousand, and the *Daily News*'s one point five million. And you lack advertising. The *News* has thirty-seven percent of the city's advertisers and the *Times* has fifty-six percent. You have only seven percent."

Garrett didn't blink. "That will change. In Britain, my newspapers attract millions of readers. It's working in Toronto, and it can work here, too."

Ian shrugged. "Perhaps. But the people who read your sleazy stories aren't the upscale types advertisers want."

Garrett smiled. "You Americans are so preoccupied with advertising. In England, circulation is what really counts, and I'll prove that's true here, too. When the *Tatler* reaches a million readers—and it will—advertisers will fall in line. Besides, I suspect many of those cherished *Times* readers are really closet *Tatler* readers. Americans are no different than the British really. They live on their little cul-de-sacs or in their tiny flats, looking for relief from their boring lives. That's what I try to give them."

Ian stared at him. "Maybe you underestimate us."

"I doubt it."

Ian rose and went to the window. Garrett's voice had shifted toward indifference, and Ian knew the moment was slipping away. Perhaps he had been wrong and Garrett couldn't be enticed. He stared down at the gray stretch of the East River. He had one more card to play.

"You strike me as a man of vision, Mr. Richardson," Ian said. "Not one to be content with such a small arena."

"New York is scarcely a small market."

"But just one newspaper here in the United States?"

Garrett sat silent for moment. Then he rose and came over to the the window to stand next to Ian, who now was making the pretense of looking at the gloomy view.

Ian, sensing the advantage, decided to let Garrett make the next move. "Which bridge is that?" Ian said amiably, pointing to the left at a plain steel structure.

"The Manhattan. Pretty homely compared to the Brooklyn Bridge there," Garrett said, pointing right.

Ian waited, saying nothing.

"They're like two sisters, one plain and useful, the other beautiful and inspiring," Garrett said. "Rather like the two bridges in your town, I'd say." He paused. "There's something about beautiful bridges."

"Yes," Ian said, fighting his urge to steer the conversation back to business.

Garrett leaned against the window frame, hands in pockets. "How does your sister feel about your coming here?"

"She doesn't know. Frankly, she's not a factor in this deal. My brother Tyler will be twenty-one soon and will have a third vote in all company matters."

"And how does he feel about selling?"

"I can convince him of the wisdom behind it."

Garrett stared out the window for a moment, then glanced at his watch. Ian noticed the gesture and, sensing that he had at least piqued Garrett's interest, decided to take the offensive. "I know you're a busy man, Mr. Richardson," he said. "But nothing has to be decided right here and now. Perhaps we could have dinner tonight."

Garrett considered Ian carefully. "All right, but it'll have to be now." He smiled. "How do you feel about pizza? I know a place nearby that serves the best pie in New York."

Ian forced himself to smile. "But only if you allow me to reciprocate . . . when you come back to San Francisco."

Garrett pulled off his tie and took his glass of brandy into the bedroom. He had had only one beer at dinner, wanting to keep his head clear when he confronted Ian. While he was convinced Ian could be manipulated, he knew he wasn't a complete fool. He had come prepared to make a deal and had laid his criteria out plainly for Garrett to consider. The asking price for all the Bryant properties was $400 million. And the figurehead title of publisher, in perpetuity, for Ian and his heirs, with a $2 million annual salary. And no involvement at all for the other members of the family.

Garrett had been only mildly surprised at the first; the price was high, but fair. But the second point had surprised him. He didn't think Ian cared about the family name being retained as a connection. Of course, that was no obstacle; a name on a masthead was only a sentimental gesture. The Bryant family would have no power if he took over.

If he took over . . . Garrett sat down in a chair near his bed, the brandy in his hand untouched. Why had he even bothered to listen to Ian Bryant? He certainly didn't need the aggravation. The Toronto operation had survived the conversion, was gaining circulation every day. But the *Tatler* was a different story. It demanded every ounce of his energies.

Garrett set the brandy aside. It annoyed him that Ian had known the circulation and advertising figures, and that, without really understanding the larger picture, he had managed to pinpoint the *Tatler*'s problems.

Five years ago, when Garrett bought the *Tatler*, he had been convinced that with belt-tightening and a change of format, it could succeed. His instincts told him that New Yorkers were ready for an alternative to the self-satisfied journalism of the *New York Times* and *Daily News*. And with his usual thoroughness, he had studied the market and found figures that seemed to back up his belief.

So Garrett had gone ahead with the *Tatler* purchase, even though his father cautioned against it. The transition had been rough. Many of the newspaper's reporters and editors had rebelled and quit; Garrett had fired others who could not be converted to the new philosophy and filled a few key positions with British editors. Garrett ordered the stories shortened and the headlines souped up. He expanded and sensationalized the crime coverage and beefed up television and racetrack coverage. The *Tatler* doled out a daily diet of sex, gore, gossip, and celebration of the nude female form. Garrett's efforts were rewarded with an immediate circulation gain of several hundred thousand readers.

But once the novelty wore off, circulation leveled off, and it had remained stagnant. Then, last year, the *New York Times* made some startling changes. It enhanced its sports, science, and business coverage. It added a new Living section and a Home section with consumer features to court the upscale readers. It investigated the best avocado in the city with the same fervor that it applied to international politics. Its readership was creeping up again, and industry insiders were predicting that the *Times* would regain its lost circulation. Garrett wasn't convinced. As far as he was concerned, the *Times* could stick to the high road, because he was sure the *Tatler* would prevail on the low one.

He thought back to what Ian had said earlier about underestimating American tastes. The man was a pompous ass who knew little about journalism, and his air of superiority had not been lost on Garrett. But then, Garrett had gotten used to dealing with snobbery. Since taking over the *Tatler*, he had become the city's publishing pariah, scorned by the city's newspaper elite. Outwardly, he ignored it, but inside, he felt resentment toward his cohorts. Hadn't he, after all, saved a doomed newspaper? That should count for something in a town with only three surviving newspapers where once ten flourished? But the prevalent feeling about Garrett Richardson was that he was not a savior or even a legitimate journalist. He was an interloper, trying to revive a dying newspaper by immersing it in the toilet.

No one seemed to realize that the *Tatler* was often truer to the city's spirit than the other papers, aggressively pursuing local stories ignored by the *Times*. And detractors overlooked the paper's positive output, such as a hard-hitting investigation of rent-control fraud, or the weekly feature Garrett created called

Wednesday's Child, which profiled children available for adoption. All anyone noticed about the *Tatler* was its dirty face.

Garrett glanced at the clock by the bedside. It was nearly midnight and he was tired, having spent the usual twelve-hour day at the newspaper office before the dinner with Ian. He rose and went into the bathroom. He turned on the shower and got in, wincing but enjoying the prick of the too-hot water on his body.

His thoughts drifted to last week's meeting of the Publishers Association of New York City. He had lost his bid to be elected its president. He had tried to shrug it off, telling himself that he was used to being excluded. But it still stung. He had always been an outsider. In prep school and then at Oxford, he had been looked down on by the sons of wealthy men or aristocrats, who saw Arthur Richardson as a parvenu who had bought his knighthood through a prime minister's favoritism and had shouldered his way to wealth via smutty tabloids. When he was a boy, such attitudes had always inspired Garrett to excel; whether at academics or sports, he was forever trying to prove he was the best. And he remained, by choice, an outsider. He often suspected that was why he was so attracted to America. It was a country of kindred souls, outsiders like himself, all bent on proving themselves.

He got out of the shower and wrapped a towel around his waist. He went to the terrace and opened the door. It was gusty, and the rush of cold air on his bare chest made him pull in his breath. He glanced south, across the dark expanse of Central Park to where the lights began again. He had bought the penthouse for its view. The rest of it, the white marble floors, the towering ceilings, and the self-consciously austere decor, he hardly ever noticed. He felt more at home in the plain dinginess of the *Tatler* office.

He left the door wide open. He couldn't sleep unless the room was icy. He got into bed and lay there for an hour, exhausted but unable to sleep. He brought his arms up to cradle his head and stared into the dark.

His thoughts turned to the Toronto paper and back to the one crucial question: Why had he been able to succeed in that market but not in New York? He had turned the facts and figures over in his head countless times to no avail. He thought about his father. Arthur had been disappointed that Garrett had lost the San Francisco deal. But at least he was keeping out of the New York business, absorbing the losses, allowing Garrett free rein. Not once had he said, I told you so. He simply ignored it. To Garrett, his indifference was worse than outright censure. It was almost as if Arthur were tolerating the *Tatler* as his son's plaything.

Garrett closed his eyes. Eight years of hard work. And the grand plan was still just that—nothing but a plan, an unrealized dream.

An unrealized dream . . .

He thought again of Ian. He was right about one thing at least: success in America had to be on an oversized scale, preferably in a glaring spotlight. Ian was right about the *Tatler*, too. It wasn't big enough. But a string of newspapers—no one could ignore that. And now Ian had reopened the door to the Bryant empire, this time with an assurance the deal could be struck. All Garrett had to do was walk through.

But what about Kellen? Her face came back to him, how she had looked the last time he saw her—so angry.

Kellen . . . Had she changed? He could see her so clearly. He could hear her laugh and feel her vibrancy. Suddenly, the sensation of her body next to his own was so powerful that he glanced over to see if she were there. Only in his mind. She was always there, in his mind. In eight years, he had not stopped thinking about her. Sometimes, preoccupied with work, he would go for weeks without seeing her face. But then, always, inevitably, she returned.

Eight years. There had been other women in that time; he was never at a loss for companionship or sex, or even love, if he wanted it. But always, after an amount of time, months, sometimes just moments, he would find himself comparing a woman to Kellen. There were times he hated her for the pull she still exerted over his life, or maybe he just hated himself for giving in to it.

Eight years. He had done what he could to exorcise her memory. He had had a photograph of her, but he had thrown it away. After he heard that she had married, he had made it a point to know nothing else about her, though he could have easily found out every detail of her life. Though she was only six hours away, she might as well have been on the moon.

But tonight . . . she was as vivid now in his mind as the last day he saw her, a time-frozen memory more enticing than any image on a photograph.

He didn't believe in living in the past. He had done that for a brief time after Susan and the twins died. Eventually, sickened by the pain, he had pulled himself out of his stupor and forced himself to go on. He resolved never to grieve for what might have been or to regret things he couldn't change.

But now, he felt himself sinking into a sad reverie, replaying scenes in his head with Kellen, thinking about what could have happened if he had been honest with her from the start, if he had realized sooner how much he loved her. The scenes played on, all leading back to the one with her standing there, her face filled with anger over his betrayal.

Had she changed? Did she still hate him?

Garrett stared into the darkness. He hadn't given Ian an answer, or even an indication that he was interested in buying the newspapers. He wasn't. He would never do anything to hurt Kellen again. But it gave him pleasure knowing he could just let the bastard twist in the wind for a while.

And yet, Ian had forced him to think about something that he had long put aside—the idea of going back. All the memories had been stirred up, along with something he could only identify as hope. But for what? She was married. She had a life without him. What could he possibly expect from her? What was he looking for after all these years?

He didn't know. But he did know that he wouldn't be able to put her out of his mind until he went back one last time. Suddenly, his mind was made up, and he made a mental note to call the agency that had cared for the house in Tiburon. He relaxed his tense muscles slightly, as he always did once he had finally reached a decision. As soon as possible, he would be on a plane to San Francisco. And no matter how Kellen felt about him, he would see her. He had to.

Chapter
Thirty-four

❋ Kellen and Stephen waited silently while the maid cleared the breakfast dishes and left. "It was just a suggestion, Stephen," Kellen said, her voice low.

"But it won't work," Stephen said. "Other afternoon newspapers have already tried it. It just won't work." He picked up his coffee, as if to shut her off.

She took a breath. She had offered her idea, thinking it was a sound one—give the news a feature slant, go with a more in-depth analytical style, instead of trying to compete with the morning *Journal*'s fresher news. She had curbed her instinct to argue, not wanting to antagonize Stephen. Ever since his suburban plant idea hadn't worked out, he had been depressed.

"Stephen, what's wrong?" she asked quietly.

"Nothing."

"Don't tell me that," she said. "Stop shutting me out."

He looked up.

"I can't even make the most innocent suggestion about the paper without you taking it wrong," she said.

He set down his coffee. "I'm sorry," he said. "It's this damn plan. I know I should forget it, but I can't. I know it would work, Kellen. If there were just a way to give it a chance."

Kellen didn't reply. It was still there between them, her refusal to sacrifice a newspaper for his plan. It had come to epitomize all the tensions surrounding their positions at the *Times*. A subtle power struggle had developed between them. She loved Stephen and wanted to support him, but she would not sacrifice what she thought was right just to appease him.

Suddenly, she froze, a thought taking form in her head. She couldn't sell a newspaper, but maybe something else. "Stephen, I have an idea," she said slowly. "What about the Napa land?"

Kellen said. "Would that bring in enough to finance the plant?"

"You mean you'd be willing to sell it?"

"It's just sitting there, for heaven's sake," she said. "I don't know why I didn't think of it before. We lease it to an adjoining vineyard, and the lease expires soon. The real estate agent sent me a new one last week. Ian and I have always just renewed and forgotten about it because it's such a small parcel. But the land has to have appreciated over the years."

Stephen brightened slightly. "It's worth exploring."

"Tomorrow's Saturday," Kellen said quickly. "Let's go up there and talk to a realtor."

"I can't. I've got a speech to give at the press club."

"Maybe Tyler will go with me. It will do him good. He's been depressed lately." She looked at Stephen over the rim of her cup. "So have you," she said softly. "Don't worry. Maybe we can trade a bunch of old vines for a new plant."

Finally, he smiled. "Maybe," he said. He finished his coffee quickly and rose. She could tell from his expression that his mind was already back on the plan, but now in a positive way. "You want me to wait for you?" he asked. They rarely drove to the office together, and his offer this morning was obviously a conciliatory gesture.

"No, you go on ahead," she said with a smile. He started for the door. "Don't forget! You have a tux fitting later."

He smiled wanly. "No way out of it?"

"This is the last one, I promise. No more charity committees. The Black and White Ball is my swan song."

Stephen left, and she sat at the table, finishing her coffee. He had looked so hopeful about the Napa land. He hadn't been so eager to get to work in a quite a while. She wished she felt the same enthusiasm. She had been struggling to clarify her role without posing a threat to Stephen. She wanted to do more than sit upstairs and push paper; she wanted to assert her authority as head of the entire chain.

She sipped her coffee, thinking of all the newspapers that came into her office every day—fourteen newspapers, one from each of the other cities in the chain. She had tried once to read them all, but it really gave her no sense of what they were like. So the papers just piled up in her office, every day faithfully coming to her.

She started to set her cup down, then paused. But what if I went to them? she thought.

She remembered what Stephen had told her once, how her father regularly visited each newspaper to keep in touch and provide a Bryant presence. She smiled. That was what she could do—go to each of the newspapers. It was the perfect idea. She would be performing a vital task, but far away from Stephen's realm of influence.

She began to map out an itinerary in her mind, filled with a sense of anticipation that she had not felt in years.

The next day, Kellen picked up Tyler and they headed out to Napa. It was a cool, cloudless spring day, and she had put the top down on the Rolls. She glanced over at Tyler, who was slumped in the passenger seat, his eyes hidden by sunglasses.

"You don't mind the top down, do you?" she said.

Tyler didn't reply.

"I'd turn the heater on, but it doesn't work when the top's down," she went on, trying to make small talk. "I called the Rolls people in England about it, and some snotty fellow said, 'Madam, it is expected that clement weather will prevail when the top is down.' "

Kellen laughed, but Tyler remained morose, so she gave up and concentrated on driving. She had hoped bringing Tyler along to Napa might snap him out of his depression over Mike Bierce. Earlier in the week, Tyler had told her what had happened. He also said he had dropped out of his college art courses. She was beginning to worry about his state of mind.

"Tyler," she said, "did you get the invitation I sent you to the Black and White Ball?"

"I can't go."

"Why not?"

"I've had my fill of balls lately," He gave Kellen a sardonic smile but saw his double-entendre was lost on her.

"But this isn't the usual stuffy ball," Kellen said.

"And who would be my date?" he said sarcastically. "I guess I could run down to Castro Street and find someone who'd look sweet in pink crepe. Would I need to buy a corsage? I'm so bad at these things. I wouldn't want to do the wrong thing and embarrass you. . . ."

Kellen curbed her impulse to strike back. "You can come alone. I've saved you a place at our table. It would really make me happy if you'd come. We see so little of—"

"All right," Tyler interrupted. "All right. I'll go if you promise to drop the subject."

They barely talked the rest of the way. The weather grew warmer and the air sweeter the closer they got to the Napa Valley.

The rolling hills of the vineyards rose up around them, an occasional discreet sign marking the entrance to a winery. Kellen spotted the stone tower that marked the beginning of the Bryant land and turned onto the property. She parked the car under a canopy of old trees, and she and Tyler got out. It was quiet except for the chirping of birds and buzz of cicadas. On the grounds were several old stone buildings, one of which appeared to be a winery. The most striking one, however, was a Victorian home. It wasn't big, only two stories, with a widow's walk, but its sweeping veranda and perfect proportions made it an elegant miniature of a grand mansion. The house was vacant and its dusty, stained-glass windows stared out forlornly.

"Why, this is lovely," Kellen said.

They went up onto the veranda and Kellen tried the door, but it was locked. "I guess we'll have to wait for the real estate agent," she said, perching on the railing. Tyler circled the veranda, peering into the windows.

"I'm glad you decided to come with me," Kellen said. "I don't know anything about real estate."

Tyler let out a rueful chuckle. "And I do?"

"Well, you can help me deal with this agent. We have to find out what this place could sell for."

Tyler plopped down on the stairs. "Why do we have to sell it after all these years?"

"Stephen needs the money for the newspaper."

"Ah, the newspaper . . ."

There was a long silence. Tyler was sitting, arms propped on knees, staring out at the vineyards. Kellen sensed that he wanted to talk. "Are you going to go back to art school?" she asked finally.

"No. I'm finished with that crap."

"But what will you do?"

He reached up and moved his sunglasses to wipe at his eyes. After a moment, he carefully readjusted the glasses. "I don't know," he whispered. "I don't know."

She hesitated, thinking about bringing up again the idea of his coming to work at the *Times*. She knew he would be dead set against it. "Well, next month, you'll be a rich man in your own right," she said.

Tyler let out a long sigh. "Did you ever think that maybe that's not such a good thing," he said softly. "The problem with being born rich is that you're already at the end, at the goal. Where do you go from there?"

Kellen heard the despair in his voice. "You could do anything you wanted, Tyler," she said.

He looked back over his shoulder at her. "No, I can't. Everything I've done in my life has been a hobby. I'm not the cause of anything, like Father was. I'm just another effect of what he did."

Before she could answer, a car pulled into the drive. The real estate agent greeted Kellen and Tyler, introduced herself, and went on for some time about how honored her company was to have managed the Bryant land for all these years. Finally, at Kellen's prodding, they started the inspection. The agent led them through an old stable, where the air was filled with dust motes and the heavy, sweet smell of hay. The winery still had much of its old equipment intact, including rows of massive oak casks. They went out into the bright sun again, walking down the rows of gnarled grapevines. Kellen and the agent talked about how the market was changing in the valley. Tyler hung back, his eyes taking in every detail of the gently curving land.

Back at the house, the agent unlocked the door, letting them in. It was cool and dark inside after the sunshine of outside, and Kellen's eyes took a few moments to adjust. The rooms were small but with soaring ceilings and beautiful carved woodwork. There was a parlor with an octagonal bay window and a red marble fireplace. The dining room had two etched-glass gas chandeliers. The few pieces of furniture were covered with white dust cloths.

"Who lived here?" Kellen asked the woman.

"I'm told it was built by a German immigrant who bottled his own wine until he was wiped out by Prohibition," the woman said. "After your father bought it, he let the man stay here until he died." The woman ran a finger along the curving banister. "Ratty old place, isn't it."

Kellen nodded absently. She glanced around for Tyler, but he had disappeared. She heard footsteps overhead and in a moment saw him walking down the stairs.

"There's a claw-foot bathtub," he said. "And a concealed staircase."

"So, what do you estimate we could get for this?" Kellen asked.

"Well, you've only got about a hundred acres here," the woman said. "And the buildings are worthless. You'd make the most by subdividing into five-acre plots for vacation homes. There's going to be a real boom here soon. Why don't we go back to the office and talk?"

Kellen followed the woman to the front door. She turned and

saw Tyler, who was still standing in the center of the front parlor. He was staring up at the intricate molding, his face bathed in the rainbow colors of the stained-glass window. "Tyler, are you ready?" Kellen asked.

He lingered, staring at the woodwork. Then he stuck his hands in his pockets and followed Kellen to the door.

Adele buzzed to let Kellen know that Clark was on the phone. Kellen wondered what Clark wanted. It was unlike him to bother her during the day when she was in her office.

"Can you spare me a minute?" he asked. "I'd like you to take a look at my column for tomorrow."

"Clark, I'd rather you talk to Stephen."

"I really want you to see this before it goes in, Kel."

She told him to come up and put down the phone, immediately wishing she had not given in. She hated the idea of skirting Stephen, even with something as apparently innocent as Clark's column. The last thing she needed now was another reason to upset him, especially after what had happened yesterday. Tyler had called and shocked her by announcing he wanted to move into the old house in Napa.

"But why?" she had asked.

"I don't know," he answered. "All's I know is that I felt at home there. Please, let me keep it."

"But what will you do there?"

He chuckled. "I saw a medium once who told me I was a shepherd in another life. Maybe that's what I'll do."

She feared Tyler's interest in the land was just another passing fancy, but he seemed so sincere, she couldn't deny his wish. Stephen had taken the news hard but stoically.

Adele buzzed to say Clark was waiting. He came in, holding several sheets of copy paper, and sat down. "I thought you should read this before I hand it in," Clark said, holding out the papers.

With a shrug, she took the column and began to read:

ABLE CABLES: A tipster from Tiburon tells me that the British are coming—again. The Belvedere aerie of Garrett Richardson is being prepared for the press baron's homecoming. Has our adopted native son finally tired of the wormy Big Apple?

Kellen looked up at Clark. "Is this true?" she asked incredulously.

He shook his head.

She reread the item. "How did you find out?" she asked.

"A guy who owns a cleaning service called me. Said he had been hired to open Garrett's house. It's being stocked with all the same stuff Garrett used to order—right down to the kind of wine he drinks."

"Is this all you know?" she asked in a strained voice.

Clark nodded. She looked away, covering her mouth with her hand. Clark sat quietly, watching Kellen's face. "Kel, what is it?" he asked. When she wouldn't answer, he added, "Good lord, you're not still in love with him, are you?"

She looked at him, still saying nothing.

"Are you going to see him?"

"No," she said quickly.

Clark leaned forward. "Kellen, maybe it's none of my business . . . tell me if it's not . . . but I think you should. I know how you felt about Garrett, but it's been a long time. You've changed. He probably has, too. You should see him. If nothing else so you can put the past to rest."

She looked at him, dazed. "Clark, can we talk later? I have some work to do."

He rose. "Sure."

She held out the column. "Go ahead and run the item," she said quietly. "Everyone will know soon enough anyway. You might as well have the scoop."

He took the papers and left. Kellen leaned back in her chair, her eyes going to the picture of her children. They lingered on Sara. How could she put the past to rest when she was confronted by it every day in her daughter's face? No, she would not see Garrett. It would only disrupt everything she had worked so hard to create all these years—her family, her marriage, her life. It would disrupt everything.

Why was he coming back? What could he possibly want? She glanced down at the *Times*, still spread out before her on the desk. It's the newspapers, she thought. Not me. The newspapers. That's what it was eight years ago. That's all it is now.

She let out a breath. The realization left her somehow calmer, liberated. He wanted the newspapers, and that was something she could defend. She thought suddenly of Ian and his recent threats to sell. She wondered if Ian had anything to do with Garrett's return. He had to. That was what this was all about. Ian and Garrett were in league again.

She realized suddenly she had forgotten to ask Clark if Stephen had seen the item yet. She had to talk to him now. It couldn't wait.

She took the elevator down to the newsroom.

Stephen's door was open and he looked up in surprise when she walked in. It was rare for her to venture down to the newsroom. Then he noticed her expression. "What's wrong?" he asked.

She shut the door behind her, sat down, and took a deep breath. "Garrett's coming back," she said.

A quick look of apprehension flashed across his face and was gone. "How do you know?" he asked.

She told him about Clark's tip. "You know how Ian's been talking about selling," she said. "I think Garrett's coming back to make another run at the newspapers."

"How can you be so sure?"

"That's all it can be, Stephen." She paused, knowing what he was thinking. "It's not me," she said. "That was over a long time ago."

"And Sara?" he asked quietly.

"I don't think he even knows about her," Kellen said.

"Will you tell him?"

Kellen held his eyes steadily. "No," she said. "Sara has nothing to do with Garrett. She's our daughter."

There was a silence, broken only by the muted noises of the newsroom. Stephen rose and, hands in pockets, walked slowly around his office. He paused before the window, looking out over the newsroom.

She watched him, then rose and went over to him. "Don't worry," she said. "We'll fight them both, Stephen. There's no way Garrett will get the newspapers."

She took his hand and held it tightly. He looked at her. There was no way he could tell her that it wasn't the newspapers he was most worried about.

Chapter Thirty-five

Sara reached out and touched Kellen's hair. Kellen sat still, watching the reflection of her own face next to her daughter's in the dressing table mirror.

"You have such pretty hair, Mama," Sara said.

Kellen smiled. "So do you."

Sara made a face and watched as Kellen twisted her red hair into a heavy plait and pinned it up. "I like it better down," Sara said. "Wear it down tonight."

Kellen looked at her own reflection. "All right," she said, removing the pins. She shook her head, and her hair fell loose about her shoulders. She picked up a brush.

"Let me do it," Sara said, taking the brush. "Where are you and Daddy going tonight?" she asked.

"A ball."

Sara's eyes glittered. "Like in Cinderella?"

"Yes, just like that."

"You should wear a crown."

Kellen laughed. "Would you bring me that black box over there on the bed?" Sara brought her the black velvet case. Kellen opened it, and Sara's eyes grew wide. "Will this do instead?" Kellen asked, holding up a necklace. It was a string of small diamonds, dominated by four large stones in the middle—a ruby, an emerald, a sapphire, and a diamond. They were all of an emerald cut, each about five carats. The sapphire was midnight blue, the emerald the color of a pine forest. The ruby was an intense blood red, and the diamond was as colorless and clear as water.

"Oooh, Mommy! It's beautiful!" Sara whispered.

"Turn around," Kellen said. Sara faced the mirror, and Kellen held the necklace around her neck. It rested against the blue flannel of Sara's nightgown, the colors dancing in the light.

"This is a very special necklace," Kellen said softly. "Your Grandfather Adam bought these stones for your Grandmother Elizabeth. And then he gave them to me." She paused. "Someday, when you're older, I'll tell you all about it. And someday, the necklace will belong to you."

Sara looked up at Kellen. "I wish I could have met them. I mean, I love Grandpa Josh and Grandma Anna, but it would've been nice having another Grandpa and Grandma."

Kellen gathered her into her arms. "I know, baby," she murmured. "They would have loved having you, too."

Sara turned back in the mirror. "Nanny Katie says I look like the pictures she's seen of Grandpa Adam. Is that true?"

"Yes, you do," she said quietly. She saw Stephen's reflection in the mirror and removed the necklace from Sara's shoulders.

When Sara saw Stephen, she spun around. "Daddy! You look so handsome!" she said. Ben toddled into the room and climbed up on the bed, the nanny following a moment later.

"Oh, I'm sorry, Mrs. Hillman," she said. "He just got away from me . . . been running me ragged all day. Too much energy, this one has."

Kellen stood and picked Ben up. "That's all right, Katie. He's just overexcited because I let him stay up to see his father." She kissed Ben's cheek. "Now, don't give Katie a hard time tonight, okay?" She turned the boy over to the nanny. "He'll probably fall asleep soon. If not, just read him that story I started today. The book's by the bed."

She bent down to kiss Sara good night. "Sleep tight . . ."

"Don't let the bedbugs bite!" Sara finished.

Stephen kissed the children good night, and Katie led them away. As Kellen walked back to the dressing table, she could feel Stephen's eyes on her back.

"Where did you get that dress?" he asked.

Kellen turned. "I found it in a trunk in the attic last week when it was being cleared out. It must have belonged to my mother." She faced the mirror. The Vionnet gown was forty years old, and its white satin had deepened to an ivory color. But its ingeniously pure design looked more modern than anything Kellen had in her closet. Kellen ran her hands over her hips, smoothing the satin. "I decided at the last minute to wear it tonight instead of that black thing," she said, gesturing toward a more demure crepe dress hanging on a closet door. She turned around slowly. "What do you think?"

Stephen stared at her. "It's . . . provocative," he said.

"Well, coming from a husband, that's a compliment, I suppose," she said lightly. She picked up the necklace. "Would you help me with this?" She held her hair off her neck as Stephen fastened the clasp.

"You haven't worn this in a long time," Stephen said.

Her fingers lightly touched the jewels. "I know. But for some reason, I wanted to tonight."

Her eyes met Stephen's in the mirror. "Thank you, Stephen," she said softly.

"For what?"

"Letting me keep this."

"I couldn't let you sell your necklace just so I could get my plant. Though the offer was greatly appreciated." He lifted up her hair to kiss her neck.

Kellen shut her eyes.

"We'd better get going," she said.

As they drove, Stephen talked about the newspaper, but Kellen was barely listening. She was a thousand miles away, in Paris, reliving the first night she had spent with Garrett, the feel of his lips on her neck in the cool, dark cavern. Stephen's kiss had awakened the memory, and now it was so sharp, the sensations so real, that her body was tensed with sexual anticipation. She glanced over at Stephen and felt sick with guilt. She had been thinking about Garrett constantly in the last week, ever since Clark had told her that he was returning. Stephen hadn't mentioned Garrett at all outside their one discussion. But she sensed an unease in him, as if he, too, were waiting to see what would happen.

The car pulled up to the opera house, and the valets helped Kellen out. The Black and White Ball was a mammoth affair, a fund-raiser started in 1956 to commemorate the 1906 earthquake, and it always attracted a diverse crowd. Everyone dressed in some variation of the black-and-white dress code. The scene in the lobby took on the bizarre look of an old black-and-white movie. Black-and-white balloons hovered in the air, anchored by white ribbons. Everywhere were huge sprays of white flowers—mums, roses, tulips. And on each table was a candelabrum with white tapers and a stunning arrangement of irises, so dark purple that they appeared black. The orchestra was playing "Moonlight and Shadows."

Stephen and Kellen made their way through the crowd, stopping to make small talk with acquaintances. Finally, they found their table. Clark Able was already seated, absorbed in jotting notes in his gold notebook. He looked up, and his face creased into a smile as his eyes traveled over Kellen's gown.

"Why Kel, you look absolutely ravishing . . . ten years younger!" he said.

"Why do your compliments always sound so suspect?" she said, but she was visibly pleased. She scanned the room. "There's Tyler!" She waved, and he headed their way.

"God, what a zoo," Tyler said, sliding into his chair. He was wearing vintage tails, and in place of a white tie, he wore a Victorian marcasite pin in the shape of a salamander.

"You certainly look dashing," Kellen said.

"We look like we've stepped out of the same era." He nodded to Stephen. "How've you been, Stephen?"

"Busy, as usual. How's the refurbishing going?"

Tyler smiled. "Great. Kitchen remodeling starts Monday."

"I still don't see what in the world you're going to do up there all alone," Kellen said.

Tyler shrugged. "I've been thinking about trying my hand at winemaking. Some of the equipment is salvageable, and the vine-yards have some prime cabernet sauvignon grapes."

Kellen frowned slightly. "But you don't know anything about growing grapes or making—"

"I can learn," Tyler said. "I've bought some books."

Kellen and Stephen exchanged glances. A waiter filled their glasses with red wine. "Besides," Tyler said, picking up his glass. "When you sell wine, you sell *two* things. The liquid in the bottle—and the mystique and image that surrounds it."

Clark took a sip from his glass and made a face. "But what-ever's in the bottle better be good, or you can forget all about mystique." He rose. "I'm going to get a real drink. Can I bring anyone anything? No? See you later, then."

Kellen listened as Tyler began to lecture Stephen on the virtues of California wines. Her attention wandered back to the black-and-white crowd. Most of the men wore tails, but the women had taken the concept of basic black and white to extravagant heights. There were couture taffeta concoctions worthy of Scarlett O'Hara and slinky black-sequined numbers. A woman waltzed by in swirl-ing white chiffon pyjamas, trimmed in ermine. Another wore black satin, the neck and hem rimmed with black pearls. White diamonds were the jewels of choice—necklaces dripping down decolletages like icicles, rings the size of golf balls, earrings hang-ing like crystal stalactites. A brave few had embraced the absur-dity of the theatrical atmosphere. A woman appeared, her face powdered white as death, her lips blackened, and hair dyed pitch black and coiled like a flame rising from her head. Another wore white bird feathers over her ears, looking like a ballerina who had wandered away from *Swan Lake*. Suddenly, the crowd seemed to part, and a woman walked through dressed in a nun's habit.

"Look at that," Kellen said, poking Stephen.

"That's Grace Slick," Tyler said, laughing.

Kellen noticed a man coming toward their table, smiling. Stephen rose to greet him, then turned to introduce him. "J. D. Waverly, this is my wife Kellen and her brother Tyler."

"It's a pleasure to finally get to meet you, Mrs. Hillman," the young man said. "My father knew your father. He told me many stories about the battles they had."

The man was about thirty, with a pleasing face and an engaging smile. Kellen suddenly recognized his name. J. D. Waverly had just been elected to the board of supervisors, the youngest person ever to hold the office. His father had also served on the board for years and had been a powerful political force in the city for decades until his death eight years before. The Waverly family was well-known around town for its political and social involvement.

She smiled at him. "My father had his share of enemies. I'm sorry your father had to be one of them."

"To the contrary," J. D. said. "My father might have been a Republican, but he was one of Adam Bryant's greatest admirers. He always said Adam Bryant was the only man in town with guts enough to stand up for what he believed in. The fact that your father was a Democrat . . ." J. D. smiled. "Well, my father forgave him for that lapse."

"But you're a Democrat, aren't you?" Tyler interjected.

"Yes, the black sheep of the family. But when I decided to go into politics, I wanted to go with people who shared my beliefs." He looked at Stephen. "Like Stephen. It was the *Times* endorsement that won me the election, I'm convinced."

"You'll do a good job, J. D., especially on the environmental stuff. That's why we got behind you," Stephen said. He pulled out a chair. "Why don't you join us?"

Kellen listened as Stephen, Tyler, and J. D. Waverly talked about politics. Every so often, she let her eyes wander to the dance floor, watching the clot of people trying hard not to look foolish while they attempted to dance the Hustle.

Clark returned and slipped into a chair next to Kellen. "I have to talk to you," he whispered.

"What is it?"

Before Clark could reply, Stephen interrupted to introduce J. D. to Clark. "I've always wanted to meet you, Mr. Able," J. D. said, "ever since you wrote that item about me, the one that called me Mr. Greenjeans."

Clark smiled. "No offense intended, Waverly. I was just poking fun at your youthful enthusiasm over ecological issues. And let's face it, we don't have many politicians who campaign in Levi's."

"I may be young, Mr. Able, but I'm serious about the issues."

Clark shrugged. "Your heart may be in the right place, Waverly, but you're a politician, just like your father. I don't think anyone, not even you, can stop the developers from wrecking this town." Clark took a drink of his martini, shaking his head. "I'm beginning to feel old. I see the city changing around me, losing its links to the past. . . ."

"Ah, the past," J. D. said with a smile. "That's this city's biggest problem. People see the past as some big, romantic pageant filled with dancing forty-niners and top-hatted troubadours. There's so much emphasis on the past that it's hard to get people to pay attention to the present."

Clark picked the olive out of his martini. "Don't knock the past," he said. "I remember the day they tore down the old Monkey Block. They tore down a perfectly good old building, one that fit in with the rest of the town, and put up that god-awful pyramid."

"I like the pyramid," Tyler offered. "It's modern. And architecturally valid."

Clark shook his head. "I'm a fossil, right, Tyler?"

"The past is a nice place to visit—"

"But you wouldn't want to live there," Clark finished.

The orchestra switched suddenly to a labored version of "Feelings." "Well, give me an anachronism any day," Clark said. He turned to Kellen. "How about a dance?"

They moved out onto the dance floor. "You are in rare curmudgeon form tonight," Kellen said. "By the way, what did you want to talk to me about?"

Clark sighed. "I just found out that Garrett is supposed to be here tonight."

"What?" She scanned the crowd. "Here? Tonight?"

"You look like a trapped rabbit planning its escape," Clark said. "You can't just leave now. Besides, it might be better if you just faced him, and it'll be easier here, in a crowd." He paused. "You'll have to, sooner or later."

"We don't have anything to say to each other," she said.

The music stopped, and they stood in the center of the dance floor. "Well, maybe you can kid yourself, but you can't kid me. I know you too well," Clark said. "You won't have a moment's peace until you see him."

The music began again, and they began to dance. "You're trembling," he said.

"I don't want to see him, Clark."

"Just go up to him, say hello, and pretend like nothing happened."

She stared at him. "Pretend like nothing happened!" She paused. "He hurt me, Clark. It may have been a long time ago, but I still feel it." Her eyes darted out across the room. "He hurt me," she repeated.

The song ended, and Clark started to steer her back to the table. "No, give me a moment first," she said. "I don't want Stephen to see me upset."

"All right," Clark said. "Let's go hit the bar. You look like you need a drink." He took her hand and led her through the crowd. Clark ordered two martinis. "Try this," he said. "It's better than a Valium." Kellen sipped her drink, her eyes searching the crowd.

"Good lord, get a load of Lilith," Clark intoned, nodding toward a nearby table. Kellen followed his gaze and saw Lilith chatting with Ian and Clarisse. She was wearing a white Grecian-style gown with a huge diamond necklace that hung like a bib on her chest. Her dark hair was pulled back in a bun, and her gaunt face was the color of mahogany.

"All gold and teeth—just like King Tut," Clark murmured. "That woman's amazing. . . ."

Clark chatted on, making bitchy comments about other women's dresses, obviously trying to divert Kellen. But her eyes continued to scan the crowd, searching for Garrett. Finally, she turned to set her drink on the bar and froze.

There he was, standing in a doorway, just ten feet away. She could see every detail of his face. His dark hair was shorter, his face tanner, his body a little thinner, as if he had lost some weight.

Her heart was pounding, and she wanted to run. But she couldn't move. She couldn't even look away.

Suddenly, as if sensing her stare, Garrett looked up. His eyes locked on hers, and in that instant, she felt like she could read every thought in them. A second went by, two, three; and eight years vanished. Sounds and colors blurred, and for one mad moment she stood poised, ready to rush to him. The dark pull was still there, as strong as ever.

She felt Clark's fingers on her arm, a gentle tug back to reality. And then she saw Enid Atherton appear at Garrett's side and slip her arm through his. A second later, another woman appeared. She was blond, pretty, and very young. She took Garrett's other arm, but Garrett didn't look at her. He was still looking at Kellen.

Clark was saying something, but Kellen ignored him. Without taking her eyes off Garrett, she took a deep breath and went toward him. Garrett watched her approach.

Enid saw her and intervened. "Why, Kellen, dear," she said, with a smile. "It's been so long since I've seen you."

A few people turned to watch. Enid was very old and frail, but she still commanded respect as the social high priestess. "I get out so seldom these days," Enid went on, "only on the most special of occasions." She smiled up at Garrett. "And this is certainly one."

"You're looking well, Enid," Kellen said. She looked at Garrett, waiting for him to speak. But he just continued to stare at her, making her feel unprotected and naked. "Garrett, it's been a long time," she said evenly.

"You look as beautiful as ever," he said softly.

Enid's glance went from Kellen to Garrett. "Kellen, I don't think you know my granddaughter, Amy," she said, gesturing toward the blonde. Kellen and the girl exchanged polite greetings. "Amy will be starting UCLA soon," Enid said. "She wants to go to New York and be a television journalist. What ideas children have today—"

"Granny Enid," the girl implored.

"It's a hard profession to break into," Kellen said. Her eyes drifted down to the girl's hand resting on Garrett's arm, but she quickly looked up into Garrett's eyes.

A few more people had sidled up to their half-circle, and Kellen felt their eyes on her. "Are you staying in town long?" she asked Garrett.

"I expect to," he said.

"This must be quite a change after living in New York for so long," she said. She was amazed to hear her own voice, so cool and neutral. Inside, she was aching, remembering what it had been like eight years ago.

"A welcome change," Garrett said. "I don't like New York, really. I feel more at home on the West Coast."

A black-and-white collage of faces pressed closer, people holding drinks, their eyes expectant. Clark was now standing at her side. She tried to think of something to say that would provide a graceful exit, but her mind was a sudden blank. At that moment, Ian edged into the circle, up to Garrett's side, with Lilith close behind. Kellen watched as Ian greeted Garrett in a familiar manner that made it clear to her that he had been in touch with him recently.

I was right, she thought. Garrett is trying to cut a deal with Ian.

Lilith peered at Kellen. "What a stunning necklace," she said, her eyes narrowing on the stones. Lilith had heard the story behind the necklace's origin and had always secretly coveted it. She wagged a finger in Kellen's face. "But you're not supposed to wear color tonight."

Kellen was suddenly aware of someone standing close behind her. She turned and saw Stephen staring at Garrett. She realized then that they had never met each other, yet an introduction now seemed absurd.

"It isn't fair," Lilith said, "for you to wear that necklace when the rest of us must make do with plain old diamonds." She glanced around looking for sympathy and caught Garrett's eye. "It's not fair, is it, Garrett?"

Garrett's eyes were focused on Stephen's hand, now placed lightly around Kellen's waist. He looked up into Kellen's eyes.

"No, it's not fair at all," he said.

His eyes held Kellen's. She felt her face grow warm. He still wants me, she thought. And after all this time, I still want him. She felt Stephen's hand slip from her waist. And Stephen knows, she thought. He feels it, and he knows.

Stephen extended his hand to Garrett. "I don't think we've ever met," he said. "I'm Stephen Hillman, Kellen's husband." The men stared at each other for a moment, then Garrett shook his hand.

"Mother, don't you have something to ask Kellen?" Ian interrupted.

Everyone's attention focused in on Lilith, who smiled, aware of the ears listening. "Kellen, dear," Lilith said, "I'd like you to come to dinner tomorrow night. Garrett will be our guest. And Stephen, you'll come, too, of course."

Kellen looked at Ian, who stared at her with a small smile as he swirled his ice in his glass.

"We're busy, Lilith," she said.

"We have some things to discuss, Kellen," Ian said. "Just

some business. Mother and I just thought it would pleasant to get the family together for a nice dinner.''

"Some other time," Stephen said.

Kellen looked at Ian, and he smiled. She realized now what he was doing. He was playing one of his mind games, and this time squarely in the public eye. He was staging a little melodrama to embarrass her and Stephen in front of those who certainly remembered what had gone on between her and Garrett eight years ago.

Stephen turned to her. "Kellen, I think we should go. The children—''

"Yes," she said quickly.

Stephen paused, then held out his hand toward Garrett. "It's good to finally meet you, Mr. Richardson," he said.

"After all these years," Garrett said, shaking his hand.

There was an awkward moment, then Kellen extended her hand to Garrett. His hand was warm, holding hers firmly. "Enjoy your stay," she said.

"I will, Mrs. Hillman, thank you," he said.

She pulled her hand away. She turned to Stephen and slipped her arm through his. The crowd parted slightly to let them through, then closed again with a soft murmur.

Garrett was sitting at the table near the window, his beer untouched. Louis's restaurant, perched above the rocky shore at Point Lobos, offered a prime view for sunset watchers, but Garrett was oblivious to the scenery. His eyes were focused on the door, and when he saw the figure in a raincoat and hat enter, he rose.

"I didn't think you were coming," he said.

Kellen glanced around the crowded bar. "Please, let's go outside."

Despite the weather, the area outside teemed with people milling around the tour buses in front of the nearby Cliff House and peering through binoculars at the colony of seals on the rocks just offshore. Kellen looked at Garrett, then started down a steep path that led away from the crowd, down to a large flat cove below. They made their way through some odd stone formations, across weather-beaten ramparts and ruined pathways. They went by several large rectangular stone pools of brackish green water, passing under the gaze of big gray gulls sitting motionless, like gargoyles, on the rocks. There was an eerie feel to the place, like that of an old shrine, tranquil yet discomforting in its abandonment. The place was called the Sutro Baths, and in the late 1880s, it had been a huge, festive public bathhouse. Over the years, it had suffered neglect, demolition, and fire, and now what was left was being slowly reclaimed by the sea and air. Only the truly curious ever wandered down to the ruins, and they never lingered. Kellen went through a stone archway, and Garrett ducked his head to follow. They emerged on a small stone balcony, exposed to the wind and the surf crashing on the rocks far below.

"I didn't want to be seen," Kellen said.

"I understand," Garrett said.

Kellen stood, looking at him intently for a long time, then slowly shook her head. "I feel like I should be able to talk to you, but I can't."

"Then why did you agree to see me?"

She paused, then looked away. "I don't know."

It began to rain, a light mist carried away by the wind. A sudden gust caught Kellen's hat, sending it flying toward the railing. Garrett lunged for it but couldn't catch it in time. He looked back at Kellen. She reached up to brush back her hair, which was tied back in a haphazard ponytail.

"You look like a young girl," Garrett said. "You haven't changed at all."

"Yes I have. I have two children now," she said. "A boy and a girl."

"Ben and Sara," Garrett said. Kellen turned to face him. "Enid told me."

"What else did she tell you?"

"That you recently went back to working at the newspaper with your husband. She sees that as a bit . . . a bit strange, and she wishes you would come back to the opera guild."

Kellen searched Garrett's face for ridicule, but there was none. Neither was there any hint that he knew Sara was his child. When he had called yesterday asking to see her, she had thought that Sara was the reason, that he had somehow found out about her. In the three days since the ball, she had thought often about what would happen if Garrett found out the truth. For eight years, she and Stephen had managed to live with the secret. But now, with Garrett back, it was threatening to move beyond her and Stephen. She didn't care for herself, but she couldn't bear to see Sara hurt. So she had come today to beg for Garrett's understanding and discretion. But apparently he didn't know. She was flooded with relief, but it didn't make it easier to face him.

"Enid's a busybody," Kellen murmured. She stuck her hands in her pockets. "Her niece is very pretty."

"Amy? She's just a kid." For the first time, Garrett smiled, a slight self-deprecating smile. "I think she has a crush on me. It makes me feel very old."

Kellen felt herself begin to smile but quickly shut it off. She reached up to wipe her damp hair off her face. "It's getting late," she said. "I have to go soon."

Garrett hesitated. His somber expression reminded her so much of Sara that she had to look away. "I had to see you," he said. "To tell you something . . . That I've never stopped thinking about you. Not once in eight years."

The strange sound of the seals barking on the far-off rocks carried on the wind, wavering loud then faint. She began to shiver, and pulled her coat tighter around her. Never, in all the moments she had thought of him in the last three days, never had she expected those words.

"It's cold," she said. "I've got to go."

Garrett took several steps toward her but stopped when he saw her begin to retreat. "I know why you came back," she said. "It's no different than before. What makes you think it is?"

He looked momentarily bewildered. "You think I came back here for the newspapers?" he asked. He shook his head slowly. "Kellen, I don't care about the newspapers anymore."

"Then why did you come?" she demanded.

He paused. "At first, I wasn't sure. I thought that maybe by seeing you one last time, I could finally put an end to it. But when I saw you at that party, I knew I couldn't. I saw something in your face that told me it wasn't over."

"What is it you want, Garrett?" she asked quietly.

"Another chance," he said softly.

"I have a husband. I love him," she said.

"Like you love me?" he asked. "Like I still love you?"

She looked away quickly. She had come to see him not knowing what to expect. An apology perhaps, but not this. Not—after all these years—an admission of love.

"Stephen and I have a family," she said. "We have . . . a history together. You and I never had anything together."

"My god, how can you say that?" Garrett said. "We had the one thing everyone looks for! We had passion, great, wonderful passion."

"That's not enough for a life together."

"How do you know? We never really had a chance to find out." He paused. "Remember that poem you used to quote to me all the time in Paris—about roman candles? That's what we could have had together. A life like that."

She took a step back and felt the rocks against her back. She had forgotten that poem and was shocked that he hadn't.

He reached up and cupped her face in his hands. His lips touched hers and, for a spare second, she forgot where she was, who she was.

She turned her head away. "Don't," she said.

"Kellen—"

"I can't, Garrett," she said. "I've got too much to lose. You've got no right to ask."

Slowly, his hands dropped, and he took a step back. He ran his hand through his wet hair. "You're right," he said. "I guess I expected you would just magically jump into my arms and that we could forget about what happened and start over. Like some old movie." He paused. "I'm a sucker for happy endings, I guess."

He smiled slightly, but she just stared at him, and his face grew somber. "I won't bother you again," he said. "But I'm going to stay here. At least until I'm sure there's no chance for us. I'll be here, Kellen, if you want me."

She pushed herself away from the rock and edged past him. She pulled the belt of the raincoat tighter around her waist and walked away, without looking at Garrett. She went through the archway and along the pathway between the pools. The rain was coming down harder now and she quickened her pace. At the base of the path leading back up the cliff, she paused to look back. Garrett was still standing there, watching her. She turned and stumbled up the path away from him.

Chapter
Thirty-six

"It's the answer to our problems," Stephen said.

Kellen looked at him from across the desk. It was late, and they were sitting in her office. Stephen got up from his chair and began to pace. He turned to face Kellen. "I can't believe you worked this out yourself," he said.

"It wasn't exactly my idea," Kellen said. "The Federal Communications Commission is forcing our hand. So, it's enough money?"

"Enough to build the suburban distribution plant and more," he said.

Kellen smiled. "Good."

"I just wish you had told me about this ahead of time."

Stephen's voice had a challenging edge to it. Or perhaps her fatigue was just making her overly sensitive. "I wanted to surprise you," she said.

"But if I had known——"

"We'll have the money for the plant, Stephen. What does it matter how it happened."

A slight sadness was edging out the excitement she had felt earlier about telling Stephen about the sale of the Oakland television station. She had worked hard to put it together. Ever since she had first heard the news last week about the FCC, she had been thinking about selling the station. To break up monopolies, the FCC had recently begun pressuring newspapers to sell other media holdings they had in the same market. She had not wanted to discuss the sale with Stephen until she could line up a buyer. It was a matter of pride to set up the deal herself, so she could finally prove to Stephen, to Ian, and to herself that she was capable of functioning in the corporate realm. Finding the buyer had not been difficult. The Oakland station—despite its small size—had always been financially solid, and the buyer wanted to turn it into a base for future cable enterprises. After three weeks of intense negotiation, the buyer agreed to her asking price.

"I can't believe Ian's agreed to this," Stephen said. "He's fought me tooth and nail on the plant."

"He doesn't know yet," Kellen said. "He's been in Hawaii for the last two weeks. I want to keep him out of this until it's too late for him to move. Now that Tyler's of age, I just need his vote, and the deal's done."

"What does he say?"

"I haven't been able to reach him. He's been on vacation, wandering through France. But I'm sure he'll side with me. He's due back tomorrow."

"So's Ian. We have a budget meeting Monday, remember?"

"Then I'll just have to get Tyler to sign this before Ian finds out. I'll drive up to Napa tomorrow." She sighed heavily. She had not been sleeping well lately, not since that day she saw Garrett, and now she could think of nothing but going home and taking a hot bath.

"Kellen, are you all right?" Stephen asked. "You haven't been yourself lately."

"I'm just tired."

He went to her side. "You've been worrying too much," he said. "Stop worrying about Richardson."

Kellen's heart skipped a beat.

"He won't get the newspapers," Stephen said. "No matter what Ian's up to, there's no way they can fight both of us."

Kellen got up slowly. "Let's go home," she said.

The next day, Kellen drove to Napa. She had not visited the property since Tyler had moved in, and she was taken with how charming it looked. The Victorian house had been freshly repainted in soft grays, and beds of flowers had been planted. A fat tabby cat, lolling on the veranda, eyed her with disinterest as she climbed the stairs. The door was open, so Kellen walked in. She saw Tyler's suitcases in the vestibule, and she called out his name. After a moment, he emerged from the kitchen. "Kellen, what in the world are you doing here?" he asked, startled.

Before she could reply, another voice called out Tyler's name, and a second later, J. D. Waverly appeared. When he saw Kellen, he froze. For a long time, no one said anything.

"I came to welcome you home," Kellen stammered. "And to talk to you about some . . . I'm sorry, I should have called."

Tyler pursed his lips, glanced at J. D., and let out a sigh. "Let's all go into the living room," he said.

Kellen sat on the sofa, and J. D. took a chair across from her. He was having trouble concealing his nervousness. Tyler sat down on the sofa near Kellen.

"Tyler, I'm really sorry—" Kellen began.

"It's okay. Just relax." He looked at J. D. "Kellen's the only one who knows about me, J. D. I didn't tell her about you. She's always been level with me. You can trust her."

J. D. just looked at Kellen for a moment, then finally smiled slightly. "Well, I have no choice really," he said.

There was a long silence.

"So!" Tyler said, with a quick smile. "I think we could use a drink. How about some wine?"

The next hour was awkward, as Kellen and J. D. eyed each other cautiously, and Tyler tried to keep up the conversation. But then, gradually, everyone began to relax. Tyler told her about his and J. D.'s trip to France. Soon, dusk closed in, and Tyler rose to turn on some lights.

"I didn't realize it was getting so late," Kellen said.

"Stay for dinner," Tyler said. "I insist."

During dinner, Tyler talked animatedly about his trips to the great wineries of Burgundy. He said he was going back in the fall for intensive study. "I have so much to learn," he said, shaking his head. "So I'm going to hire good people to help me. J. D.'s already got me going on that."

Kellen looked at J. D., who had been watching Tyler with a small smile, letting him do all the talking.

"All I suggested was that you get a good business manager and a lawyer so that you won't get taken advantage of," J. D. said. He looked at Kellen. "Your brother is the typical artist. It's hard to get him to listen to the mundane aspects of running a business."

"He's a dreamer," Kellen acknowledged.

"Has he told you the ideas he has for this place?"

Kellen shook her head, glancing over at Tyler, who was now quiet. "Well, go get your sketches," J. D. said to him with a smile. Tyler left and returned with a portfolio, placing it before Kellen. "I think," he began, pulling out sketches, "that someday California wines will be just as popular as French wines. Some of them are just as good now, but people are too snobbish to realize it. Or too intimidated to know the difference. So, I'm going to produce the best wine I can. And make it irresistible . . . but accessible."

The sketches showed the old winery and nearby stables refurbished, with the grounds tastefully rearranged to accommodate parking and picnic areas. "The winery will be redone so people can take tours and classes," Tyler said. "The stable will be a gift shop. We'll sell the wine, some cheese, maybe some good glasses."

"But no T-shirts," J. D. said.

Tyler grinned. "No T-shirts."

Kellen stared at the sketches in disbelief. "Tyler," she said softly. "This is remarkable."

"Show her that other sketch you did," J. D. said.

Tyler pulled a small sketch from the bottom and handed it to Kellen. It was of a wine bottle label, a simple design in blue and gray that showed a stylized bird in flight, and in silver letters: Ingram Hills.

"That's what I'm calling it," Tyler said. "I didn't want to trade on the Bryant name, so I'm using your mother's maiden name. I hope you don't mind."

Kellen looked at Tyler. "I like it, Tyler. I really do."

Tyler gathered the sketches together. "I'll put these away and be right back," he said, leaving the room.

Kellen and J. D. sat silently for a moment. "I wish I had one ounce of your brother's creativity," J. D. said with a small smile. "Maybe I'd be a better politician."

Kellen smiled and took a drink of her wine. J. D. cleared his throat. "Kellen," he said hesitantly, "no one knows about Tyler and me. No one knows I'm gay."

"J. D.—"

"Tyler thinks I shouldn't try to hide it. He's coming out, and he thinks I should, too." He paused. "I want to, for him if nothing else. But I've worked very hard to get where I am. Contrary to what a lot of people think, I haven't been able to ride into office on my family's coattails." He took a breath. "I love what I do, and I'm vain enough to think I can somehow make a difference."

He took a sip of wine. "I've only known your brother for a short time, but I've come to care about him very much." He smiled slightly. "I'm a driven, self-centered man, and Tyler's been good for me. He brings something out in me, an unselfishness, like I want to be there for him."

Kellen smiled. "I know what you mean."

"I'm not ashamed of what I am," J. D. went on. "But I can't count on people understanding. I don't even know how you feel about it, so I have to trust you. I have to keep this part of my life secret. I've got too much to lose."

J. D.'s gray eyes were locked on hers, and Kellen realized he expected some kind of response from her. She believed J. D. was sincere. And in just this one evening, she had seen for herself the trust and affection between her brother and this man. A part of her clung to the idea that something was wrong with Tyler; perhaps she'd never get over that. But she recognized now that he had found something with J. D., a contentment that she had always assumed would be denied to him. "I understand," she said.

Tyler came back in the dining room. "So what were you two talking about in my absence?" Tyler said.

"Politics," J. D. said, with a smile. "Just politics."

Soon after, J. D. left the room so Tyler and Kellen could discuss the business about the radio station. Tyler signed the sales contract. It was almost ten by the time Kellen got ready to leave. She said good night to J. D., and Tyler walked her out to her car, carrying his wineglass.

The air was warm, and it was quiet except for the crickets. The stars were strung together like transluscent white ribbons in the clear, black sky.

"I like him, Tyler," Kellen said.

Tyler looked at her, his finger tapping the edge of the empty glass, a gesture of nervous joy. "I've given you a lot to worry about over the years, haven't I," he said.

She shrugged slightly. "That's what family's for."

Tyler glanced back at the house. "I know I've only known J. D. for a little while, but it's different this time, Kellen. It's like we've always known each other. Like we just belong together." He gave her a puzzled smile. "You have any idea what I'm talking about?"

She stared at her brother. "Yes," she said softly.

His face creased into a big, sudden smile. "I'm so happy," he said, his voice soft with incredulousness.

Kellen took a breath. "I'm sorry I've been so, so unaccepting, Tyler," she said. "It's hard enough to find someone to care about without . . ." Her voice trailed off.

"Forget it. I'm glad you know now."

Kellen hesitated, then put her arms around Tyler, hugging him tightly. Finally, Tyler pulled away, his eyes on the ground. "Drive carefully," he said.

She nodded and got into the car. She steered the car out of the drive and onto the street. Hers was the only car on the road, and she rolled down the window to let the warm, fragrant air rush over her. It was a moonless, pitch-black night and the headlights seemed inadequate pinpricks in the dark ahead. She wished suddenly she had accepted Tyler's invitation to stay the night. The drive ahead seemed too long, the road too dark. And she felt an emptiness that she finally recognized as envy—a great longing for the fulfillment her brother had so unexpectedly found.

She groped on the passenger seat, and her fingers found a cassette. She quickly thrust it in the player. A second later, the sounds of Puccini's *La Tosca* spilled out. After a moment, she reached over and turned the volume up high, then even higher, filling the car and night with music.

Lilith stood staring out the window, down at the people in Union Square. After a minute, she turned back to face Ian, sitting at his desk. "She outmaneuvered you," she said.

"There was nothing I could do," Ian said tersely. "That's the way Father set it up. One vote for each of us."

"But why didn't you see it coming? Why didn't you know about the FCC thing?" Lilith heaved a big sigh. "That station made a lot of money."

"I know, Mother! I was the one who set it up to do exactly that!"

"I just don't see why you—"

Ian slammed his hand down on the desk. "It's gone! Sold! Let's forget it, all right?!"

Lilith stared at him, wide-eyed. Then she walked regally to a chair and sat down, wearing a hurt look.

"I'm sorry," Ian said.

"You're awfully tense, dear."

"I have a lot on my mind." Ian began to sift through some papers as a way of hinting to Lilith that he wished she'd leave. But she just sat there, and after a moment he noticed Lilith's eyes wandering around the room intently and that she was frowning. "What is it?" he asked in exasperation.

"Do you plan to see Richardson today?" she asked.

"No, he left for New York two days ago."

"Without giving us his answer?" she asked, surprised.

"He's coming back next week," Ian said flatly. "But I get the impression he's not interested."

"Nonsense. I think he's just stringing us along to get a better price. Perhaps if you were more aggressive—"

"Mother, I've talked to that man until I'm blue in the face. I just don't think he wants the papers."

"Well, despite what all the gossips say, I don't think he's here just to renew old acquaintances, although I certainly wouldn't put it past Kellen.'' She paused thoughtfully. ''I think we should lower our asking price. This sale has to go through.''

Ian stared at her for a long time. ''I don't get it,'' he said. ''I've listened to you complain for years about how Father stole your family's newspaper. And you keep telling me how important it is for me to run things so Robert can sit in this office. But now, you're ready to just turn around and hand it to an outsider. I don't get it, Mother. I just don't get it. What in the hell do you want?''

Lilith opened her purse and pulled out a gold compact. She opened it and looked at her reflection, smoothing a stray black hair away from her heavily powdered cheek. She put it away and leveled her dark eyes at Ian. ''I want to hurt Adam the way he hurt me,'' she said.

For one fearful moment, Ian thought he saw tears form in Lilith's eyes, and he froze, not having any idea of what to do. But then Lilith's mouth drew into a firm line.

''He left me for that woman,'' she said. ''He's dead, and I have to hurt him—both of them—the only way I can, through their daughter. Kellen won't get the one thing he wanted her to have most.''

Ian could think of nothing to say. Finally, he picked up some papers on the pretense of stacking them in a neat pile. ''Richardson said he's coming back next week,'' he said. ''I'll present him with a new offer.''

Lilith smiled.

''You know, Mother,'' Ian said, ''even if Richardson bites, there's no guarantee we can count on Tyler. He's obviously aligned himself with Kellen.''

Lilith began to button her jacket. ''I wouldn't worry about Tyler. He can be persuaded. You just have to find the right button to push. If I'm right about my hunch, Tyler has a secret that might prove very embarrassing if it got out.'' Lilith smiled, enjoying Ian's expectant, bewildered look. ''Why, didn't you know, dear? Your little brother's a homosexual.''

''Tyler? A faggot? I don't believe it!''

Lilith frowned. ''I so dislike that word.'' She rose, picking up her purse. ''Well, as unbelievable as it might sound, I really think it's true. And what's more, I think his . . . his . . . *friend* is that politician, Waverly.''

Ian's mouth fell open. ''How do you know that?''

''I saw them together at the Black and White Ball. By the end of the night they seemed awfully friendly.'' She shook her head at Ian's incredulous face. ''One just has to be observant, dear.''

Ian recovered slightly. "Well, if you're planning to go into the blackmail business, Mother, you'd better have more than a hunch. Besides, you know Tyler. He probably couldn't care less if anyone knew."

"Yes, I know. But I wonder how Mr. Waverly might feel. He has a family image to protect. I've seen him in public with women, so he's obviously not out of the cupboard."

"The closet," Ian said.

"Whatever."

She glanced at her watch. "Well, I must run." She went to the door, then turned back to Ian. "You know, you're right, dear. We do need something more than just my hunch. I think we should hire someone to watch them."

"A detective? Good lord, Mother."

"Just to gather some information," Lilith said. "Just in case we need it. You'll do it for me, won't you, dear? Of course you will. You're such a good son. . . ."

Chapter
Thirty-seven

In the next month, Kellen relied on work to keep her from thinking about Garrett. But the words he had said to her that day at the Sutro Baths remained in her head, and she turned them over repeatedly, carefully, like pages in a book, looking for insight to his feelings and her own. True to his word, he didn't contact her. And she didn't call him. She finally admitted to herself that she was afraid to, afraid seeing him again would melt whatever resolve she had.

So she worked. The sale of the television station went through smoothly, and Stephen's plan for the plant was resurrected. It was projected the plant would take a year to be completed, but Stephen, working at a furious pace, was flogging everyone toward a nine-month completion date. He was away from home and the office often, and Kellen turned his long absences to her advantage, maintaining her own heavy schedule at work. She concentrated on the unsolved problem of the *Times*'s flagging city circulation, but a solution remained as elusive as ever. Then, on a routine trip to the loading dock, she stumbled on an idea. She overheard the conversation of two delivery men. One man said he had quit his job delivering the morning *Journal* to come to work for the *Times*. She approached the men and introduced herself and asked the man why he had quit. He explained that he had been forced to leave the *Journal* because he needed to work afternoons to accommodate his wife's schedule.

"But you sound like you'd rather be back at the *Journal* instead of working here," Kellen said.

"It's nothing against this newspaper, ma'am," he told Kellen. "It's just that trying to run a truck through the afternoon traffic in this town is impossible. It was easy delivering the *Journal* at three in the morning." He gestured toward a truckload of the *Times*. "But this is driving me crazy."

"Me, too," Kellen said ruefully.

The man smiled. "Maybe you should switch the *Times* to the morning."

Kellen nodded absently but then paused. Switch the *Times* to the morning . . . could it be as simple as that? She returned to her office, the idea burning in her mind. She began jotting down notes about production schedules, deadlines, press configurations. She called various departments gathering information. By six, she leaned back in her chair staring at her scribblings on the yellow pad. It could be done, she thought with rising excitement. The *Times* could be converted to a morning publication. It *was* as simple as that. She quickly packed her briefcase. She couldn't wait to tell Stephen about her idea.

Stephen set the yellow pad down on the table, taking off his glasses. He looked up at Kellen. "It seems like a good idea, but I don't know," he said slowly. "There are a lot of things you haven't taken into consideration."

She stared at him in consternation. She had hoped for more enthusiasm, but so far Stephen had given her mainly reasons why it shouldn't be done. It was just his cautiously pragmatic side emerging, but right now she didn't want to hear it. Right now she wanted a spontaneous show of support.

"I know that," she said. "So we'll form a project committee, like the one for the suburban plant."

He shook his head. "Kellen, I've got all I can handle with this plant. Maybe when it's up and running—"

"We can't afford to wait another year. Something has to be done now." She paused. "I'll head the committee."

He stared at her. "This would mean tremendous changes for editorial. I can't give you the input you need right now, Kellen. Be reasonable. Let's tackle one thing at a time."

She took a deep breath. "I know editorial well enough to act on your behalf." She paused. "I want to do this, Stephen. I'm going to call a meeting of the vice presidents for tomorrow. Can you be there?"

"I was planning to go back to the plant site. But I'll be there if you want me to."

"I'd appreciate it."

He pushed himself out of the chair. "I'm tired," he said. "I think I'll go to bed early."

She sat there, her eyes focused on the yellow pad lying on the desk. Stephen paused at the door of the study. "Are you coming up?" he asked.

"Not right now," she said. She heard him go up the stairs and for the next half hour, she sat there without moving, staring at the yellow pad.

Kellen glanced down the long conference table at Stephen, then at each of the other vice presidents. She could read their reactions to her idea in their faces—everything from amazed skepticism to barely disguised scorn. "That's about all I have to say, gentlemen," she said. "Perhaps you have some questions?"

The men glanced at each other. Finally, Dennis Dingman cleared his throat. "You'll have to excuse us, Mrs. Hillman. We're all just a little shocked by your proposal."

"I can appreciate that," Kellen said. "Converting the *Times* from an evening to a morning newspaper is an audacious move that would no doubt cause upheaval and some problems. But I'm convinced it is the only way we can stem our circulation loss and regain our dominance over the *Journal*."

George Avare looked puzzled. "But how?"

Kellen looked to Stephen. "Stephen has talked about how hard it has become to get the paper delivered on time because of traffic problems," she said. "This will solve them. It also accommodates trends toward morning readership."

Harry Beebe shook his head. "But we're sure to lose circulation if we switch to morning. Readers are creatures of habit."

"Some readers will be angry and leave us," Kellen said. "But most people view the newspaper as an old friend. You get angry at the friend once in a while, but you don't desert him. I'm confident most of our subscribers will stay with us. We will continue to put out a late edition to satisfy the afternoon need."

She glanced at the vice president of promotion. "One of the keys will be a good promotional campaign. It has to start at least six months before the switch."

Avare, who had been hired by Ian and had never liked Kellen, stared at her. "What about your brothers, Mrs. Hillman?" he said. "How do they feel about this?"

"I told them both about it this morning. Tyler has backed my recommendation." She paused. "Ian, on the other hand, feels the move would jeopardize any chance there might be to sell the company, which you all know has been his intent for some time now. That's why he refused to be at this meeting."

She closed the leather folder in front of her and folded her hands on top of it. She stared at her hands for a moment, then looked up. "I have something to say about that," she said. "Most of you knew my father. He hired four of you and guided your rise here. You know he published newspapers that stood for something—integrity, truth, the best values of the reader. And he always did it with a great passion." She paused. "I can no longer stand back and watch any of that be compromised. and I will not allow this company to be sold. I will do whatever is necessary to prevent it."

The room was quiet. "Our next step," Kellen said finally, "will be to form a project committee to research this. I will head it, and I'd like each of you to appoint someone from your division. We have to move fast on this."

The men looked at each other. "If there are no other questions," Kellen said, "then I think we can call it a day."

The men rose and filed out of the room, talking among themselves in low tones. Kellen lingered, watching Stephen out of the corner of her eye. The tension that had begun last night was still unresolved.

Stephen rose from his place at the far end of the table and came over to her. "You handled that well," he said.

"I could have used your help."

"You didn't need it."

She looked at him, closed her briefcase with a snap, and started for the door. He followed. They said nothing as they walked down the hallway.

"I know this can work," she said finally. "But not if they're not on my side."

"They're used to Ian calling the shots, Kellen. Now all of a sudden, you come on strong. They feel like they're caught in the middle of a family feud and are probably afraid to take sides. Also, you've issued a direct command. They might be feeling a little threatened."

She stopped to face him. "Is that how you feel?"

Stephen stared at her. Her question hung in the air, and she wished she could take it back.

"No," he said finally.

"Then why do I feel like you're fighting me on this?" she asked.

"I told you last night that I thought it was a good idea, Kellen. But I also think you're moving too fast. I know how much you want to solve the problem, but I don't want to see you do something impetuous that you'll regret later. If you'd just wait until I have more time to help——''

She shook her head in exasperation. "Stephen, stop it, please. You're treating me just like you used to when we were kids. 'You don't think things through, Kellen. . . . You're too impetuous. . . . You need my help. . . .' '' She looked at him imploringly. "I'm not a kid anymore, Stephen. Stop treating me like one.''

Her outburst had startled him into silence. She looked at her watch. "I've got to get going or I'll get caught in the rush hour traffic," she said quickly.

She went toward the elevator. Stephen paused, then followed her. She pushed the button and they waited, neither saying anything.

"Don't go," he said.

"I just want to be alone, Stephen. I want to think."

"You don't have to go down to Carmel to do that."

"Yes, I do. I want to get away for a few days."

He was staring at her, but she wouldn't look at him. Her eyes were trained above the elevator, watching the floor indicator move slowly, too slowly. "I'm sorry, Kellen," he said. "I didn't mean to sound like I'm patronizing you. I'm sorry about last night, too.''

Her eyes stayed on the elevator indicator lights.

"Don't go," he said. "We'll talk about it. Whatever it is that's bothering you, we'll talk about it.''

Her eyes dropped to the carpet.

"If it's something I've done——" he began.

She shook her head. "It's not you, Stephen, it's me.''

The elevator door opened, and she got in. She pushed a button, but Stephen held the door open. He seemed to want to say something, but finally he just let the door go.

The little gull-wing Mercedes hugged the road, heading south away from the congestion of the city. Soon, the urban sprawl gave way to open, hilly land and amorphous coastal towns. She knew the road well and tried to lose herself in the simple pleasure of driving, but she could not stop thinking about Stephen.

She glanced up at the clear blue sky, then over to her right. She knew from experience that just beyond the road there was a cliff, and that far below was the ocean, pounding on the rocks. But today, a heavy fog bank had moved in and lay nestled against the cliffs. Nothing was visible but the top of the fog, resting atop the ocean like miles of meringue. The sight was disorienting, a strange distortion of the reality she knew was there, just beyond the guard-rail.

Disoriented . . . that was how she felt right now about Stephen. It was as if their marriage was shifting slightly. It was like the time when she was twelve and had felt her first real earthquake tremor. She had felt the floor of the house move slightly under her feet, and when it was over seconds later, she had looked up and seen cracks in the walls of her bedroom. The sturdy old house on Divisadero, she had realized, was only as solid as the ground it was built on.

Was that what was happening to her marriage? Was the ground on which it had been built undermined by some fault?

Last night, when she told Stephen she was going to Carmel, he had been exasperated and even a bit angry at her reluctance to explain why. She couldn't explain it to him.

The car screeched around a curve, and she gripped the wheel tighter. The road dipped down a hill and through a tunnel of trees, and the fog engulfed the car. Kellen switched on the headlights.

If it's something I've done—

It's not you, Stephen. it's me. . . .

"It's not you," she said softly. "It's not me. Maybe it's just *us*."

An hour later, she steered the car onto the turnoff to the exclusive community of homes in the Del Monte Forest north of Carmel. She waited for the sense of peace that always came over her when she returned to the house. But instead, the disorienting feeling remained, now coupled with an anxiety. The sun had almost set by the time she pulled up to the dark house. She hurried up to the door, unlocked it, and went in. The house was stale from being closed, and she went immediately to the glass doors leading to the deck and threw them open. She stepped out into the rush of fresh salty air and closed her eyes, breathing in deeply. For several minutes, she just stood there, watching the sun disappear. She heard a sound behind her and turned.

"I wanted to be here when you arrived," Garrett said. "You beat me."

"I drive too fast." She paused. "After you called, and we agreed to meet here, I changed my mind. I wasn't going to come. . . ."

"But you did," he said.

For a moment, neither of them moved. Then, Garrett came toward her. He held out his arms, and Kellen stepped into them.

He held her, not tightly, and then she felt his hands go up under her hair to cradle the back of her head. She closed her eyes, waiting, expecting his kiss. Instead, she felt the brush of his lips over her eyelid.

"A long time," he whispered. "Such a long time."

His arms tightened around her, and his lips touched her temple. She leaned into him, wanting to feel every part of him touching her. Then he kissed her, almost shyly.

She pulled away, her eyes on him. She took his hand and led him to the bedroom. In the murky light, she could barely make out his face, but she steadfastly held his eyes as she slowly undressed. Then, she crossed the room and, without a word, unbuttoned his shirt. She bent her head to kiss the hollow of his throat. He slipped free of the shirt, and her hands moved up over his waist and across the hard expanse of his back, her fingers greedily rediscovering his body. This time, when his lips found hers, his kiss was fierce and biting. And when he grabbed her hips and pulled her toward him, she gave out a cry, half laughter, half sob.

He struggled out of his pants, and they fell on the end of the bed. She was aware of nothing but his lips and hands moving over her body, touching her everywhere at once. Every time he tried to ease her back toward gentleness, she kissed him bruisingly, urging him on. Finally, he laid back in surrender. She straddled his hips and guided him inside her. She moved against him, slowly at first, then faster until her breath was coming in gasps and sweat beaded on her breasts. He watched her, swaying above him, her hair caressing his chest. He watched her face, entranced. And when she cried out and collapsed against him, he clasped her to him as his own body tensed, then went limp with a thunderous release.

It was a moment before he realized she was crying. He held her more tightly, and her fingers dug into his arm. After a moment, she stopped and lay quietly on his chest. Finally, she got up and without a word, put on a robe. She switched on a small light. She stared at him for a moment, then ran a hand through her disheveled hair.

"I don't like myself for doing this," she said. "But I'm here. I don't know why, but I have to be."

Garrett said nothing.

"There are two things," she said softly. "We won't talk about the newspapers."

"All right," Garrett said.

She took a slow, deep breath. "And the other thing," she said.

"This is just sex. Don't expect anything more from me." After a moment, she looked away. "There's a robe you can use in the closet," she said quietly, and she left the room.

Garrett found the robe hanging amid the other men's clothing, but he shut the closet and put on his own clothes. When he went back out into the living room, Kellen was curled up in a chair. She looked up at him with wary eyes.

"I'll go get the bags," he said.

When he returned, she was in the same position, staring vacantly at the dark windows. He went to her, kneeling beside the chair. "Kellen, don't do this," he said.

"What?" she said without looking at him.

"This coldness. Don't do this to me."

"You said you wanted what we had before. Well, this is it. This is what it was."

"No, it's not. Before, there was a joy in what we did."

"It was sex, Garrett," she said sharply. "That's all there was between us. Just sex. And that's all it can be now."

"That's not true. You know it's not."

She closed her eyes, shutting him out.

He took her hand. "We loved each other," he said.

"Stop," she said, trying to pull her hand free, but he gripped it harder.

"We loved each other as completely as two people can."

She pulled her hand free and covered her face. "It's different now," she murmured.

"It doesn't have to be. Give me a chance to prove it. Let me love you."

Kellen's hands dropped to her lap, her eyes closed. "I'm here. That's all I can promise you." She looked at him. "Please, Garrett, don't pressure me. Please."

He rose. "All right, Kellen. Whatever you want."

They scarcely spoke to each other for the rest of the evening. Garrett drove into town to buy groceries and then made a supper of steak and salad. Kellen hardly touched it and sat at the table looking at him. They went to bed early, without making love, and Kellen fell asleep immediately in his arms. She was awakened in the morning by the press of Garrett's lips on the back of her neck. When he made love to her, slowly and tenderly, it felt like the delicious, lingering moments of a dream. They spent the day walking the beach, reading, and listening to music—sometimes together, sometimes apart. Kellen knew Garrett was giving her wide emotional breadth, and gradually she began to relax. She felt something unfamiliar around him—a calmness that before had been overpowered by the omnipresent current of sexuality.

Saturday night, she decided to try her own hand at making dinner. She was an inept cook; nothing in her upbringing had prepared her for the mysteries of the kitchen. But she remembered watching the cook make an omelet, and she attempted one, which she garnished with fresh fruit and brought to the table.

Garrett stared at the huge blob of egg for a moment. Kellen took her place across from him and waited, expectantly.

"That's the ugliest damn omelet I've ever seen," he said with a smile.

After that, the tension eased more, and their conversation was relaxed though still cautious. She cleared the dishes, and when she returned from the kitchen, she saw Garrett standing near a desk, looking at a display of framed photographs.

"This must be your mother," he said, holding out a frame as Kellen came over to him.

"Everyone says I look just like her," she said.

"Yes. Just as beautiful." He picked up a photograph of Adam. "This is your father?"

Kellen nodded. Garrett put it back in its place. There was a cluster of several other photographs, of her with Stephen and with the children. Garrett studied them for a moment, then picked up a small one in a silver frame. Kellen held her breath.

"That's Sara," she said.

It was a recent school portrait, and it captured Sara in a rather formal pose, her dark hair neatly pulled back with a blue bow, her blue eyes serious. Garrett looked at the picture for a long time. Then he carefully returned it to its exact spot between pictures of Ben and Stephen.

He looked up at Kellen, and her heart skipped a beat. She saw the question in his eyes.

"Would you like some coffee?" she stammered. "Oh, that's right. You don't drink it." She went to a liquor cabinet. "Maybe some brandy. I think I've got some here. . . ."

She poured two glasses and brought them over to the sofa where Garrett was now sitting. She waited, her heart pounding, waited for him to ask about Sara. But he didn't. He just sat there, staring at the fire, sipping his drink.

"You have a beautiful family," he said quietly.

She shut her eyes.

"Stephen's a lucky man," he said after a moment.

She heard the sad envy in his voice and knew he would not ask her about Sara. She felt a strange sense of relief. He knew the truth; he had to. But he was, for some reason, allowing it to remain unspoken between them. True to his word, he wasn't going to pressure her in any way. Everything would be on whatever terms she wanted.

"I miss having a family," he said.

She glanced over at his profile. Her heart, which she had set so hard against him, softened. "Why didn't you remarry after your wife died?" she asked softly.

It was a moment before he answered. "I don't know. I probably should have while I was still young enough. Now I'm forty-three, and I know too much." He smiled wryly. "I'm not so brave anymore."

She looked away toward the fire.

"Besides," he added, "I have this strange, middle class notion of romantic love. And you're the only woman I have ever loved enough to want to marry."

"Garrett, please . . ."

He cupped her chin in his hand. "I know. I said I wouldn't pressure you. But I didn't say I'd lie to you." She tried to turn away, but he wouldn't let her. "Listen to me, Kellen. I'm getting older. I want a family of my own."

Why doesn't he ask about Sara? she thought frantically.

"Things didn't work out for us the first time," Garrett went on. "But they could now. I know that you and Stephen have a history together. But do you really love him?"

"Yes," she said.

"Then why are you here?" he said. "No matter what you say, I won't believe it's just sex."

She looked at him, her eyes brimming. "I don't know. . . ."

"I've loved you from the day we met," Garrett said. "And I know—I know, dammit—that you love me. I feel it in the way you touch me, the way—"

The phone rang, and Kellen jumped. It rang several more times before she finally rose and answered it. Garrett watched her as she picked it up.

"Hello? Oh, hi, baby," she said. Her voice was soft but artificially light. "I know . . . Mama misses you, too. . . ." Kellen slumped slightly, closing her eyes. "You did? That's great. . . . Soon, I'll be home real soon." There was a long pause. "Don't let the bedbugs bite," Kellen said softly.

Another pause. And Kellen turned her back to Garrett. "You shouldn't let her stay up so late," she said.

Garrett looked away, at the fire. He knew from the tone of her voice that she was talking to Stephen.

"Sunday . . . I'll be back Sunday. I've got to go. I . . . I'm really tired and want to get some sleep." Kellen murmured something else and hung up the phone, but she made no move to return to the sofa. When Garrett looked back at her, she was just standing there, staring vacantly, her hand covering her mouth. Finally, she looked at him.

"Was that Sara?" he asked.

She nodded, the guilt etched in her face.

"Kellen, I—"

"You've got to leave, Garrett," she said softly.

"What?"

"Please. Please just go."

He started to object but then saw her eyes fill with tears, and he realized how hard she was trying to contain them. He had done exactly what he said he wouldn't; he had pressured her, and now the call from Sara had driven her to the edge. The wrong move from him now would push her over and away from him forever. He rose and went into the bedroom. A few minutes later, when he emerged with his suitcase, she was still standing in the same position.

"There's an inn down the road," she said distractedly.

"No, I'll just drive back to the city," he said.

He went to the door, opened it and paused, turning back to her. "Can I see you again?" he asked.

She shut her eyes. "I don't know," she said.

He left the house and got in his car. He sat there for a moment, his hands resting on the wheel. He wanted to go back in the house, but he knew there was nothing he could do or say right now to persuade her. He realized suddenly the magnitude of what he was asking of her—to give up everything just because he said he wanted her. Why should she? Why should she believe anything he said after what had happened eight years ago?

But he was not going to give up. Not now. He had come back to see if whatever it was that had once bound them together was still there. It was. He knew it now. But there was something more. Sara . . . Seeing that photograph had sent a searing jolt of shock through him, and his mind had quickly calculated back the years. Sara had to be his daughter! Somehow he had hid his reaction and resisted the surge of questions that had come to him. He didn't want to ask; he wanted Kellen to tell him. He had given her several chances, but she hadn't.

He looked back at the house one last time, then started the car. He felt a strange, sad elation. . . . He had a daughter! Kellen and he were bound together in a way he had never anticipated. But what did it mean? Nothing, unless Kellen was willing to acknowledge it. He pulled out of the drive, glancing back once again at the house. He would wait until she was ready to trust him again. That was all he could do. Just wait.

Chapter
Thirty-eight

Kellen stood by the copy desk in the middle of the newsroom. Surrounding her, in a quiet semicircle, were most of the editorial employees of the *San Francisco Times*—reporters, editors, columnists, photographers, secretaries, and clerks. More than three hundred pairs of eyes were leveled at her, waiting. Kellen scanned the faces, recognizing a few from her stint working in the newsroom ten years earlier. Clark was standing off to one side, smoking one of his brown cigarettes, watching her with a small smile.

She straightened her shoulders. "I know many of you are nervous about this move to morning publication," she began, her voice strong and clear. "I'm here today to try to explain why it's necessary to the survival of the *Times*."

She went on to talk about the ongoing circulation drain, the delivery problems, and the loss of market share to the *Journal*. She told them about the need for the new suburban plant, and that Stephen was currently in San Mateo developing the plant site. She explained that she would be honest with them, that they had a right to know what was happening. When she was finished, she paused. "I'll be glad to answer any questions," she said.

After the topic of the conversion was exhausted, there were other questions about salary and budget freezes. "I know you've all been patient," she said. "And I have to ask for you to be patient for a little longer. Most of our resources must now be directed at bolstering circulation and the new plant. But no more salary freezes. We are budgeting a modest five-percent increase for salaries this year."

There were murmurs of surprise. Ian had instituted a newsroom salary freeze eighteen months ago, and now Kellen, with one quick stroke, and Tyler's vote, was wiping it out.

The questions kept coming. Most were about small concerns,

but Kellen answered each one patiently. She had purposely not been much of a presence in the newsroom during recent years, and she sensed now that perhaps she had pulled back too far. As empathetic as Stephen was, it was different for employees to have the owner's ear. Just as with the other newspapers, they needed to know a Bryant still cared.

A reporter who had driven in for the meeting from a suburban bureau talked about feeling isolated and unappreciated. A photographer complained about having to ration his film. The baseball writer bemoaned budget cuts that prevented him from covering spring training. A copy editor asked if the *Times* was going to start using computers, which triggered a long and lively debate about technology.

Kellen was listening to the exchange when she noticed Ian standing off in a far corner. He was watching her, his arms folded across his chest, his dark eyes glaring at her.

"Mrs. Hillman," a voice called out. "I have a question." A young man took a step forward. He was about twenty-five, with keen eyes. Kellen had never seen him before.

"I grew up reading the *Times*," he said. "I admired it and always wanted to work for it. During the year I've worked here, I've heard lots of rumors about your selling, and like a lot of people around here, I get the feeling this is a rudderless ship."

"What's your question, Bailey?" It was the managing editor, Ray, bristling slightly.

The young man looked at Kellen. "Every great newspaper should have a vision, a concept of what it stands for. What's yours, Mrs. Hillman?"

All eyes, which had been locked on the man, turned toward Kellen. "I believe," she said slowly, "that a newspaper is unlike any other business, that it must somehow transcend its preoccupation with profit and loss to focus on a greater goal. I believe that a newspaper is a sacred trust, that it has an obligation to serve its readers first." She smiled slightly. "And its owners second, if necessary."

She looked around the crowd, focusing on Ian. "I know the *Times* has lost something, that some of its substance has drained out," she said. "But I know, too, that we can get it back. I see the *Times* as a paper that stands for what's best in people, as a newspaper of great passion. And I see it soon taking back its place as the single most important source of information in this community. I don't have to tell you that this is a special city, with a unique personality. Nothing can reflect that better than a good newspaper. And no one—certainly not the *Journal*—can do it better than we can.''

The young reporter was still staring at her. "Vision is a difficult thing to articulate," Kellen said with a smile. "That is the best I can do.''

The room was silent for a moment. Then Ray stepped forward and asked if there were any other questions. There was none, so the crowd slowly dispersed throughout the newsroom. Clark came over to Kellen and Ray.

"I'm going to break that kid's neck someday," Ray said, jerking his head toward Bailey, who had returned to his desk.

Kellen watched the young man, who was now on the telephone. "Where's he from?" she asked.

"The *Oakland Tribune*," Ray said. "He's real talented. But a smart ass. I still oughta break his neck.''

"Don't," Kellen said with a smile. "He's hungry, Ray. Besides, a healthy disrespect for authority is good in a reporter. And it was a good question.''

She turned to Clark with a sigh. "How about buying me a cup of coffee. I need it after that.''

They went over to the coffee maker in the corner. Clark handed her a plastic cup. "This stuff'll jump-start a corpse," he said.

Kellen took a sip and grimaced. "Just what I need. I'm really beat.''

Clark leaned against the wall. "You know, you handled that really well," he said. "Just like your old man." Kellen murmured a thank you, and Clark was surprised at the look of gratitude in her eyes.

"It's funny. I get more nervous talking to them than I do the vice presidents," she said. "But I survived this, so I guess I can survive the next month. I'm going to visit each of the papers in the chain. It's time that the other rudderless ships got to see that someone's still at the helm.''

"You'll be gone a month?" Clark asked. "What does Stephen say?''

"He doesn't like the idea very much.''

Clark noticed, for the first time, the dark circles under her eyes. "I'm worried about you, Kel," he said softly. "You've been working too hard lately.''

"I'm all right.''

"There's something bothering you," Clark persisted. "Something you're not telling me." He paused, weighing whether he should press on. "It's Garrett, isn't it," he said quietly. "You've seen him again?"

Kellen bit into the edge of the cup, avoiding Clark's eyes. "No, not since Carmel."

Last week, not long after the weekend with Garrett, Kellen had confided in Clark. She had needed to talk and knew Clark could be trusted. She had told him everything, even about Sara. Clark had told her that he had always suspected it. And he cautioned that perhaps Garrett did, too.

"What's wrong then?" Clark persisted.

"I've been thinking a lot about what you said, about telling Garrett about Sara. I've been thinking that maybe he does have a right to know about her. But I just don't think I can do it. I don't know if I trust him. I don't even know how I feel about him."

"What about Sara?" Clark said. "If Garrett has a right to know about her, she certainly has a right to know about him."

"I don't know," she said softly. "I thought once it was better if she didn't ever know the truth, but now I'm not sure. I thought once that I loved Stephen, but how can I if I'm constantly thinking of another man? I thought I knew myself, but I don't."

The sound of the wire machines filled the silence. Clark knew he had to get her back to safe ground. "How's Tyler?" he asked. "I haven't seen him in a while."

It took her a minute to focus on his question but then she smiled slightly. "He's happy. Truly happy."

Clark shook his head. "Living all alone in the middle of that vineyard . . . The boy's still a lost soul."

"Tyler?" she said softly, staring out over the newsroom. She tossed the unfinished coffee in the wastepaper basket. "He's not as lost as most of us."

Kellen tipped the bellboy, and he left her standing alone in the middle of the suite. She kicked off her shoes, opened the suitcase, and carefully took out the framed photograph. She glanced around the suite and then set the frame on a bureau, positioning it so she could see the faces of Sara and Ben from wherever she was in the the room. Her eyes drifted to a large bouquet of white roses on a nearby desk. She picked up the card: Hurry home. We miss you. Love, Stephen.

She went to the window, pulling back the draperies. Downtown Portland was spread out below her, its lights just beginning to break through the dusk.

She knew that the roses were Stephen's way of apologizing.

Last night, they had had an argument on the phone. He wanted to know when she was coming home. Considering that she had been away now for four weeks, it had been an innocent enough question. But in her fatigue, she had interpreted it as an accusation. They had argued, and finally, Stephen had said her trip was only an excuse to get away from him. You're pulling away from me, he had said. The conversation ended, angry and unresolved.

Now, alone in the hotel so far from home, she realized that Stephen was right. She was pulling away from him. Every day she felt herself drifting farther away, yet she felt unable to stop it.

She turned away from the window and went to her suitcase. She quickly unpacked and ordered a light dinner from room service and a copy of that day's *Portland Press*. She changed into a robe and popped open her briefcase, extracting a thick folder labeled "Portland." When the food and newspaper arrived, she set the tray on the bed and sat down, cross-legged, to begin work. She first read the newspaper thoroughly, then tackled the folder, which was filled with status reports on the newspaper's finances, circulation, market position, and general health. Her routine had been the same for each newspaper she had visited. She had guessed beforehand that she would be perceived as a dilettante owner making a token visit to the fiefdom. So she made sure she was prepared. She read the reports so she could handle the management; she read the newspapers so she could talk to the employees.

In each city, she had been greeted with wariness. No one from the Bryant family had been to the newspapers since Adam's death ten years before. But by the end of each visit, Kellen had won the respect of those she met. And slowly, each newspaper took focus in her mind, no longer just a line on a balance sheet or a paragraph in a corporate report, but separate entities, each with its own personality and set of problems. In Phoenix, reporters complained of salaries that had been frozen for two years. In Seattle, she discovered Ian had imposed a ridiculous "two-take rule" in an effort to force shorter stories to conserve newsprint. In Sacramento, she discovered presses in dire need of modernization. In San Diego, she discovered Ian had reduced the size of the comics so much they could barely be read. Everywhere she went, she found good newspapers, but also a legacy of neglect. For more than a decade, Ian's laissez-faire management and his insistence on a high profit margin for the sake of personal income had stifled the newspapers. Adam Bryant's dream had been undeniably compromised. Ian had taken a chain of powerful, vibrant newspapers, joined by a singular vision, and turned it into a disconnected scattering of impotent profit machines. The realization had left Kellen deeply saddened. But it had also crystallized her resolve. She would, she promised each person she talked to, do all that she could to restore the lost vitality.

She was doing it for the newspapers and all the people who worked for her. But she was also, she knew, doing it for herself. After so many lost years, so many false starts, she finally felt as if the newspapers were truly becoming hers. They were no longer something she had inherited. They were something she had earned anew.

Kellen set the Portland folder aside, her thoughts going back to Stephen. She wished that she could make him understand that better. Lately, he had tried hard to be more supportive, but she still felt that deep down, he did not understand. To him, the *Times* was his profession, a certain part of his identity, to be sure, but something separate. But to her, the *Times* and now all the other newspapers were as essential as Ben and Sara, an extension of her, like family. It was not something she could explain in rational terms. Perhaps it was not something Stephen could ever understand.

Suddenly, she felt very lonely. She glanced at the bedside clock. It was too late to call the children. Besides, she had already talked to them that morning from the airport in Seattle. Benjamin talked about his toys. Sara had been excited about going off to summer camp tomorrow. Their cheerful preoccupation with their own worlds made Kellen wonder briefly if they missed her at all.

She was tired but still keyed up. Finally, she got dressed and went downstairs to the newsstand in the lobby, hoping to find a diverting book. To her surprise, she found the newsstand stocked with out-of-town papers. She saw that day's *San Francisco Times*, its filigreed gothic nameplate as welcoming as a smiling friend. She scanned the front page. The lead was a story about the linkup in space of the American Apollo capsule and the Soviet Soyuz.

Kellen was about to turn away when a huge, black headline on another newspaper caught her eye: TERROR FROM THE SKY. Good grief, she thought, a plane crash? Why isn't it on the *Times*'s front page? In the next instant, she saw the nameplate, the *New York Tatler*. She picked up the paper and thumbed to the story, and as she read, her mouth tipped up in a smile. The "terror from the sky" was an air-conditioning unit that had fallen out of a Manhattan apartment window, narrowly missing a lady but squashing her dachshund. The story was written in straight news style, with no hint of irony, and by the time Kellen finished it, she was laughing. She paid for both papers and took them back to her room.

She sat down on the bed and spread the *Tatler* before her. She turned the pages slowly, shaking her head and smiling at the tabloid's insouciantly lurid mix of stories.

"I will say this for you, Garrett," she said softly. "You made me buy the thing."

She leaned back against the headboard, then glanced over at the phone. After a moment, she picked up the receiver and dialed Garrett's house in Tiburon. After ten rings, she hung up. She reached for the *Times* but then paused. She picked up the phone again and dialed Garrett's office in New York. It rang seven times and she was about to hang up when Garrett's voice broke in with an impatient "Hello."

She gripped the receiver. "It's me," she said. "Kellen."

"I was just going out the door," he said. "I wasn't going to answer the phone. I'm glad I did."

Kellen's mind went blank. Her impulse to call was dissolving into uncertainty. "What are you doing at work so late?" she asked casually.

"Working hard. Trying not to think about you." There was a long pause. "Why are you calling, Kellen?"

"You made me laugh. The story about the killer air conditioner."

"Ah, yes. Wrote that headline myself."

She took a breath. "I want to see you again, Garrett."

"I can be there tomorrow."

"No, I'm not in San Francisco. I'm in Portland on business. I'll be here two days, then I'm going to Las Vegas."

"I'll meet you there." His voice, the familiar, elegantly accented deep murmur made her shut her eyes. "Las Vegas," he said. "I've always wanted to see it. I've never gambled before. Have you?"

"No," she said softly.

"Well, we'll try our luck together," he said.

Kellen sat in the car, searching for Garrett in the crowd exiting the airport, afraid she would miss him. But she spotted him easily, standing out from the Bermuda shorts crowd in his three-piece suit and tie. She honked the horn to get his attention and, as she watched him make his way toward her, her pulse quickened. If she had had any doubts about calling him, they had evaporated with the sight of him.

He tossed his suitcase in the back and got in. "It's eight o'clock at night, and it's like a bloody oven!" he said.

"Welcome to Las Vegas in July. Maybe I should have asked you to meet me in Seattle instead."

They looked at each other, and for a moment Kellen tensed, waiting for his kiss. But he leaned back in the seat and yanked off his tie. "No, this is fine," he said with a smile. "I'm just happy you called. I'd have gone to hell itself if you'd asked."

She maneuvered the car into the traffic. "That's exactly what some people might call this place," she said.

As they drove toward the Strip, they were both quiet. Kellen could see that Garrett was tired, but she knew that he was waiting for her to set the mood and pace. She was the one who had called him. It was up to her to set the ground rules. She glanced over at him. I'm the one who has to decide what this is going to be, she thought. I have to decide what it is I want from him.

As they pulled onto the Strip, the sun was going down. The overwhelming, kinetic neon of the casinos competed with nature's own show, a sky streaked with blazing bands of red, orange, and purple.

"My god," Garrett whispered. "This is like being trapped inside a kaleidoscope."

"I know," Kellen said. "It doesn't even seem real. Nothing in this town does."

Garrett continued to gape as Kellen led him through the faux-rococo lobby of Caesar's Palace, through the clamor and congestion of the casino. Upstairs, in the suite, she closed the door, and it was quiet. Garrett glanced around the suite with a small smile. It was enormous, furnished in white and royal blue with chandeliers, marble, gilt, and statuary, including a cherub fountain.

"How wonderfully decadent," he murmured.

She smiled. "Why don't you shower? I'll order dinner."

A half hour later, Garrett emerged from the bedroom wearing a bathrobe, toweling off his hair, and looking considerably revived. He looked at the dinner, at the candles and the bottle of wine. Kellen poured a glass and handed it to him.

He smiled. "Haute Brion. Plump white bathrobes. Gold telephone in the loo. You stage a fine seduction."

He leaned in to kiss her softly. The smell of his skin, so clean, was intoxicating. She brought her arms up to encircle his back. He pulled back slightly to look at her.

"No pressure this time," he said. "I promise."

They stood, holding each other for a moment, both nervous, both uncertain what to do next. "Let's start with something easy—dinner," Garrett said finally.

At first, conversation was strained while they ate, but gradually, helped along by the wine and by Garrett's stories about the *Tatler*, they both began to relax. By the time Garrett came to the end of a long, funny story about one of his reporters, Kellen had tears in her eyes from laughter.

"It's good to see you laugh," he said. "Even if it does come at the expense of my fine publication."

"Oh, Garrett, how do you expect me to take the *Tatler* seriously when you don't?"

"But I do take it seriously," he said. "Very seriously. I want the *Tatler* to succeed." He paused. "So much so that I may have to finally admit that I'm wrong about its approach."

"What do you mean?"

He took a drink of his wine. "The formula isn't working here like it does in England or Toronto. Strangely enough, your idiotic brother understood that better than I did."

Kellen tensed. "Ian?"

"Yes. He told me once that I underestimated American tastes. And he was right in a way. In London, the *Sun* is popular because the working class likes to shock the establishment. But in New York, the working class likes to think of itself as middle-class. So scandals and bare-breasted women don't sell. Especially to advertisers." He smiled. "I did all my research about America but failed to take into account the upwardly mobile American ego."

"Is the *Tatler* in trouble?" Kellen asked.

"It loses money. But its circulation has stabilized, so I suppose it can go on living off the British operation. The question is, how long can my ego continue to take a bruising? I was picturing myself as quite the media mogul."

He was smiling in a self-deprecating way, but Kellen sensed he was more bothered by the *Tatler*'s situation than he wanted to admit. "So what will you do?" she asked.

"I'm not sure. I still believe the city needs a good, blue-collar newspaper. Maybe I just need to rethink how the *Tatler* should fit in." He grinned. "What do you think I should do with my smutty rag? Should I clean it up and go after my share of the brie-and-chablis set?"

"I think you should trust your instincts. That's what my father always said about running newspapers."

"Sound advice." Garrett poured out the last of the wine. "Shall we get another?"

Kellen smiled, shaking her head. "I'm half-drunk now." She leaned back, closing her eyes and stretching her arms languidly above her head. She looked back at Garrett in time to see him watching her, and she resisted the urge to pull the gaping neckline of her blouse together.

"So what were you doing in Portland?" he said.

She hesitated. Since Garrett's return, they had not once discussed the newspapers. All she had was his one declaration that he now wanted her, not them. She stared at him, wanting suddenly to believe him, not just for the security of the newspapers but for her own sake. She realized in that one moment that she had called him in the belief that they would take up where they left off in Carmel—an affair, purely sexual and uncomplicated. But seeing him now, she knew that was not what she wanted at all. She wanted, with all her heart, to trust him enough to love him again.

"Learning," she said finally. She went on to tell him about her visits to the papers, about the problems she saw and the solutions she was considering. She told him, too, about the morning conversion plan to help the *Times*. He listened intently to all of it, then leaned back in his chair.

"Your brother called me the other day," he said. "He's pressuring me to buy again. He's lowered his asking price."

She couldn't hide her surprise. "What did you say?"

"The same thing I told you. That I'm not interested."

"You were right about him, Garrett. He's crippled the newspapers."

"But you'll change that."

She looked back at him, surprised.

"Eight years ago, I didn't think you could," he added. "Which is one reason I came in and tried to take over. But you've changed. I don't know what it is exactly. . . . You're more confident, as if you've finally grabbed ahold of what's yours instead of just waiting for someone to hand it to you."

His words were so unexpected that she could only stare at him. "But Ian's hard to fight," she said. "I feel like I'm running behind him, trying to undo the harm he's done, cleaning up his messes. I just hope it's not too late." He saw with surprise that her eyes were rimmed with tears.

"Sometimes I'm so angry at my father," she said softly. "For leaving me with . . ." Her voice faltered.

She got up abruptly, went to the sofa and sat down, her back to him. After a moment, Garrett came over to her.

She turned to him, dry-eyed. "I'm sorry," she said. "I don't know where that came from. I've been thinking about him a lot lately. Going to his newspapers, hearing so many people talk about him in the past few weeks . . ."

He took her into his arms and kissed her.

She looked at him. "Make love to me," she said softly.

He eased her down on the sofa, his lips moving down to her neck. He undressed her slowly, then took off his robe. She gave herself over to the luxury of selfishness, allowing him to do what he wanted. It was a new sensation for her; their lovemaking before had always been tinged with an urgent, competitive tension. Now, he just wanted to please her, and she wanted to let him. When it was over, she lay against Garrett's chest, thinking about many things. About how much they had both changed in the last eight years. About Sara. And about how one thing had not changed: the strange powerful bond she had felt with Garrett that first time in Paris was still there. She stared up at the blue-and-gilt ceiling, thinking about all of it. It was only after she was about to drift off to sleep that she realized that not once had she thought about Stephen.

The next day, Garrett chartered a plane, saying he wanted to see the Grand Canyon. They sat silently, faces pressed to the window, as the plane swooped over the panorama of russet gorges and purple shadows. Far below, the Colorado River was a winding gold ribbon, glinting in the sun.

"I've never seen such colors," Garrett murmured. He was leaning over Kellen to look out the window, and she reached up and ran her hand slowly through his hair. The tender, possessive gesture surprised him, and he looked at her.

"I have to go home tonight," she said.

He sat back. "I was hoping we'd have more time."

"I have to get home. I've been away more than a month."

"Well, I didn't even get a chance to lose some money," he said, trying for lightness. He smiled. "But I guess I can do that in New York, right?"

She turned away, on the pretense of looking out the window. He took her hand. "I love you, Kellen," he said.

She leaned her forehead against the glass, shutting her eyes. Her fingers intertwined tightly with his.

"I don't know yet what I want from this, Garrett," she said

softly. "I don't know what I'm going to do. I just know I have to be with you." He looked at her, saying nothing. "We've got to be careful," she said. "I don't want to hurt Stephen. Please understand."

Garrett looked at her for a moment, then leaned forward and picked up the intercom. "We're going back now," he said to the pilot. The plane banked to the left and headed south. They were silent, both staring absently out the windows until Las Vegas appeared below, in the daytime just a smear of dull colors in the khaki-colored desert.

"Kellen, listen to me," Garrett said. "I know I said I wouldn't pressure you, but there's something I have to say." He paused. "Maybe you don't know what you want out of this, but I do. I don't want you to just fall in and out of my bed whenever you feel the need. I don't want just your body. I want all of you. I want a future with you. Why in the hell do you think I came back after all these years?"

He paused again, choosing his words carefully. "I know you don't want to hurt Stephen," he said. "But sooner or later, you're going to have to make a decision. I love you. And though you won't admit it yet, I know you love me."

She stared at him, surprised by his vehemence and afraid of the truthfulness of his words. "I have to have some time, Garrett. Please. You've got to give me that."

He turned back to the window. The plane was circling toward the airport. After a moment, he reached for Kellen's hand again. "All right," he said. "I can wait for a while."

He looked back out the window, down at the Strip's silent lights, then back at Kellen. "I guess I'm more of a gambler than I thought," he said.

Chapter
Thirty-nine

Ian lit his cigarette and looked around the Big Four dining room. The lunch crowd was the usual amalgam of well-known faces, and Ian felt a glow of self-satisfaction over the prime placement of his table. He caught the eye of a pretty young woman and allowed himself a flirtatious half smile. Why shouldn't he? He knew what she saw. At forty-six, he was a man worthy of admiration—handsome, well-dressed, socially confident. Especially confident today because he was about to close the biggest deal of his life, one that would provide him, Clarisse, his son Robert, and new baby Hillary, with permanent financial security. He looked across the table and conferred a smile on Lilith.

"That's an attractive suit, Mother," he said, feeling magnanimous. "Is it new?"

She ignored him, her eyes trained on the entrance. "Where is he?" she asked. "He's late."

"Richardson will be here, Mother. Stop worrying."

"Well, I just don't understand what's taking him so long," she said with a frown. "He's kept us dangling for months, and now suddenly he's interested again."

"He's shrewd. He knows how badly we want to sell, and he waited us out. When I called him yesterday and lowered the price again, he finally had an offer he couldn't pass up."

"Three hundred and thirty million . . . We're giving it away," Lilith muttered.

"So now you want to forget about selling?"

"No, it has to go through." She glanced around the room. "God, I'll be glad when this is finished. At least I don't have to deal with that detective anymore. . . . Dreadful man. Did you read the report he sent?" Ian nodded. Lilith shook her head. "I always suspected Tyler was, well, not normal."

"You didn't have to send me those pictures," Ian said under his breath. "They were disgusting."

"They may be useful when the time comes." She glanced to the door. "He's here," she murmured.

Garrett came up to the table. "Sorry I'm late," he said, giving Ian a cursory handshake and Lilith a nod.

"Would you like a drink?" Ian asked.

"No, nothing."

"Mother?"

"A martini would be nice." She turned to Garrett. "It's a shame you couldn't come to dinner last week. It must be quite tiresome, all this flying back and forth to New York."

"I don't mind it," Garrett said. "I spend the week in New York, then come out here on the weekends to relax."

"Yes," she said with a smile. "It must be so nice over in Tiburon. Close to the city, yet so secluded, so far from the madding crowd . . . all by yourself."

Ian leaned back, allowing Lilith to handle the small talk, marveling at her audacity. He could see that her innuendo about Kellen had not been lost on Garrett. Ian glanced around at the nearby tables, noting the other diners eyeing him and Garrett with curiosity. He wondered if anyone else suspected, as he and Lilith did, that Garrett and Kellen were having an affair. Ian looked at Garrett and felt a grudging spurt of respect for his ability to carry on with Kellen while deceiving her again about the sale. He wondered idly if Stephen knew. Probably not, he thought. Serves him right for marrying the crazy bitch in the first place. Ian's gaze drifted to the nearest table, whose occupants, three businessmen, gave him a nod of fraternal recognition. Well, he thought with satisfaction, soon they'll have even better things to talk about than poor old cuckolded Stephen.

"Do try the salmon, Garrett," Lilith purred.

"I won't be staying long," Garrett said.

Ian and Lilith exchanged glances. "Well," Ian said quickly. "Then perhaps we should get on with what we came here for. You've had time to consider our latest offer?"

"More than enough time," Garrett said. He folded his hands, resting them on the tablecloth.

Ian finally prompted, "And you've found it enticing. . . ."

"I found it insulting," Garrett said quietly.

Ian glanced quickly at Lilith.

"It's an insult to your sister," Garrett said, "and to your entire family, especially your father's memory."

Lilith nearly spilled her drink. Ian managed to keep his face impassive.

"I came here today," Garrett said, "only to tell you that I'm not interested in buying your company."

"I thought we were going to do business," Ian said, his voice low. "After all these months—"

"Once and for all," Garrett interrupted. "I'm not interested. And I'd greatly appreciate it if you didn't try to contact me about it again." He glanced at Lilith. "Frankly, your persistence is becoming a bit embarrassing."

"Well, of all the nerve," Lilith said.

"Mother, let me handle this," Ian said sharply. His eyes locked with Garrett's. "Me embarrassing you? That's truly amusing, Richardson, considering what you and Kellen have been up to. I thought you were smarter than this, allowing her to manipulate you."

"You're a fool," Garrett said evenly. "You've exploited your corporation for short-term personal gain—mismanaged it into impotency. You've done all you could to undercut Kellen, when you should be grateful to her for trying to salvage it."

"Now wait a minute, Richardson—"

At that moment, the waiter appeared and placed salads before Lilith and Ian.

"You were handed an empire and you pillaged it," Garrett went on, not bothering to lower his voice. "You're an incompetent fool, Bryant. Even if I wanted your company, I wouldn't do business with you. I don't deal with fools." Garrett rose. "I have a plane to catch." He nodded to Lilith, who sat frozen, her face white. "Enjoy your lunch."

Ian and Lilith didn't move. The waiter stared at Garrett's retreating figure, then turned to Lilith. "Would Madame care for some pepper?" he asked, holding out the mill.

"Go away," Lilith said through clenched teeth.

Ian sat there, eyes trained straight ahead. His face burned with humiliation. "Now what?" he muttered to Lilith.

She picked up her fork. "Eat your salad," she hissed.

Ian speared a piece of romaine but couldn't bring it up to his mouth. "That fucking limey prick," he murmured.

"You know I can't stand that language," Lilith said.

"Let's get out of here," Ian said angrily.

"No, we will stay and have our lunch." Lilith said, with a discreet look around. She took a bite of salad and rolled her eyes.

"Good lord, can't anyone make a decent Caesar anymore? This is absolutely crawling with anchovies. . . ."

"How can you just sit there and eat after what he said to me?" Ian said. "To say nothing of the fact that we've lost our best chance to sell, for chrissake."

"Pull yourself together and listen to me," she said calmly. "And eat your salad. People are staring."

With a petulant frown, Ian began to eat.

"We don't need him," Lilith said. "Perhaps there's another way. I was thinking about something Enid once told me. Must have been eight years ago. Time does fly these days. Anyway, Enid had just returned from England and had visited the Richardsons. They're close friends, you know."

Ian continued to eat morosely, his eyes sweeping the room, wondering who had heard Richardson.

"Well, it seems Arthur got to talking about San Francisco," Lilith went on, "and he told Enid he tried to buy a newspaper here, but the deal fell through. . . . " She paused. "You're not listening, you're not hearing what I'm saying."

"What *are* you saying, Mother?"

She leveled her dark eyes at him. "That perhaps we've been courting the wrong Richardson. That perhaps we should have been talking to the father all along."

"Why would he—"

"Enid said he was very disappointed that Garrett couldn't close the deal. There's no reason to think Arthur Richardson has changed his mind, especially if the price is lower than it was eight years ago."

Ian focused on Lilith for the first time. "Do you really think—"

The waiter placed a salmon in dill sauce in front of Lilith. She took a bite. "London in October," she mused. "It's probably terribly rainy. Perhaps we can pop over to Paris when we're finished with business. I could do with a new Chanel or two. What do you think, dear?"

Ian glanced around the room, at the sea of gray business suits. The sting of Garrett's words was still fresh on his face. He forced himself to take a bite of the salmon. "I think," he said slowly, "that if you can pull this off, Mother, I will buy you all the Chanel you want."

The hurdy-gurdy music rose beguilingly on the breeze, mixing with the sound of children's laughter. Sara dashed across the playground toward the carousel. Benjamin let go of Kellen's hand and ran after her.

"Sara, wait for your brother!" Kellen called out. But Sara was already out of earshot, a blur of blue and dark streaming hair. By the time Kellen and Stephen caught up, she had already positioned herself on a painted horse. Ben waited patiently until Stephen hoisted him up onto a smaller one and showed him how to hang on to the brass pole.

The carousel started up, and Kellen and Stephen stood watching each time the children came around. Ben was clinging to the pole, his face reflecting his cautious excitement. Sara was standing up in the stirrups, laughing.

Kellen shaded her eyes from the bright sun. "She's going to break her neck one of these days," she murmured.

"She'll be fine," Stephen said.

The flat tone in his voice made Kellen turn, but he had already walked off to a nearby bench. He sat down, leaning his forearms on his knees, staring at the ground. Kellen went over and sat down next to him. It was a beautiful day, and Golden Gate Park was filled with people. She watched a group of men in white nearby playing a courtly game of lawn bowls, the gentle thuds of the steel balls punctuating the chatter of the children in a nearby sandbox. She glanced at Stephen. All morning he had been locked in some private contemplation. He was often preoccupied about the plant these days, but today his mood had been impenetrable.

"I'm glad you could come with us today," she said.

Stephen didn't look at her. The carousel music carried over to them on the breeze. "Kellen, we have to talk."

He hadn't moved, but now his hands were clamped tightly together. She focused on his ring, glinting in the sunlight, then looked away quickly, knowing suddenly what was coming.

"I know about you and Garrett," Stephen said.

She closed her eyes. In the last few weeks, she had thought often about this very conversation, about what she would say. But she had thought about it only from her viewpoint, of how she intended to tell Stephen.

"Stephen, I—"

"No, let me talk." His voice was firm. "I've been thinking about this for a week now, trying to figure it out, trying to understand why." He paused, taking a deep breath. "I know you haven't been happy. I thought going back to work would change that. But I guess it wasn't enough."

He stared at the carousel. "When I finally realized what was going on, I blamed myself," he said. " I thought there had to be something I wasn't doing, something I wasn't giving you. But then I realized it's not me at all."

He looked at her. "It's you, Kellen. It's just the way you are. You need this . . . this excitement in your life."

The matter-of-fact emptiness of his eyes and voice rendered her speechless. "I didn't mean to hurt you, Stephen," she said finally, knowing how weak it sounded.

He shook his head. "Oh, Kellen," he said quietly. "I've spent most of my life running behind you, and I long ago stopped expecting you to turn around to see how I'm doing." He stared vacantly ahead. "You never had to. You always knew I was there right behind you. Good old reliable Stephen."

Kellen started to say something, but suddenly Sara came bounding over. "Daddy, can we go again?" she exclaimed. Stephen pulled some change out of his pocket and handed it to her. She ran off to buy more tickets, leaving Kellen and Stephen sitting in silence.

"It sounds like I'm feeling sorry for myself." Stephen said calmly. "But I'm not. Not anymore. I'm just fed up, Kellen. I won't just sit back with everyone else and watch you and Garrett make a fool of me and a mockery of our marriage."

"Stephen," Kellen said softly. "It's not as simple as—"

"Yes, it is as simple as that," He interrupted, turning to face her. "It's black and white. It's him or us. It's Garrett or your family."

Kellen looked over at the carousel. "Don't use them like this, Stephen. It's not fair."

"Fair? What the hell is fair about any of this?" The anger had finally burst free, and he looked at her accusingly. "I've been patient, Kellen, for years, hoping you'd forget him. I thought you had. But I was wrong. And obviously this is not just something you need to get out of your system." He paused, his eyes locked on hers. "So you tell me what it is. Do you love him, Kellen? Is that it?"

She closed her eyes. "I don't know."

He looked away. "You don't know," he repeated flatly. After a moment, he looked back. "Well, do you love *me*?" he asked angrily. "Maybe you can tell me that at least."

"Yes," she said softly, still unable to look at him.

He sat there, staring at the carousel. He ran a hand over his eyes. "What about Sara? Have you told him?"

"No."

His eyes did not leave the carousel. "In all the ways that count, I'm Sara's father," he said, his voice now quiet and firm. "This is our family. You have to decide if you want to keep it together." He stood up. "Until you do, I'm moving out of the house." He looked once more toward the carousel. "Tell the kids what you want for now. I'll talk to them later."

She looked up at him. He had stuck his hands in his pockets, and he was squinting in the sun, staring off at some distant point. "You take the car," he said. With a last glance at the carousel, he turned, went up the path through the playground, and was gone.

Kellen sat motionless, her senses painfully acute. She could feel the sun hot on her bare neck, could hear the click of the metal balls on the lawn and the rippling calliope music. She looked at the carousel, and it metamorphosed into a blur of color and motion. The sun refracting off mirrors, the lulling gait of the wooden horses, and a flash of blue ribbon, going round and round and round.

Chapter
Forty

Kellen stood at the window, watching the storm as it moved inland. The afternoon sky was heavy with gray clouds and green foaming waves crashed on the kelp-littered beach.

"Kellen? Is something wrong?"

She turned toward Garrett, who was building a fire. They had just arrived at the house in Carmel, and their bags still stood by the door. She clasped her arms around herself and shivered, then turned back to look out the window.

"This'll get rid of the chill in a moment," Garrett said. He came over and wrapped his arms around her. "I think we're in for a bad one," he said, looking out at the ocean.

It began to rain, first just a few huge drops pelting the glass, then a steady beat.

"Garrett, Stephen knows," Kellen said. "He's moved out of the house."

"How did he find out?"

She slipped out of Garrett's arms and went over to the fire. "Apparently, it's been no secret," she said softly.

"But we were so careful. We were together only here and at my house."

"It doesn't matter now. It's out in the open. Maybe it's for the best." She looked at him despondently. "I just don't want Sara and Ben to be hurt by this."

"Do they know what's happening with you and Stephen?"

She shook her head. "Stephen has been down in San Mateo so much lately that they haven't questioned his absence. I have to tell them soon, before they hear lies from someone else." She paused. "I don't know how I'm going to explain."

"They'll be all right, Kellen," he said. "Children are tougher than we think. They know you and Stephen love them. That's all they need to get through this." He paused, trying to smile. "But I'm the last person to give you advice right now. I'm rather prejudiced about the outcome."

She sat down on the sofa and looked up at Garrett. He had been so patient, letting her deal with Stephen in her own time. But now she knew she owed him something. He had a right to know where they stood. And he had a right to know about Sara. It was time to tell him.

A rush of emotion filled her. "I love you, Garrett," she said softly.

For a moment, he just looked at her. But then he smiled. It was a smile unlike any she had seen from him before, not calculated to charm, not tinged with irony. Just a slowly unfolding expression of joy. Before he could say anything, the doorbell rang. They glanced at each other.

"Did you tell anyone you'd be here?" Kellen asked.

"No one," Garrett answered.

The bell rang again. Kellen rose and went to the door. She looked back at Garrett, and he moved out of sight. She opened it, and her mouth fell open. It was Ian.

"What do you want?" she asked.

"You could at least ask me in from the rain," Ian said flatly.

"You're not welcome here," Kellen said.

"We have business to discuss." He pushed by her and paused to take off his raincoat, tossing it on a chair. He picked up his briefcase and went into the living room. Garrett looked at him in shock, and Ian gave him a sour smile. "Well, look who's here. I was hoping you would be," Ian said. "Makes the drive down here almost worth it." He hoisted his briefcase onto a desk and snapped it open. "Poetic justice, you might say," he added under his breath.

He pulled out a folder and tossed it on the sofa. He looked at Kellen. "Some papers for you to sign," he said.

With a glance at Garrett, Kellen picked up the folder. She opened it slowly and began to read.

"Just sign it," Ian said quietly, staring at Garrett.

Kellen looked up, first at Ian, then at Garrett. "This is a purchase agreement," she said. "From Richardson Newspapers Ltd. to buy out the Bryant Newspaper Corporation."

"What?" Garrett exclaimed. "Let me see that."

Kellen made no move to give it to him.

"Kellen," he said. "I haven't the faintest idea what this is about!" He turned angrily to Ian. "What are you trying to pull?"

Ian ignored him. "Sign it," he said to Kellen.

"Get out of here," she said quietly.

Ian shrugged. "Is that the thanks I get? I come all the way down here to save you the trouble of having to do this on Monday. And you will have to deal with it—now or later—whether you like it or not, little sister. Now sign it . . . bottom of the last page, right next to Tyler's signature."

Kellen flipped to the last page. The color drained from her face, and she slumped down on the sofa. Garrett grabbed the papers from her limp hand. There was the signature: Tyler Landon Bryant, right next to Ian's.

Garrett froze. There was a third signature: Arthur Richardson. "Oh god," he said softly.

Ian pulled a pen out of his breast pocket and held it in front of Kellen's face. "Sign it," he said.

Garrett slapped Ian's arm away, sending Ian reeling backward. He threw the contract into the hearth. "Get out," he murmured.

Ian straightened and glowered at Garrett, then at Kellen, who was still sitting motionless, staring at the floor. "Fine," he said. "We have plenty of copies. We'll do this Monday, with a lawyer, if necessary."

He picked up his briefcase, went to the foyer, and put on his raincoat. "I'll see you bright and early Monday morning, little sister." He smiled coldly at Garrett. "It's been a pleasure doing business with your family, Mr. Richardson."

With a slam of the door, he was gone. Garrett sat down next to Kellen. For a long time, there was nothing but the sound of rain on the roof and the snap of the fire. Garrett looked at Kellen. Her eyes stared dully ahead.

"Kellen," he said softly. "I swear to you, I knew nothing about this. Please believe me."

"It doesn't matter," she murmured, without looking at him. "Ian's won. I've lost the newspapers." Her mouth quivered. "I don't understand why Tyler would—"

He reached for her but she pulled away. "Kellen, don't," he pleaded. "It wasn't me who did it."

She looked at him, eyes brimmed with tears. "It was your father. He signed the papers. You can't separate yourself from that. I can't separate you from that."

"Kellen . . ." He felt helpless, watching her slowly slip away from him. "This has nothing to do with you and me."

"It won't work," she said softly. "Not now."

"I know what you're feeling," he said softly, "But don't let it destroy what we've got. I'll go to my father. I'll talk to him. We can work this out. What does it matter who owns—''

The look in her eyes caused him to stop in midsentence. ''What does it matter?'' she repeated. ''These newspapers have been in my family for years. They were given to me in trust to care for. They *are* my family, as much a part of me as Sara and Ben. It *does* matter who owns them.'' She paused. ''If you don't understand that, you don't understand me.''

''Kellen, I didn't mean—''

''You'd better leave,'' she said. When he didn't move, she closed her eyes. ''Please, Garrett. Leave. Right now. I just want to be alone right now.'' He rose slowly, standing above her, waiting. ''Just go,'' she repeated softly.

He went to the door and picked up his bag. He looked back, waiting for Kellen to stop him, but she didn't even look up. He left, closing the door softly behind him.

The rain came to a sudden halt, leaving the house eerily quiet. Kellen sat staring into the fire. The contract lay in a corner of the hearth where Garrett had tossed it. A log fell with a snap, and Kellen watched the flames slowly eat into the curling edges of the paper.

With a spray of gravel, Garrett pulled his car to an abrupt stop in the driveway of Durdans. He let go of the steering wheel, his fingers aching from the viselike grip he had exerted during the drive. He was exhausted, having flown nonstop from California to New York, then catching the first plane to London. But now, he was also fueled by the surge of adrenaline and a rage that had been building since he had left Kellen twenty hours ago.

He went quickly through the front door, surprising a maid sorting mail in the foyer. ''Where's my father?'' he demanded.

The stunned woman, new to the household, stared at the disheveled stranger. ''I d-don't . . .'' she stammered.

''Mr. Richardson. Where is he?''

''In the sun room, having his breakfast . . .''

Garrett brushed by her and headed toward the back of the house. His father was sitting alone at the table, amid the potted red geraniums, about to bite into a sausage. His fork stopped in midair when he saw Garrett. He stared at him for a moment, then slowly put down the fork. ''Well, Garrett,'' he said quietly, ''What a surprise. Although not an altogether unexpected one, I might say.''

''I want to talk to you,'' Garrett said.

"Yes, well . . . how about some tea?" Arthur said. When Garrett didn't reply, he added, "Do sit down at least."

Garrett took a chair, his eyes locked on Arthur. Arthur poured a cup of tea and put it in front of Garrett. "You look dreadful," he said slowly. "Perhaps you'd like a bath and a shave first."

"Why did you do it?" Garrett asked evenly.

Arthur poured himself more tea to buy time before he answered. He was deliberately slow as he filled his cup from the silver service and added sugar and cream. He picked up a spoon and stirred his tea. The silver clicked musically against the thin porcelain. "It was an opportunity," Arthur said finally. "An excellent one. I took it."

"You didn't even bother to consult me."

Arthur carefully put the spoon down. "I didn't think you were in a position to make a clear decision, Garrett."

"What in the hell are you talking about?"

Arthur stared at him for a moment, his face reddening slightly above his pristine white collar. "When Mr. Bryant and his mother came to see me last week," he said, "they told me about your involvement with his sister. They said they had been eager to consummate this deal with you for some time, but that because of your feelings for this woman, you had failed to respond."

"My feelings for Kellen are none of their business. Or yours for that matter," Garrett said, struggling to keep his anger in check.

Arthur took a sip of his tea. "I understand this woman is married, with two young children."

"That is none of your damn business either!" Garrett said, his voice rising.

Arthur looked up suddenly, beyond Garrett. Garrett turned and saw his mother standing at the door. She looked at Garrett, her hand at her throat, her eyes wide. "Garrett . . . I thought I heard your voice," she murmured.

"Helen, please leave us alone," Arthur said. She continued to stare at Garrett, making no move to leave. "Helen, please!" Arthur said. With a stricken look at Garrett, she left.

Garrett stared at Arthur, waiting for him to say something. After a moment, Arthur sighed. "I can appreciate your anger with me, Garrett," he said. "But you've got to understand that I did this for you."

Garrett laughed. "For me? You did this for yourself! For your own bloody ego!"

Arthur looked at him calmly. "I did it for you." He paused, frowning slightly. "I'm seventy-five, Garrett. I won't be around forever to run things. I wanted to make sure I had enough to pass on to you. A real empire. This acquisition will make you one of the richest, most powerful men in America. It will certainly offset your bad situation in New York." He paused again. "It was your own plan. I only carried it out for you, son."

Garrett stared at him, incredulous, and for a brief moment, the words he was thinking nearly burst from his mouth. Son? he thought. I'm not your son. I have no connection to you. Instead, he looked away quickly.

"I had to do it," Arthur said, "because you never would have." He looked at Garrett thoughtfully. "You've always let your heart rule your head, Garrett, ever since you were a boy. I couldn't let you do it in this case."

Garrett rubbed his hands over his eyes.

"Do you remember Blue Boy?" Arthur asked. "Do you remember what happened when he broke his leg jumping over the hedge? He was suffering, but you wouldn't let me put him down. I know you hated me for that, but I had to do it." Arthur paused. "I know you blame me for what happened to Susan and the twins, too."

Garrett looked up at him in shock. Never, not once in twenty years, had his father ever mentioned his deceased wife.

"You blamed me because, at the time, you needed someone to blame," Arthur said.

"You drove her away," Garrett muttered.

Arthur stared at him. "She was leaving you, Garrett. You just didn't want to face up to that fact."

"She left only because you and Mother did everything you could to break up the marriage," Garrett said angrily. "Your constant interference, your condescension . . . Do you think she didn't feel it? It got so even she believed she wasn't good enough for me. That's why she left. That's why she took the twins and ran off that night. It was your fault!"

"It was an accident," Arthur said, "A lorry driver who—"

"You drove her to it," Garrett said, his teeth clenched.

Arthur blinked rapidly. "We were only looking out for you, Garrett," he said quietly. "She was seven years older than you, a divorced woman of no background with two children. You were just twenty, too young. We thought you deserved a chance to have your own family."

"They *were* my family," Garrett said, his voice cracking.

For a moment, neither man moved. Garrett was fighting to bring himself under control. He focused on the silver teapot sitting in the middle of the table, gleaming in the sun. He could hear the tapping of a branch on the glass overhead and then the muted whir of a vacuum cleaner starting up somewhere deep within the house. He pushed himself up wearily from the table, leaning on it for support.

"You told me once you needed something of your own," Arthur said, almost under his breath. "I thought this is what you wanted." He looked up at Garrett, his expression prideful and pleading.

Garrett looked at him, shaking his head. "You have no idea what you've cost me," he said.

He stood there for a moment, wavering with fatigue. He looked around the room. He saw Helen hovering outside the doorway, her eyes wide with alarm. He took a step to leave.

Arthur rose quickly. "Garrett, stay, please. We'll talk about this. You'll—"

"No, I'm going back. I'm going home," he said.

He left, walking by Helen without a word, and without looking back at Arthur, standing alone in the sun room.

On Monday morning, Kellen received the final papers from Ian. She had already spoken to Josh who had explained that Tyler's consent made it binding and that she had no legal recourse. But she had waited until now to call Stephen in San Mateo. She told him what had happened, and for a long time the phone was silent, so great was Stephen's shock.

"There's got to be something we can do," he said.

"There's nothing you or anyone can do, Stephen."

"Have you talked to Tyler?"

"I can't find him," Kellen said. "There's been no answer at his house for days. I haven't seen him in a month." She had also tried to reach J. D., with no success. "Stephen, I don't know what's going to happen next," she said, her voice wavering. "Ian's lawyer sent a letter saying that after tomorrow, I'm not allowed in the office." She paused. "I've got to get to the paper. I've got to tell everyone before they hear it from somewhere else."

"I'll be there as soon as I can," Stephen said.

Kellen got to the Times building just before ten and went quickly upstairs to the city room. When she stepped off the elevator, she froze. A large crowd was gathered around the bulletin board, and she knew that somehow the news had gotten out. She made her way to the managing editor's office. Ray looked up at her vacantly.

"They know, don't they," she said.

''The wire services got it. Someone put it on the bulletin board a few minutes ago.'' He motioned her in and shut the door. Kellen dropped into a chair.

''Ray, I'm sorry. I wanted to be the one to tell you and everyone.''

Ray shrugged despondently. ''You want a drink?'' He reached behind his desk to a minirefrigerator and pulled out a can of diet soda. ''Too bad I don't stock some hard stuff, for real catastrophes,'' he said with a weak smile.

Kellen looked out through the windows. People were milling around with stunned looks on their faces or talking in quiet knots. All work had stopped. She turned back to Ray. ''You know I didn't want this to happen.''

He nodded. ''I know it was Ian's doing. All of us old-timers know you were on our side. And we were on yours, too.''

Kellen glanced back at the crowd outside. ''I've got to talk to them,'' she said, rising. ''Help me get them together.''

She went out into the newsroom, Ray trailing behind. He made an announcement, and soon everyone had gathered around the main copy desk. Kellen stood before them, just as she had four months ago to explain the morning conversion plan. Then, she had confronted them with confidence and optimism. Now, she was numb with defeat. She glanced around at the stunned faces, feeling their fear and confusion. Suddenly, she had no idea of what to say. Only two words came into her head.

''I'm sorry,'' she said quietly.

She paused, no other words coming to her. There was no sound except the efficient tapping away of the wire machines and a phone ringing. ''I'm sorry,'' she repeated. ''I betrayed your trust, and I owe you all an apology.''

Her throat constricted, and she blinked rapidly to fight off the tears. She couldn't break down. She had to leave them with something hopeful, something positive. She spotted Clark standing in the back of the crowd. He looked as shocked as anyone, but he smiled slightly and gave her a half-hearted thumbs-up sign. She took a deep breath, which gave her the second of control she needed.

''I know what a shock this is,'' she said. ''I know you're all worried about what will happen to you, what will happen to the *Times*.'' She paused. ''I wish I could tell you. But I don't know.'' She stopped again, afraid her voice would not hold. ''I do know, however, that you are the finest group of people anyone could ask for, and I've been proud to work with you. You put out a hell of a newspaper. A great newspaper. No one can take that away.''

She paused again as the faces before her began to blur through her tears. "For that," she said softly, "you'll always have my sincerest gratitude.''

With a last look at Clark, she turned and went quickly to the elevator. When the doors closed, shutting off the newsroom, she leaned against the wall, the tears falling silently down her face. No, she thought, not here. Do your crying at home. No one needs to see your tears right now.

She wiped her eyes and pushed a button. The elevator took her to the top floor. She went slowly down the quiet, wood-paneled hallway. Adele rose slowly when she saw Kellen.

"Kellen, I just heard," she said, her voice breaking.

"It's all right, Adele," Kellen said. "I'm sure there will still be a place for you here.''

"But it won't be the same," the woman said, beginning to cry. "I worked for your father for twenty years. And now . . .''

"Everything will be all right," Kellen said softly. She walked away quickly, not trusting her own composure. She went to her office and opened the door.

She froze. Lilith was standing there, behind Kellen's desk, and turned to face her. Kellen stared at Lilith and at first didn't notice the strange man in a suit standing at the window, holding a yellow tape measure across the window.

"What are you doing here?" Kellen demanded.

The man just stared at her in curiosity. Lilith smiled. "Just taking some measurements for new draperies. We'll be finished in a moment.''

"Get out," Kellen ordered.

Lilith turned to the man. "Wait for me outside, Paul. I'll only be a minute." He left, and Lilith turned to Kellen. "You don't have to worry about your things, dear," she said. "We'll box them up for you and send them to the house." She picked up a plaque, one of Adam's that Kellen had salvaged from Ian's office. "Of course, you probably don't want all this tacky bric-a-brac.''

"Put it down," Kellen said.

The ominous tone in Kellen's voice made Lilith set the plaque down. She walked slowly toward the windows, her eyes wandering over the walls and furnishings.

"Get out of my office, Lilith," Kellen said.

"This isn't your office anymore," Lilith said casually, looking out the window. "Actually, Ian and I were thinking of turning it back into a conference room. Unless, of course, Mr. Richardson wants to use it.''

''Until tomorrow this is my office. And my newspaper,'' Kellen said angrily. ''Now get the hell out before I have you thrown out! You have no right to be here.''

Age had left Lilith diminished, eroding her once formidable presence. But now, as she stared at Kellen, her dark eyes still had a malevolent power. ''I have every right to be here,'' she said. ''This newspaper belonged to my father. Adam stole it from him.''

''The *Times* would have died if it weren't for my father,'' Kellen said. ''He saved it.''

Lilith shook her head. ''Oh, Kellen. I thought after all these years you'd finally given up this hero worship of yours. It's quite unnatural, you know. Maybe you should try analysis. I can give you the name of a good doctor.''

''Get out,'' Kellen said quietly.

Lilith ignored her, moving back to the desk. She sat down. ''Shall I tell you the truth about your father? Shall I tell you what kind of man he really was?'' She paused. ''He was a cold, ruthless bastard who used people to get what he wanted. He worked his way into my father's trust so he could steal his newspaper. He married me . . .'' She paused, cocking her head to one side, like a bird. ''Because I was part of the deal. And he wanted me to produce his sons.''

She paused. ''He had no use for women, you see. They were nothing but wombs or whores to him. Look at what he did to your own mother. She gave him all her money, but she couldn't give him what he really wanted—more sons.'' She shook her head. ''He obviously drove the poor woman mad. And that made it rather sticky for him. He couldn't just divorce her. So he just, well, did away with her. . . .''

The pent-up emotion of the morning suddenly spilled out of Kellen, and she began to cry. ''Get out!'' she said.

Lilith rose and went to the door. She turned back to Kellen. ''I'm only taking back what's mine,'' she said flatly.

She left, leaving Kellen standing alone in the middle of the quiet office. For a few minutes, she didn't move as she struggled to control herself. She scanned the office, and the memories crowded around her. Memories of her father in the full flush of his power. Memories of the newsroom, the people, of the closeness she and Stephen had shared in the early days. Now, with the simple act of signing a piece of paper, it was over.

She went to her desk and began to gather up papers. She picked up files and documents haphazardly, slipping them into her brief-case. Then she paused, realizing suddenly she no longer had use for any of it. None of the work needed her attention anymore. She glanced around and finally took a few of Adam's plaques off the wall and put them into her briefcase. To that, she added the photographs of the children and the one of her mother and father. She closed the briefcase. At the last moment, she picked up a copy of that day's *Times* and glanced at the headlines. Juan Carlos was calling for unity in Spain after the death of Francisco Franco. Squeaky Fromme had been found guilty of the attempted assassination of President Ford. And California Governor Ronald Reagan had announced he would run for president. The Reagan story had been given second billing to Juan Carlos.

Misplayed, Kellen thought idly, I'll have to talk to Stephen about that. She paused, realizing that, too, was over. She stuck the paper under her arm and picked up her briefcase. With one last look around, she left the office.

Outside, she paused at Adele's desk to pick up a pile of messages. There were three from Garrett in New York. She stared at his number for a moment, then crumpled them up and tossed them in the trash. She glanced at Ian's office. "Is he in?" she asked.

"No," Adele answered. "He left about two hours ago. He said he'd be at his home in Hawaii for three days."

Kellen shook her head sadly. A rudderless ship, she thought. She looked at Adele. "It's been good working with you all these years, Adele," she said softly.

"I'll miss you, Kellen," Adele said.

They embraced, and Kellen pulled away for fear she, too, would start crying. "Good-bye," she managed, and turned quickly and went down the long hall to the elevator.

That evening, at home, Kellen sat alone in the study. The house was quiet. She had dismissed the servants and sent Sara and Ben over to Josh and Anna's to stay overnight. As she sat in the dim light of the study, her mind was blank, her emotions spent. She felt only a deep fatigue and a great emptiness. The mantel clock chimed nine times. She glanced at the telephone, thinking about calling Stephen. He had called earlier in the day, offering to come by the house. But she had told him she wanted to be alone. Now, in her loneliness and despair, she was thinking again of turning to him.

She closed her eyes. No, don't do it, she thought. Don't use him again. It's not him you really want right now.

At that moment, she heard the sound of the front door being

unlocked and sat up in the chair. She heard soft voices in the foyer and wondered if it was Stephen. A tall figure appeared at the door, silhouetted in the foyer light. It was Tyler. He just stood there, as if waiting for an invitation.

"So, you finally decided to show up," she said, with more weariness than anger.

Tyler came tentatively into the room. "I wanted to talk to you," he said. "To try to explain."

"It's a little late, don't you think?" Out of the corner of her eye, she saw another figure hovering in the doorway. It was J. D., who looked extremely ill at ease.

"Wait for me in the living room, will you, J. D.?" Tyler asked. J. D. left, and Tyler turned to Kellen. He shifted uneasily from foot to foot.

"Where have you been?" she asked flatly. "I tried to reach you."

"I know. I didn't want to face you." He wouldn't even look up at her now. "I'm sorry, Kellen," he whispered. "I had to do it."

"Oh, Tyler, please," Kellen said, looking away. "Don't try to tell me that . . ."

He came over to the desk. "You've got to understand. Ian made me do it. He found out, somehow, about J. D. and me. He threatened me. He, he showed me these, these . . . pictures." Tyler paused. "I didn't care about myself, but he said he'd ruin J. D.'s career." The words spilled out, tumbling over each other. "I didn't want to do it, Kellen, but I kept thinking about J. D., how it was my fault. That just because he loved me, he was going to pay for it." His voice wavered. "I didn't even tell J. D. what was going on. He didn't find out until the sale was done. He knew something was bothering me and forced it out of me."

He looked at Kellen, pleadingly. "God, I'm sorry, Kellen. I should have come to you first. But I was scared."

Kellen looked at Tyler. He was distraught, fighting to stay in control. "I'm sorry," he repeated. "I didn't want to lose him, Kellen. You've got to understand that. I didn't want to lose everything . . . everything I—"

"Lose everything?" Kellen said softly. "Tyler, don't you see what you've cost me? I've lost the newspapers—"

"But you've still got Stephen and the kids," Tyler said plaintively. "You've got a family, someone to love you. Please don't blame me because I wanted that, too."

Kellen looked away. "Stephen's left me," she said. "We've separated."

Tyler's face registered his shock. "God, I'm sorry, Kellen," he said.

There was a noise at the door, and they both turned to see J. D. He had obviously heard most of their conversation, and he looked embarrassed and disconsolate.

"Kellen, can I say something?" he asked softly. She nodded, and he came into the room. "I feel like I'm the one who should apologize," he said. "When I found out what Tyler had done, I told him we had to talk to you." He paused. "I know what kind of sacrifice has been made. I just wish I had known beforehand so I could have stopped it. I hope you believe that."

Kellen looked at J. D. and at Tyler, whose eyes were bright with anxious tears. She realized suddenly how overwrought he looked, as if he were on the verge of emotional collapse. She rose wearily. "It's late," she said softly. "I'm going to bed."

She started past Tyler, then paused, placing a hand gently on his arm. She looked at J. D. "It's a long drive home. You're both welcome to stay," she said. Her eyes locked on Tyler's for a moment. "Really, you are."

She went to the door and looked up the staircase, at the procession of carved faces in the balustrade leading up to the darkened rooms. "It's a big house," she said softly, "and there's plenty of room."

Chapter
Forty-one

❧ It was Christmas week, and a scrawny tree had been set up near the copy desk, festooned with strung-together paper clips and old ornaments. But the atmosphere in the newsroom was decidedly unfestive as everyone went about their usual routines of putting the *Times* together. For two months now, ever since the sale had been announced, there had been a gloomy cloud over the city room. Although Garrett had made no changes and had kept an extremely low profile, everyone was nervously awaiting his first move as new owner. A few people had already quit, vowing they would not work for a smut tabloid, and the talk in bars after work invariably escalated into bravado declarations to follow suit. Many of the best reporters and editors already had begun sending out résumés, but mostly everyone was simply lying low, waiting.

Now, two days before Christmas, Garrett was making his first appearance in the city room, stepping off the elevator with Ian at his side. As his people saw him, word spread as if by telepathy, and work ceased. They walked through the newsroom, two dark-haired men in business suits, Garrett drawing stares of intense curiosity and hostility.

Ian led Garrett to Stephen's office at the far end of the city room. Stephen's secretary, staring at Garrett, informed Ian that Stephen was expected back soon from a meeting. "Tell him we were here," Ian said imperiously. He and Garrett went to see Ray, who rose in astonishment from his desk when he saw them.

"Mr. Richardson has asked for a tour before he settles in upstairs," Ian announced. "Apparently, Stephen's busy, so I thought you could help him."

"Sure," Ray said, stunned.

Ian left, leaving Ray and Garrett staring at each other. Ray's eyes traveled over Garrett's suit, and he nervously adjusted his loosened tie. "Where would you like to start?"

"The city desk would be fine," Garrett said.

They went out to the desk. Everyone tried to look busy. "We're just starting work on the first city edition now," Ray began. "We have six editions—"

"San Mateo, South County, and Marin for the suburbs," Garrett said. "And two for the city. And, of course, the token afternoon run." He saw the surprised look on Ray's face and added, "Printed in that order, right?"

"Yeah," Ray said. "That's right."

They continued through the newsroom, stopping at the business department, where Garrett surprised the financial editor by suggesting that the business coverage should be expanded. In sports, Ray introduced Garrett to the football writer. "Another bad year for the Forty-niners," Garrett said to the man, amiably. "Any chance they can turn it around next year?"

The man looked at Garrett. "I doubt it. Three losing seasons in a row," he grunted. "You like football?"

"Yes, but the Forty-niners are making it tough for me."

"Welcome to the club," the writer muttered, but his animosity showed through the attempt at banter.

Ray and Garrett went down a hallway toward the features department, Garrett drawing stares from passersby. Those who recognized him deferred to him as they might a foreign conqueror, almost flattening themselves against the wall to allow him to pass. In features, Garrett introduced himself to editors and reporters, making knowledgeable comments about their sections. Ray felt a begrudging respect for Garrett's diplomatic skill, but he knew how useless it was against the wall of resentment the employees had erected. The tour over, they paused outside the newsroom entrance. "That's about it," Ray said. "That's the *Times*."

"You've been a great help," Garrett said. "I'll need to call on you again until I can find my way around."

"You seem to know a lot about this place already."

Garrett looked at the city room. "I'm an outsider, Mr. Coffey. I have a great deal to learn." He glanced toward Stephen's office. "If you'll excuse me, I see Mr. Hillman is back in his office now. It's been a pleasure meeting you."

Garrett went across the newsroom. Stephen saw him coming and came out from behind his desk, setting his face in a stony mask. "If you have a moment," Garrett said, "I'd like to talk."

Stephen motioned Garrett in and shut the door. Out in the

newsroom, necks craned to see what was happening behind the glass partition.

"I'll get right to the point," Garrett said. "Ian told me this morning that you're resigning."

"That's right," Stephen said.

"I'd like you to reconsider. The change of ownership has been traumatic, and your presence here—"

"I can give you two weeks," Stephen interrupted. "That will give you plenty of time to bring in your own man."

Garrett paused. "I have no right to ask anything of you—"

"No, you don't," Stephen said brusquely.

The two men stared at each other. "I'd like you to stay for a while to ease the transition," Garrett said. "I don't plan to make any big changes with the *Times*, at least not initially. Your presence here would reassure the staff."

Stephen smiled bitterly. "They're not stupid, Richardson. They know what kind of newspapers you run in England and in New York, and they know what you are going to do here. You may look like some squire fresh from the fox hunt, but they know you're a smut slinger. Nearly all of them are looking for jobs. In a couple of months, you won't have anyone worthwhile left out in that newsroom." He paused. "Of course, that's probably what you want. Clear the place out and bring in your own mercenaries."

Garrett looked at Stephen evenly. "This company has had some grave problems," he said calmly. "Because of some recent good moves, it now could possibly turn around. The conversion to morning has already brought about a circulation gain, and the suburban plant was a good investment. Two gutsy but brilliant moves . . ." Stephen looked at him, waiting. "But this is a crucial turning point," Garrett went on. "Any sudden changes or instability could hurt the *Times*'s recovery. I have no plans to do anything that could jeopardize it. But you, the example you set with your staff, could. Your support—or desertion—of the *Times* right now will send out a powerful message to those people out there."

Stephen was silent, his eyes shifting from Garrett out to the newsroom.

"You have reasons to hate me," Garrett said. "I'm asking you to put that aside for the time being."

The office was silent. Only a few muted sounds from the newsroom could be heard. The soft rasp of the wire machines, the ring of a telephone, and a random bolt of laughter.

"I would think you'd like me out of your hair," Stephen said finally. "It would make everything a lot easier."

Garrett stared at him for a moment. "So your answer is no, I take it." He rose and went to the door.

Stephen let a beat go by. "I'll stay. For two months," he said. "But not because of anything you've said. I'm staying here because I care about this paper and the people here." He paused. "I care about Kellen, too. I don't have to tell you what this has done to her. She's . . . she's worked very hard in the past year. And she's worried about what is going to happen to everyone who works here. And to the *Times* itself."

Garrett stood, his hand resting lightly on the door frame. He seemed to want to say something, but after a moment he simply turned and went back through the newsroom.

He went upstairs to the executive suite. Adele rose when she saw him and handed him a sheaf of papers. "Here are those figures you wanted, Mr. Richardson," she said. "The travel agent is sending over an itinerary for your visits to the other papers. And Mr. Bryant wants to see you."

He took them absently, muttered thank you, and went toward his office.

"What about Mr. Bryant?" Adele called out.

"Tell him I'm busy." He shut the door of his office behind him. The office still smelled of fresh paint. It had been outfitted with sleek furniture and touched by the hand of a tasteful decorator. When Ian had first shown it to him, he had announced, with perverse pleasure, that the office had belonged to Kellen. It had seemed to Garrett, on first glance, an accommodating office. Yet now, as he looked at it, it felt too stark and impersonal, like a fine hotel suite, primed for the next temporary visitor. He found himself trying to imagine what it had looked like when Kellen was there. She was never far from his mind, but today, for some reason, her presence was everywhere—down in the newsroom and lingering now in the office.

He forced her from his mind and sat down behind the glass-and-chrome desk. The early editions of that day's *Times* had been placed neatly on the corner, and he reached for the San Mateo one. One of the front-page stories was about a bomb that exploded in the LaGuardia Airport terminal, killing fourteen holiday travelers. The story, by the *San Francisco Times*'s New York correspondent, was a well-reported, dispassionate account of the horror. Garrett found himself thinking about how the *Tatler* had undoubtedly handled the same story: a screaming headline, a horrific picture, lurid quotes, all carefully choreographed to boost street sales. He glanced back at the *Times*. The way the *Times* reporter had written the story, it was deprived of its dramatic, human-interest edge. A lost opportunity to nab readers.

Shaking his head slightly, Garrett picked up a red marker and read other stories, stopping frequently to scribble remarks or cross out paragraphs. But after a while, he put the pen down and began simply to read. He read a well-written analysis about what soaring real estate prices were doing to old downtown neighborhoods. He read a colorful feature about the last of the little jitney buses, doomed to the city's history books. He read a news story about a conflict between a young Chinese architect who wanted Chinatown preserved as a landmark and Chinese residents who objected that the area was nothing more than an ethnic ghetto. He read, with a smile, Clark Able's "Of Cabbages and Kings" in which Clark opined that in the event of an earthquake, government would endure because the state is twenty miles thick "especially in the state capital."

Then, he went back to the front page and reread the *Times*'s version of the New York bombing story, seeing it now in its context of the paper's sedate, thoughtful format. He had been ready to condemn the *Times*'s treatment as a lost opportunity, but now he realized it was appropriate—for the *San Francisco Times*.

Garrett stared at the red-marked pages before him. He had read the *Times* so often when he was researching it as a takeover prospect and always with a calculating eye to what he needed to change. But now, for the first time, he realized that he was reading it with the affection of someone who knew and loved the city.

Of course, there were things he could change that could make the *Times* better. He could shorten some of the news stories, demand less sycophantic writing from the sports reporters and less self-indulgent writing from the feature staffers. But he realized now that the *Times* accomplished its most important task better than any newspaper he had ever read: It reflected the city's heart and soul.

And I'd be a fool to tamper with that, he thought.

He rose and went to the window, looking down to the people in the square, just spots of color diffused by a dissipating fog. The sight made him think, not for the first time lately, of how much he dreaded leaving San Francisco. Soon he had to return to New York and to the *Tatler*. He could look ahead and see what his own life would become—a transient existence, continuously shuttling from coast to coast, diluting his time and energies.

He stared at the fog, an idea taking shape in his mind. Perhaps . . . perhaps, he thought, it doesn't have to be like that. Perhaps I can just stay here. I could run the *Times* just as it is, keep its present format. Just because one type of journalism works well for one paper doesn't mean I must impose it on another. I could run the *Times* as Kellen would have. . . . Perhaps she would even . . .

He paused. No, it wouldn't work, he thought, his spirits sinking. His father would never allow it; he wanted the *Times* converted quickly to bring up the profit margin. Garrett knew he would do what he could to protect the *Times*'s essence. But in time, the precious individuality would be lost, sacrificed to the bottom line and lowest common denominator. Eventually all the other Bryant properties would evolve into efficient fiefs, in service to the Richardson Ltd. system of journalistic feudalism.

He knew he was thinking of more than just trying to preserve the *Times*'s identity. He was also trying to preserve his own chance for happiness.

I don't want to be just a visitor here anymore, he thought. I want to stay. He turned away from the window and stood for a moment, staring out at the sterile office. And I still want Kellen, he thought. She's lost to me and, God help me, I still want her.

The house on Divisadero was brightly lit, its yellow windows beckoning through the foggy night to those who came up the long, curved drive. Inside, the rooms were warm and filled with the smell of food and the sound of voices. There was a party, a reason to celebrate. Josh Hillman was retiring, and Kellen was honoring him with a dinner party. People milled through the house, longtime friends and associates, those who had worked with Josh at the *Times* during his thirty-eight-year tenure.

The mood was merry, but almost forcibly so, like picnickers hellbent on reveling beneath a thundercloud. Though Josh had often joked about retiring, everyone knew he didn't really want to leave. But the sale of the *Times* had forced his hand, and everyone present shared his sadness. Most also knew about Stephen and Kellen's estrangement. Still, the determinedly upbeat mood prevailed, helped along in no small part by Clark and by Tyler, who had taken over the party planning from Kellen and orchestrated it into a diverting wine tasting. Kellen knew it was Tyler's way of trying to get back in her good graces, but having overestimated her own energy, she was grateful for his help.

By midnight, most of the guests had left, but a core of Josh's oldest friends remained, clustered around the fireplace, smoking cigars, talking about bygone days. Kellen sat off in a corner, half listening. Occasionally, hearing her father's name mentioned amid the reminiscing, she would listen, but then drift away again. She was tired; the party had drained away the last of her energy that the events of the week had already depleted. Her eyes traveled over the room, to the large Christmas tree standing in one corner and the menorah on the mantel. She lingered over the familiar faces. Tyler sitting along on the sofa, drinking a cup of tea. Josh laughing at some remark with Anna sitting quietly nearby. And Stephen sitting on the edge of his mother's chair, unsmiling, lost in his own thoughts. She watched Stephen until he looked up and met her gaze. She saw many things in that one moment. Hurt, confusion, and anger, but also an emotion new to the catalogue of their estrangement—resignation. She sensed in that moment that Stephen, like she, had finally admitted that their marriage was finished. Perhaps it had been dying for a long time, and her affair with Garrett had just finished it. She didn't know. The only thing she knew for sure was that now only the pain of the final ending blow was left. With a deep stab of sadness, she looked away.

She felt someone at her side and looked up to see Clark. "Listen to those guys," he said with a smile. "They're having the time of their lives dredging up old ghosts." He paused. "This was a good idea, Kellen, having this for Josh. May be a good idea for the rest of us, too."

He studied her pale face. "Is something wrong?"

She shook her head, her eyes on the others. "I was just thinking, remembering. This house holds so many memories."

"Good memories," Clark said.

She looked up at him and smiled slightly. "Remember the solstice? What a good time we all had together?"

He nodded. "The Summer of Love . . . a hundred years ago . . ."

Kellen turned to watch the others, but suddenly her eyes brimmed with tears. "Excuse me, Clark," she murmured, rising before he could see. She went into the foyer and paused by the staircase to collect herself. For a moment, she just stood there, then she went into the study, closing the door behind her. She had wanted so much to put up a cheerful front for Josh tonight, but the front was finally cracking. She knew the despair she was feeling arose from more than just the loss of the newspapers and the end of her marriage. It also came from fear. She had felt the same thing when first her mother died and then her father. She had depended so on each of them for support and then, suddenly, they were gone. Now, it was happening again. Stephen, the newspapers—the things she had depended upon to give her solace, to give her life shape, were gone.

She went to the desk and sat down wearily. She had not allowed herself to cry all week. She had not shed one tear over the loss of the newspaper or over the failure of her marriage. She had not allowed herself to even think about Garrett. But now, it all closed in on her, and she began to cry. She gave in to it, her body shaking with great waves of sobs, and her chest and throat ached until finally, she could barely breathe. Then, slowly, it subsided, and she laid down her head on her folded arms and closed her eyes.

She didn't hear Josh come into the room. He closed the door softly and came over to her. He touched her arm.

With a start, she looked up at him, then away.

Josh took her chin and gently turned her face toward him. He smiled slightly. "You always did it this way," he said softly. "In private. Even when you were a girl you hated to let anyone see you cry."

Josh held out a handkerchief, and she took it. He sat down on the edge of the desk. "I saw you with tears in your eyes only once," he said. "The day you went off to boarding school. You were only eleven, trying so hard to be brave."

"I was scared," Kellen said.

"And angry, too."

"Yes," she murmured. "I was."

She looked away, and Josh saw she was staring at the photograph on the desk of Adam and Elizabeth. "I've been thinking about my father a lot lately," she said softly.

"It's only natural, with what's happened," Josh said.

She stared at the picture. "You know, he never told me why he sent me away, Josh," she said. "He never told me why he did it. He just sent me away. I thought I was being punished, but I never knew what for."

"Oh, Kellen," he said softly. "He didn't do it to punish you. He just . . ."

Kellen looked up at him, and he paused, seeing in her eyes that an old wound had been reopened. She obviously wanted him to go on, but the right words eluded him. It had been so long since he had thought about the events surrounding Elizabeth's death. They were distressing memories, and he had buried them. But the look on Kellen's face was compelling him to face them.

"He sent you away," Josh said gently, "because you reminded him so much of Elizabeth. After she died, he fell apart. Just the sight of you deepened his grief. He finally realized he needed you near him and brought you home. But for a while, he was a drowning man."

Kellen stared at Josh for a moment, then turned back to the photograph. "Then he really loved her," she whispered.

"What?" Josh asked.

"He really loved my mother." She looked up at Josh. "Didn't he?"

The question struck Josh as so strange that it took him a moment to realize she actually expected an answer. "He loved Elizabeth with all his heart and soul," he said. "Whatever made you believe otherwise?"

Kellen stared at him unwaveringly, and suddenly Josh knew what was coming next. He had thought about it often over all the years, and he had always believed he would be able to handle it if it ever surfaced. But now, as he stared into Kellen's eyes, he was afraid.

"How did she really die, Josh?" Kellen asked.

In that instant, all the events surrounding Elizabeth's death came back in a flash of memories. The awful sickness, the funeral, the lurid stories in the newspaper about the will, the police investigation, the relentless gossip. Then in rapid-fire sequence, his mind tripped back in time to his first meeting with the young Adam Bryant, and of their friendship built over the decades, of favors asked in friendship and promises given. The memories came to a halt on one drizzly cold night in May, 1952. Adam had called him to the house, as he had so many times before, and asked for his counsel. Josh gave it, and then, at Adam's bidding, vowed an oath of silence. It had held for twenty-three years. Josh looked into Kellen's eyes and knew now he had to break it.

"Elizabeth wanted to die," Josh said. "Your father helped her to do it."

He watched her face for reaction, but none seemed to register. Then, after a moment, she whispered, "Go on."

"Your mother was gravely ill," he began slowly. "For a long time, we didn't know what it was. The doctors said it was depression, and they gave her drugs. The drugs caused other depressive reactions, and she was given more drugs. One doctor diagnosed her as manic-depressive, another said she was schizophrenic. Another all but accused her of being an addict. It got progressively worse, and your father kept bringing in more doctors. Finally, he was told the only thing he could do was have her committed.''

Josh paused, his shoulders caving inward. ''Your father couldn't bear the thought of Elizabeth locked away somewhere. So he kept her at home, trying to help her as best he could. It was very hard on him. He sat here and literally watched her go slowly out of her mind, helpless to do anything. Sometimes, she would be lucid. . . . He lived for those moments; they gave him hope that she'd recover. But they grew rare and then stopped. Two days before Elizabeth's death I remember Adam telling me that the woman he loved was already dead.''

Again, Josh paused. His eyes drifted over to the photograph, then out over the study, focusing on nothing in particular. ''The next night, he called me to the house,'' he went on, his voice cracking. ''He was sitting in this room, alone. He was calm, but I could see he had been crying. He told me that Elizabeth had had one of her good moments . . . that she told him she wanted to die and begged him to help. Until that point, he had believed Elizabeth had no conception of her condition. But that night, he was convinced she knew. She was suffering. He couldn't stand that . . .''

He looked back at Kellen, tears in his eyes. ''He asked me to help find a doctor who would grant her wish. He was distraught but had obviously given it great thought. We found a doctor who supplied the drugs for an overdose. Adam gave them to her himself. Elizabeth went into a coma and died quietly while Adam held her. I was there. I saw them.''

Kellen continued to stare at Josh, as if in a trance.

''It wasn't until later, after the autopsy, that the true cause of Elizabeth's illness was uncovered,'' Josh went on. ''They called it presenile dementia. It's rare in a young person, and it's often misdiagnosed as mental illness. It can be caused by a number of underlying things—in Elizabeth it was an undetected brain tumor.'' He sighed. ''By then, Adam was so angry about all the publicity that he demanded the autopsy results be kept secret. I advised him to make it public, to clear his name if nothing else, but he refused. I remember what he said: 'No more newspaper stories. I just want her left alone.' ''

He glanced at Kellen. She still had the same blank expression on her face.

''I thought then,'' he went on, ''that after they'd put a name to her illness, Adam would cope with Elizabeth's death better. But he didn't. He blamed himself for the misdiagnoses, saying he should have found her better care. He was never the same man. I think he blamed himself until the day he died.''

Kellen looked up at him suddenly, and the opaque veil lifted from her eyes. Josh's heart ached when he saw her pain. ''He may have blamed himself,'' he said gently. ''But I don't think he ever regretted his decision. He loved your mother more than he loved life itself, and he couldn't stand to see her suffering. I watched what he did that night, and I can only say it was an act of utterly selfless love.''

Tears fell slowly down Kellen's cheeks. She was holding the picture frame, and now she set it down carefully on the desk, tilting her head slightly as she looked at it.

''Oh, Josh,'' she said. ''Why didn't he tell me?''

''He couldn't, Kellen. After the scandal died down, he just wanted to put it behind him.''

Kellen continued to stare at the picture. ''All those stories I heard when I was growing up . . .''

Josh's eyes returned to the picture of the young Adam. ''I was closer to your father than any man, Kellen, but I don't think even I really knew him. He was a complex, private person. Who knows why he did the things he did? But I saw him with your mother, and I know for their short time together, they had a great love. A wonderful, rare, grand passion. Isn't that all that matters really?''

Kellen closed her eyes. ''Perhaps.''

The room was quiet, and from out in the foyer came the sounds of the last guests gathering to leave. She felt the warmth of Josh's hand covering her own, and she looked up at him. ''You've always been so good to me, Josh,'' she said.

''I've always thought of you as part of my family, Kellen.''

''I hope you won't hate me for what's happening with Stephen and me.''

''He's my only son,'' Josh said. ''It's hard to see him hurting.'' He paused. ''But I'm trying to get him to talk about it. He'll be all right. He's a strong man.''

''I didn't mean to hurt him. Or you and Anna.''

Josh saw the guilt in her eyes. ''Perhaps just as some things are not meant to be, some people are not meant to be together.'' He shrugged, a bit sadly. ''You and Stephen have been together your whole lives. Like brother and sister. Maybe that is your special bond.''

He paused. ''The idea of family is a strange thing. Most people think of a family as a solid, never-changing thing, but it's not. It's always expanding, shrinking, changing shape to make room for the needs of everyone in it.''

He looked at Kellen. ''You are still part of my family, Kellen.'' He smiled slightly. ''And so are Benjamin and Sara, I hope. Anna and I rather like this grandparent bit. You'll make sure we see them from time to time, won't you?''

Kellen grasped Josh's hand. ''Of course,'' she said, her throat constricting.

They embraced. ''Good,'' he said softly when they pulled apart. ''And you'll do something else for me?''

''Anything.''

''Try not to dwell on the newspapers. You did your best. I'd say you gave it a hell of a shot.''

''I'll try. Thanks . . . for everything, Josh.''

The door opened, and Kellen and Josh both looked over to see Stephen standing there. He looked at them with curiosity. ''Everyone's leaving, Dad,'' he said. ''I thought you'd want to say good-bye.''

''Yes, of course,'' Josh said, rising. He gave Kellen a final smile and left the room. Stephen paused, looking at Kellen. Finally, he turned and went out into the foyer.

When Kellen came out a few moments later, Stephen was already outside waiting in the car. She said good night to Anna and Josh and they left. Kellen closed the front door, and the house was suddenly very quiet.

Tyler came in from the kitchen. ''Where is everyone?''

''They've gone.''

''I didn't get a chance to say good night.'' He glanced at the living room, littered with half-filled glasses and empty plates. ''What a mess,'' he murmured, starting toward it.

''Leave it, Tyler,'' Kellen said. ''It'll wait until morning.''

He peered at her puffy eyes. ''Are you all right?''

She nodded.

''Are you sure?'' he asked. ''I can stay here tonight if you want.''

Kellen shook her head. ''You go on home. I know you want to get back. I think I'd rather be alone tonight anyway.''

Tyler wavered. ''All right,'' he said, picking up his coat from a chair. He went to the front door, and Kellen held it open. She shivered and wrapped her arms around herself. Tyler started across the porch, then turned back to her. ''I don't feel right leaving you alone,'' he said.

"Go home," she said, managing a smile. "I'm fine. Really. And Tyler . . . thanks for your help tonight."

He smiled broadly and, with a small wave, went down the drive to his car. Kellen stood at the door, watching his car until it disappeared down the hill, then she went back inside. She closed the door and locked it. She turned and stood in the foyer, looking out over the living room. The fire was now just a pile of glowing embers. She went across the foyer and flicked off the lights, leaving only the towering Christmas tree lit. She stood there, staring at it for a moment as the quiet reverberated in her head. Her ears strained to pick up a sound, any sound in the huge house, but there was nothing, just the cold sweeping silence. She shivered, drawing her arms tighter about herself.

Her thoughts went to Ben and Sara, asleep upstairs in their bedrooms. She stared at the tree, thinking about the gifts she had hidden away for them. Slowly, she stopped shivering, and after a few moments, the quiet grew less threatening. She smiled slightly imagining the look on Ben's face when he saw his new bike, and how Sara would react when she found out a pony waited in a stable for her.

Kellen turned off the switch for the tree lights, and the rooms were dark. She went across the foyer, the click of her heels on marble echoing through the house. She paused at the staircase, looking up at the light she always left on in the hallway outside the children's bedroom. By reflex, she glanced down at the frowning carved face in the balustrade, then at the next one, which was turned up in the beginning of a smile. She started up the stairs toward the light.

Chapter
Forty-two

Kellen sat on a bench, watching Ben and Sara chase a flock of ducks. It was late afternoon, and the lawn in front of the Palace of Fine Arts was still speckled with parents and children. She glanced up at the sun slanting through the trees and, when she looked down, she saw Stephen. He came toward her with his usual quick strides, hands stuffed in his corduroy jacket. "I'm sorry I'm late," he said.

"It's all right," she said. "I've just been sitting here enjoying the day."

He sat down, and they were both silent, watching the children play. They had not seen each other in three months, not since Josh's retirement party. Kellen had been surprised when Stephen had called earlier and said he wanted to meet. She glanced over at him now as he sat there, hands clasped. Ben's laugh drifted over to them.

"Kellen, I thought we should talk," he said finally. "We probably should have sooner, but it's taken me this long to put aside my anger about Garrett." She waited. "I still haven't entirely," he said. "But I've been doing a lot of thinking about us."

"So have I." She paused. "Ben asked me yesterday when you were coming home."

Stephen let out a long breath. "I think it's time to tell them that I'm not."

There it was. The words were spoken. It really was over. Stephen had taken the initiative to announce the end. Now all she had to do was acknowledge it.

"I'm sorry, Stephen," she murmured. "I wish it could have been different."

His eyes dropped to his hands. "Yeah, me, too," he said.

She wondered why she couldn't think of anything else to say.

She had been turning this over in her mind so much in the past few weeks, looking for the right words, for some way of explaining to Stephen, and to herself, why things went wrong. She had thought about saying that they were simply too different. Or that the newspaper had gotten in the way. But she came back most often to what Josh had said—that they were like brother and sister. That spoke to the love she still felt for Stephen. But it also said much about what had always been missing. Garrett had only served to point it out. She and Stephen had been joined together by so much—their childhoods, their love of the newspapers, and, of course, by Benjamin. But their souls had always been separate. And she knew she couldn't live without that essential connection.

"It's nothing you did, Stephen," she said softly.

He gave her a smile. "Maybe it's something I didn't do, then."

"You can't think of it that way."

"That's what Dad keeps telling me. We've been doing a lot of talking these past few days." He paused. "I'm beginning to think I should listen to his advice. He's pretty smart. For a lawyer."

"For a father," Kellen said.

Stephen was silent, looking around the park now. "I haven't been down here in a long time," he said quietly. "We used to come down here together all the time, remember? Bring our books to study on the lawn."

She smiled. "Well, *you* studied."

His eyes traveled over her face. "You know, you haven't changed. It's strange, but I look at you right now and I see this girl—"

"She grew up," Kellen said.

"That doesn't mean I won't miss her."

There was an awkward silence. The breeze blew Stephen's hair across his forehead, and he brushed it aside. He was watching Sara and Ben intently. "Would you mind if I had the kids for a couple of days? My mom and dad are going to Tahoe and invited me along. They'd like Sara and Ben to come."

"No, of course not," Kellen answered.

He looked over at her. "When we get back, I think we should tell them. Together, if that's all right with you."

She nodded. She blinked rapidly and let out a breath. "How is everything at the office?" she asked, to change the subject.

He shrugged. "No change, really. A couple more people quit. But it's been quiet. Too quiet. Like everyone's waiting for the other shoe to drop."

She sat there, unable to think of anything else to say. As intensely curious as she was about the newspaper, she knew Stephen probably couldn't tell her much. Not even Clark had been able to tell her more than Stephen just had. Apparently, Garrett had been keeping a low profile.

"I've quit the paper," he said. "Today was my last day."

She looked at him in surprise.

"I've got a couple of good offers," he said. "One from the *Washington Post* that would put me in line for editor. Also got a call from a buddy at Knight-Ridder who wants me to be publisher of their paper in Charlotte." He paused. "And believe it or not, *Newsweek* has approached me about running one of their European bureaus."

Kellen's eyes dropped to the ground. It was one thing to accept the idea of divorce, but she had thought that despite it somehow Stephen would still always be there. Now she realized that he would not be.

"You'll never guess who else called," Stephen said. "Chandler at the *Los Angeles Times* is courting me for managing editor." He smiled slightly. "A step down . . . bad for the old ego. To add insult to injury I'd have to move to L.A. . . ."

She still stared at the ground.

"I'm going to take the L.A. job," Stephen said quietly, "so I can stay near the kids."

Kellen looked up, her eyes bright with tears. "You'll be great in the job," she said. "And I'm glad you'll be near."

The quacking of ducks drew their eyes to the children. Ben spotted Stephen and came running over. "Daddy!" he cried. Kellen watched as Stephen hugged him tightly, closing his eyes. Sara came walking up, and as usual, waited until Stephen beckoned. He clasped her to his chest.

"How'd you two monsters like to go to the lake with Grandma and Grandpa and me?" he asked them.

Ben whooped with delight, but Sara glanced at Kellen. "What about Mommy?"

Kellen gave her a quick smile. "I have a lot of things to do, baby. I can't go."

Her eyes remained with Kellen. "Then I'll stay home and keep you company."

Kellen reached over and pulled a few leaves out of Sara's hair. "No, you go with Daddy. I'll be fine."

Sara looked at her dubiously, but she finally smiled. "I would like to see Grandma and Grandpa," she said.

Stephen nudged Ben off his knee and stood up. "I've got to

go,'' he said. He looked at Ben and Sara. "I'll pick you two up bright and early Monday morning, okay?"

He looked down at Kellen. "Take care," he said softly.

She pulled Ben and Sara toward her. "You, too."

She watched Stephen walk across the lawn. When he was gone, she looked at Ben and Sara then hugged them tightly to her. "It's getting late," she said. "Let's go home."

Garrett was just leaving the office to catch a flight to New York when Adele buzzed to tell him he had a call. "It's from London," she said.

Garrett paused. He had not spoken with his father in months. "Tell my father I'll call him tomorrow."

"It's not your father. It's your mother."

Garrett glanced at his watch. It was nearly ten at night in London. And why would his mother even call him from the city? She never left Durdans. "Put it through," he said.

"Garrett? Are you there?"

"Yes, Mother. What is it? Why are you calling so late?"

"It's your father. . . . He's had a stroke."

Garrett slowly shifted the phone to his other ear.

"Garrett?

"Yes, I'm here."

"He was at the office." Though the connection was good, Helen's voice sounded thin and very far away. "I'm at the hospital with him now," she said. "He asked for you. . . . Can you come, Garrett?"

"I'm on my way," he said. She gave him the name of the hospital, and he hung up. For a moment, he didn't move. Then he grabbed his raincoat and left the office. He arrived at Kennedy Airport in the middle of a snowstorm. At the British Airways counter, the clerk told him the storm had delayed all outbound flights and that he could wait in the VIP lounge.

In the lounge, Garrett ordered a scotch and stationed himself before the window. There was nothing to see, no planes moving, just a mad swirl of snow in the black sky.

He picked up a copy of the *Wall Street Journal*, but soon tossed it aside, unable to concentrate. He kept seeing Arthur just as he had left him three months ago, standing in the sun room, surrounded by a blur of red flowers. Garrett had been so enraged about the sale that he hadn't been able to bring himself to talk to his father since that day. Arthur had sent Garrett a formal letter saying that he expected him to act on his behalf as owner of all the

Bryant holdings. Since then, Arthur had conveyed everything to
Garrett through intermediaries in the corporation. The arrangement had suited Garrett fine; he wanted no part of his father. He
just wanted to live his life as best he could.

The last three months had been hell. He had tried to contact
Kellen many times, but she would have nothing to do with him.
At the newspaper, he tried to persevere in the hostile atmosphere
as resignations kept coming in. Recently, he had received a call
from an editor of the *London Sun* inquiring about opportunities at
the *Times*. The day after, Garrett received a letter from his father
extolling the man's virtues. Between the lines, Garrett could read
the real message: Hire this man. . . . Get things moving in San
Francisco again. The letter infuriated Garrett. He almost felt as if
he were defending the *Times* against an invader. I'm going to do
this my way, he thought, whether he likes it or not. I'm not going
to allow this paper to be systematically trashed.

Garrett raised the glass of scotch to his lips. If only he'd just
leave me alone. He drained the scotch and set the glass aside. Why
should I expect anything different from him? It's just the way he
is. I did it for you, son—that's what he said. But I'm not his son.
And he's not my father. I don't have a father.

A stroke . . . Helen hadn't really said how bad it was. Garrett
sat there, trying to picture Arthur in a hospital, but the image
wouldn't come. He could only see variations of the same Arthur
he had always known—barrel-chested, bellicose, larger-than-life,
and somehow eternal. Arthur . . . Father. The only father he had
ever known.

Garrett stared at the white snow beating frantically against the
black windows. A waiter came by, and Garrett grabbed his arm.
"The flight to London," he said. "Is there any word of when it's
leaving?"

The man gave him the easy smile he used to placate all impatient businessmen. "Not yet, sir," he said. "But I'm sure it will
be soon."

Garrett turned back to the window. "I must get there as soon as
possible," he murmured.

When Garrett finally arrived in London, it was late afternoon,
a dismally cold, rainy day. He went to the hospital and was
directed to a private room in the intensive-care ward. The room
was dim, but his eyes went immediately to the motionless figure
on the bed. He paused, staring at the tubes and machines. A small
sound drew his eye to a darkened corner. It was Helen, sitting in

a chair. Garrett's eyes went quickly back to the bed and his heart skipped a beat.

"Is he . . .?"

Helen rose slowly and came over to the door. In the harsh light from the hallway, she looked ghastly, as if the last of her muted color had drained from her skin, her eyes and hair. Garrett stared at her. She looked like a stranger, like a lost stranger. Without thinking, he gathered her in an embrace, and for a moment she leaned heavily against him. When she pulled away, she wavered.

"He had another stroke early this morning," she murmured. "There's been no response since. Nothing." She looked up at Garrett. "He wanted to talk to you. He . . ."

Garrett glanced at the bed then back at Helen. "Have you been here since yesterday?"

She nodded wearily.

"I'm here now," he said softly. "Why don't you at least go get a cup of tea." When she started to protest, Garrett interrupted. "I'll stay here with him," he said.

With a deep sigh, Helen nodded and left the room. Garrett stood motionless staring at Arthur, then he made a slow half circle around the bed, keeping as far away as he could. His eyes kept going back to the tubes and monitors. Being in a hospital, with the smells, sounds, and ugly machines, had brought back all the bad memories of Susan's and the twins' deaths. He forced himself to approach the bed and look down at the man lying there. He was shocked by Arthur's appearance. He had expected that he would be wasted looking, but he wasn't. Arthur was pale, and his eyes were closed, but he looked as if he were simply asleep. Garrett stood over the bed, staring at Arthur.

"Can you hear me?" he said.

There was no response.

"Can you hear me?" he repeated, more loudly.

A nurse came in at that moment. "He can't answer," she said briskly. "His brain is functionally dead." She went to the monitor to check something, then turned to Garrett with a frown. "No one's supposed to be in here," she said. "Who are you anyway?"

"I'm his son," Garrett said, staring at the figure in the bed.

The nurse pursed her lips. "Oh, I'm sorry," she said, her tone softer. "Please don't stay long. It's really not allowed." She left, closing the door behind her.

The room was dark, except for one small bedside light, and quiet except for the gentle blip of the machines. Garrett drew a chair close to the bed and sat down. For several minutes, he just stared at the man in the bed.

"I know you can hear me," he said.

Silence.

"I hate you," he murmured.

Suddenly, his eyes filled with tears. They poured down his face. He picked up Arthur's hand.

"I love you," he said, gripping his father's hand between his own. "I love you. . . . I love you. . . ."

Garrett was standing at the mantel in the drawing room of Durdans. Helen sat in a chair nearby. Four days had passed since Arthur's death and cremation. Helen had retreated immediately to Durdans, but Garrett had stayed in London to assure that business went on as usual at the newspaper. He had returned only that morning, and now they were waiting for Arthur's lawyer, Charles Lassiter.

Garrett looked at Helen. She was pale but composed. "I hope you don't mind my asking Lassiter to come today," he said softly. "But I have to get back to the States soon. And I thought you'd want me here to handle the will."

She smiled wanly. "I understand, Garrett. And I appreciate it."

The silence between them was strained. "It's all happened so quickly," Helen said quietly. She looked up at Garrett. "I'm most sorry that you didn't have a chance to talk to him. He wanted to talk to you so badly."

"It doesn't matter now," Garrett said. He went to the window and pulled aside the drape to look out.

"It mattered to—" Helen began.

"He's here," Garrett said, letting the drape fall. "Now we can get this over with." He went out to the foyer to greet the lawyer and escort him in. Garrett introduced his mother, and Lassiter took a seat, placing his briefcase on the floor beside him. Garrett returned to his spot at the mantel.

"I'm sorry we've never met before, Mrs. Richardson," Lassiter said. "I was your husband's solicitor for ten years, but I guess I never had the chance to come out to the country." He glanced around the room. "Lovely home you have here, by the way."

Helen nodded cordially. Garrett sensed her strength had been taxed, and he wanted to hurry business along. "I don't mean to be abrupt, Mr. Lassiter," Garrett said. "But we'd really like to get on with the matter of my father's will."

Lassiter gave a strange little shrug. "There is no will," he said.

Garrett looked at him in disbelief. "That can't be," he said. "My father would never have been so careless. He was very meticulous about his business affairs."

Lassiter nodded. "Yes. But he was also a bit of an egoist, if you'll pardon my saying so." He paused. "I was constantly on Mr. Richardson about drawing up a will. He kept saying he'd get to it, but he didn't." Lassiter shook his head. "To be honest, I think he didn't do it because he sincerely believed he was going to live forever."

"So what does this mean legally?" Garrett asked. "That the estate will be tied up in courts for years?"

Lassiter shook his head. "No, not at all. It's quite simple, really. In these cases, the spouse inherits everything. I'll have it worked out for you by week's end."

Helen looked up first at Lassiter, then at Garrett.

The lawyer pulled a sheaf of papers out of his briefcase. "It's all delineated here for you, Mrs. Richardson. All the property and corporation holdings in this country, France, Canada, and the United States." He gave her a smile. "Your husband left you an exceedingly wealthy woman."

Tears formed in Helen's eyes. Seeing her distress, Lassiter set the papers down on the table and closed his briefcase. "I'll just leave this with you," he said, rising. "I'll be back in touch in a few days."

"I'll show you out," Garrett said.

When he returned, Helen was still sitting in the chair, a vacant stare on her face. Garrett picked up the papers Lassiter had left and thumbed through them slowly. It was all there—and more. The eight newspapers in Britain, the Toronto paper, the New York *Tatler*, the fifteen Bryant newspapers, and other holdings. An apartment in London, property in France, the bank accounts and insurance policies, the healthy portfolio of incredibly diverse investments—and Durdans, of course. Arthur Richardson had left an estate worth more than £250,200,000. About $600 million, almost half of it the Bryant holdings, Garrett estimated.

He shook his head in sad wonderment. No will . . . He could claim nothing as his. Even in his death, Arthur cast a shadow. Garrett set the papers down in front of Helen. After a moment, she picked them up and began to turn the pages.

He wondered what she was thinking. All during her marriage to Arthur she hated the newspapers. It seemed logical that she would now sell them, wash her hands of the grimy endeavor forever. He stared at her. He knew he couldn't let that happen, and he would do whatever he had to—beg, plead, or steal enough to buy them back from her—anything to prevent them from slipping through his grasp.

She glanced at the paper. "I don't want any of this," she said softly. She looked up at Garrett. "It's yours," she said. "He always meant it to be."

He stared at Helen. "What?"

"It may not be in any will, but he told me he wanted you to have everything when we were gone," she said.

"When?" Garrett asked.

"About three months ago. He had never said one word about it before, but one day, out of nowhere, he just said, 'I did it all for my son, and when I'm gone it will be his.' "

Garrett's mind went back to the last day he had seen his father at Durdans, that morning he had come to confront him about the sale. Garrett looked at Helen's wan face. He went to the sofa and sat down beside her.

"It was the day I came here, wasn't it," he said. "That morning we had the fight in the sun room."

The memory seemed to distress Helen. "Yes," she said softly. She looked at him. "Your father was very upset by the whole thing. He kept saying that he only did what he did for your sake, and that he was sorry he hurt you. He said that often in the last few months."

"I wish he had told me that," Garrett said quietly. His eyes traveled around the room, and he could see Arthur standing by the fireplace, one arm propped on the mantel, a tumbler in his hand, playing the role of a country squire. He closed his eyes and could see Arthur in the dirty newsroom of the *Sun*, shirt smudged with newsprint, baying at some unfortunate wretch, playing the role of publishing titan. He could see him walking down the lane to the races, shortening his stride to match that of a little boy's, playing the role of father.

"I wish," Garrett said, "I had talked to him more."

Helen was still holding the papers. "All I really want is enough to live decently on . . . and Durdans," she said. She held the papers out to Garrett. "The rest is yours. I know you'll care for it the way he wanted."

He nodded and took the papers. There was an awkward moment of silence between them.

"You'll be going back to the States soon?" Helen asked.

"Yes, but I don't know when. There will be a lot for me to do here, I suspect.'' He stared at the papers in his hand. "Then I'll go on to New York.''

"What about San Francisco? I thought that's where you live now.''

He let out a breath. "It wouldn't really be practical anymore. I need to be able to get back here quickly to watch over things. New York will be a better base for me, I think.'' He smiled rucfully. "The empire is suddenly too big.''

"What about that woman in San Francisco?'' Helen said. "I thought you were in love with her.''

It seemed strange to hear such a direct and personal statement from Helen, and Garrett looked up in surprise.

"It didn't work out,'' he said.

Helen hesitated. "I know what you and your father were arguing about that morning. I heard everything.'' She sighed. "I don't expect you to ever forgive us for what happened to Susan. In a way, you are right. It was our fault. We did push you two apart.'' She paused again, and Garrett was surprised to see tears form in her eyes. "But I don't want to see it happen again, Garrett. I don't want to see you unhappy like that again. It broke my heart.''

She reached out and took his hand. "If there's any chance you could get this woman back, then do it. If you love someone that much, don't give up. With love, one must never give up and just make do.''

Garrett sat there, stunned. Was this Helen talking like this? This cool, pale woman who he had always assumed to be so passionless? He stared into her gray eyes, trying to see beyond what he had always seen before. Suddenly, he wanted to ask her questions—he wanted to ask her everything. Why had she married Arthur? Had she loved him? Why had she chosen him to be her son when it could have been anyone? Who was she, this woman who had been his mother?

Her fingers were cool and soft on his, and he looked into her eyes, knowing there was no way he could ask her any of these questions. Not now, at least. Perhaps later. He realized with a growing sense of peace that "later" was possible. He would make time to find out who this woman, his mother, was.

He embraced her. Surprised, she resisted at first, but then returned the embrace. They pulled apart, with an awkwardness.

"I think some tea would be nice,'' Helen said.

"Yes, it would.''

She rang for the maid. While they waited for the tea, the room fell silent again. "It's gotten chilly," Helen said, pulling her sweater over her shoulders.

"I'll get the fire going again." Garrett rose and went to the hearth to put a new log on the fire. He stood there, feeling the warmth of the flames on his face. He turned back to Helen. "I have to leave tomorrow for Paris," he said. "I have some important business to take care of."

She nodded, looking away.

"But I'd like to come back for a visit," Garrett said, "Maybe in spring when everything's green. Would that be all right with you, Mother?"

She looked up at him, and a smile spread across her face. "I'd like that very much, Garrett," she said softly.

Garrett went quickly down the rue St-Andres des Arts. It was a cold, overcast day, and the gray, opalescent light made the streets and buildings look like a smudged charcoal drawing. Garrett turned a corner and came to the three-cornered intersection. The café was open, and its yellow lights beckoned warmly, and he went quickly toward it. He searched the terrace, but it was empty, except for a large tan dog sleeping in the doorway. He peered in the window, but there were only a few workmen standing at the bar. He was about to turn away when he saw her.

She was sitting at a table in the corner, drinking from a large coffee cup. Just as she set the cup down, she looked up and saw him. He went over to her table.

"I didn't think you'd come," he said.

"I wasn't going to," Kellen said. "When you called and asked me to meet you here, I thought you were crazy. I changed my mind at least ten times. I even got off the plane in New York just before it took off."

"I thought it was the only way you'd agree to see me, if I met you on neutral ground."

She looked around the café, her eyes guarded. "This is hardly neutral ground," she murmured.

They were both silent. "How's your family?" Garrett asked, trying to get beyond the awkwardness.

"The children are with Stephen." She paused, debating whether to tell him that she and Stephen were divorcing. She decided not to. What difference would it make now?

"I heard about your father," she said. "I'm sorry."

He nodded, and they fell into another silence. "What did you want to talk to me about, Garrett?" she said. "You said it concerned business."

The crispness in her voice made him hesitate. "Yes, it's business," he said. He reached into his breast pocket, pulled out a folded paper, and held it out to her.

With a puzzled frown, she opened it and read it. She looked up at him, incredulous. "You want to sell back the corporation to me?" she whispered.

"Yes," he said. "I'll sell it back to you for $220 million, the equivalent of what my father paid for it, minus Ian's share."

She gripped the paper. "But why? Why would you do it?

"It's not mine. I didn't build it. I didn't earn it. It's yours. You're the person who rightfully should have it."

She stared at the paper. "Garrett, I don't know what—" she said quietly.

"Things happened between us to make you mistrust me," he said. "Some of it was my fault, but some of it was not. I didn't want your newspapers, Kellen, I wanted you. This is the only way I can convince you."

She stared at him, then looked at the paper in her shaking hands. "You don't know what this means to me," she said softly.

"Yes, I do."

She shook her head slightly. "But it's not right. I'll agree to it only if you take the full price your father paid." She paused. "I don't have all of it right now, but I can arrange annual payments for Ian's share."

He saw the pride in her eyes, and he nodded. "I'll have a new contract drawn up when I get back to London."

Her eyes didn't leave his face. "Are you going to be living in London now?" she asked.

He hesitated, trying to find something in her face that would give him encouragement. He shook his head. "I don't know yet, either there or in New York. I have a lot to keep me busy now with the corporation."

They fell silent. Kellen picked up her coffee and took a sip, but it was cold. She stared into the cup, not wanting to look at Garrett, not knowing what to say.

"Kellen, there's something else," he said. "I have to know if there's any chance left for us at all."

She looked up at him. Suddenly, in that one moment, everything closed in around her—losing the papers, going through the divorce, getting the papers back again. And now the possibility of Garrett back in her life. It was all too quick, too confusing, too much to absorb. Her emotions, so battered by the events of the last four months, were short-circuiting, and she knew she could not handle the intensity Garrett would bring. It was strange; all her life the thing she had feared most was being alone. But suddenly, that was what she craved. Solitude.

"I have to be alone for a while," she said.

He started to say something, but she held up her hand. "Please, Garrett," she said. "Give me some time."

He let out a breath. "You keep asking for that," he said. "You keep expecting me to wait until you're ready. But I can't do that forever. I can't keep putting my life on hold waiting for yours to fall in step." He paused. "I love you, Kellen, but we seem always to be out of sync. I guess it wasn't meant to be otherwise."

He rose and waited for her to respond, but she didn't even look up at him. "I'll send you the new contract from London," he said quietly.

She stared at the paper on the table before her. By the time she looked up, there was no one to be seen on the street. Garrett was gone.

Chapter
Forty-three

❧ Kellen paused outside the Gothic building and looked up at the gilt letters above the entrance. The *San Francisco Times*. She went into the lobby, and the security guard recognized her immediately. "Mrs. Hillman!" he said with a smile. "I haven't seen you in months! What brings you down here?"

"Business," she said with a small smile. She started toward the elevator, but the guard stopped her. "Gee, I'm sorry, Mrs. Hillman, but you gotta have an ID badge to go upstairs," he said sheepishly. "All visitors do now, order of Mr. Bryant. He says we got a security problem. Sorry." He held out a plastic badge, and she took it.

"That's okay, Charlie." She pinned it to her lapel and went to the elevator. Once inside, she put the badge in her pocket. She pushed the button for the executive suite, then on impulse pushed the one for the newsroom floor.

The doors opened, and she stepped out. It was nearly noon and the city room was quiet. It seemed strange to her for a moment, then she had to remind herself that the *Times* was now a morning newspaper and that activity would not pick up until late afternoon. She stood there, savoring the sights and sounds nonetheless. The muted sounds of the wire machines, the ring of a telephone, a reporter lounging at his desk in a corner near the police monitor eating a doughnut.

She turned back to the elevator. The doors opened and Clark, reading a newspaper and not watching where he was going, stumbled into her.

"Kellen!" he exclaimed. "What are you doing here?"

She smiled and pulled him back into the empty elevator. "Come on," she said, "Let's go for a ride and I'll tell you."

By the time the door opened on the top floor, Clark was standing there with his mouth hanging open. "You're the only one who knows, except Tyler," she told him. "So keep it quiet until I tell you otherwise."

Clark smiled, then burst into a laugh. "Kellen, this is incredible. I'm so happy for you! For me! For the newspaper! Do you realize what this means? I won't have to go work for the *Journal* now!" He hugged her. "Let's celebrate! Let's go over to the Washbag and have lunch. We'll get drunk!"

She smiled. "Maybe later. Right now, I have something very important to take care of." She nudged Clark back into the elevator and pushed the down button. "I'll call you later. And keep your mouth shut, you old gossip!"

The door closed, and she stood alone in the quiet hallway of the executive offices. She looked around, taking in every detail: the feel of the carpet beneath her feet, the smell of the polish on the wood, the quiet tapping of someone typing. She took a deep breath and went slowly down the hall.

Adele looked up as Kellen approached. "Kellen!" she said. "How good to see you! It's been so long."

Kellen smiled. "It's good to see you, too, Adele." She tightened her grip on her briefcase. "Is my brother in?"

"Yes. Shall I tell him you're here?"

"No," Kellen said evenly, heading for the door. "I want to surprise him."

"Kellen—" Adele interrupted. "His mother's with him. They were just about to leave for Mr. Bryant's club to have lunch together."

Kellen smiled slightly. "I'm sure they won't mind being a little late."

She opened the door. Ian looked up from his desk, his eyes widening with surprise. Another pair of dark eyes swiveled to see what he was looking at. Then Lilith looked quickly back at Ian.

"What are you doing here?" Ian said.

Kellen closed the door. "I just thought I'd pay you a little visit. Hello, Lilith."

Lilith gave Ian a sour, questioning look.

"You're not supposed to be up here," Ian said. "In fact, you're not even allowed in this building."

"Don't worry, I have my little badge," she said, taking it out of her pocket. She tossed it on Ian's desk. "Is this what you're reduced to these days? Playing office police?"

"You'd better leave," he said, his voice low.

She shook her head slowly, smiling. "Not this time."

"Ian, call security," Lilith said.

Ian stared at Kellen. "That's not necessary, Mother. Kellen's a reasonable woman."

"No, she's not," Lilith said. "She's crazy."

Ian folded his hands in front of his face. "What do you want, Kellen?"

Kellen took a paper out of her briefcase and held it out to Ian. With a cock of an eyebrow, he took it. Slowly, his expression changed, passing quickly through disbelief and into anger as he comprehended the contract's contents.

"This is crazy," he said, tossing it onto the desk. "Do you expect me to believe this is real?"

Lilith snatched up the paper and read it. "Ian!" she exclaimed in horror. "This says that Richardson has sold the corporation back to her!"

"It's not possible," Ian said with a shrug. "Arthur Richardson would never allow it."

"Arthur Richardson is dead," Kellen said. "You should read the newspaper, Ian. You ran the obit."

Ian stared at her incredulously. "It's not p-possible," he stammered. "You don't have enough money to buy it back."

"Tyler gave me half. The rest is being made in annual payments."

Ian's mouth fell agape, then his face blackened. "That goddamn faggot," he muttered. "I'll kill him for this. I'll make sure everyone knows about him and his fucking little—"

"Tyler doesn't care anymore," Kellen said. "And neither does J. D. They've both decided to come out. You can't do a thing to either of them anymore."

Lilith was white with shock. "Do something," she hissed at Ian.

"Do *what*?" he shouted.

Lilith jumped and stared at him.

"What in the hell do you want me to do, Mother?" Ian screamed. He grabbed the contract and crumpled it into a ball and flung it at Kellen. "What do you want me to do, Mother? *What . . . do . . . you . . . want?!*" He jumped to his feet and swept his arm across his desk, sending everything on it crashing to the floor—papers, pens, a brass lamp, a crystal ashtray.

Lilith drew back into the chair, and Kellen stood there, frozen, staring at Ian. His face was pale, and his chest was heaving. She felt a ripple of fear go up her spine.

"All my life I've listened to you," he said, staring at Lilith. "Listened to you bitch about Father, how he stole the newspaper, how he hurt you! How I had to fix it all for you! Well, I'm sick of it! I'm sick of you using me to get back at him!" He glanced at Kellen, then back at Lilith. "What am I going to do about this?" he said with a horrid smile. "I'll tell you, Mother. I'm not going to do a fucking thing! I've had it! I'm leaving!"

He stormed out of the office, slamming the door. For a moment, it was perfectly still. Lilith sat frozen in her chair, staring at the mess on the floor. Finally, Kellen went over, picked up the lamp, and put it back on the desk.

"You won't get away with this," Lilith muttered. "In the agreement we made with Arthur Richardson, it said that Ian would remain publisher here in perpetuity. This sale does nothing to negate that." She paused. "Ian will still be here, and so will Robert after him."

"I know," Kellen said. "But it doesn't matter. I own these newspapers now. Ian's name may remain on the masthead as publisher, but mine will always be above his as owner. He'll never have any power." She glanced at the rubble on the floor. "As his mother, I'd think you'd be more concerned for his state of mind than his position here."

Lilith shrugged. "He'll be fine. He's always had a temper. He'll get over it, and he'll be back. By rights, all this is his."

Kellen shook her head slowly. "Not anymore." She leveled her eyes at Lilith. "This is my office now, Lilith. And I'd like you to leave."

Lilith stared at her for a moment. Slowly, she withdrew a mirror from her purse, checked her reflection, then put the mirror away. With a last look at Kellen, she rose and walked out of the office, leaving the door open.

Kellen went slowly across the room and closed it. She turned and leaned back on the door, looking over the office. It looked different than it had when her father had occupied it. Ian had changed it too much. But there was still a feeling about it that he had not been able to erase, a presence, as if her father were still there. The feeling was so strong that it brought unexpected tears to her eyes.

Quickly, she went back to the desk. She knelt down and gathered up the papers that Ian had flung aside. There was nothing important among them, so she dropped them all into the trash. The crystal ashtray, in two pieces now, was also dropped in, along with a few knickknacks. There was a copy of that morning's

Times, which she put on the desk. Just as she was about to stand up, something caught her eye under the desk. It was a frame, and she picked it up, staring at it. It was a picture of a somber, dark-haired boy—Robert. She stood up and put the picture in her briefcase. She would have it sent to Ian's home.

She reached into her briefcase, withdrew another silver frame, and set it on the edge of the desk. She sat down behind the desk, staring at it. Adam and Elizabeth stared back at her, smiling.

Her gaze went to the newspaper. Slowly, she unfolded it and ran her hands lightly over the front page, almost in a caress. She raised her hands, turned them over, and looked at her palms. They were smeared with ink. She thought of what her father had said a long time ago. I don't want my daughter dirtying her hands with the business. She glanced at his photograph, and she knew that if he could see her, he wouldn't mind it at all now.

She looked at her hands and smiled. Neither did she.

Ian stood high on a cliff, staring down at the ocean far below. He watched the breakers crashing on the rocks and the rhythmic advance and retreat of the waves. He closed his eyes and drew in a deep breath of the ripe, humid air, then let it out slowly. He repeated the exercise ten times, just as the doctor had told him to do. Then he opened his eyes.

It didn't work. He still felt bad. Usually, coming to the house on Hana gave him an immediate lift. But now, three weeks after his arrival, he still felt . . . so empty. In the last few days, he had come to a revelation: he could do anything he wanted. He didn't have to go back to Clarisse if he didn't want to. He never had to talk to Lilith again. He could stay right here in Hana and never go back. He was, for the first time in his life, truly free of responsibilities and everyone else's expectations. He could do whatever his heart desired.

He glanced back at his magnificent house. Whatever his heart desired . . . But it desired nothing, really. As he stood there on the cliff, he realized he couldn't think of one thing he wanted to do or one person he wanted to be with.

He stuck his hands in his pockets, and his fingers closed around a wadded letter. He unfolded it and read it again. It was from Lilith, a rambling appeal to come back and resume his figurehead role of publisher. "Not for my sake, Ian," Lilith wrote, "but for your son's." It went on and on, ending with a discordant note of sentiment: "Please come home, dear. You know I love you and want you to be happy."

Ian folded the letter in half. Happy . . . what a strange word for Lilith to use. What in the hell did she mean? He couldn't think of any moment in his life to which he could apply the word happy. Contented, satisfied . . . that was how he usually felt here at Hana. But not happy. Never happy.

No, that wasn't entirely true. . . . He could remember feeling happy twice in his life. When he was with Chimmoko. And a faint memory of that day he had gone to look at the new bridge with his father.

His thoughts went to his son Robert. He had not seen him now in weeks, and he realized suddenly that he almost missed him. The boy was a mystery to him, a stranger really. But there was some sort of connection there, something he felt with no one else on the face of the earth. Whenever he looked into Robert's eyes, he could see a reflection of himself as a boy there. But it was growing dimmer, always dimmer. He was losing Robert, too. Just as assuredly as the business now belonged to Kellen, Robert belonged to Clarisse and Lilith. He had . . . nothing.

He glanced at Lilith's letter in his clenched hand. Slowly, he tore it into pieces and threw them into the wind, watching them swirl down to the water below. He looked out at the ocean and then down to the rocks. He closed his eyes and slowly raised his arms, holding them straight out. His body swayed, caught in the wind, and his senses became suddenly sharpened by the salty smell, the pounding waves, and the delicious vertigo. His lips parted in the beginning of a smile. Then he opened his eyes, squinting at the glint of the sun off the water. Slowly, he lowered his arms and took a step away from the cliff's edge. He knew suddenly that he would go back. He had to. He had to make sure the connection was maintained. For Robert. For his son. For himself.

The afternoon sky was overcast, but inside the beach house there was laughter. Kellen sat at the dining room table talking with Clark, Tyler, and J. D. Out on the deck, Sara and Ben were seated at a table, engrossed with their crayons, paper, and scissors.

Tyler reached for another bagel. "I didn't even know you could cook," he said with a smile.

"Only omelettes," Kellen said. "The kids and I live on them when we come down here."

J. D. leaned back in his chair. "This is a great house," he said. "Thanks for inviting us, Kellen. It was good to get away for a couple days before the crush starts up again. I'll need all the strength I can get this time around.''

J. D. was up for reelection to the board of supervisors and was about to set out on the campaign circuit. Last week, he had called a press conference and made his homosexuality public.

Clark raised his glass. ''To Mr. Greenjeans's reelection,'' he said with a smile.

They all took a drink. Kellen turned the wine bottle around to look at the label. It was the same as the sketch Tyler had once shown her: a gray gull on a field of blue with silver letters spelling out Ingram Hills.

''So, tell me again how much you like our wine,'' Tyler said with a smile.

Kellen took a sip of the chablis. ''A presumptuous little domestic,'' she said. ''The perfect complement to runny omelettes.'' Then she smiled. ''I'm kidding. You know I'm proud of you. And you know I know nothing about wine. But I really do like it.''

Tyler turned to Clark. ''You, on the other hand, have not said a word. So what's the verdict, you old snob? After all these years of taking your grief, I can take one more insult.''

Clark raised his glass, peering at the wine in the light. ''Kellen's right. It's presumptuous, but it has a certain insouciant charm. Reminds me a little of a Montrachet I had in France once, from a vineyard called Les Pucelles.''

''That's as close to a compliment as Clark will get,'' Kellen said with a smile toward Tyler.

They were all silent for a moment, happily satiated by the meal and company. Ben began to fuss that Sara wouldn't give him a crayon. ''Sara, share with your brother,'' Kellen called out.

''But I need the black one,'' she protested.

''Break it in half and give him a piece,'' Kellen said.

The kids became quiet again. Tyler watched them for a moment, then turned back to Kellen. ''How are they taking the divorce?'' he asked.

''As well as can be expected,'' Kellen said. ''They were upset at first, but Stephen's been great. He comes up to see them nearly every week and calls all the time.'' She looked over at them. ''They both know we both still love them very much.''

''And how's Stephen doing?'' Clark asked.

''He likes the new job, says he has a real challenge ahead of him trying to shake the *Los Angeles Times* out of its complacency.'' She paused. ''He seems happy.''

Tyler stared at her. ''What about you? Are you happy?''

She looked at the children. "Yes. Things are turning around at the newspapers. I have everything I want."

They all fell silent again. J. D. glanced at his watch. "It's nearly three, Tyler," he said. "We'd better get going."

"You're right. It's a long drive." They all rose, and Tyler helped Kellen clear the table while J. D. put the suitcases in the car. Kellen walked them out to the car. J. D. got in the car, but Clark said he had forgotten his coat and went back into the house.

Tyler and Kellen stood there for a moment without saying anything. Then a small smile tipped Tyler's lips. "Strange, isn't it, how things turned out," he said.

"What do you mean?" she asked.

He shrugged slightly. "Oh, I don't know. All the time when I was growing up, I never felt like I was part of the family. I always felt like an add-on to Father's life. I never really felt he loved me." He looked at Kellen. "I always envied what you and he had. And I envied your love of the newspapers because it was your connection to him, something I never had."

"Oh, Tyler," Kellen said softly.

"But a couple months ago I realized something really important," he went on. "I have a connection, too. Father left me something without even knowing it."

"The vineyard," Kellen said.

Tyler smiled slightly. "Yes, the vineyard. But also a sister. Who loves me enough to forgive me for what I did."

Kellen stared at him, then embraced him. They held each other tightly for a moment, then pulled apart.

Clark came toward them. "Okay, let's get going," he coaxed. "I've got a date tonight."

Tyler got in the car. Clark hung back to say good-bye to Kellen. He hesitated. "Something wrong?" he asked.

"No. Nothing. Why do you ask?"

"I don't know. Just a hunch."

She smiled. "Quit trying to read my mind, Clark."

"Well, you've gone through a lot the last few months. I'm just concerned about you."

"I'm fine. Everything has turned out fine."

"You've left one thing out. You haven't mentioned Garrett once since you got the newspapers back."

She looked toward the house. "When I saw him in Paris, he said we were out of sync. I think he was right." She looked back at Clark. "I don't even know where he is. I think he finally just got tired of waiting for me, Clark."

"Good grief, Kellen, what are *you* waiting for? Why don't you call him?"

She shook her head. "He's got a corporation of his own to run now in Britain. His life is there now. There's no reason for him to be here anymore."

Clark sighed. "You're here. Sara's here. Two damn good reasons, I'd say."

She shifted from one foot to another.

"What about Sara?" he asked. "Are you ever going to tell her about him?"

"She's got enough to handle right now with the divorce," Kellen said quietly. "I don't want her feeling like she's lost one father and suddenly there's a new one to get to know."

"But the longer you wait, the harder it will be. Kids can forgive you for a lot of things, but not being lied to."

Tyler beeped the horn. "Better get going," she said.

Clark kissed her cheek. "I'll see you at the office Monday," he said, getting in the car. She waved and waited until the car disappeared down the road. Then she went inside to clean up. Her thoughts bounced between what Tyler said about feeling connected by a sense of family and what Clark said about Sara. She knew Clark was right, that someday soon she would have to tell Sara about Garrett. Secrets within a family were only destructive. Hadn't her own and Tyler's and even Garrett's experiences borne that out? She somehow had to find the courage to tell Sara the truth.

Ben came up and tugged on her hand. "Mommy, can we go see the seals?"

"I don't know, sweetheart, it's getting late," Kellen said. Then she saw the look on Ben's face and smiled. "Go put your jacket on." When Ben reappeared, Kellen led him out to the deck toward Sara, who was absorbed in her drawing.

"Want to come with us to see the seals?" Kellen asked.

"I'll stay here. I want to finish this," Sara said.

"All right. We'll be back in a little while." Kellen started down the beach, holding Ben's hand.

Sara watched them head toward the rock jetty, then returned to her project. She didn't hear the knock at the door when it came ten minutes later. When she finally looked up, she saw a tall man standing at the sliding glass door, watching her. She wasn't afraid; there was nothing in the stranger's kind face that made her feel that.

"Who are you?" she asked, her crayon poised in midair.

Garrett stared at her. "A friend of your mother's."

"You should have knocked," she said, giving him an even stare. "It's not nice to just come into someone's house."

He smiled slightly. "You're right. I'm sorry. But I did knock. I guess you were too busy to hear me."

"My mother took my brother for a walk," she said. Garrett looked down the beach to where Sara was pointing. "They'll be back in a minute," she said, going back to her crayons and paper. "You can wait if you want."

"Thank you," Garrett said. He came over to the table. "What are you making there?" he asked.

"A newspaper," she said.

"Ah, yes, of course it is," Garrett murmured, looking over her shoulder at the paper on which Sara had penciled in stories and drawn photographs. She had drawn a nameplate across the top that proclaimed THE CARMEL TIMES.

"You run color pictures in your paper, then?" Garrett asked.

"Sure," Sara said, looking up at him. "My mother says black-and-white newspapers are old-fashioned."

"Your mother's right."

Garrett stared at the girl sitting before him. She was pretty, her glossy black hair streaming down over her blue sweater. Her deep blue eyes looked back at him steadfastly. He could feel his heart beating against his chest. It was the first time he had ever seen his daughter. He felt strange, almost nervous, but exhilarated. His daughter . . . his and Kellen's daughter.

"You talk funny," Sara said. "How come?"

He laughed, surprised by her directness. "I'm from England. Everybody there talks funny."

She smiled slightly, then returned to her paper.

"What's your big story there?" he asked.

"It's about the baby seals. They were just born." She looked up and smiled. "Would you like to see them?"

Garrett nodded. "Yes, I would."

She slid off the chair and took his hand. "Let's go," she said. They started down the beach together.

Kellen stood near the rock jetty watching Ben, who was mesmerized by the family of seals bobbing in a kelp bed offshore. She turned back toward the house and saw two figures coming down the beach. She recognized Sara immediately, but at first she couldn't figure out who the man was holding her daughter's hand.

Then she froze. She watched Sara and Garrett as they came closer, unable to take her eyes off their interlocked hands. In all the times she had thought of Garrett during the last eight years, she had never been able to picture him with Sara. Despite the fact their resemblance was startling, she had kept their images separate. It had always been a defense of sorts against the truth. But now, seeing them made her heart ache.

Sara brought Garrett to her. "Mommy, this man says he's your friend. I brought him out here to see the seals."

Kellen stared at Garrett for a moment, then looked down at Sara. "Okay, sweetheart," she said, "But first we need a few minutes to talk. Would you go watch your brother for a little while?"

Sara looked up at Garrett, then gave him a shrug and smile. "Okay," she said. She ran off toward the rock jetty. Kellen's eyes remained on the children.

"I was going to call before I came," Garrett said. "But I was afraid you wouldn't talk to me or allow me to see you."

Kellen wouldn't look at him.

"I know about the divorce," he went on.

She focused on the children, now climbing on the rocks. For a long time, she was quiet. "Garrett, I have something to tell you," she said softly, "It's about Sara."

"I know. She's mine, isn't she?"

She turned to face him, her expression searching. "You knew? But why didn't you ever say anything?"

"It wasn't up to me, Kellen. It had to come from you."

She looked back to Sara. "Eight years," she murmured. "I wanted to tell you then, but I couldn't. And after that . . ." Her voice trailed off. "I guess I did what I had to do to protect her . . . and myself." She paused. "I'm sorry, Garrett. I should have told you a long time ago."

It began to rain lightly. The barking of the seals mixed with the children's laughter.

"What happened in the past doesn't matter," Garrett said. "What matters is, I know she's my daughter. I want to be with her. I want to be with you. I want a family. We can still have it, Kellen. Don't turn your back on me again."

She wouldn't look at him.

"You said you needed time," he said. "Two months is enough. Eight years is enough. I've waited. I've been patient. But now I deserve an answer."

At that moment, Sara came running up. Her face was pink from the chilly air, and her hair was beaded with rain. "Come on, Mama," she laughed, out of breath, "come on and look at the seals!" She grabbed Kellen's hand, tugging on it.

Kellen looked at Garrett, then down at Sara. Yes, she would tell her the truth . . . soon. Suddenly, with Garrett there, it seemed less frightening. It seemed right. They stood there, neither saying a thing. Slowly, Garrett smiled.

"Come on!" Sara implored. "What are you waiting for?"

Kellen returned Garrett's smile. "What am I waiting for?" she repeated. "Nothing anymore."

Sara took Garrett's hand and started pulling them both toward Ben. "Then let's get going," she said.

About the Author

Kristy Daniels is a husband-and-wife writing team from Fort Lauderdale, Florida. Daniel Norman is Deputy Managing Editor/Features-Sports of the *Fort Lauderdale News/Sun-Sentinel*. Kristy Montee worked full-time in the newspaper business for thirteen years before resigning to become a free-lance writer and dance critic. *Jewels of Our Father* is their third novel.